The
Second Sister

Center Point
Large Print

Also by Marie Bostwick and available from Center Point Large Print:

Apart at the Seams

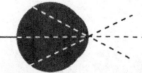

The
Second Sister

MARIE
BOSTWICK

CENTER POINT LARGE PRINT
THORNDIKE, MAINE

This Center Point Large Print edition is published
in the year 2015 by arrangement with
Kensington Publishing Corp.

The text of this Large Print edition is unabridged.
In other aspects, this book may vary
from the original edition.
Printed in the United States of America
on permanent paper.
Set in 16-point Times New Roman type.

ISBN: 978-1-62899-588-6

Library of Congress Cataloging-in-Publication Data

Bostwick, Marie.
  The second sister / Marie Bostwick. —
    Center Point Large Print edition.
      pages cm
  Summary: "Political campaign advisor Lucy Toomey is forced to return
to her hometown when her mentally impaired sister dies. In order to
inherit their family home, her sister's will requires Lucy to reside there
for eight weeks. Her return to Nilson's Bay, Wisconsin, is a time of
reflection, healing, acceptance and romance"—Provided by publisher.
  ISBN 978-1-62899-588-6 (library binding : alk. paper)
  1. Large type books. I. Title.
  PS3602.O838S56 2008b
  813'.6—dc23
                                                        2015011151

With Thanks . . .

To my wonderful editors, Audrey La Fehr, whose experience, wisdom, and humor have been a gift to me for more than a decade, and Martin Biro, whose energy, enthusiasm, and attention to detail have inspired me with renewed zeal and made this a much better book. To Liza Dawson, who is, without question, the best literary agent on the face of the earth and who makes the experience of writing a joyous adventure. Honestly, dear Liza, I don't know how I'd do this without you. To my Sparkly Assistant, Lisa Sundell Olsen, who keeps me organized, on schedule, and smiling. To beta readers John Walsh and Molly Skinner, for their keen editing eyes. To Anne Dranginnis for advice and counsel regarding legal matters in the story. And, of course and always, to the readers.

Behold, I am with you and will keep you wherever you go, and will bring you back to this land; for I will not leave you until I have done what I have spoken to you.

—Genesis 28:15

❧ Chapter 1 ❧

November 1, 2016

Wherever I am, in California, Pennsylvania, Ohio, New York, or Texas, as well as those rare occasions when I actually sleep at my spartanly furnished apartment in Denver, the last thing I do before turning out the light is make sure my cell phone is fully charged and within easy reach on the nightstand.

So when the phone rang at 1:48 a.m., I already knew who was calling and why.

"Can't sleep again?"

"I woke up," my sister replied. "Freckles jumped off the bed and I had to get up and feed her."

I shouldn't sigh when she says things like that, but it's hard not to.

"Alice. Why don't you close the door to your room at night? I sent you that nice cat bed. Why can't the cats sleep out in the living room?"

"But how would I know when Freckles is hungry? Lucy? I was thinking. Why don't you come home for Christmas this year?" Alice's voice brightened, as though this brilliant idea, which she had voiced every time we'd talked in

9

the last three weeks, had only just come to her.

I swallowed to banish the dryness in my throat, a side effect of my usual sleep aid, three fingers of single-malt scotch over ice administered shortly before retiring, and then crooked my right arm across my eyes to block out the glow of the streetlamps from the boulevard below.

I keep promising myself that I'm going to buy some drapes to draw over my standard-issue apartment blinds, but I keep forgetting. At this point, it probably isn't worth the expense. In another week or two, I might be moving. Or not. And if not, everything I've done in the last three years has been a complete waste of time.

But I won't think about that, not now. If I do, I'll never be able to get back to sleep.

"Alice, we've been over this before, remember? We're going to go someplace warm for Christmas. Maybe Disney World."

Alice loves Disney World. I took her there for Christmas two years ago and booked us into a room overlooking a man-made savannah populated with African wildlife; giraffes grazed not ten feet from our balcony. Alice was so entranced that I had to coax her to leave the hotel and visit the parks.

"Or maybe," I said, clearing my throat and then drawing out the phrase, trying to add a tantalizing note to my tone, "depending on how things turn out Tuesday, we could spend Christmas in

Washington. The decorations at the White House are gorgeous. The tree in the Blue Room is eighteen feet tall."

"Is Washington warm?" Alice asked, suspicion creeping into her voice.

"Not in December," I admitted. "But the National Zoo has pandas. And I could book us into a very fancy hotel with a Jacuzzi. And a spa. We could get pedicures and massages."

Alice was quiet for a moment. I could tell she was tempted. Alice loves Jacuzzis. And pedicures. And how many times had she told me that, someday, she wanted to see a panda?

A near-drowning accident at the age of eighteen had permanently altered my sister's intellect, abilities, and personality. But at the core of her being she's still a Toomey, shackled by the weight of responsibility and the Protestant work ethic. It's pretty ironic, considering we're Catholic. Well, Alice is. At this point, I consider myself religiously abstentious. Nothing against it if that's what works for you, but I choose not to participate.

Of course, Mom was born Lutheran. She converted when she married our father, solemnly promising to raise her children according to the tradition and teachings of the Church of Rome, faithfully following through on her vows. So maybe the whole Protestant work ethic thing came from her side of the family? That made sense and explained why the inexorable pull of duty proved greater to Alice than the promise of pleasure. I wasn't really surprised.

"I can't leave Freckles and Dave home again at Christmas," Alice said. "They get too lonely. You come here, Lucy. We could go to the ice sculpture contest," she said, adopting the same wheedling tone I'd been using a moment before. "And we could decorate our *own* tree, a really big one. I still have Mom's ornaments. You could meet my friends and we could go to midnight mass, with all the candles. It's so pretty. Lucy, you should go to mass more often."

As wheedling edged toward scolding, Alice sounded so much like Mom that for a moment it was as if Sally Toomey had risen from her grave and pulled the phone from the hand of her older daughter to give the younger a good talking to.

"I know. But I've been very busy," I said, giving the same excuse I'd always used on Mom. "We'll go to mass at Christmas, I promise. We can go to the National Cathedral. It's about twenty times as big as St. Agnes's and has all kinds of stained glass in the windows."

The National Cathedral is an Episcopalian congregation, but services there are so formal and the liturgy so similar to the Catholic rite that Alice wouldn't know the difference. And I love the architecture of the building. It feels more like visiting a museum than going to church, which,

12

as far as I'm concerned, is infinitely preferable.

"No," Alice said firmly. "I want to have Christmas in Nilson's Bay. You haven't been home since the funeral, Lucy. That's eight years."

Eight years? Had it really been that long since our parents died?

I did a little calculation in my head, counting back to 2008, a terrible year. The year when both our parents were killed in a freak, single-car accident, also when my boss lost his job and I lost mine in turn and we both returned to Colorado, the year everybody expected him to fade into the background and never be heard from again. Except he hadn't. I made sure of it.

Sixty-, seventy-, and even eighty-hour work-weeks, so many frequent flyer miles logged that I could take Alice on a trip around the world for Christmas, first class, if I wanted, and close to three hundred nights spent in hotel rooms in the previous year alone. No wonder I've lost track of the time.

"Lucy? Did you get the card?"

Though I was sometimes annoyed by my sister's habit of abruptly dropping one topic and taking up another without any kind of transition or lead-in, I was only too happy to suspend discussion of Christmas plans, though I knew we'd revisit the subject during Alice's next wee-hours wake-up call. It's the same every year. Alice always wants me to come home for Christmas and I always resist and, in the end, get my way. I know how bad that sounds, but it really is better this way, for both of us. Think of all the things Alice would have missed otherwise. Without my influence, my sister might never have traveled farther than Milwaukee.

And as far as me missing Nilson's Bay? I don't. I spent the first stifling eighteen years of my life in Door County, tucked up in the remote reaches of Wisconsin, and don't need to make a return trip, not ever. Nilson's Bay never changes. But I have, thank God.

I yawned, my eyes still shut. "What card?"

"The *card,*" Alice replied, sounding a little testy that I wasn't following her line of logic. "There's a picture of a red panda on the front, also known as a lesser panda, which doesn't seem like a very nice name. I don't know why they call it a panda at all. It looks more like a fox, a teddy-bear fox. It was hard to draw. I mailed it on Wednesday so it would get there in time for your birthday. Did it?"

"Oh, the *card!* Yes. Thank you, Allie-Oop," I said, using our dad's old nickname for her. "It's beautiful. I'm going to put it up on the bulletin board at my office with the others."

Truthfully, I hadn't opened or even seen Alice's birthday card or, until this moment, remembered that today is my birthday. When I came home from my final East Coast swing, not quite three hours before, I poured myself a scotch and sat staring at nothing while I consumed it, trying to empty my head and calm down enough to sleep, then got undressed, plugged in my phone, and collapsed into bed without bothering to open the mail or even my suitcase. I'd look for it tomorrow and, just as I promised, pin it to a bulletin board alongside her other drawings.

The fact that Alice's ability to draw was not impaired and has even improved since the accident is one of the oddities of my sister's condition. In many ways, she's just like anyone else. People meeting her for the first time, people who don't know what she was like before, often have no clue that anything is amiss with Alice. They just think she's a little slow. That's one of the reasons, aside from the obvious career complications it would cause, that I've never urged Alice to move in with me. Alice loves Nilson's Bay; they suit each other. Both are a little slow.

"Will they give you a party at work?" Alice asked.

"No. Maybe a cake," I said, once again stretching the truth for my sister's benefit.

At thirty-seven, Alice is seventeen months older than I am, but in regard to certain subjects, including the celebration of birthdays, her mentality is still that of the teenager she'd been at the time of the accident.

"Just a cake?"

"Jenna is taking me out to lunch," I lied.

"What about the governor? Will he come to lunch too?"

"No." Much as I know Alice would relish the picture of me enjoying a birthday lunch with the possible next president of the United States, I'm willing to stretch the truth only so far. "He's too busy. The election is next week, remember?"

"I know. I put a red circle around the date on my calendar so I wouldn't forget."

I smiled. "Good. Who are you voting for?"

"Governor Thomas W. Ryland for president of the United States, Lindsay R. Bell for governor of Wisconsin, Charles Skoglund for mayor, and Peter J. Swenson and Arlene Bloom for Village Council."

"Be sure to tell your friends to vote too."

"I will."

I rolled onto my side and opened one eye. The red numbers on my digital clock were blurry without my glasses, but I could still see that it was 2:06 a.m. In two hours and twenty-four minutes the alarm would sound, rousing me for another sixteen-hour workday.

"Alice, I've got to go back to sleep now. You should do the same."

There was a pause on the Wisconsin end of the line, followed by a deep, drawn-out sigh, the kind of worrisome exhalation that I hadn't heard from her in a long time.

I opened both eyes, wide-awake now. "What's wrong?"

"Nothing. But . . . Lucy? Are you happy?"

"Sure. Of course I am." I propped myself up on the pillow. "Are you?"

"I miss you."

"We'll see each other soon. Christmas will be here before you know it."

"I just wish you'd come home for Christmas. I really, really do," Alice said, a teary rasp in her voice.

I closed my eyes again and rubbed my forehead. I couldn't deal with this right now. I didn't have the energy.

"We'll talk about it later. But not tonight, okay? Let's wait until after the election."

Alice went on as if she hadn't heard me. "Come home. There are things I want to show you, things I want to talk to you about. . . ."

I sighed again, tired of disjointed conversations that lead nowhere and night after night of interrupted sleep.

"What things?"

"Things," she repeated. "Nilson's Bay things. It's not all bad here, Lucy. You're remembering wrong."

Remembering wrong? I very much doubted that, but it wasn't a debate I wanted to have at two in the morning.

"Alice," I said, "I just got home. I've been up

for twenty hours straight. I have *got* to get some rest."

"I'm sorry."

"It's okay," I said more gently, regretting my impatience. It wasn't Alice's fault. She didn't want to be like this. "Just go to sleep now, all right?"

"All right. Lucy? Just one more thing. . . ."

I felt my jaw clench. "What now?"

Alice took in a breath and, after a moment, began to sing "Happy Birthday" in a clear, soft soprano. When she was finished, I smiled.

"Thanks. Good night, Allie-Oop."

"Good night, Lucy."

❧ Chapter 2 ❧

After I hung up with Alice, I went right back to sleep, but I didn't get much rest. I had the dream again.

It begins like it always does. Walking across the edgeless white plain.

No trees. No buildings. No houses. No means to measure the distance I have traveled or the miles yet to come. No way to judge my relative weight or volume within this space. Just hard white earth beneath my feet, hard blue sky turning to starless black above my head. And the shadow that follows me.

No. Not a shadow. More the sense of one, because though I turn around repeatedly, I see nothing. But I know it's there.

What I've left behind is the same as what lies ahead. I have no thought of destination. I keep walking because that's what I've always done and because if I stop to think, the shadow will overtake me.

I take another step, no longer or shorter or harder or softer than the others, and without warning, the white plain beneath my feet cracks like a broken mirror and swallows me whole, plunges me into frigid waters that rob me of breath.

Torpor turns to panic. I thrash and twist, fighting to find my way back to the white-flat world above, breaking briefly through the surface, gasping for air, clawing for purchase at the jagged white teeth of the edge, my hands blue and bloodless, fingernails snapping off as, again, and again, and again, I clutch desperately at the diamond-hard ice until exhaustion over-takes me and I slip beneath the surface.

Terror gives way to surrender, and I begin the descent, unable to breathe or think. I begin to lose feeling in my frozen limbs and my connection with the world above.

The shadow is below me now, shrouding my feet,

my legs, my breast, pulling me close, drawing me down. I open my mouth to speed the inevitable, welcome cold, black water into my lungs with my face turned upward in farewell, catching a last look at the fast diminishing circle of light.

And then a hand appears in the center of the circle, frantic fingers opening and closing on empty water, searching. It reaches lower, becomes an arm, brushes against trailing tendrils of my hair and snaps shut, a reflex, and yanks hard, pulling at the roots. I jerk away, a reflex. Pain jolts me from my stupor and I reach up, grab hold, and feel the hand clamp closed over mine.

Just before breaking through, my lidded eyes open wide and through the ripples of troubled water I look up and see Alice.

She has saved me again.

But tonight is different. Tonight the dream doesn't end there. Though my hair and clothes are still wet, suddenly I'm the one on the surface and Alice is in the water.

I lie prostrate on the ice, arm submerged almost to my shoulder, my frozen fingers pulling frantically on Alice's arm, straining with all I have to bring her up from the depths. She slips from my grasp. I scream, reach down into the black again, even deeper than before, but I can't feel anything. I've lost her.

I plunge forward, submerging my head and

shoulders into icy waters, and see Alice's face turned toward mine, her eyes placid and blue as she slowly sinks into the shadows, beyond my reach.

And then it is done and I am on the surface again, lying on my back this time, shivering. Everything is like it was before. The world is cold, white, and boundless. The sky is hard blue. The crack in the ice is sealed over and smooth, as though it never existed. Alice is gone.

But the shadow is still with me. And it speaks.

"Where have you been?"

I open my mouth, but can't answer. A bell rings. The dream splinters.

I sat up, confused and breathless, panting. The bell sounded again, rude and demanding. I reached for the phone, but there was no one there. Finally, I realized the noise was coming from the alarm clock. I leaned across to the far side of the bed, smacked the black button to silence the bell, and then collapsed back against the pillows, taking big breaths and exhaling slowly.

I stared into the middle distance of the darkness, collecting myself, and pressed my hand on my chest to measure the gradual slowing of my pounding heart, thinking about Alice.

I couldn't go home for Christmas this year, I reasoned. If we won, I'd have to go to Washington

21

to help with the transition. And if we lost—a possibility I never liked to admit, not even to myself—if we lost, I'd need to start looking for a job.

But Alice's voice was so pleading, so plaintive. And so persistent. She'd never let it go. Alice never let anything go.

Even so, I couldn't go home for Christmas, not this year. I just couldn't. I had to make her understand. But . . . maybe next year? Yes. With some advance planning, and as long as it was just for a couple of days, I could do that. I didn't want to, but I could. I would. For Alice's sake.

I sat up on the edge of the bed, yawned, and looked at the clock. It was quarter to five, too early to call Alice. I'd tell her later, the next time she called.

Which, I calculated, would be in about twenty hours.

Groaning, I flopped backward onto the mattress and closed my eyes. *Just five more minutes.*

❧ Chapter 3 ❧

After five smacks of the snooze button, I finally hauled myself out of bed.

Getting out the ironing board would have required rising after only two snooze cycles, so I

22

pulled the least creased of my standard-issue blue suits from my still unpacked suitcase and hung it on the back of the bathroom door. Hopefully, the steam from the shower would take care of the wrinkles—the big ones. At this point, washing and drying my hair wasn't an option either, so I took a curling iron to the top layer, fluffed it out with my fingers so it wouldn't look quite so flat, then did a quick backcomb and spray job to cover up a recently sprouted crop of dark roots, promising myself that I'd go to the salon the minute the election was over and go back to brunette. Pretending to be blond was just too much work.

With wardrobe and hair more or less under control, I turned to makeup and accessories. Humming "A Hard Day's Night," my usual predawn anthem, I slathered on a coat of tinted moisturizer, a little blush, and some mascara. I didn't bother with lipstick. It'd be gone before I finished my first cup of coffee. I put on some earrings and a scarf, slipped my feet into a pair of blue pumps, grabbed my car keys, phone, purse, briefcase, and two cookies to tide me over until I got to the restaurant, and headed out the door.

It was 5:42 in the morning. I was already running late.

Whenever Joe Feeney comes to Denver on business, we meet at Syrup, the best breakfast spot in Cherry Creek, to eat eggs and catch up.

Even with his face shielded behind news-papers, I knew the guy at the corner table was Joe. People in Denver don't drink Bloody Marys at six a.m. on a Tuesday, and nobody else would be so engrossed in the pages of the *Washington Post*, with copies of the *Wall Street Journal*, the *New York Times*, and *Roll Call* sitting at the ready. Joe, who began as a staffer for late, legendary senator Daniel Patrick Moynihan of Massachusetts in the mid-seventies, eventually leaving to open his own lobbying firm in the mid-nineties, is old school and still reads the papers in print.

Hearing my greeting, he lowered his paper.

"Lucy. It's bad enough that you buy blue suits five at a time off the clearance rack. Couldn't you at least hang them up at night? Did you sleep in that thing?"

I plopped into a chair and nudged a second one out from the table with my foot so I could dump my purse, briefcase, and coat onto the seat.

"I just got back from New York. Haven't had a chance to do laundry."

I reached for the carafe, filled a coffee cup, and gave my order to the waiter without reading the menu. I always get the Kitchen Sink: scrambled eggs and maple-peppered bacon on an open-face biscuit, layered on hash browns, and covered in sausage gravy. Joe ordered a spinach egg-white omelet with wheat toast, dry.

Joe folded up his paper, then unfolded his napkin and laid it over the knife-edge crease of his perfectly pressed pants. I took a muffin from the bakery basket.

"There's this new thing out there, Lucy—dry cleaners. Heard of them?"

"I have," I replied, buttering a muffin. "I also heard they charge fifteen bucks to press an outfit you can iron yourself for free."

"Except you never do."

Joe stirred his Bloody Mary before taking a bite from the celery stick.

"Not everybody can afford to send their custom-made suits to the cleaners," I said. "Some of us have to work for a living."

Washington is full of well-dressed men—lawyers, lobbyists, lawmakers—but even in DC, Joe stands out. His suits come from London and his shoes from Italy. The links in his French cuffs always match his tie, and the snowy-white handkerchief peeking from his pocket matches the thick, perfectly coiffed shock of snowy-white hair on his head. He is as dapper as I am disheveled and twenty-five years my senior. Our only common interests are politics and baseball. And yet, we are friends. In fact, Joe Feeney may be the best friend I have.

I've always found it easier to relate to men than to women. Even when I was growing up, the only girl I was really close to was Alice. She always watched out for me. Now I watch out for her, which I'm glad to do. After all, I owe her. But that's not the same thing as friendship, is it?

Joe is a better listener, and gives better advice on everything from career and romance to nutrition and fashion, than any woman I know. Plus, he doesn't get his feelings hurt when I choose to ignore that advice. Nor does he gossip. He can hold his liquor and his tongue and looks good escorting me to weddings and New Year's Eve parties when I'm between boyfriends—what more could I want?

"What's in the news?" I asked, nodding toward his discarded newspaper. "I didn't have time to turn on the computer before I left the apartment."

Joe flipped over a section of the paper and cleared his throat. "It says here that Women for a Better Tomorrow is endorsing Tom Ryland for president. Sounds like somebody had a success-ful trip to New York."

I shrugged off his praise. "Getting them to endorse a month ago would have been a success. At this point, it's just averting disaster."

"Averting disaster *is* success," Joe said. "But you went to New York and calmed everybody down. Disaster averted and Tom Ryland is still in the fight."

"In it," I said, shifting back in my seat as the waiter set a plate in front of me, "but trailing by three points."

26

Joe gave me a look over the rim of his coffee cup. "Quinnipiac says it's five."

"Quinnipiac is wrong. They're not giving enough weight to the new voter registration. Or to voters under thirty."

"Voters under thirty don't show up to the polls."

"Which is why I'm back in Denver," I said, cutting into my breakfast, carefully composing a perfect bite, with equal parts egg, bacon, biscuit, and hash brown, before putting my fork in my mouth, "to oversee the final get-out-the-vote push—"

"Should have happened weeks ago," Joe said, as he took a bite of his overly pale omelet. "But it didn't because Miles and the rest of those ivory-tower idiots from the party don't know a thing about retail politics. They spent two point six million on a consultant who told them they needed to buy more yard signs! Do you know how many actual yard signs they could have bought for two point six million?"

"Half a million," I said, dragging another perfectly composed bite through a pool of gravy, making sure it was evenly coated. "And we do need more."

"See? You don't need a consultant to tell you that. If they'd have left you in charge of the ground game instead of sending you off to placate pissed-off women's groups. . . . Why waste your talent with that? You don't even *like* women."

"That's not true. I like women." I frowned. "I don't *dislike* them. Anyway, let's not play armchair quarterback right now, okay? I'm trying to eat."

Joe took another sip of his Bloody Mary and stayed silent—for two seconds.

"I'm just saying, if Miles wasn't such an insecure, egocentric jerk, if he'd been smart enough to keep you in a position where you could play to your strengths—"

"It was my idea to bring Miles on board, remember? Well, maybe not him specifically, but somebody with experience running national campaigns."

"You've worked on tons of campaigns," Joe said, gnawing on dry toast.

"Six," I said. "Always for the same candidate. And the first one doesn't count. I was just a junior staffer answering phones and handing out bumper stickers."

"And next time you were running the show. What does that say about you?"

"That Ryland couldn't afford anybody better—that's what. Listen, it was a small district in Colorado. It's not rocket science. Shake enough hands and you win. If the sitting governor hadn't slept with his babysitter, Tom wouldn't have won."

"But he did," Joe countered. "You were successful in four out of six races. If you were playing baseball, you'd be an all-star."

"In the minor leagues. Triple A. Maybe double."

Joe drained the bloody dregs of his glass and munched morosely on his celery stump, but kept eyeing the muffins. I thought about taking the last one, just to torture him, but decided it would be too cruel.

"Does Ryland understand what he has in you?" he asked. "You're the one who got him in the race to begin with. You're the one who came up with the strategy that brought him in second in the Iowa caucuses!"

"Strategy?" I laughed. "Please. You mean the five-point plan I scribbled on the back of a cocktail napkin from that dive bar in Georgetown? We didn't come second in Iowa because of strategy; we just worked harder. You can do that in a caucus. Again, not rocket science. And as I recall, when I first showed you my plan, you said it would never work and called me some very unflattering names."

"Yeah. And then I wrote a two-thousand-dollar check to the Ryland Presidential Exploratory Committee. None of this would have happened without you, Lucy. Tom Ryland might not know that, but I do."

I held the bakery basket out to him. "Thank you. The last muffin is yours."

"I'm serious, Luce. What is it you see in him?"

"In Tom?" I asked, confused by the question and that Joe should be the one asking it. "Well, he's a strong leader. Always on the right side of the issues that matter, puts people ahead of party. After years of political divisiveness, Americans are ready for a new kind of leadership. He'll bring the country together again and—"

Joe rolled his eyes. "Yeah, yeah," he said. "I don't need to hear you spout the latest campaign commercial. What do *you* see in him? Are you in love with him?"

"In *love?*" I let out a short, sharp laugh.

He leaned closer and lowered his voice. "Seriously, did you sleep with him? *Are* you sleeping with him? You can tell me."

"Joe!" I hissed, feeling a flush of heat on my face and neck. "No! Absolutely not! How can you even ask me a thing like that?"

"Sorry." He shrugged. "I wasn't trying to insult you. I just don't get it. Anybody else would have bailed after what they did to you post–New Hampshire." He took the muffin, broke it in two, and put one half on my plate. "I thought maybe you had a crush on him or something."

"A crush? What am I? Twelve?" I gave him a pointed look and bit into my muffin half. "You still think of me as a green kid from Wisconsin."

"Naw." Joe broke his muffin half into four parts and started eating them one at a time. "You're a long way from that earnest, young legislative aide I met thirteen years ago, talking about the marvel of democracy, ordering strawberry daiquiris, and expecting people to take her seriously." He smiled. "But in some ways, you're still that girl. You still care. You still believe that public service is a noble calling and that it's better to fight and lose than not to fight at all."

"Well, it is," I said defensively. "Don't you think it is?"

"Not the way you do. Not anymore. That's one of the things I like about you, Lucy. You remind me of my better self. You know what else you remind me of?" he asked, sliding the butter dish across the table and applying the last of it to his muffin. "One of those chicken things my sister's kids always get at Easter. The ones nobody ever eats? And then, three weeks later, they end up in the trash?"

"You mean Peeps? I remind you of marsh-mallow Peeps?"

Joe, his mouth full of muffin, raised a finger and bobbed his head.

"Peeps!" he exclaimed after swallowing. "That's it! You remind me of Peeps. Take them out of the protective packaging—the sheltered girlhood in rural Wisconsin—expose them to the air and elements—the harsh reality of partisan politics—and they develop this tough, thick skin. But when you break them open . . ."

". . . they're all sweet and squashy inside. I get it. That's the dumbest analogy ever. Having ideals doesn't mean you're a marshmallow any more

31

than staying on a campaign after they demote you means you're sleeping with the candidate."

"Fair enough. So you're not in love with Tom Ryland. Who are you in love with?"

I scowled at him. I was getting really tired of this.

"I'm seeing Terry Boyle. You know that."

"The media consultant. Uh-huh. And how's that going?"

I shrugged. "Oh, you know. He lives in Alexandria and travels. I live in Denver and travel. We don't see each other much. Plus, he has terrible taste in movies—loves all that apocalyptic garbage. I don't see it working out. After the campaign—"

"You'll end it," Joe interrupted. "Like you always do. Every new campaign brings a new boyfriend, also a politico, just as busy as you, who, more often than not, lives out of state. You have fun for a few months, but when the campaign ends, the relationship does too. See a pattern here, Luce?"

I let my jaw go slack. "Oh my gosh! I do! I see it now! Thank you, Dr. Phil!"

Joe smirked at me and I smirked back.

"So the cycle of my relationships coincides with the election cycle," I said. "Big deal. I'm out there looking for the right guy. When I discover that the guy I'm with *isn't* right, I move on. No point in wasting time. But just because my biological

32

clock is ticking doesn't mean I'm going to settle."

"Not suggesting you should." Joe popped the last bite of muffin into his mouth. "But who is the right guy? What would he look like?"

I squirmed in my seat and looked at my watch. "Joe. Can we do this another time? I've got a conference call with the Chicago field office in forty-five minutes. In fact, I wanted to talk to you about that. I've been studying our polling in-house. We've got better support in the Southwest than people realize. If we win Texas—" Joe raised his eyebrows to make his skepticism clear. "*If* we win Texas, then it's going to come down to Illinois. But we'd need to win Chicago *big*. So I was thinking—"

He picked up my thought and ran with it. "You double your media buy in Cook County. Double up on phone banks. Schedule one last Chicago rally, maybe on the Northwestern campus. You rev up the college kids, solidify your under-thirty turnout, and recruit fresh volunteers all in one fell swoop. But run another poll in Texas. I've got doubts about your numbers."

"See?" I said, spreading my hands and grinning. "You know what I'm thinking almost before I do. No wonder I haven't fallen in love. Who could measure up to Joe Feeney? Thanks, buddy."

I started to get up, but Joe reached across the table and grabbed my forearm.

"Hang on. I know you've got to go, but I flew

out here specifically to talk to you. Just give me five minutes."

Reluctantly, I settled back down into my seat. Of course I would listen to whatever he had to say, but I hoped we weren't going to delve into more of his psychological theories about me. I wasn't in the mood.

"Lucy, I want to see you happy."

"I am happy."

He shot me the same look he'd tossed in my direction when I said we'd win Texas, but he didn't contradict me, just kept talking.

"When the election is over, I want you to come work for me. Ah! Hear me out! Lobbying isn't all graft and influence peddling. People can lobby for good things. I'm adding a department focused on social issues. It'll elevate the public image of our corporate clients. I want to put you in charge of it."

"But . . . I don't have any lobbying experience. Why would you want me?"

"Because you're passionate and organized and you know how to inspire passion in other people. You'd be great. And it'll give you a chance to have a life. Lobbying pays a lot better than law making. You'll be able to buy some decent clothes and even send them to the cleaners. I never want to see you in a wrinkled blue blazer again," he said in a tone of mocking superiority, "not in my office. You'll be able to buy a real house and real furniture. No more renting. You can put nail holes in the woodwork and paint the walls any color you want.

"You'd have to travel, but not too much. You'll have weekends off, nights too. Not all the time, but more often than you do now. And you'll meet regular people—civilians, not politicos. Washington is full of eligible bachelors."

"Joe? Are you trying to set me up?" I couldn't keep from grinning.

"Well," he said with a little shrug. "I know a couple of guys. One just divorced. One never married. You might like them. Look, you're going to need to find work after the election, so why not work for me? We have doughnuts on Monday morning and an open bar on Friday night. What more could you want?"

"Very tempting," I said. "But if Ryland wins . . ."

Joe's smile disappeared. "Lucy, he's not going to win. Quinnipiac has you down by five. You can't close the gap in a week. Even if you could, why would you stay on? Ryland won't give you a big job, Lucy. You know that. Otherwise, he'd never have let Miles push you out of the spotlight."

He leaned forward, his expression absolutely solemn. "I know you don't like to talk about it, but just this once, let's lay it all out there. You pulled off a miracle in Iowa and for a week you were a hero. You were interviewed on CNN. The *Washington Post* called you Ryland's secret weapon, the architect of a brilliant but bare-bones campaign based on jobs, jobs, and more jobs that appealed to disaffected moderates who'd given up on voting and catapulted a candidate no one had ever heard of into a front-runner. For a week, you were a genius. Money poured in, big donors got on board, the party elite started paying attention, and the media was giving Tom the kind of coverage money can't buy. For a week."

He paused, giving me a chance to fill in the blank.

"And then came New Hampshire," I said. "And we came in second to last."

Joe nodded slowly. "Uh-huh. And the people who sang your praises after Iowa started throwing rocks after New Hampshire. They said you were in over your head, too inexperienced to run a national campaign."

"And I was! I knew that!"

I pushed away my plate, wishing I hadn't eaten so fast. The food had given me indigestion. Or maybe it was the conversation.

"The plan was to do just well enough in Iowa and New Hampshire so Tom would be seen as credible," I said. "Then we could attract larger donors and afford real advertising and a manager with national experience. I'd *always* planned to step aside!"

36

Joe gave me a "get real" sort of look. "It's one thing to take a step to the side, Lucy. It's another thing to get sent down. If you hadn't done quite so well in Iowa, built up expectations, and done a little better in New Hampshire—"

"We didn't have an advertising budget! The donations came in too late!"

Joe held up his hands. "Hey. You don't need to defend yourself to me. I know what you were up against. But, fair or not, you were the one who was held responsible. Let me ask you something. Did Tom stand up for you?"

Joe was staring right at me, his eyes practically boring through me. I stared right back. I wasn't going to let him get to me.

"Look. It wasn't his idea. He was getting a lot of pressure from the big donors. We had to make changes or the money would have dried up."

"You didn't answer the question," Joe said, still staring. "Did Tom Ryland stand up for you? Did he tell them that New Hampshire wasn't your fault?"

I turned my head away. He already knew the answer.

"Exactly," Joe said. "It might not have been his idea, but he let them push you aside because by that time, he started to believe he really *could* win. And he wants that, very much."

"We both do," I said. "There's no point in running if you're not in it to win."

"Lucy," he said in a chiding tone, "you should have walked away after Iowa instead of sticking around and letting Miles shuffle you off to organize coffee klatches for women's groups. I see you killing yourself . . . working ninety-hour weeks . . . Why? Some misplaced sense of loyalty? Are you trying to redeem yourself in the eyes of the world? In your own eyes? What's in it for you? I don't get it."

I grabbed the edge of the table, but really, I felt like smashing it with my fist.

"First off, what's wrong with loyalty? And second, is it possible that I stayed because I believe in what we're trying to do? Okay, sure. Is there a part of me that decided to hang in there to prove everybody wrong? Probably. I'm only human. But a Ryland administration will put people and jobs first, politics second, and fix what's been broken in the country since I was a kid. And when that happens, I want to be part of it!"

Joe just looked at me. I think he was trying to give me time to cool down.

"Well," he finally said, "you almost pulled it off, Lucy. Without you, Ryland would never have gotten this far, would never even have been in the race. You should be proud of that. But it's not going to happen. Even if it did—"

"Joe," I interrupted, "you don't need to say it. I won't get a big job in a Ryland administration. I already know that. But I've spent almost my whole career with Tom. If he goes to Washington, I go with him. Regardless of the title."

Joe moved the napkin from his lap to the table. "Ryland doesn't deserve you, Lucy. He really doesn't."

"Well, neither do you. God help the man who *did* deserve me. He'd be in for a world of trouble. I've got to go."

I reached into my purse to find my wallet, but Joe waved me off.

"I'll expense it. With a little imagination, I can figure out how to charge two clients for the same breakfast. You know how crafty we lobbyists can be." He smiled. "Don't think I'm done with you. Let's talk after Tuesday. If Ryland loses . . ."

"*If,*" I said, refusing to be defeatist.

"If he does," Joe said, "then promise me you'll think about my offer."

"Promise. Thanks for breakfast." I kissed him on the cheek. Joe stood up, watching me leave.

"Hey, Luce?" I turned around at the sound of his voice. "I forgot to tell you—that's a nice scarf."

"Yeah?" I fingered the blue and bottle-green fabric draped across my shoulders, pleased by his words. Positive comments from Joe regarding my wardrobe were rare. "Thanks. I found it in a thrift shop in Brooklyn."

"Uh-huh. And the shoes," he said. "Did you get those in a thrift shop too?"

I frowned. "No. Why do you ask?"

Joe grinned and looked at my feet.

"Because you're wearing two different ones."

❧ Chapter 4 ❧

The week leading up to the election was exhilarating and terrifying by turns. Office morale soared and plummeted with the arrival of every new poll. We were closing the gap—but slowly.

Campaign veterans wanted to be optimistic, but couldn't quite bring themselves to it. They'd been to the rodeo before.

Another week and we'd have this thing in the bag. But by Tuesday? I don't know . . .

The campaign virgins, recent college grads hoping their unpaid internships would lead to jobs with the administration, perhaps as secretary of state, or maybe the guy who carried her briefcase, anything with a paycheck, were exuberant.

Dude! I borrowed money from my mom for a deposit on an apartment in Foggy Bottom. But I need two roommates. You in?

Campaigning is a young person's sport, so by rights I should have been in the camp of the cautious. But I continued to believe that our position was brighter than the polls painted it. Miles, the campaign manager, disagreed.

"It's over, Lucy. We're short two million votes. If we only had another week . . ." He grimaced. "But we don't. Time to polish up the résumé. I'm talking to people at CNN. It's gotta be easier to talk about campaigns than run them, right? I'm getting too old for this crap."

He'd already given up. It was a fight to get him to agree to go ahead with the rally on the Northwestern campus—he said it was a waste of money—but I refused to leave his office until he gave in, so eventually he did, just to get rid of me.

I would have liked to fly out to Illinois for the rally, but I couldn't spare the time away from the office. Illinois could be the straw that broke the back of the Gardner campaign camel, but we had to stay strong in the other states too. We couldn't afford to let anything slide.

Normally I find those final days leading up to an election energizing. But this time, I just didn't feel the usual rush of adrenaline. Maybe I was getting too old for this too.

I kept thinking about my conversation with Joe. Obviously, he thought Tom didn't place the value on me that I placed on him. I really didn't think that was fair. When Tom brought Miles in to run the campaign, he was only doing what he had to do.

Okay, yes. It might have soothed my ego if

he'd fought a little harder for me, made Miles give me something more substantial, but that wasn't the real issue, not for me. What really bugged me was that Tom wasn't listening to me anymore.

Miles came on board just three days after the debacle in New Hampshire. After that, I almost never saw Tom. Unless it was a conference call, we rarely even talked on the phone. And when Miles and I had a disagreement about strategy or policy, Tom would just sit there, watching Miles and me go at each other, never taking sides, but never coming to my defense either.

The equal-pay thing was a perfect example. Miles wanted him to back off. I disagreed, vehemently. But in the end, Tom did what Miles told him to do.

Look, I understand that a ship can have only one captain, but that doesn't mean the owner of the ship shouldn't at least consider other points of view. Tom was wrong to flip on equal pay, and not just because it cost us support with women. It was just a mistake to back off on something he'd gone on the record as supporting for his entire career. It made him look indecisive. And if the whole thrust of your campaign is making sure that people have good-paying jobs, then it only makes sense that those policies apply equally to everybody. That's just common sense.

If he asked my advice, I'd tell him to flip right

back as soon as the election was over. Maybe even put a reference to equal pay in his inaugural address. He wouldn't be the first president to change his mind once the votes were counted.

But he hadn't asked for my advice. Not for months.

Every waking moment of that week was spent calling field operatives and offices, state and county chairs, making sure that every detail of our get-out-the-vote strategy was perfectly understood and executed. I worked unceasingly, going to my apartment just long enough to change into my cleanest dirty clothes or catch a couple of hours of sleep before being woken right in the middle of a REM cycle by yet another phone call from Alice, who was still going on about Christmas.

Exhausted doesn't even begin to describe how I felt by Monday.

I didn't bother going back to the apartment that night. Instead, around two-thirty in the morning, I went into my office, closed the door, dimmed the lights, kicked off my shoes, and, after a moment of hesitation, decided that, just this once, I'd leave my cell phone off.

Lying down on the couch, I fell instantly asleep and didn't wake until Jenna, my assistant, knocked on the door and said the polls were about to open in the East. Also that the lobby had called to say two Secret Service agents were on their way up, which meant the governor would be right behind them, arriving at any minute.

"What!" I bolted upright and started frantically raking my fingers through my hair. "Why'd you let me sleep so long?"

"Because you needed it. You look like complete crap, Lucy. So does your office." She shook her head and looked around at the piles of papers, files, boxes, half-empty cups of cold coffee, and other debris. "How can you work in this mess?"

"You know, if I needed a mother . . . I know where everything is in here; I have a system." Unable to see without my glasses, I slid my bare feet over the office carpeting, searching. "Where are my shoes?"

Jenna shot me a look, then stooped down and retrieved two scuffed pumps from under the sofa.

"Here," she said, holding out my missing footwear. "Hang on a second. Don't put them on yet." She reached into the left shoe, pulled out a pair of eyeglasses, and handed them to me.

I frowned. "I put them in there so I'd be able to find them later."

"I know. You have a system."

"That's right."

I stood up, slipped my feet into my shoes and my arms into the sleeves of my jacket, and smoothed my hands over my hair and lapels.

"Do I look okay?" I asked hopefully.

Jenna looked me up and down. "Maybe after some coffee."

I followed her a few steps into the outer office, which, in spite of the early hour, was already starting to buzz with activity. Jenna started down the hall toward the kitchen, but came face-to-face with two very tall, very fit, very serious-looking men dressed in dark suits. Without speaking, one of them started opening closet doors and peering around corners. The other walked up to her and asked, "Is Miss Toomey alone in her office?"

Secret Service agents make Jenna nervous. She says that the way they look at her, faces like flint, makes her feel like they suspect her of something.

She called out over her shoulder, "Luce!"

"He's here?" I asked. "Why? He's supposed to be at the TV station."

Hearing my voice, the agent looked across the room to me and repeated the question, "Miss Toomey, is there anyone else in your office?"

I shook my head. The agent lifted his sleeve to his mouth, mumbling the all clear into a tiny microphone hooked to the cuff of his starched white shirt before he and his partner moved into position on either side of the hallway, standing as still and stalwart as two stone lions. A moment later, a door opened and Governor Thomas W. Ryland came striding down the hallway.

"Happy Election Day!" he boomed.

Bleary-eyed staffers, their faces suddenly bright, looked up from what they were doing, got to their feet, and started to clap. The governor flashed his famous smile and waved, hand high over his head, calling out to them over the applause, thanking them in advance for all their hard work.

"It's going to be a great day! Historic! We couldn't have done it without you. Now, let's everybody go back to it, eh? See you tonight at the victory party!"

His pronouncement brought another brief wave of applause, but it died off quickly as everyone returned to work. Tom walked up to Jenna and shook her hand. She'd been working for me for more than a year, and she still blushed every time he spoke to her, but hey, she was only twenty-four. He had that effect on people. I got it.

He dropped her hand and turned toward me. "Morning, Luce! Beautiful day. Who are you voting for?"

"Still trying to make up my mind," I said, and crossed my arms over my chest.

I'm too old to be charmed.

"What are you doing here?" I asked him. "You're supposed to be recording interviews for the East Coast morning shows."

I really hadn't expected to see him until tonight. There were about two hundred other places he needed to be that day.

"We finished up a little early," he said brightly. "So, thought I'd just drop by and rally the troops before we drive back to the hotel to pick up Leah and go vote. After that, I've got a photo op, then a breakfast speech to the teachers' unions, then back to the station to record more interviews for the West Coast morning shows, followed by another speech, three more photo ops, and two rallies before we go to the hotel to watch the returns. See? You can quit scowling at me anytime, Lucy. I know where I'm supposed to be as well as you do. And even if I didn't, is that any way to talk to your future commander in chief?"

"You're not commander in chief yet."

I stood aside to let him pass and then looked at Jenna. "Coffee ready?"

She nodded. "I'll bring it in."

"Hold my calls for a few minutes, will you?"

I followed him inside and closed the door behind me. As soon as I did, the governor slumped into a chair, the hail-fellow-well-met persona of a moment before melting away like a morning mist. Suddenly, I understood why he was there.

It was Election Day. Tom Ryland had come looking for me, as he had on so many other Election Days, nervous, anxious, afraid of wanting this win too much, afraid he'd already lost, in need of reassurance. He'd come, not to rally the troops, but so the troops—so I—could rally him.

For a moment, I had to fight back the urge to get up from my chair and kiss the top of his head.

Instead, I opened my top left desk drawer, which held six identical boxes of Girl Scout cookies, took a cookie for myself, then held the open box out to him.

"Want one?"

Still slumped in his chair, he lifted his hand, waving off the offer. "How are you able to eat so many of those things and not gain weight?"

"I've got the metabolism of a rabid wolverine," I mumbled through a mouthful of coconut, chocolate, and caramel. "When I was little, my mom was worried I was too skinny, so she started feeding me Girl Scout cookies. It worked. I gained seven pounds and developed a lifelong addiction to Samoas."

He leaned forward and picked the box up off my desk, frowning as he read the package. "Samoas? Then why does it say Caramel deLite on the box?"

"The name is different depending on which bakery the cookies ship from. But to me, they'll always be Samoas. Caramel deLite is a stupid name. Sounds like a stripper in a cheap night-club."

He smiled a little. "You're never shy about giving your opinions, are you?"

"I'm in the wrong line of work for that."

48

His smile faded. "According to last night's Quinnipiac poll," he said glumly, sinking back into his seat, "I'm not going to be commander in chief. They still show us down by four points."

"They're wrong. It's going to come down to Texas, Illinois, and the weather. If the rain holds off and we get a good turnout in Chicago, we've still got a chance."

"So that's it?" he huffed. "After three years of campaigning and billions of dollars, the question of who gets to be president comes down to whether or not it rains in Cook County? Insanity." He laced his fingers behind his head, looked up at the ceiling, and blew out a long breath.

"Sure you don't want a cookie?"

He shook his head and sat up straighter in his chair, his expression solemn.

"Lucy, the reason I came by is . . . I just wanted to say that, no matter what happens today, I'm glad we made the trip. We changed some attitudes and moved the debate. Even a Gardner administration is going to have to pay attention to the issues we raised and try to be more bipartisan. That ain't nothin'," he said, his voice becoming a little emotional. "And I'm truly grateful to you for making it happen."

He held out his hand so I could grip it.

"Stop it."

He frowned. "Stop what?"

"Stop making concession speeches. I mean it." I

raised a single finger to stay his protestations. Tom withdrew his hand.

"If it comes to that, I'll be the first one to say so, but now is not the time. You've got to keep your game face on and believe. Believe in yourself. Believe in the smart people who helped you get this far. Believe in the voters."

"Believe in the weatherman?" He cocked an eyebrow at me.

"Him too.

"Governor," I said, "you and I have been down this road plenty of times. I could sit here for the next fifteen minutes and pump up your confidence, tell you how brilliant you are, how brilliant your campaign strategy is, how your message has resonated with the voters, but frankly, neither of us has time for that today. I could pull out a bunch of charts and graphs to try to convince you that I know what I'm talking about, but I don't have time for that either. You've known me long enough to know that I'm not just trying to pump sunshine up your kazoo. I've always told you the truth, and the truth is: We've still got a chance."

I leaned toward him, both hands flat on the desk. "Quinnipiac doesn't know what I know. And what I *know,* with every ounce of political instinct in my body, is that you're still in this thing!"

I smacked my hand so hard on my desk that the plastic cup holding my pens tipped over. The governor flinched, which was good. I had his attention.

"So quit making speeches, all right? Because it's really starting to piss me off."

He raised his hands as if to protect his now smiling face from my ire. "All right! Don't go upsetting yourself."

I smiled back, and for a moment it was like the old days, when it was just Tom and me, making it up as we went, before the arrival of the entourage.

"Now, get out of my office and get back to work. I'll see you at the party."

There was a knock on the door. The governor straightened his shoulders and tie.

"Can't I sit and drink my coffee first?"

"I'll have Jenna put a lid on it. You can take it with you."

I got up from my desk and opened the door. Jenna was standing there with empty hands and anxious eyes.

"Sorry, Luce. I know you said to hold your calls, but Barney Purcell is on the line. He says it's urgent."

Barney Purcell? I knew that name. He was . . . a field operative?

"He's calling with updated polling data?"

Jenna shook her head, her face somber. "Barney Purcell. Your cousin. He's calling from Wisconsin. Lucy, there's been . . . an accident. It sounds pretty bad."

❧ Chapter 5 ❧

I bit my lower lip, the phone pressed to my ear, as Barney, who sounded shaken, described what had happened.

"They don't know how long she's been unconscious. One of the neighbors came over this morning and found her in bed, unresponsive, with an open bottle of sleeping pills on the nightstand. She was barely breathing."

An overdose? Oh, dear God. I thought we were past all that.

"How many did she take?"

"Nobody knows," Barney said. "The doctor said it could have been an accident. Maybe she woke up, forgot she'd already taken the pills, and took more."

I pressed my hand to my forehead and closed my eyes, picturing Alice awake and alone in the night, dialing my number, getting no answer, getting no rest, reaching for the bottle of pills. *Why hadn't I left the phone on? Why?*

"But she's okay? The doctor said she's all right?"

"He said her respiration is good."

I breathed a sigh of relief. *Thank you.*

"They're running some blood work. I'm here in

the waiting room, but I don't know what I'm supposed to do. I think you'd better come out here."

"Sure, sure," I said quickly, my mind racing, a little less panicked now that I knew Alice was breathing without a problem. "Hang on a sec, Barney."

I tucked the phone tight between my shoulder and ear, grabbed a pen, scribbled *Flights to Wisconsin* on a yellow Post-it, and handed the note to Jenna, who hurried off as soon as she read it.

"Okay. I'll catch the first flight out tomorrow morning."

"Tomorrow?" Barney sounded frantic. "Lucy, you've got to come *now*. I can't handle this! You're the one who should be making the decisions, not me."

I propped my elbow on my desk and rested my forehead in my hand, eyes closed, trying to focus. "I know, Barney. I know. I'll be there just as soon as I can, I promise. The election . . ."

The weight of a hand on my shoulder interrupted my words. I opened my eyes. Tom Ryland stood over me.

"Tell him that you're catching the next plane out of here."

"But, Governor . . ."

"You're going. If I have to drive you to the airport myself, you're going right this second.

This is your sister we're talking about, Lucy. You've *got* to go."

Looking into his eyes, stern and as gray as granite, I knew he was right. The realization splashed over me like icy water, shocking me back to sensibility. What had I been thinking? Alice was breathing, thank God. She would be all right. But she was frightened of hospitals. When she woke up, I had to be there.

Phone still to my ear, I stood up and grabbed my coat off the back of my desk chair.

"Barney, I'm leaving right now. I'm not sure about the flight schedules, but I'll call you when I change planes in Chicago. If they'll let you in the room, tell Alice she got her way. Tell her I'm coming home."

All the outgoing flights from Denver to the Midwest were full—there was a snowstorm coming and everybody was trying to get out of town before it hit—but I headed to the airport anyway, figuring I could just go standby. Surely a seat would open up for me. It did, but not until five o'clock.

By the time I finally boarded a flight to Chicago, the snow was starting to fall. We taxied to the runway only to be told that air traffic control had just declared that visibility was too low to allow takeoffs. Rather than return to the gate, we sat there waiting for the runway to open. By the time it did, ice had built up on the wings, so we got to sit some more, waiting for the ground crew to de-ice us.

I'm sure I'd been more frustrated in my life, but it was hard to remember when. Having my phone battery give out did nothing to improve my mood, not even after we were finally able to take off. For the next two hours and thirteen minutes, there was nothing for me to do but drink scotch, eat pretzels, and think.

I thought about Alice, of course. I felt incredibly guilty for leaving my phone off the night before, for possibly being the catalyst for Alice's accidental overdose. But . . . was it accidental? Could she have taken those pills on purpose?

Alice had had a tendency toward depression since her early twenties, after returning home from a disastrous and ill-advised year at college. Once, she swallowed a whole bottle of some over-the-counter painkillers and had to be hospitalized. But that was a long time ago. The doctor put her on medication after that, and her mood swings became less pronounced, but it wasn't always enough, especially during the winter. That's why I always leave my phone on. I can usually gauge Alice's mood by listening for the twitches and repeated phrases that signal anxiety, the sighs that accompany a rising tide of depression. I can usually pick up on those things, but I hadn't heard anything worrisome lately.

No, that wasn't true. Not really.

On the night before my birthday, Alice told me she was sad. I'd felt a flash of unease when she sighed, but dismissed it as a ploy to convince me to come home for Christmas. I love my sister, but when she puts her mind to it, Alice can be a master manipulator. But . . . isn't everybody? At least sometimes?

I should have left my phone on. From here on out, I promised myself, I would, no matter how exhausted I was. It would be easier once the election was over; I'd have more time. Well . . . probably not. Especially if we won. But I'd just have to figure it out. Once Alice was out of the hospital and feeling better, I would.

The plane shuddered and bounced and the "Fasten Seat Belt" light came on. The pilot announced that we'd begun our initial descent and advised the flight attendants to pick up any remaining cups and glasses quickly, then buckle up for the remainder of the flight. It was going to be a bumpy ride, he said; there were thunderstorms in Chicago.

Thunderstorms in Chicago? *Damn it!*

Rain was coming down in sheets. Pushed by side winds, the plane skidded to the right as we made contact with the tarmac, but we made it.

Sprinting up the Jetway and into the terminal, I started digging through my purse for my phone and charger, scanning the walls of waiting areas and corridors for an unoccupied charging station. There were people everywhere, and every one of them seemed to be tethered to an electrical outlet, captives chained to the walls by power cords. The storm had all but closed the airport; planes were being allowed to land but not to take off. Stranded travelers trying to phone their families or access the Internet to rearrange their plans were making use of every available power source.

A man in the waiting area of gate C22 wearing earbuds and a T-shirt that said, "Another Day with No Plans to Use Calculus" sat cross-legged on the floor waiting for his iPod to charge. I squatted down next to him, but his eyes were closed as he listened to his music. I shook his shoulder to get his attention.

"Hey!"

He jumped, surprised to see a strange woman staring at him, and pulled the buds out of his ears.

"Yeah?"

"I'll give you five dollars if you let me use that outlet to charge my phone."

He frowned and looked around as if he thought this might be a joke and someone might be filming us. "Uh-uh. I've gotta charge up before my flight leaves. Can't fly to LA without my tunes."

"Just let me use it for a little while," I begged. "Fifteen minutes. Ten."

"Dude, I already told you. I don't want to be stuck on a plane to—"

I reached into my purse and got out my wallet. "Twenty bucks," I said. "Two dollars a minute. Please? I've got a very important call to make. My sister is in the hospital and I'm trying to get home. Seriously, dude. I'm not kidding."

The man looked at the money, then at me, and shrugged. "It's all yours."

I plugged my phone into the socket, pressed the "on" button, and sat down on the floor with my back against the wall, chewing on my thumbnail while I waited for the phone to power up. I knew Barney would be anxious to know where I was, but I'd spoken to him not long before leaving Denver. Alice was doing fine then, so I wasn't quite as concerned about talking to him as I was about getting in touch with headquarters. I'd check in with Jenna first, then call Barney. She'd be able to give me the latest on wins, losses, and projections . . . *if* my phone would just finish booting up! Why was it taking so long?

Glancing up, I spotted a television tuned to CNN on the far side of the waiting area. A red, white, and blue video graphic with the words "Decision: 2016" came on the screen. I asked the guy in the T-shirt to watch my phone for a minute and crossed the room to the television without waiting for him to respond.

A small cluster of other travelers stood under the television set, just as transfixed as I was, watching two anchors exchange backchat about it being a historic evening and an exciting race. I'd met the younger anchor, Sam, on several occasions. Right after Iowa, we'd gone out for a couple of drinks. I thought it was just a work thing, but the more we talked, the more I realized he thought we were on a date, so I said I had to get up early the next day, insisted on paying for my own drink, and headed up to my hotel room. I can't date journalists. And he did this thing, constantly reaching up and smoothing his hair, that got on my nerves. Plus, he was shorter than me. Anyway, that was after Iowa. I'm sure he'd have found me less fascinating after New Hampshire.

He was harkening back to the Iowa race now, saying it had been a game changer, had awakened the imagination of a previously apathetic electorate, thanks to the entry of dark-horse candidate Governor Thomas Ryland, the first successful presidential nominee from the state of Colorado, who had not only won New York and all of the New England states as expected, but also Pennsylvania and North Carolina, surprising everyone.

"Everyone but me," I said under my breath, studying the electoral map graphic that appeared on the screen, clutching my hands into fists, mentally adding up the figures. It was close. Very close. My palms started to sweat.

Sam and his sidekick exchanged more banalities, eating up time and commenting about how Senator Gardner's big electoral wins in Florida and Ohio meant this was still anybody's race.

The older anchor, with a gray mustache and a grizzled voice, looked to his counterpart and said, "It's a tighter contest than anybody could have guessed, Sam, but I predict that the outcome is going to come down to one state, which was still too close to call in our last segment—Illinois."

"I already know that!" I shouted. "Come on, guys! Let's just get to the results!"

"Seriously!" barked a middle-aged man who was standing next to me. "Cut the chatter and tell us who won!"

As if in response to our protests, the grizzled anchor lifted his hand to his ear.

"The polls have just closed on the West Coast. We are now ready to predict that Senator Robert Gardner will win the states of Michigan, Indiana, Missouri, and Iowa," he intoned, the gray patches on the map behind him turning to red and blue as he spoke. "However, Governor Tom Ryland has all but run the board in the West, even squeaking out a surprising win in Texas *and*," he said, his voice rising with excitement, his face splitting into a grin, "the state of Illinois! Which means that Tom Ryland is going to be the next president of the United States!"

"Yes!" I screamed. "Yes! Yes! Yes!"

People surrounding the television broke into cheers or groans, depending on their political proclivities. I grabbed the man standing next to me and hugged him as hard as I could. Fortunately, he was wearing a Ryland button. He laughed when I let go of him, then whooped and hugged me back, actually lifting me a couple of inches from the ground and dancing around in a circle.

I didn't mind.

I felt like raising a flag and ordering a twenty-one-gun salute to *my* candidate, Governor Tom Ryland! No! *President* Ryland! President of the United States of America! Tears came to my eyes. I actually started to cry! It was like Christmas, New Year's, and Mardi Gras had all fallen on the same day. For about sixty seconds, I was having the best day of my life.

The man with the Ryland button put me back down. He laughed again, and so did I. I probably would have hugged him again, but felt a tap on my shoulder and turned around. The guy who didn't like calculus was standing there with my phone.

"Dude, your phone kept ringing, so I went ahead and answered it. Somebody wants to talk to you. Says it's important."

"Sorry! I mean, thanks!" I laughed, breathless and flustered, grinning as I took the phone from his outstretched hand, certain it was Jenna calling to tell me the news I already knew. Or maybe even the governor—No! The president-elect!

"Hello? Jenna?"

I heard a voice, but the connection was bad and there was so much noise in the terminal that I couldn't make out what it said.

"What? Jenna, what did you say?"

"Where are you?"

"Oh, Barney!" I laughed. "Sorry, it's kind of noisy here. Listen, I'm still in the Chicago airport. There were a bunch of thunderstorms, so my plane was late getting in and all the outgoing flights are delayed. The board still shows my flight to Green Bay leaving on time, but I bet they end up delaying or even canceling. It'd probably be faster to rent a car and drive. I should be there in about five hours. How's she doing?"

"The doctor just came out to see me," Barney said, then fell silent, pausing for so long that I said his name again, thinking the call had been dropped. When he spoke again, his voice was hoarse.

"Oh, Lucy . . . Oh God. She didn't make it, Lucy. The doctor just came out to tell me." He choked out a sob. "Alice died about twenty minutes ago."

✄ Chapter 6 ✄

For the next thirty-six hours, I felt like I was underwater. My reactions were slow and laborious, and the whole world was muffled and blurred at the edges.

I pointed my rental car north and drove to Door County in the dark, submerging my thoughts into the white noise of rubber on asphalt, drawn into the current of traffic that swirled through and past the city, eventually spilling out onto country roads, taking me past landmarks that had been familiar for the entire first half of my life but that now were so disconnected from who I am that they seemed like mirages, objects and places that might melt away at my touch.

Barney met me at the hospital. He'd been waiting for me, holding vigil, I suppose, his eyes red from crying. Barney, my last living relative, an apple farmer and lifelong bachelor, is about twice my age, his hair completely white and his leathery face lined with wrinkles. He'd always been nice to Alice and me when we were little, teaching us to drive the tractor, saving the best apples to give us as treats, pretending he couldn't find us when we played hide-and-seek, comforting me when Alice would challenge me to a race through the orchard and I would inevitably lose, assuring me that I'd get bigger and catch up someday, drying my tears and carrying me back to the farmhouse on his shoulders. But that day, I was the one comforting him.

He was an emotional wreck and so exhausted. I hugged him, thanked him, absolved him, and sent him home to get some rest, promising I could take it from there and would join him at the farm as soon as I could. After he left, I talked with the attending physician, tried hard to focus as he explained what had happened, the damage done to Alice's liver, the complications caused by the length of time between the ingestion of the pills and the discovery of her unconscious form, and the possibility that her other overdose, all those years before, had caused some previous damage.

It was hard to understand, but I nodded as if I did, absolving him as well without quite believing it was my place to do so, wondering why I wasn't crying and worrying about what that meant.

There were papers to sign, calls and arrangements to make. I phoned Jenna to let her know that I would have to stay in Wisconsin for a few days, then sat in the waiting room waiting for the men from the mortuary to arrive, drinking bitter coffee and working on an obituary for the newspaper, going through five drafts before putting it aside, realizing I had no idea what to say.

By the time I dealt with the most pressing concerns, it was nearly dawn. I drove the rental car to Barney's house, surprised that I still remembered exactly how to get there, and went to sleep in his spare bedroom under a blue-and-white granny-square afghan my mom had crocheted and given him for Christmas in 1989.

I remembered that too. Strange how it all comes back.

❧ Chapter 7 ❧

I woke up around noon. Barney made me a plate of bacon and eggs; that and spaghetti were the only things he knew how to cook that didn't come from the frozen-food aisle.

When I finished eating, I drove to Sedgwick's Funeral Home. Father Eugene Damon, pastor of St. Agnes of the Lake, the parish I'd grown up in and out of years before but which Alice had attended faithfully, met me there.

Something about the sight of a clerical collar makes me feel instantly exposed, as though any person wearing one can see right through me, knows all my secrets and failures. In the case of Father Damon, this was probably true. He'd been the priest and confessor to my sister as well as my parents and probably knew more of the

Toomey family secrets than anyone in town, perhaps even more than me. It was a disconcerting thought.

But when George Sedgwick, the funeral director, started asking questions about the service, the interment, the disposition of the remains, I was glad Father Damon was sitting next to me. He stepped in, answering questions I had no answers to, making me feel as though I were doing well and that everything was being handled properly.

"Saturday is better for the service. That way people won't have to take off work to attend. But solid brass handles won't be necessary," he said, shaking his head when Mr. Sedgwick made the suggestion. "And a simple hardwood casket will be fine, don't you think so, Lucy? Maybe with the cherry stain? It's a nice, warm color. Or the pecan?"

I nodded and said "pecan" not because I felt certain of my choice, but because it was the last word I had heard and I couldn't remember what the other options were.

Father Damon smiled encouragingly. "Good choice," he said. "Alice wouldn't have wanted to spend the money on a bronze or copper casket. She liked to keep things simple."

Mr. Sedgwick set his lips into a line, nodded tersely, and made a notation on the pad in front of him. He clearly didn't appreciate the priest's interference with his profit margins, but couldn't say so.

"I assume burial will be in the family plot?"

I was confused, so George explained further.

"When your folks purchased their plots, they bought some for you and your sister as well. They wanted the family to rest together for eternity. When the time comes, you'll know you always have a home here in Nilson's Bay."

He gave me a liquid sort of smile, as if he couldn't imagine a more thoughtful expression of parental regard.

They'd bought me a plot?

I could understand my parents making such a purchase for themselves or even Alice. But for *me?*

Of all the things of value my parents could have given me—and there had been precious few over the years—why would a burial plot rise to the top of the list?

Maybe the folks had gotten a group discount for buying all the plots at once—a four-for-the-price-of-three offer? I wouldn't put it past Dad. He never paid retail for anything if he could help it, aside from groceries, and he did his best to get around even that. I was in college before I knew what less-than-day-old bread tasted like.

I suddenly had a vision of my father sitting in this very room, in this very chair, talking to Mr. Sedgwick, saying, "Well, what about that plot on the end? Throw that in as a sweetener and you've got yourself a deal. I know it's six inches too short for a regular casket, but Lucy's small; she can squeeze in."

The corner of my lip twitched, threatening a smile, but I quickly cleared my throat, keeping my expression neutral.

"Well, it's good to have that settled in advance."

"Isn't it, though?" the mortician said earnestly, leaning across his desk. "You'd be amazed how many people go through their whole lives without giving a thought to the hereafter." He sighed regretfully before picking up his pen and moving on. "Now, what would you like to do about flowers?"

"Do about them?" I asked, looking at the priest for clarification. "Don't people just send them?"

"They do," Father Damon replied. "And a spray of roses on the casket is nice, perhaps a wreath or standing arrangement as well, but you only need so many flowers. After the service they just wilt and get thrown away. You might want to give people the option of doing something more lasting by making a donation to a charity instead. Perhaps to the pet rescue?"

Why hadn't I thought of that? Alice loved her work at the pet rescue. It only paid minimum wage but, realistically, it was one of the only jobs in town she could have handled. And she adored working with animals. When she was young, she wanted to be a vet, just like Dad. If not for the accident, she probably would have been.

"Yes, a memorial fund for the pet rescue. Alice would have liked that."

"I'll add that to the notice in the paper," Mr. Sedgwick said, scribbling a note before looking up at me. "One more thing. Do you want to add a satin pillow and coverlet to the casket? To give the impression of her being asleep? People sometimes find that comforting."

"Yes to the pillow," Father Damon said, answering for me. "But the coverlet won't be necessary. The FOA is making a quilt to go into the casket. They'll deliver it first thing on Saturday, before the service."

"The FOA?" I asked. Was this some kind of community group or association? Friends of Animals? That made sense, since we were talking about my sister.

"Friends of Alice," Father Damon explained. "Rinda Charles, Daphne Olsen, and Celia Brevard. All three of them moved to town within the last few years, and you know how Nilson's Bay can be—slow to accept strangers. Anyway, Alice sort of adopted them, just the way she did with animals, like they were strays. They were all very close. One day, somebody made a joke about them forming their own club, the Friends of Alice Society, and the name stuck. Now people just say FOA. Alice never mentioned them to you?"

I'd never heard of the FOA, but the names—Rinda, Daphne, and Celia—were familiar. I knew they sometimes did some sewing together. Alice had taken up quilting during that time in the psychiatric hospital—occupational therapy—but I couldn't remember much else about her friends.

Alice talked so often about so many people, animals, and events that it was sometimes hard to follow the conversation. The world was very immediate for Alice and also very small. She sort of assumed that everyone she knew, knew everybody else and so didn't offer much in the way of explanation. Honestly, I hadn't asked for any. In my defense, it didn't help that she tended to call me in the middle of the night. I'd just lie there with my eyes closed and the phone to my ear and let her talk; every now and then I'd mumble, "Oh?" or "Really?" or "Uh-huh." But I wasn't truly listening. I was too tired to pay attention. Now I wished I had.

Rinda, Daphne, and Celia . . . At least one of them had children—of that I was sure. I remembered Alice sometimes said something about one of the daughters coming over, but I didn't know more than that. And one of them was a teacher of some kind and one had moved from Chicago. I didn't remember anything more about the FOA, but, obviously, they were very close to my sister. Closer than I'd been.

"You never see one without the other three,"

Father Damon said, and then stopped for a moment, his Adam's apple bobbing as he swallowed back his emotions. "Well, not until now."

When we were finished with the funeral arrangements, Father Damon walked me to the car. The day was bright and crisp. A gusty wind stirred up piles of dry leaves and sent them skittering across the pavement.

"Thank you for coming, Father. You made this a lot easier."

"Not at all," he said, waving off my thanks. "Funeral arrangements can be overwhelming. It's good to bring a wingman along. And, you know, Alice was dear to me. She was dear to a lot of people in town. If you didn't know that before, you will on Saturday. I predict a full house.

"Of course," he said with a smile, "any funeral in Nilson's Bay attracts a crowd. Being such a small town, people feel more or less obligated to attend even if they didn't like the deceased. But people *did* like Alice. You'll see. I know that you hadn't spent much time with her in the last few years, but when she was feeling herself, your sister was easy to like."

"What about when she wasn't feeling herself?"

I don't know where that came from; I honestly don't. The minute I said it, I looked at the ground, then clicked the key fob to unlock the door of the car, too embarrassed to face the priest, hoping he hadn't heard me. But he had.

"Lucy," he said after an uncomfortable pause, "is there something you want to ask me?"

"No. Not really. I was just . . . I guess I was wondering . . ."

"You were wondering?"

He looked at me straight on, his gaze so solid. I couldn't get away from it.

"When I was growing up, the church had . . . certain rules about conducting funerals. I think things have changed since then, but you've been in the priesthood a long time, Father, and I . . ." I bit my lower lip, trying to figure out how to phrase the question. "I guess I was just wondering if you felt any hesitation in performing the service on Saturday?"

"Lucy. If you're asking me if I think Alice committed suicide, the answer is no. She suffered from depression on and off for many years; I'm not telling you anything you don't know. But was she depressed enough to end her life?" He shook his head. "Absolutely not. Alice wanted to live and to live happily; she just didn't always know how."

He lowered his head slightly, his eyes boring into me again. "Nothing you said or did or didn't do caused or contributed to Alice's death. It wasn't your fault. Nor was it Alice's. It was an accident."

I nodded and swallowed back tears. My first instinct about the old priest was correct; he could see right through me.

"Thank you," I whispered, pressing a clenched fist to the corner of my eye.

Father Damon nodded, then shoved his hands into his pockets and changed the subject. I was grateful for it.

"How long will you be staying in Nilson's Bay?"

"I'll be leaving right after the funeral. Sunday at the latest."

Father Damon frowned. "But won't you need to stick around and help clear up the estate? You're Alice's closest living relative. I don't think she had much in the way of worldly goods, but there is the cottage. Surely she must have left it to you."

The cottage? He was right. Who else would Alice leave the family home to? How had I forgotten about that? But death has a way of re-ranking your priorities and clearing your mind of debris. Maybe that is part of its purpose. On the other hand, maybe death is just death.

"You should stay in town for a while, a few days at least. From the look of you," the old priest said, "you're long overdue for a vacation. But the election must have been very exciting. You know, I saw you on television once, right after the Iowa caucuses. You were very good. Don't tell anyone," he said, glancing from left to right. "As a priest in a small parish, I've learned it's best to keep your politics to yourself—but I voted for Ryland. He's a man who can bring the country together again."

"Thank you, Father. When I see him, I'll tell him you said so. But that's why I've got to go back as soon as I can. There's a lot of work to do. I should get to Washington and help with the transition."

"So you'll be getting a job in the new administration? You don't look too happy about it."

"Oh, I am," I assured him. "Who wouldn't want to work for the president of the United States? They can't offer me a big job, of course. Even though I ran the campaign . . . for a while. I don't have any White House experience or the kind of technical knowledge required for the top positions."

I stopped myself; there was no need to go into specifics.

"Anyway," I went on, "with my background, I won't get an offer for anything that important. Maybe an assistant to an assistant undersecretary in some department. Which is fine," I said, resting my backside against the door of the car. "It all matters. But, between you and me, I'm not crazy about the idea of going back to Washington."

Father Damon shoved his hands even deeper in his pockets, looking puzzled. "Really? I visited once and it seemed like a wonderful city. There's so much to do. All the museums and monuments—"

"I'll never get to see any of them. Politics is a great career, especially if you win. But, if you'll forgive the analogy, it's also something of a mad monk society."

Father Damon laughed.

"No, seriously," I said. "If you work in politics, there is this silent agreement that you will have no personal life, no outside interests, no outside anything. People who sleep more than four hours in a night are considered slackers. It's a competition to see who can kill themselves quickest.

"It's not so bad when you're doing a campaign, because there's this . . ." I looked up into the branches of the nearest maple tree, trying to find the right word. ". . . this adrenaline rush. I think that's why they call a campaign a race. That's what it feels like, like racing.

"You're pushing yourself as hard as you can toward the goal, throwing everything you've got into it. It's as if your whole body is flooded with endorphins and you feel powerful, like you've got a chance to change the world! Your mind is so sharp, your thinking so clear. You know exactly where the goal line is and nothing else matters. The difference is that instead of lasting for one hundred yards, or a mile, or a marathon, the feeling lasts for weeks or months or, if the finish line is the White House, even years! But the feeling of winning is . . ."

I stopped myself again.

If I told him that in the middle of rushing to my dying sister's bedside, I had, for a moment, been having the best day of my life, Father Damon would think I was a terrible person. Maybe I was.

"Well . . . it's hard to describe. It's amazing. And fleeting. As soon as the win is over, you start racing again. Governing is just as intense, but the course is even longer and the goal is harder to define. And you know when you finally reach the finish line, four years later, or even eight," I said, thinking that in eight years I'd be forty-four years old, "there is no way you'll be able to match the high of that first victory. Nothing could top that."

"Why not join a new campaign?" the priest asked. "Find a new candidate."

I shook my head. He didn't understand. How could he? Even with his imposing white collar and wise gray head, he was still just a civilian.

And I was a card-carrying member of the Mad Monk Society.

"It doesn't work like that, Father. Not for me. I've spent my whole career with Ryland. There will never be another candidate like him, not for me. I'll follow him anywhere. Even to Washington—the city with the largest per capita population of pompous, self-absorbed horse's asses in these United States." I laughed nervously. "Sorry. I guess I shouldn't say 'ass' to a priest."

He smiled. "I've heard the word before. And met more than a few right here in Nilson's Bay. Don't ask me to name names. But you think that our nation's capital has more than its share?"

I opened the car door and sat down in the driver's seat, rolling down the window so I could continue the conversation.

"Definitely. And I'm not just talking about members of Congress—though some of them definitely qualify. Do you know that when you go to a cocktail party on Capitol Hill, nobody makes eye contact? I'm serious!" I declared, countering the silent skepticism in Father Damon's eyes.

"When you are talking to somebody at a party in the district, the person you're talking with is always scanning the room behind you to see if they can find somebody more important or more useful. It's true. You could be baring your soul to someone, and right in the middle of your sentence, they'll interrupt and say, 'Excuse me. The secretary of the interior just came in. Call me and we'll do lunch.'

"And just like that," I said, snapping my fingers, "they're gone and you're standing there alone in the crowd, swirling the ice in your glass and looking like a wallflower."

I turned the key in the ignition, bringing the engine to life.

"And you know what the worst part is? That I completely get it. I'm just as bad as all the rest of them, Father. And yet," I sighed, "I'm planning to go back there for the next four years, possibly eight. Voluntarily."

I put my foot on the brake, shifted into drive, and looked up at him.

"Do you think there's something wrong with me?"

Father Damon worked his lips for a moment, weighing the question.

"Probably," he said.

❦ Chapter 8 ❦

My cell phone rang at 5 a.m. on Saturday. Eyes still shut, I reached up and groped the top of the nightstand, a reflexive response after all these years, and answered on the fourth ring.

"Can't sleep?" I mumbled, my voice raspy. "Alice, can't you leave the bedroom door closed? The cats won't starve during—"

"Miss Toomey?"

The voice on the other end of the line didn't belong to Alice. I opened my eyes, saw the blue-and-white afghan on the bed, remembered where I was and why and that I would never again wake in the darkness to the sound of my sister's

78

voice, and experienced the stab of loss anew, a vacancy in my center.

"Miss Toomey?"

"Oh . . . Yes. I'm sorry. This is Lucy."

"Please hold for the president-elect."

I rubbed the sand from the corners of my eyes, then grabbed the afghan from the end of the bed and wrapped it around my shoulders. It didn't seem right to hold a conversation with the next leader of the free world in a state of semi-undress, not even over the phone.

A moment later, he was on the line.

"Lucy?"

I cleared my throat. "Good morning, Mr. President-elect."

Groggy as I was, I couldn't help but smile as I addressed him by his new title, thinking how much better it would sound in just a few weeks' time, after we subtracted the suffix.

"How are you this morning, sir?"

It came to me automatically, this new formality of address. Of course, I'd always spoken to him this way in public. Anytime there were people present, he was sir, or Congressman, then Governor, but when it was just the two of us in the room, he'd been Tom. But things were different now. Aside from his wife and immediate family, he had no familiars.

This was what I had wanted, what *we* had wanted. Knowing it had come to pass made me proud. But also a little sad. We'd never be just Tom and Lucy again.

"Doing well, doing well. You sound a little rugged, though. Did I wake you?"

"No, sir." I blinked a few times, trying to bring the room into focus. "I was just getting up. Where are you, sir?"

"In the car, heading over to the Pentagon for a security briefing. I know it's early, but this is the only open spot in my day. I'm sorry I didn't get in touch sooner."

"No need to apologize, sir. I know you've been booked every second since the election. Thank you for sending the flowers. They're just beautiful."

I switched on the bedside lamp so I could see the arrangement of orange lilies with yellow roses with the card that read, "In our thoughts and prayers, Tom and Leah Ryland."

"Leah picked them out especially. I'll tell her you liked them. The funeral is today, isn't it? How're you holding up?"

"I'm fine," I assured him, sitting up a bit straighter and clutching the afghan tighter around my body. "I still have a few loose ends to tie up, but I'll be in DC sometime next week, hopefully by Thursday."

"There's no rush," he said. "In fact, that is part of the reason for my call. I think you should stay out there for a while, Lucy. Take some time off."

"You're very kind, sir, but that really won't be necessary—"

"Lucy," he said, cutting me off. "Hear me out for a second. This is a big deal. Your parents are gone, now your sister. You're all alone in the world, an orphan. It might not have hit you yet, but it will. And when it does . . ." He took in a breath and let it out. "You remember what it was like when Mike passed."

I did.

His brother, Mike, his last surviving relative, who had suffered a traumatic brain injury during his service in the First Gulf War, died of heart failure four months before the Iowa caucuses. The governor went home to Colorado for the funeral and was back on the campaign trail the next day. At first he appeared to be handling the loss well, but after a few days he started snapping at the staff, very uncharacteristically. He seemed unfocused, too, lethargic. He definitely wasn't himself.

At that stage in the race, every minute away from the campaign was a lost opportunity, but I cleared the schedule and sent him home to the ranch for a few days, over his strenuous objections, but I insisted.

"Everybody needs time to grieve," I told him at the time. Now he quoted my own words back to me.

"I appreciate your concern, sir, but the

best thing for me will be to get back to work."

"When was the last time you took a vacation?" He answered for me. "Never."

"Not true. I take my sister on vacation every Christmas. I did."

"Three days," he scoffed. "Four at the most, and you spend the whole time on your phone or answering e-mail."

"I went to Europe in 2013."

"Yeah, I remember because I was there; five countries in eight days, six major speeches, a dozen interviews, and thirty-three photo ops. That wasn't a vacation, Lucy. It was a 'fact-finding' tour designed to boost my international bona fides. I'm talking about you taking a real vacation."

"Sir, I appreciate your concern, but I'm doing just fine. I can't afford to take any time off now. There's so much to do before the inauguration. Somebody has to sort through all the—"

"I've already got the transition team in place. Miles is taking that job at CNN, but that's just as well. Drew, Natalie, and Steve are staying on through January, and we've already got short lists for all the cabinet posts and have begun vetting the candidates. Jenna is helping with that. Hope you don't mind . . ."

"Of course not, sir. But I just don't think this is the time for me to—"

"If not now, then when? You think things are

going to slow down after January twentieth? You have got to take some time for yourself, Lucy, and you've got to do it now. A month, maybe more."

"A month!"

My feet hit the cold wooden floor and the afghan dropped from around my shoulders. I stood there with the phone clutched to my ear, wearing nothing but a University of Wisconsin T-shirt, polka-dot underpants, and, I'm sure, an expression of panic.

"Mr. President-elect! I'm . . . I don't understand. Sir, if you're trying to tell me something or if you're unhappy with . . ."

I stopped, took two big breaths, trying to slow the pounding in my chest.

"Tom, are you firing me?"

"Firing you? No. Dammit, Lucy! I'm trying to do you a favor!"

He huffed in exasperation. "I didn't want to have to say this, but you look like hell. Seriously, Luce. Veterans returning from combat zones look less worn-out than you did when I last saw you. You need to take some time off and get a rest, a real rest. You need to sleep late, breathe deep, go on some long walks, eat some decent meals—something besides cookies and black coffee—and spend some time thinking about your sister and what you really want to do with your life."

What I wanted to do with my life? He *was* trying to fire me!

I plopped onto the edge of the bed, too shocked to speak. It felt like somebody had smashed a fist into my stomach.

"When you sent me out to the ranch that week," he continued, "I spent a lot of time thinking about Mike and all the things he never had a chance to do. Life goes so fast, Lucy. You shouldn't waste it doing anything but the things that speak to your heart. While I was home, I started really thinking about why I got into the campaign. I came to realize that, at least partly, it was because I didn't want to disappoint you."

"What?" Suddenly, I found my voice again. "Pardon me, sir, but that's a stupid reason to run for president. You've got to want it for yourself!"

"Can I finish my story?"

"Sorry," I said, hearing the rebuke in his voice and remembering I was talking to the man who would soon have access to the nuclear launch codes. "Go on, sir."

"One day while I was out there, I saddled up Diamond and went for a long ride, thinking it all through, sorting out what I had to offer to the country and what I really wanted to do with what was left of my life. I was gone all day. It was dark by the time we got back to the barn, but when I did, I knew that I wanted to run for president. And I knew that I wanted to win."

"And you did."

"*We* did. I couldn't have done it without you,

Lucy. Come January twentieth, our team needs to be rested and ready to govern because it's going to be a grueling four years. Exciting, but grueling."

"Four?" I asked, smiling as I bent down to pick up the afghan, then draping it over my shoulders again. "I'm counting on at least eight."

"All the more reason for you to take some time to decide if this is really how you want to spend the next eight years of your life. I don't want you signing up for this just because you're afraid of disappointing me. No!" he barked, silencing my protests before I could even voice them. "Don't say anything now. We'll discuss it in a month, after your vacation."

"Sir, I don't need a whole month. Maybe a week. Two at the most."

"Four at the *minimum*," he retorted, using the tone I recognized so well, the immovable "I carried fifty-one percent of the vote and you didn't" voice, the voice that tolerates no negotiation.

"And if you decide you need more time, that's fine. All I ask is that you be back in Washington by January second, refreshed and ready to move into your office in the West Wing on January twentieth."

I almost dropped the phone.

"I . . . I'm sorry . . . I—Did you say the West Wing?"

"I did," he replied, and I could almost hear his

grin, the pleasure he took in springing the surprise on me.

I was more than surprised. I was stunned.

For a career political operative, a job in the West Wing—*any* job in the West Wing—was the pinnacle, the thing we all aspired to. After Iowa, I'll admit that I'd entertained a few fantasies about working there, becoming one of the few, the chosen, an insider's insider. But New Hampshire had brought me back down to earth.

"Sir, I'm flattered. You know I am. Don't you think you'd catch a lot of flack for appointing me? What if—"

"What if what?" he snapped. "What if some deep-pocket donor or party hack tells me that you're a liability? That I can't afford to put my trust in somebody so untested? That I need to hire people who've been on the inside? I'll tell 'em to get the hell out of my Oval Office!

"My office. My White House. *My* rules. I listened to those idiots once. I won't do it again. They damn near cost me the election! But I did win, Lucy. *We* did! I'll be damned if I let anybody make me act like we didn't. Anybody who gives me flak about you had better get ready for a fight. I'll sic my FBI on them. Better yet, I'll invite 'em into the Oval Office for a chat, stick a knife in their hand, and scream for the Secret Service. We'll see how that goes!"

I put my hand over my mouth, covering a smile

that threatened to swell into a giddy laugh. Tom Ryland has a long fuse and you have to work pretty hard to light it, but he was on fire today. And on my behalf! I was touched, I really was, but I couldn't let him talk like that, not even in jest.

"Okay, sir. Let's just calm down a little bit. I know they record phone conversations in the Oval Office. Do they do the same thing when you're in the motorcade? If anyone is listening," I said in a loud voice, "he was just kidding."

"Not by much," he grumbled.

"Sir, I really am honored by your offer, but be practical; you don't want me in the West Wing. I'm an organizer, somebody who greases the skids and makes sure the wheels keep turning. What you need are policy wonks. I don't have any expertise in foreign relations, national security, or economics—not at that level. I'm not even a lawyer. And I've never held a job in the White House."

"Neither have I," he said. "That's why I want somebody I trust close by, somebody who understands how I think and has a complete grasp of what our message was during the campaign and why the voters sent us to Washington. That's why I'm going to appoint you deputy assistant for intergovernmental affairs, because I need somebody who can make sure everybody plays nice with everybody else. I don't want any hidden agendas in my administration. We're all going to pull in the same direction. I need you, Lucy. I do. I can't imagine doing this without you."

The walls of my throat felt thick. In all the years we'd been together, he'd never spoken to me quite like that, never come right out and said he needed me. Until that moment, I hadn't realized how long I'd been hoping to hear him say so.

"You don't have to give me an answer," he said. "Not today. Just tell me you'll think about it."

I bobbed my head and swallowed hard. "I will."

"Are you all right?" he asked, picking up on the rasp in my voice. "I'm sorry. Maybe I shouldn't have said anything, not on the day of your sister's funeral."

"No, no," I said, swiping at the corner of my eye. "It's fine. I'm fine."

"Take some time, Lucy. Mourn your sister. Get reacquainted with yourself and your hometown. Wisconsin must be a beautiful place to spend the holidays."

"The holidays?" I choked out a laugh. I couldn't help it. "Mr. President-elect, I have no intention of spending the holidays in Nilson's Bay."

"Then where will you go?"

"I don't know. But I can tell you this; the second I've wrapped up my business, I'll be on the next plane to anywhere that isn't here."

❧ Chapter 9 ❧

We say that we mourn the dead, and there is some truth in that.

We lament the flower frozen in full bloom, cut off at the moment of promise, or another long wilted, whose slow fading and drawn-out, painful diminishment cast a shadow over a vibrant and glorious past.

And yet.

Once the eyes are closed and the heart is stilled, we come to understand that the worst of the pain has passed. For them. The dead have no more use for pain, for memory or regret. Regret is for the living.

And so when we stand at the bedside, the graveside, the casket, our mourning is less for the beloved departed than it is for ourselves. We mourn the missed opportunity, the word unspoken or spoken in haste, the hole in our lives and the unsettling of our souls, our own disappointments and the loss of innocence. We gaze upon the stillness that is unending and feel our self-importance crack and the myth of our immortality smash. We stare upon the face of death to see ourselves more clearly, to satisfy our curiosity, to make peace with the inescapable.

We hold our breath, try to imagine what it would be like never to take another and what the departed know now that we don't. We try to conjure what the life we have left would look like if such knowledge were ours. We try to imagine ourselves kind and expansive and giving, balanced and patient, more honest, more thankful, more peaceful, content with what we have, mindless of what we have not.

We imagine ourselves happy. For a moment, we believe we can be.

And then, because we can't help ourselves, we breathe and, breathing, are reminded of the many other things we cannot help.

The faith of a moment fades and hope is replaced by the intimate knowledge of our imperfections. Lonely, weeping, we stand with our feet anchored to the ground, watching our better angels fly above us and beyond us to time out of mind, and we mourn.

❧ Chapter 10 ❧

I heard the clearing of a throat.

"Lucy? May I close the lid now?"

My heart clenched like a fist inside me. I bent my head over the still form in the casket, brushed my fingers across the brown curls spread across the satin pillow. Her face was so still and pale, an expression carved from ivory, like the face of someone who reminded me of someone I used to know.

I wanted to say something, but couldn't remember what. I took a step back, trying to think what it could be. Mr. Sedgwick moved into the vacancy and placed his hands on the coffin lid.

"Wait!" The sound of my voice stayed his movements. "Wait a minute."

I reached out and plucked a pink rose, still in bud, from the spray of flowers that stood nearby and carried it to the casket. I lifted the edge of a quilt of pink, green, and white, bound with periwinkle blue, and slid the long stem of the rose underneath so the flower was just peeping out, then pressed the fabric smooth across Alice's chest, tucking her in for the night ahead.

"I'm sorry," I whispered and kissed my sister's forehead.

I lifted my head, took a last look, and turned to face the mortician and his sober-suited assistants.

"All right. You can close it now."

I wasn't that surprised by the number of people who came to Alice's funeral; Father Damon had prepared me for that. But he forgot to mention the dogs.

Alice's part-time job at the pet rescue involved

cleaning cages, walking dogs, feeding cats, administering routine medications, that kind of thing. I didn't realize she had also become a sort of unofficial adoption coordinator, going to great lengths to find homes for recently rescued or abandoned animals, a sort of human-animal yenta. Judging by the scores of her clients, both two- and four-footed, who came to pay tribute to her match-making skills, she must have been a good one.

People brought cages with cats, birds, even a rabbit. The dogs were on leashes, every breed and size, from a shivering Chihuahua that peeked nervously out of Amanda Lane's shoulder bag, to a lumbering Newfoundland named Bruce, who sat on his haunches in a seat instead of lying on the floor and took up half a pew.

I was nervous about the presence of so many four-footed mourners, but they all behaved; no fighting, barking, or peeing. In fact, until the end of the proceedings, there wasn't a peep out of any of the animals, except for the snoring of an elderly, jowly bulldog who fell asleep almost as soon as things began and that of his elderly, jowly owner, Mr. Coates, who ran the little upholstery shop that was housed in the basement of the hardware store.

When the organ prelude began I went into the church and sat in the front row, on the right-hand side. Barney sat with me, blowing his nose through the whole thing. There was no one else in the family pew. We are all that's left now.

Three women came in soon after and walked to the front, sitting in the first pew on the left.

The first was tall, probably five foot ten, looked to be in her late forties, and had sandy-colored hair cut in a short, layered bob that stuck out at odd angles. It was hard to tell if the style was intentionally edgy or if she had just neglected to comb it that morning.

The next woman was thin, almost wiry looking, about my height, five foot six, probably in her early to middle fifties, and had a determined set to her jaw, as though daring anyone to try to make her cry. She had dark brown eyes, close-cropped black hair, and coffee-colored skin, which, frankly, surprised me. When I was in high school, our class didn't have a single African American student. Time marches on, I guess, even in Nilson's Bay.

The last member of the trio, who couldn't have been more than twenty-five, was a petite little thing, barely topping the five-foot mark, with bright blue eyes and a unicorn tattoo on her forearm. In contrast to the somber suits worn by her companions, the young one wore a dress of hot pink with a turquoise belt and turquoise cowboy boots. Clearly, she was one of those people who preferred to approach funerals as celebrations of life, but she was sobbing uncontrollably.

This was the FOA: Friends of Alice—I was sure of it. And if I'd had any doubts, they were banished when I saw how many of the mourners gave them pitying glances as they passed through the aisle, reaching out to pat their hands and mouth words of condolence, a consideration no one had offered me when I had passed by.

Father Damon reminded me that people in Nilson's Bay can take a long while to accept strangers. Apparently, the policy also applied to people who had been gone so long they had become strangers.

Perhaps I deserved it.

I folded my hands in my lap and looked at the blush-pink spray of roses, thinking how much Alice would have loved them. I sent her pink roses every year for her birthday, and she always called to gush over them, as if she were surprised by their arrival. She may have been—Alice lived in the moment. I always felt very pleased with myself after those calls. Much as she loved flowers, what she'd have loved more was for me to deliver them in person. I didn't. And now I couldn't.

I felt a hand on my shoulder and looked up and into the face of a man about my age, tall, with chestnut-colored hair and a beard, both neatly trimmed, and sympathetic brown eyes. His face seemed familiar.

"Lucy, I'm so sorry," he whispered, and squeezed my shoulder.

I ducked my head to acknowledge his words, wishing I could summon up a name to go with those eyes, wondering if I should say thank you or just keep silent. It seemed so odd to respond with thanks in a situation that was clearly so sad. I looked up again, but he was already walking toward the back of the crowded church, looking for a vacant seat.

I looked at Barney, who was wiping away tears with the back of his hand. "Who was that?"

Barney glanced over his shoulder. "Peter Swenson. Did you hear? He was just elected to the village council."

"That's Peter Swenson? Not the—"

The organ stopped abruptly. A bell rang and everyone rose. Father Damon, dressed in his violet vestments, entered to begin the mass.

I hadn't been to mass ten times in as many years. But the words of the liturgy, lodged in the deepest recesses of my memory, fell easily from my lips. There was some comfort in that, in submerging my voice into the murmurs of two hundred voices, in sinking to my knees and rising as one with the others. It made me feel less alone.

We had decided against the custom of opening the floor to allow people to say a few words about the deceased. Father Damon had urged me not to, saying it could take hours, Alice being so beloved in the community. He gave a eulogy instead. He'd asked if I'd like to do it, but I'd passed, saying I wasn't sure I'd be able to get through it without breaking down.

Father Damon made a good job of it. When he told the story of how she'd snuck into the feed store and freed a flock of baby chicks just before Easter, everyone laughed, including me. Though I didn't laugh quite as hard as the others. I'd never known anything about her staging a poultry prison break.

It suddenly occurred to me that almost anyone in the room would have given Alice a better eulogy than me, especially the three women sitting in the front left pew. I couldn't help but notice how Father Damon split his gaze equally between my pew and theirs as he spoke. It wasn't intentional, I was sure of that, but it was clear to me that he, like the others, considered the three Friends of Alice to be chief mourners at this funeral, those who had lost the most on this terrible day.

They were wrong.

Those three women, intimates to Alice but strangers to me, were mourning the loss of what they once had. I was mourning the loss of what I could have had but never would, the chance to really *know* my sister, to amass my own collection of funny, tender, and memorable Alice stories to treasure even in the void of death. I had no one to blame but myself.

As I cast my eyes forward to the polished wooden box, blanketed in pink roses, something cracked inside me. The tears I had been unable to shed flowed freely now. Barney, his own eyes red and raw, put his arm around me.

Father Damon finished his remarks, and I sank to my knees with the others, still weeping. Words of contrition I'd learned as a child emerged from my memory.

Through my fault, through my fault, through my most grievous fault . . .

For all I have done and all I have left undone . . .

Mercy. Mercy. Mercy.

The words played an unending loop inside my head, rising from my mind and falling ineffectually back to earth, bringing no mercy, no relief. And then it was over; the mass was ended and we were instructed to go in peace.

If only it were as easy as that.

Barney and the other pallbearers came forward. The pianist began playing that old Carpenters song, "Bless the Beasts and the Children," and a stubby-legged beagle in a pew near the back began to bay and every other dog in the room took up the cry, howling mournfully as the casket was carried down the aisle and out the door.

It was an odd way to end a funeral, but also strangely appropriate. As I watched the rose-covered casket carrying my sister's remains being loaded into the hearse for the journey to the cemetery, I couldn't help but think that Alice would have approved.

❦ Chapter 11 ❦

Sitting in the back of a black sedan for the return trip from the cemetery, I felt drained. I wanted nothing more than to go back to Barney's house, crawl under the covers, and not speak to anyone for two or three days. But there was one more piece of the ritual yet to be performed, the post-funeral reception.

The car pulled up in front of St. Agnes's. Mr. Sedgwick's eldest son, Danny, jumped out of the driver's seat and ran around the car to open the door for me. The chill November air was startling after sitting in the warmth of the sedan. I stood on the sidewalk and watched as a long line of cars, stretching all the way around the corner, pulled into the church parking lot. One of those cars carried the FOA, who I really needed to talk to, so I could thank them for the quilt. Another carried Peter Swenson, who I really hoped to avoid.

In Nilson's Bay, funerals are potluck affairs. People brought Crock-Pots of baked beans, trays of whole sliced hams, pans of lasagna, casserole dishes of Swedish meatballs, and platters of deviled eggs, as well as bowls of layered salads, cabbage salads, gelatin salads, pasta salads, and untold numbers of desserts. They laid them out on the waiting tables, set up by some women who had stayed behind during the graveside service to make sure everything was ready for our return. Almost immediately, a line formed and people began helping themselves to the buffet, piling their plates high.

Looking over the heads in the crowd, I saw Peter Swenson talking with Mr. Coates, who was holding his bulldog in his arms and shaking his jowly face in response to whatever it was Peter was saying. They were deep in conversation, so I took the opportunity to study my old high school classmate from the back.

He was a little taller than I remembered, maybe an inch, but he was not quite as muscular as he'd been back in the day. He looked good without quite so much muscle, less hulking. I wondered if he was still as cocky as he'd been in high school. Probably. Is there anything as cocky as a small-town athlete with real talent? Of course, our high school was so small—a total enrollment of fewer than three hundred even though it was the only school for the whole northern part of the county and served seventh through twelfth grades—that we didn't have any real sports teams aside from cross-country. Peter was the captain. In the winter he played "shinny hockey" on Kangaroo Lake with Clint Spaid, Jimmy Schrader, and whoever else they could round up for a scrimmage. He was a catcher in the summer baseball league, too, and held the record for home runs and stolen bases.

I remember how he'd crouch down like a crab during the game, skittering from right to left to right along the baseline, rattling the pitcher and charming the crowd, letting the anticipation build. Having seen him do it so many times before, they were waiting for that moment when he'd explode from the bag, run like the wind, and slide safely to the next base just ahead of the ball, drawing a hail of curses from the pitcher and an outburst of applause from the stands, before hopping to his feet, dusting off his pants, and settling his cap back on his head with an easy grin that said, "Didja like that? Wanna see me do it again?"

Of course they did. They never, ever got tired of seeing Peter Swenson swing a bat or steal a base. Generally, people in Nilson's Bay could never be accused of being overdemonstrative or throwing away compliments, but after the final inning they'd crowd around Peter, slapping his back and reliving the highlights of the game. Little kids sometimes even asked him to sign their baseballs.

No wonder he'd been such a cocky kid, the kind of kid you didn't see often in Nilson's Bay, a town that considered working hard, humility, and not drawing attention to yourself to be life's greatest virtues. But I guess every town needs a hero, somebody to be proud of. Peter Swenson had been ours.

But that kind of attention at such a young age generally isn't good for a person. I mean, how many washed-out former football stars reach their peak in the fall of their senior year and spend the rest of their lives growing a beer gut and going on about carrying the ball up the middle and winning a game ten, twenty, thirty years before? It's really pretty sad.

Except Peter Swenson didn't look sad. Nor did he have a beer gut. Was he still cocky?

Feeling my gaze, he turned his head and flashed me a grin, the same "I know you're watching me and I don't blame you" grin he'd had as a kid.

Yes. Still cocky.

He put his hand on Mr. Coates's shoulder, as if he might be excusing himself to come and talk to me. I slipped away before he could, heading to the opposite corner of the room, where I spotted the three members of the FOA sitting at a table in the corner. Barney had explained who was who among them. Rinda Charles, the African American woman, was the eldest. Daphne Olsen, the one with the stick-out hairdo, was about my age, though she looked older. And the young one with the unicorn tattoo was Celia Brevard, who was sitting with her head buried in her hands, still crying. Rinda and Daphne were trying to comfort her, patting her shaking shoulders and leaning down to whisper into her ear, but it didn't seem to be helping.

Before I could speak to them, I was waylaid by two silver-haired matrons, Betty and Carol, cochairs of the bereavement committee, who approached to press a plate of food upon me. I wasn't very hungry. Even if I had been, there really wasn't time for me to sit down and eat.

Though it seemed like people had gone out of their way to avoid me before the funeral, now that it was over they couldn't wait to talk to me. I'm not sure if it was because people in Nilson's Bay just take time to warm up to newcomers or because seeing my tears during the service had aroused their sympathy. Whatever the reason, they approached me now, eager to wring my hand and let me know how much Alice had meant to them.

A few also wanted to discuss the outcome of the election—some with approval, others with disdain. I'd never known people in Nilson's Bay to be that engaged politically, but it was clear that they'd been paying attention this year. Maybe having someone they knew once upon a time involved in such a high-profile campaign had piqued their interest. Most, however, wanted to talk about Alice.

Carla Erickson was among the first. She fought

back tears as she told me about how Alice had come to her aid after her husband's death, two years before.

"I was a wreck after Fred died. The house was so empty and the days were so long. I almost didn't know how I could go on; I was that depressed. I hardly ever left the house. One day, Alice showed up on my doorstep with a basket of kittens. I never had a cat in my life," Carla said, shaking her head to convey her surprise, "so I can't think why Alice would have thought to come to me, but the next thing I knew, I'd picked two kittens from the basket, sisters, marmalade with patches of white, and named them Mabel and Hilda."

Carla paused in telling her story and swallowed back tears, dabbing at her eyes with a handkerchief.

"Honestly, I just don't know what I'd do without my girls or what might have become of me if Alice hadn't knocked on my door that day. Some people might say that Alice wasn't too bright, but she knew what I needed even before I did. She was such a blessing."

Larry and Linda DeVine, the parents of two little boys, Daniel and Dylan, born just sixteen months apart, were next to seek me out. Elvis, their yellow Labrador, was with them. He made himself patiently comfortable on the floor as we talked, chin resting on his paws.

"The last thing I thought we needed was a dog," Larry said. "I mean, with two boys who were constantly battling for our attention, things were chaotic enough. Then Alice showed up at our house with Elvis. She said that they didn't have any room at the pet rescue and that, if she couldn't find a family to take care of him for a week or so, just until they had more space, they might put him down." Larry smiled and shook his head. "Like I said, the last thing we needed right then was a dog; that's what I thought, but . . . how could I say no to that face?"

Larry looked down at Elvis, who gazed at him with adoring eyes and started thumping his tail. Linda picked up the story.

"Before the end of the week, we'd completely fallen in love with Elvis and wouldn't have dreamed of sending him back. Instead of adding to the chaos, he actually helped calm things down. He's just so mellow and easygoing. The boys are so happy taking him for walks or playing ball with him that they don't have as much interest in picking on each other now. I think Alice knew exactly what she was doing when she came to our house that day. Your sister might not have been as . . ." Linda hesitated, frowning a little as she searched for a word. ". . . as quick as other people, maybe not sharp, but she was wise in her own way. And good. She had a big, big heart."

Linda choked up as she finished, and her eyes filled with tears. So did mine.

"Thank you. I'm so happy you shared that with me," I said.

The guilt and regret that had overcome me during the funeral, the sense of being surrounded by people who knew my sister better than I did, was still sharp. But when Mrs. Erickson, Larry, Linda, and others shared their stories, they became my stories, too, memories to cling to and smile over, to pass on to someone else, or would have been, had there been anyone left. I was the last Toomey. When I died, those memories would die with me. But they were alive for now, and knowing that helped dull my despair, at least a little.

I conjured an image of Alice in my mind, standing on the DeVines' front stoop with Elvis on a leash, her face as placid as always, her eyes calm and unblinking, as she related the doomed dog's fate and made a straightforward appeal for clemency, her voice as flat as her expression.

Once upon a time, Alice had been animated, even dramatic. But the accident had narrowed her emotional range and robbed her of all sense of irony. She talked in simple, concrete, utterly honest terms, telling it exactly as she saw it, lacking the ability to lie. Or so I thought. But the pet rescue was a no-kill shelter. Alice told me that no healthy animal was ever put down there.

Had she stretched the truth to get Larry DeVine to take Elvis in, knowing ahead of time how the scenario would play out? Maybe.

I smiled to myself. Maybe, as Linda said, Alice was wiser than she appeared.

Larry shook my hand again and looked at his wife, saying they should give some of the others a chance to talk to me. I looked up, glancing across the room and to the table where the FOA still sat, Celia looking more composed now, sipping a cup of punch while Daphne and Rinda talked with Father Damon and a couple of other people. I wanted to go speak with them, but couldn't break away yet. I was surrounded by a ring of people waiting for a word.

Peter Swenson was among them, standing just a little back, but trying to catch my eye. I pretended not to notice and shifted so Peter was removed from my line of sight and started talking to Mrs. Lieshout, the town librarian, who explained how Alice helped her adopt Mr. Carnegie, the fat and friendly library cat.

The story was similar to other tales of Alice's uncanny ability to match humans with just the right pet. But Mrs. Lieshout, being a reference librarian, embellished her story with interesting facts and figures, explaining that Mr. Carnegie was named after Andrew Carnegie, the wealthy industrialist and philanthropist who, between 1883 and 1929, built more than sixteen hundred public libraries throughout the United States, including the one in Nilson's Bay, a two-story, cut-stone edifice, built in the Scottish baronial style, and that since Mr. Carnegie had "joined the staff," library visitation was up by 13 percent, which had enabled her to get a fifteen-thousand-dollar grant to buy new computers and add to the children's collection.

"None of that," she declared, "would have happened if Alice hadn't shown up in my office three years ago and plopped Mr. Carnegie right down in my lap. She knew he was the right cat for the job. Alice had a way with animals. She understood them. Better, perhaps, than she did people. Or than people understood her." A look came into her eye, one that said she must just have said too much; then she quickly added, "Nilson's Bay just won't be the same without her," before giving me a squeeze and scurrying away.

There were more conversations after that. When I got through the last of them, I turned to my right, relieved to see that Peter was gone, and then to my left, looking across the room to an empty table in the corner. The FOA was gone too.

I was irritated at myself for letting them slip away. They'd been closer to Alice than anyone else in town. I wanted to thank them for the quilt, but even more than that, I wanted to talk to them about Alice, to know what she'd been doing during the last few weeks, if she'd seemed at all sad or out of sorts. Father Damon had assured me that Alice's overdose was accidental. I wanted to believe him, but still . . . I would just have to find them later.

I was anxious to leave Nilson's Bay as soon as possible, but knew I'd be stuck here for at least a few days, perhaps a week, wrapping up Alice's financial affairs and closing up the cottage. I planned to go over and start cleaning things out the next day. I needed to find a Realtor too. It was a little late in the year to put it on the market, but maybe some wealthy guy from Chicago or Milwaukee would decide that a lakeside cottage in Door County would make a good Christmas gift for his wife.

The crowd was beginning to thin out. The apron-clad church ladies had cleared the buffet tables of entrées, salads, and savories and were in the kitchen wrapping up the leftovers. But the dessert table was still intact, loaded with tray upon tray of "bars," the rectangular cookies Midwesterners are raised on.

In Nilson's Bay, the baking of bars had evolved into something of a competition. Every woman in the village had her own family recipe, passed down in great secrecy through generations. The names of these confections—Dream Again Bars, Better Than Yours Bars, Chubby Hubby Bars, Princess and the Pea Bars—almost never listed the ingredients or described their flavors, an attempt to throw would-be recipe thieves off the trail.

Growing up, I thought my mother's You Like-A Me Bars, made with chocolate chips, cream cheese, coconut, and chopped dried apricots, were the most delicious bars on the planet. Mom was busy with volunteer activities at the parish and didn't spend much time in the kitchen (that's why she bought so many Girl Scout cookies every year), so when she did bake, it was something of an occasion. Alice and I would sit on stools at the counter while she worked, hoping to lick the spoon, enduring exquisite agony as we waited for the oven timer to ring, tortured by the aroma of baking butter and melting chocolate. I can still see Mom doing a little shuffle across the blue-and-white-checked linoleum, cradling a green ceramic bowl in her left arm and warbling an old song as she stirred the batter with a wooden spoon.

"If you like-a me, like I like-a you
And we like-a both the same
I like-a say, this very day,
I like-a change your na-a-ame . . ."

Mom had a terrible voice, just awful. I used to shrink down in the pew from embarrassment during mass because, as tone deaf as she was, she loved to sing hymns at full volume.

I walked to the dessert table, picked up a bar frosted with chocolate, and took a bite. It didn't hold a candle to You Like-A Me Bars.

Though I hadn't been to the cottage yet, I was sure there wouldn't be much I cared to salvage aside from a few family photos. But if I could find the recipe for You Like-A Me Bars in the kitchen, I'd hold on to it. Maybe I'd even try baking a batch myself.

❧ Chapter 12 ❧

After the reception at the church, Barney offered to make me dinner at home, but I passed. Three straight nights of my cousin's spaghetti and meatballs was enough. Plus, I really wanted a drink. I zipped up my jacket and pulled my car keys from my pocket, but then changed my mind and decided to walk to town. The fresh air would do me good.

St. Agnes sits on the side of a hill, just three blocks from downtown. The beautiful sand-colored edifice was constructed from native limestone in the late 1800s. Back then it sat alone, surrounded by empty, untouched acres of land; I've seen the pictures. Since then a neighborhood has sprung up around the church, modest bungalows and colonials, some with porches and some without, all with tidy and well-trimmed lawns and gardens. There's always been a gentle pressure to "keep your yard up" in Nilson's Bay, so much so that if you neglect your mowing, you might just wake up one morning and see a neighbor outside doing it for you. These little houses, like the church and so many other places in Nilson's Bay, have wonderful views of Lake Michigan.

The town was laid out to maximize that view, and whoever created that original plan did a good job. Walking down the hill from Erie Street to Bayshore, watching the sky over the water just begin to turn pink, it was easy to see why tourists have made their way to this tiny town in the northern reaches of Door County for nearly a century. It is the picture of picturesque.

I hadn't appreciated that as a child, but now I could see why people think it's so pretty.

Bayshore, the main commercial street in downtown Nilson's Bay, is shaped like a C, tracing the shoreline of the bay that gives the town its name. There are buildings on both sides of the road, but fewer on the lake side, with trees, benches, and little pocket gardens between the shops so you can't take more than a few steps without catching a glimpse of the water or finding a place to rest and enjoy the view.

Fishing was the original industry in Nilson's Bay, the reason for its existence, so it isn't surprising that the pier, set directly in the middle of Bayshore and marked by a parklike stretch of grass with benches on either side and a tall, white-painted flagpole in the middle, is the anchor of the town. It's the spot where people sit to watch the Fourth of July fireworks explode above the water, and where gray-haired leaders of the VFW, dressed in uniforms that fit a little more snugly than they did in earlier decades, gather on Memorial Day to salute the flag, read speeches, and kick off the annual parade. Though the water is deep here, the bay entrance is fairly narrow, and the docks can accommodate fewer and smaller vessels than can the larger towns on the opposite side of the peninsula, towns such as Fish Creek or Egg Harbor, where the warmer waters of the great Green Bay attract more tourists and pleasure boaters. Even in July and August, Lake Michigan is really too cold for swimming. That's why the tourist traffic here, while steady, isn't quite as frenetic as it is on the Green Bay side. But the people who do vacation in Nilson's Bay tend to return year after year. I guess it's something of an acquired taste.

The commercial areas of the town, such as they are, run north-ish and south-ish from the pier, in that C shape I mentioned before. The public library and the town hall sit at opposite ends—a stretch of only about eight blocks. There are a few empty buildings here and there; the old Herzog building, which once housed a furniture store, has had a "For Sale" sign on it for as long as I can remember, and Schrader's Antiques—which was really more of a junk store—seemed to have closed since I was last here. But the rest of the town looked to be doing pretty well.

Most people coming to visit stay in very small, very rustic vacation cottages that locals rent out in the summer, but there are also a couple of big, painted Victorians along Bayshore that house B and Bs, as well as the Surfside Motel, which has a small pool and a swing set on the grass and looks pretty much like it did when it was built back in 1963.

There isn't a ton of shopping in Nilson's Bay, but Ferguson's Book Nook sells used books as well as a small selection of new bestsellers and local-interest titles, and if you're looking for gifts, you can get handcrafted wooden toys, puzzles, puppets, dolls, and games at Oma's Toy Chest, costume jewelry, purses, scarves, and candles at the Sparkle Boutique, and all kinds of Scandinavian-themed knickknacks and memorabilia, everything from coffee cups emblazoned with Swedish, Danish, Finnish, or Norwegian flags to expensive hand-woven linens and red-painted wooden dala horse figures, at the Viking Trader. Of course, the usual and more necessary commercial enterprises are present as well, the gas station and minimart, post office, drugstore, hardware store, feed and garden center, and the Save-A-Bunch Market, none of them very big, but stocked with the basics that full-time residents need year-round.

If you've got a sweet tooth, you can stop into Heller's Ice Cream Haven for a cone, get candy or caramel corn at The Peppermint Twist, or visit Dinah's Pie Shop, presided over by, you guessed it, Dinah, who opened the place back in the late seventies and still bakes all the pies herself. If you want a quick snack, you can get hot dogs, chips, and sodas at a little shack near the pier called The Last Stand, or if you're looking for something more substantial, you can go to the Hot Spot Supper Club for surf and turf, twice-baked potatoes, and Caesar salad prepared tableside in a dark-paneled dining room from a menu that has been unaltered since 1955.

But, if you're in Nilson's Bay and you want a drink, there's really only one place to go, The Library.

The Library was opened years before I was born, back in the sixties I think, by Cliff Spaid, a then-young man recently returned from Vietnam who needed a job. People in town said he used to drink up the profits, trying to forget things he'd seen and done in the war.

I'd never been inside The Library before. I moved away before I was twenty-one, and when I was growing up it was considered a mostly male bastion, the name a wink toward wayward husbands who wanted to explain their whereabouts to "da wife" without actually telling a lie. It wasn't a particularly original name—I'd seen several similarly named taverns in my travels— but when I was growing up people always thought it was pretty funny. I wondered if they still did.

The familiar blue-and-red neon sign depicting a martini glass with an open book lying next to it blinked bright above the doorway. The grimy, dark glass windows on either side of a heavy wooden door with a worn brass handle had "The Library" painted on them in gold, the letters a little chipped. The outside looked exactly the same as it always had, like your basic small-town dive.

But when I opened the door and went inside, I was pleasantly surprised. The right-hand wall was exposed brick from floor to ceiling. The lighting was dim but warm, and the flames from a fire-place centered on the wall cast dancing shadows across the heart-pine floorboards. Several small tables and chairs, painted shiny black, were grouped around the fireplace, and there were four black-painted booths against the back wall, two on each side of the swinging door that led to the restrooms and kitchen. The long bar that lined the left wall was painted in a rusty red, a little unexpected after all the black, but it added a welcome touch of color and cheer to a room that might have been overly gloomy otherwise. A man dressed in jeans and a green flannel shirt sat on a chair in the corner near the window, strumming an acoustic guitar, providing background music for the hum of conversation and occasional outbreaks of laughter.

It was a fairly small space—a placard on the wall stated that the maximum capacity was fifty-five—and as I looked around I figured the crowd was pretty close to that number. The tables, booths, and seats at the bar were occupied, and I felt uncomfortably obvious standing there alone. I recognized a good portion of the faces that were looking up at me, wondering what I was doing there. They knew me and I knew them—one or two even raised their hands in a sort of half wave, acknowledging my presence—but no one invited me to join them.

I was just about to leave when I heard someone calling my name and saw the bartender waving to me.

"Lucy? Hey, der! C'mon over here, why don'tcha? Got an open spot here on da end."

The Wisconsin accent was thick and very familiar.

"Clint?" He was a lot heavier and the beard obscured his features, but when he smiled, revealing a wide gap between his front teeth, I knew for sure the man behind the bar really was Clint Spaid, Cliff's son.

I walked to the end of the bar, hung my purse over the back of the vacant barstool, and sat down. "Clint, is this your place?"

He nodded and smiled a little wider, his pride of ownership obvious.

"It's great. Not at all what I expected. I was picturing a dark little dive with a bunch of hunched old guys in feed caps sitting at the counter, drinking Pabst and staring at ESPN."

Clint laughed. "Well, until four years ago, dat was about it. After Dad died I decided t' spruce da place up a little. I couldn't make a livin' selling Pabst and cheese curds t' old guys. Dey kept dyin' off, don'tcha know. And I didn't wanna spend da rest of my life helpin' sad, old drunks get sadder and drunker."

He filled a glass with beer from the tap, tilting it to control the foam. "We do all right in tourist season; practically got a line out da door. In winter we get a lotta locals, guys lookin' for someplace nice to take da wife or girlfriend. Or find one."

He winked and walked away, carrying the beer to a customer at the other end of the bar.

I looked around the room and saw that Clint was right. The tables and booths were occupied mostly by couples, and the barstools were mostly singles; at least that's what it looked like to me. There was a lot of flirting going on at the bar.

"Well, it's a nice place," I said when Clint returned. "Real nice."

"Thanks. So how you holdin' up, eh? I'm sure sorry about Alice."

"Oh, I'm doing okay," I said with a small shrug. "It was a shock, though. I just never thought . . ."

I let the rest of the sentence fade away. In the last few days, I'd started to understand how many things I'd never thought about, too many to list. Way more than Clint Spaid would want to hear about—that was sure.

"How long you in town for?" he asked.

"A few days. Just until I can get the estate organized."

"Oh, yeah. Bet you got a lot to do now dat da election is over." Clint picked up a bar towel and started to polish a row of highball glasses.

"You know, I saw Alice just a couple of weeks ago, walking some dogs from da shelter. She crossed da street when she saw me, gave me a Ryland button, and said not to forget to vote. She said dat Lucy said Ryland was da best guy runnin' and dat you wouldn'ta said so if it weren't true. I figgered she was right, so I went ahead and voted for him. Got da wife to vote for him too," he said, smiling and jerking his chin toward a woman who was just coming through the swinging doors.

I looked in her direction and she gave me a smile of recognition, lifting her eyebrows as a sort of greeting, her hands occupied as she carried trays of food to the tables.

"Is that Roberta Bechdorf?"

He grinned. "Roberta Spaid now. We got two kids. Ricky is twelve and Kayla is ten."

"Yeah?" I asked. "Gosh, that's great. So you still playing hockey?"

He nodded. "I'm coaching now. Couple of us old guys started a league for da kids. Not shinny; dis is da real deal. We got nets and rules and everything. My Ricky's a decent goalie, but dat Kayla," he said, his smile expanding with fatherly pride. "You should see 'er skate. Fast. Loves hockey. Got a thick skull like her old man, don'tcha know.

"Anyway," he said, setting the polished glassware up in a shining row on the bar, "you don't want ta hear me goin' on about my kids. What can I getcha, Lucy?"

"Have any Macallan?"

"Ran out. Got an Old Fettercairn ten dat's good. Straight or rocks?"

"Straight."

"Hungry? We got nachos, cheese curds, mozzarella sticks, beef or chicken wraps, Caesar salad, Greek salad, chili, sliders, and wings—buffalo or barbecue. Oh, and Parmesan fries with garlic aioli. Roberta just added 'em to da menu last week. Dey're real good."

"They sound good," I said, realizing my appetite had returned. "I'll have some fries and an order of buffalo wings."

119

"You got it," Clint said, filling a glass with scotch and setting it in front of me. "This one's on da house."

"Clint," I protested, "you don't have to . . ."

He waved me off and headed toward the opposite end of the bar.

"Thanks!" I called out to his retreating form.

I picked up the glass and took a long, slow sip, grateful for the peaty flavor and warming sensaion of the liquor as it went down my throat, grateful that the man in the blue sweater and the woman in the too-tight T-shirt were so engrossed in each other that they didn't notice me, grateful for the chance to sit here quietly and not have to speak to anyone, and, most of all, grateful that this long, hard day would soon come to an end.

Roberta brought out my food just as the guy in the blue sweater left with the girl in the tight T-shirt, leaving the stool next to me empty.

The wings were good, but the fries were amazing, cut so small they were almost matchsticks, quick-fried so they were crispy without being greasy, and generously sprinkled with real grated Parmesan cheese, tangy and slightly grainy. And when I dipped the tip of the fries into that creamy, garlicky mayonnaise . . . wow! Every bite was a little piece of French fry heaven, especially if you washed it down with a little scotch.

So here I was sipping single malt and eating upscale pub grub made with really good Parmesan in Nilson's Bay, Wisconsin. Go figure. It wasn't until I left home and went out for Italian food with some friends at a small, now defunct restaurant in Georgetown that I realized Parmesan cheese didn't come out of green cans.

There was about a finger's worth of scotch left in the glass. I was staring into it, thinking about ordering another, deciding I shouldn't, when a man's voice said, "Mind if I sit here?"

"Go ahead," I said automatically, but then stopped, my jaw going slack when I looked up and realized that the voice and the face that went with it belonged to Peter Swenson.

❧ Chapter 13 ❧

Now that he was sitting there, I had to talk to him. I took a big swig of my drink, bigger than I normally would have, nearly draining the glass. The sooner I was done with it, the sooner I could excuse myself and leave.

"It was nice of you to come to the funeral," I said, looking in his general direction without specifically making eye contact.

He ducked his head to acknowledge my words.

"I'm sorry we didn't get a chance to talk at the reception."

Peter lifted his left eyebrow. "That right?" he said. "Because it looked to me like you were mortified to see me and going out of your way not to talk to me."

So much for tossing back the rest of my drink as quickly as possible and getting out of there. Now I was going to have to sit there and talk just to prove him wrong.

Clint caught sight of Peter and came over to ask what he was drinking and if I wanted a refill. I ordered a second scotch. Peter asked for a Fat Tire and some pretzels.

"You got it, buddy. Oh, wait. Or am I supposed to call you Your Honor now?"

Peter made a face. Clint laughed and started pouring a beer from the tap.

"Pete's a big shot now," he told me. "Got himself elected to da village council."

"I heard," I said. "Congratulations."

"Ha! You wouldn't say dat if you'd ever been to a council meeting," Clint replied. "Buncha people gripin' and shoutin', throwin' insults. And that's just da councilors. Dose guys hate each other. Makes a hockey game look like a Sunday school picnic."

Clint gave Peter a pitying look and put the beer down in front of him.

"Don't know why you'd sign up for dat kinda misery, buddy. Not like you don't have plenty to do already." Clint looked toward me again. "Petey coaches hockey too. Da real little guys, age four to six."

"Really? That must be fun."

"They're cute kids," Peter said, keeping his eyes on Clint. "Timmy Schrader scored two goals last week—for the other side." He grinned and shook his head. "I enjoy it—the hockey part. As far as the council . . . well, somebody's got to do it."

Clint made a sucking sound with his teeth. "Better you den me, buddy."

Clint went off to tend to his other customers. Peter pulled his cell phone out of his pocket, scrolling through his e-mail. I shifted my eyes sideways, taking advantage of his momentary distraction to examine his features.

I'm not usually a fan of facial hair on men, but his beard wasn't a heavy one, more of a generous stubble. It looked good on him. His nose was different, displaying a small but definite bump, as though he might have broken it sometime in the past. Even that looked good on him, added to his . . . masculine aura, for lack of a better phrase. I feel kind of silly saying that, but there wasn't a better way to put it, and as I sat on my barstool, sipping a second scotch, it occurred to me that I hadn't spent time with a really manly man in quite a while. Peter was cut from a different cloth than the men I'd met since leaving Wisconsin.

He was handsome, too, always had been. That was why, when I was sixteen, I'd decided that Peter should be the boy who would rid me of my virginity. Well, that was part of the reason.

The fact that I was the only girl in my class without a steady boyfriend had led me to the conclusion that I was the last innocent left and that I was missing out on all the excitement. It helped that Denise Thorsen, who had been sitting next to me since first grade because our last names were closest in the alphabet, told me the same thing.

I know. It sounds stupid now. And let's face it, it was. But I thought and did a lot of stupid things at sixteen. Deciding that I needed to clear this awkward hurdle of adolescence as quickly as possible and making up my mind that Peter Swenson should do the deed wasn't even close to the stupidest of them.

Why Peter? Because that cocky attitude of his gave me the idea that he must be more experienced than the other available candidates and I figured it would be less awkward if at least one of us knew what we were doing. Also because Denise bet me that I couldn't get him to do it. After that it was game on. I've always been competitive.

And, of course, he had the most beautiful brown eyes. That had not changed.

Peter slipped his phone back into the pocket of his jeans. I snapped my eyes front so he wouldn't catch me staring. Clint returned carrying pretzels, plus a little bowl of cashews roasted with rose-mary and cracked pepper.

"Another of Roberta's new recipes. Try 'em," Clint said proudly, setting the bowl between us before walking away.

Peter popped a few cashews into his mouth.

"Not bad. So," he said, taking a swig of beer and then *thunking* his glass down on the bar. "Why were you avoiding me?"

"I wasn't avoiding you. It's just that there were so many people. By the time I could get away, you'd already left." I laughed nervously. "I mean, not that I blame you. You must have been standing there forever, and I'm sure you had plenty of other things to—"

Peter interrupted me. "I don't mean today," he said, frowning so his brows moved closer, creating a momentary crease between them. "Well, maybe that too. But you've been avoiding me for a lot longer than that. You barely spoke to me for the whole last two years of high school, ever since the day Alice got hurt. That's pretty hard to pull off when you only have forty-five people in your graduating class."

Now that the fries were cold, the aroma of Parmesan cheese was overpowering and made me feel a little sick. I pushed them away.

"Look, I avoided a lot of people after that," I said, after taking another sip of scotch. "Not just you. Once I knew that Alice was going to be okay, or as okay as she ever would be, I wanted to get out of here and never come back."

"Well, you just about pulled it off," he said with a slightly bitter edge. "I know how much Alice wanted you to come home. And I know how persistent she could be when she really wanted something—like a dog with a bone."

Just about everybody in town knew Alice in some sense, but he was talking like they'd been closer than that, like he was intimately acquainted with Alice in all her stubborn, single-minded splendor. His description of her persistence once she'd made up her mind about something was spot on: "a dog with a bone." That was Alice, all right.

"So, if she couldn't talk you into coming home after all these years," Peter said, "I doubt she ever would have. Almost seems like Alice had to die just to get you to show up."

My chest and cheeks went suddenly hot—from anger, not embarrassment. I had to fight back the urge to throw my drink in his face. Instead, I took another swallow, a big one, grabbed my purse, and jumped up from the barstool.

"I have to go."

"Lucy! Wait!"

He reached out for my arm, but I pulled away. He grabbed my purse strap instead, jerking at it, accidentally making me stumble. I tripped over my own feet and ended up on the floor.

There was a gasp from some of the onlookers, then a little rumble of laughter when people realized I was okay, then a man's voice chuckling and saying it looked like somebody'd had one too many, then a woman's voice hissing, telling him to shut up and quit being so mean, that my sister had just died.

Now I was angry *and* embarrassed.

I crawled up onto my knees. Peter was at my side, trying to help me up, but once again, I jerked my arm from his grasp.

"Leave it!" I snapped. "I'm fine."

"Luce, I'm sorry. I shouldn't have said that. I don't know why I did. I'm really sorry. Sit back down," he said. "Please."

I shook my head. "It's late and I'm tired. I'm going to walk back to the church, get my car, and go home."

"You can't drive," Peter said. "Not after two glasses of scotch. What do you weigh, about a hundred and thirty?"

I weigh one thirty-seven, but saw no reason to correct him.

"Your blood level is way over the legal limit. I know because about twenty percent of my law practice is defending DUIs. Seriously, Lucy. You can't drive. I won't let you."

I picked up my purse again and placed it back on my shoulder.

"Fine," I said. "I won't drive. I'll take a taxi. Clint, call me a cab, will you?"

Clint took his eyes off the foam of the beer he

was drawing and stared at me. "A cab? In Nilson's Bay? Boy, you really have been gone a long time, haven't you?"

"Let me drive you home," Peter said.

The look on my face must have told him that definitely wasn't happening. After what he'd said to me, I'd have walked the five miles to Barney's farm first.

"Well, then, why don't you just sit here and wait for a while, until you're sober enough to drive? I'll buy you a ginger ale or a cup of tea or something. We really have to talk anyway. Might as well do it now."

I barked out a laugh. "I don't have to talk to you about anything! Not ever!"

The apologetic expression fled from Peter's face. His brown eyes bored into mine. "You're wrong about that, Lucy. I'm Alice's lawyer. I wrote her will."

❦ Chapter 14 ❦

Barney speared bacon with a fork and lifted the pieces out of the frying pan and onto a paper towel, then picked up a spatula and flipped over the eggs.

"I don't understand it," he said as he stared at the frying pan, waiting for the egg yolks to set.

"Why would Alice do a thing like that? I know she loved animals, but you're her sister. More coffee?"

I held out my cup. He filled it to the brim and then put a plate with three eggs, six pieces of bacon, and a toaster waffle slathered with butter and syrup down on the table in front of me before returning to the stove to fix his own plate.

I closed my eyes. The sight of those runny eggs and that greasy bacon made me want to heave.

Why, oh why, had I ordered that third scotch? The third scotch that was responsible for my pounding head and sandpaper tongue and meant I'd had to let Peter drive me home?

Actually, I hadn't *let* him drive me home; he simply had. I didn't remember the details of the transaction, only that Peter had his arm hooked under mine, half dragging me down the sidewalk to his car, saying not to worry about my car, that it'd be fine parked at the church until tomorrow. I didn't remember the drive home either. Except for the part where I told him to pull over so I could . . .

So humiliating. I deserved to feel this awful. Three scotches. What could have driven me to do something so stupid?

Not a what. A who. My sister.

I shoved a piece of bacon into my mouth and chewed methodically, ignoring the lurching in my stomach, knowing I would feel better if I could just get this down. Barney, still looking perplexed, put his own plate on the table and took a seat.

"It doesn't make sense. Why would Alice want to leave the cottage to the pet rescue instead of her own flesh and blood?"

I coughed, trying to clear my throat and mind enough to formulate an answer. I was interrupted by the sound of footsteps on porch planks, the squeak of Barney's back kitchen door opening, and Peter's voice.

"Alice *didn't* leave the cottage to the pet rescue," Peter said. "She merely stipulated that Lucy had to fulfill certain requirements in order to inherit. Should Lucy fail to do so within a year, then the ownership of the house would revert to the pet rescue."

What was it with this guy? Did he always just appear out of nowhere like that? It was irritating, but under the circumstances, I was almost grateful to let Peter do the talking.

Even when I'm at the top of my game, I don't like to have conversations before my second cup of coffee. Barney had a lot of questions, but my head hurt too much to go into details. If Peter wanted the job, he was welcome to it.

I sat there with one elbow on the table and my head resting in my hand, eating eggs and willing myself not to be nauseous. Barney took another coffee cup off one of the hooks suspended below the plate rack, filled it, and handed it to Peter.

"Want some breakfast? Won't take me five minutes to fry more eggs."

Peter shook his head. "No, thanks. I already ate."

Barney sat back down and resumed eating. "What kind of stipulations?" he asked.

"It's really just one, and it's not that complicated. Lucy has to stay in Nilson's Bay, living in the cottage, for a period of eight weeks. They don't even have to be consecutive," Peter said. "She could come for a week or two at a time. Alice did insist that Lucy be here for Christmas week, but, aside from that, she can show up anytime it suits her. Once she finishes those eight weeks, that's it. The cottage will belong to Lucy, free and clear. She can do what she wants with it."

I reached for my coffee cup. Barney glanced in my direction.

"Well, that doesn't seem too bad. It's kind of an unusual request, but Alice always was— unusual, I mean."

I turned my head, looking straight at my kindhearted cousin, a man much nicer and more soft-spoken than I.

"Crazy," I corrected. "Alice was absolutely, certifiably, bat-belfry crazy. Not unusual. Crazy."

I shoved another piece of bacon into my mouth and glared at Peter, talking with my mouth full.

"Anybody who spent five minutes with Alice knew she was crazy. And any competent lawyer should have realized that Alice was incompetent to write a will. Especially after hearing the wing-nut requirements of that will! If you think I'm not going to fight this, Peter Swenson, you're just as crazy as my sister was. I'm going to hire a lawyer—a *good* one—and contest this thing in court! Ow."

I clamped my hand against my forehead. Shouting made my headache worse.

"Get a lawyer if you want, Lucy. I'll even give you some names. But I'm telling you right now that you'll be wasting your money. Alice was legally competent. She held down a job, paid her bills, and managed her own affairs. Yes, the terms of her will are a little unusual, but that's not a legal basis for declaring it invalid. Plenty of smart people have weird wills. One of my clients, who had an IQ of one hundred and fifty-six and an estate worth more than three million, insisted that he be buried sitting on top of his Harley-Davidson motorcycle. Do you know what his family did about it?"

Barney, who had been listening far more intently than I, leaned forward and said, "What'd they do?"

"They buried the bike," Peter deadpanned, and then looked at me. "Lucy. You're not going to be able to fight this. Alice's will is ironclad. I made sure of it."

"It was bad enough the first time," I said quietly,

speaking more to myself than anyone else. "At least then I could tell myself that my parents cut me out of their will out of concern for Alice, to make sure that she'd always have a place to live and because they knew I'd be able to take care of myself. Logically, I understood it, but that doesn't mean it didn't hurt. But I never contested the will, because I cared about Alice too. No matter what anybody else says or thinks, I cared about Alice. I did."

I turned my head toward the wall and screwed my eyes shut, blocking out the light, refusing to cry, knowing that it would just make me hurt worse than I already did, addressing my words to Peter even though I couldn't see him.

"I don't care what Alice told you; it wasn't my fault that she got hurt."

"What are you talking about?" I could hear the confusion in Peter's voice. "Alice never said anything . . ."

Barney was on his feet and at my side, patting me awkwardly on the shoulder.

"It was an accident. Alice never thought you were to blame. Nobody thought that."

I opened my eyes and looked at my cousin, but said nothing, letting my stare be my contradiction. He knew my father.

Barney crouched down next to me, grunting a little as he lowered himself toward the floor, and grabbed both my hands. "Honey," he said gently, "you're reading too much into this. Alice never blamed you. I know she didn't. Don't let an old grudge between you and your dad keep you from getting what's rightfully yours.

"The cottage isn't fancy, but it has the best view in Nilson's Bay. If you fixed it up a little, it'd be just great. And I'll even help you if you want. I'm not the best carpenter around, but I know how to handle the business end of a hammer and saw. You know something?" he said, face brightening as he considered the possibilities. "If you put a new window in the living room, a bigger one, you'd be able to see the lake from every room on the main floor. And you could add a deck to the back of the house, maybe get yourself one of those big grills. Better yet, dig a fire pit and put a grate on top. It'd sure be a good spot for a—"

I stopped him. I had to. I couldn't let him go on like that, getting his hopes up.

"Barney, I know you mean well, but . . . it's too late for me to come home even if I wanted to. And I don't want to. I have no good memories of this place."

Barney frowned, dropped my hands, and hauled himself to his feet. He began collecting dirty plates and silverware.

"Then you're remembering wrong," he mumbled under his breath.

"What?"

He turned to face me. "You're remembering

wrong," he repeated, enunciating each word, making sure I didn't miss a one.

"Lucy," he said, "your dad was a card-carrying SOB. We all know that. But that doesn't mean that everybody in Nilson's Bay is. I'm not!" He dumped a stack of dishes into the sink and pointed to Peter, who was still sitting at the table, obviously uncomfortable to be listening in on such an intimate conversation, staring into the bottom of his coffee cup. "Peter isn't! In fact, there are some real nice folks around here. And you had some good times here, Lucy. Happy times. If you'd give it a chance, you might remember that."

He spun around toward the sink and turned the faucet on full blast, his face mottled red, and started rinsing grease and syrup off plates.

I stood up and crossed the kitchen, wondering if I should try to hug him. I handed him a dish-rag instead.

"Do you know those are the most words I've ever heard you string together at one time?"

He grunted, took the dishrag from me, ran it under the water, and squirted it with green soap.

"Maybe that's because you haven't been around much. I can talk a blue streak if there's some-body around worth talking to."

"Barney. I know you'd like me to stay, but I just can't. I've got to get myself to Washington. The president-elect needs me."

I squeezed his shoulder, then took a wet plate and started wiping it dry.

"No, he doesn't," Barney said in a low voice. "He told you to take some time off. A month, he said. You don't have to be in Washington until after the holidays."

"What?" I put down the dish and the towel, put a hand on my hip, and turned to look at my cousin. "How do you know that? Were you eavesdropping on me?"

Barney's face turned red. He cast his eyes to the floor.

"I wasn't . . . I didn't mean to . . ." he mumbled, then lifted his head and looked me in the eye, his voice defensive. "I wasn't eavesdropping. I just happened to be walking past your bedroom door at the same time you picked up the phone in the bedroom. And then I just . . . hung around for a while."

Now I had both hands on my hips.

"And you don't call that eavesdropping?"

He didn't answer the question.

"Eight weeks," he said. "That's as long as you'd have to stay here to inherit the cottage. If you took your things over there today and stayed until January first . . ."

Barney walked to the other side of the kitchen and flipped through the pages of a wall calendar with advertisements from Swan Cleaners, Fratelli's Towing, and Dinah's Pie Shop.

"That'd be seven weeks right there. Seven! You'd only have to come up for one more week after that and the place would be yours. Just a week!" He turned and gave me a triumphant look.

"People in my world don't take weeklong vacations."

"How about weekends? They take weekends, don't they?"

"Sometimes," I admitted. "But not often. And I just don't—"

Barney leaned to his left, looking around me to address Peter.

"Could she do it on weekends?"

"Sure," Peter said, "weekends work. As long as it adds up to eight weeks total, she can come and go as she likes."

Barney stood up straight and grinned. "Did you hear that? You make up the last seven days by coming up for weekends, three weekends. Two if you decided to come on a national holiday— Fourth of July or something. Remember how nice the Fourth is in Nilson's Bay? We got the parade and the picnic. And then the fireworks show. Remember?"

I sighed and dropped my arms to my sides. How could I make him see?

"Barney, I know that you'd love it if I moved home, but—"

"That's never going to happen," he interrupted, his grin fading to neutrality. "I know. But be practical, Lucy. That cottage has got to be worth a couple hundred thousand dollars. You don't want to walk away from that kind of money."

Peter cleared his throat.

"Actually," he said, "it's worth double that. I checked with a couple of the Realtors in town. The lowest estimate was four-fifteen."

I gasped. "Four hundred and fifteen thousand? Dollars?"

Peter nodded, confirming that both the figure and the currency were correct.

"For the cottage? It's tiny! The kitchen hasn't been remodeled since 1972 and it only has one bathroom!"

"A bath and half," Peter said, correcting me. "But that doesn't matter. Nobody cares about the house. The value is in the land, two acres of prime lakefront property. Whoever buys it will probably bulldoze it."

Barney's face fell. "You mean they'd just tear it down?"

"Well," Peter replied slowly, obviously reluctant to acquaint my cousin with the truth, "I suppose it's possible that someone might consider remodeling the existing structure or maybe adding on to it, but . . . not likely. Anybody investing that kind of money is going to want something much larger and more modern. They might even build two houses on the site. There's room enough to subdivide."

He got up from his seat and carried his empty coffee cup to the sink.

"You could consider doing that yourself, Lucy. You'd get more money for two smaller lots than you would for one big one, around a half million. Assuming you stick around long enough to collect the deed, that is."

Peter slipped one hand into the front pocket of his jeans and stood there staring at me, looking smug. Barney wrung out the wet dishrag and hung it over the edge of the sink.

"My grandma and grandpa built that cottage," Barney said quietly. "When I was little, we'd go there after church and Grandma would make a big dinner for the whole family—pot roast or ham or chicken. In the summer, when it was hot, my brothers and I would ride our bicycles out to the cottage and swim in the lake. Sometimes Grandpa would join us. When we got tired, we'd climb out of the water and lay on the grass in the sun to dry off. Grandma always came out with a big pitcher of cold lemonade and a plate of bars for us, her special recipe. You Like-A Me Bars, she called them."

"That was my great-great-grandma's recipe?" I asked. "I never knew that."

"Uh-huh," Barney confirmed as he sank down into one of the kitchen chairs, looking across the room at nothing in particular.

"And now somebody is going to buy her house

and bulldoze it. Half a million dollars," he said softly. "I guess money counts for more than memories."

I crouched down next to my cousin's chair.

"Nobody is going to bulldoze the cottage, because I'm not going to sell it. But I'm not going to live in it either. If Alice wanted the pet rescue people to have it, then fine. Let them have it. I'm not going to uproot my whole life just because my sister was crazy."

Barney frowned and the wrinkles around his mouth deepened.

"Uproot your life? You have no life, Lucy. You said so yourself. You're always at work or traveling. You don't have time for yourself or anyone else."

"I never said that," I countered impatiently. "Yes, I'm busy. Yes, I work really long hours. But I never said I have no life."

Peter cleared his throat again. This seemed to be his preferred method of inserting himself into conversations that were none of his business.

"Yes, you did. You said the same thing to me last night when I was driving you home. You repeated it three or four times."

I got back to my feet, giving Peter my absolutely nastiest glare, the glare that had been known to make interns cry. It had no effect on him. He just stood there, leaning against the kitchen counter.

"Why are you here? Do you always show up at people's homes uninvited?"

"I told you last night that I'd come by in the morning to bring your keys and give you a ride back to your car. Don't you remember?" he asked sweetly, knowing full well that I didn't.

Peter reached into the back pocket of his jeans, pulled out two sets of keys, and set them on the table.

"I brought the keys to the cottage too. Thought you might want some help getting settled in."

"No! I don't! Because I am *not* moving into Alice's cottage! I am not allowing my sister or anyone else to manipulate me into disrupting my—"

Cousin Barney groaned and I turned quickly, worried that something might be wrong with him, but he looked fine. The faraway expression was gone from his face. He was clear-eyed and obviously unhappy with me.

"Boy, you are just your dad all over, aren't you? Stubborn as a mule. Lucy, if you turn down a half-million-dollar inheritance just because you don't want to let your sister have the last word, then you're the biggest fool on God's green earth! What good would that do? You don't think that letting the pet rescue get the house is going to save it from being bulldozed, do you?

"Sure, I had dreams of you coming home for

good. You can't blame an old man for wanting some family around, but I know that's not going to happen. Just like I know that nobody is ever going to live in the house, not ever again. But if it's got to come down, then I'd just as soon see somebody I care about get the money. You say you don't have a life? A half a million dollars would go a long way toward getting one. Wherever you land—Washington, DC, or someplace else—you could afford to get yourself a nice house, a real home of your own."

He paused for a moment. "Who knows? You even might want something with a guest room so your country cousin could come visit you every now and then. But the main thing is, I want you to be happy. Whether you believe it or not, that's what Alice wanted for you too. And if you've got any arguments against that, then you go ahead and trot 'em out. I've got nothing to do today but listen."

I looked at Barney, then at Peter, then back to Barney, who looked right back at me, eyebrows raised, waiting for my decision. When I reached it, I took in a big breath, let it out with a whoosh, and snatched both sets of keys from the table.

"Eight weeks," I said, raising a cautionary finger. "But that's it. That's as long as I'm staying. Not one day more."

Barney's eyes misted and he walked to the table and gave me a hug. Peter watched us, still leaning against the counter. I saw one corner of his lip tug into a lopsided grin.

"Eight weeks," he said. "That should be enough."

❦ Chapter 15 ❦

I tossed my suitcase into the back of Peter's truck.

"Is that all you brought?"

"I hadn't planned on being here very long."

I was quiet as we drove toward town, embarrassed as I recalled, however vaguely, the details of my last ride in this vehicle. But five miles is a long time to keep silent. After a couple of minutes I said, "Thanks for coming out to pick me up. And for bringing me home last night. I hope it wasn't too much trouble."

Eyes on the road, Peter shifted the truck into a higher gear.

"No problem. I hosed out the cab as soon as I got home."

I gasped. "Oh, no! Peter, I am *so* sorry. . . ."

He glanced quickly from the road to my face and back, a grin on his face.

"Calm down. I'm kidding. I was able to pull over in plenty of time, remember?"

"You jerk!" I swatted at the air next to his

head. "What a mean trick to play! Like I wasn't already humiliated enough about last night."

"Sorry," he said.

But he didn't look sorry. In fact, he looked pretty pleased with himself. I stared out the window. I'd had enough of Peter's jokes. Law degree or not, he obviously hadn't grown up a bit since high school.

"Lucy?" Peter looked at me, but I didn't say anything. "Oh, come on. It was just a little joke. You can't be mad at me. After all, I'm the guy you picked to deflower you."

My head snapped toward Peter like it was spring-loaded. He was still looking at me. The nausea I felt when I first opened my eyes that morning returned, but this had nothing to do with my hangover. Yes, you can actually be so humiliated that it makes you want to throw up.

"I *told* you about that?" I said weakly.

"Afraid so." Peter shifted the truck into another gear and shook his head. "Boy, you really don't remember, do you? You really shouldn't drink that much."

"Tell me something I don't already know." I groaned and buried my face in my hands.

"Oh, come on. Don't be so hard on yourself. It was right after your sister's funeral. You were emotional and you had too much to drink. Could have happened to anybody." His words might have been sympathetic, but his buoyant tone of voice made it clear that he was enjoying my humiliation. "And, hey, I was *honored* to learn that you picked me as your stud of choice. Really. I'm only sorry that we never got to go through with it."

He reached across the seat to pat my shoulder. I pushed his hand away.

"Leave me alone. I am not talking to you."

"Oh, come on. Don't be mad. I was just teasing. Lucy?"

I shook my head, hands still covering my face. Peter said my name again, but this time his tone was different, softer, and there was no laughter in his voice.

"Lucy. Look at me."

Reluctantly, I lowered my hands from my face, straightened my back, and turned my head to the left. Peter wasn't grinning now. He wasn't even smiling.

"I won't joke about it anymore. But you know something? Even though it never happened, I really was proud to know you'd wanted me to be the first. You know what a huge crush I had on you in high school."

"Oh, stop it. You did not."

"*Huge* crush," he repeated. "I actually wrote poems to you, terrible, lovesick, teenage poems that I kept hidden under the mattress in my room."

I rolled my eyes. "Sure you did. Right next to

the ragged copies of *Playboy* you stole from the drugstore, no doubt."

He shrugged. "Just one copy, an October issue. And I didn't steal it. I borrowed it from Jimmy Grinell's older brother. Actually, Jimmy and I dug it out of the trash can when he was packing his room to go to college. He let me have it."

I sat back in the seat, relaxing a little, smiling to think that adolescent Peter, who I had thought of as worldly and experienced, had been just as awkward, confused, and driven by hormones as any other teenager.

"So what happened to them?" I asked.

"The poems?" He laughed to himself. "One day while I was at school, my mom went in to clean my bedroom and found the poems. And the copy of *Playboy*."

He removed his eyes from the road and tossed me a stricken glance. I laughed. I couldn't help myself.

"What'd she do? Wash your mouth out with soap? Make you go to confession?"

"Naw. She came into my room, closed the door, and showed me what she'd found. That was humiliation enough. I wished the floor would open up and swallow me. She told me that the magazine was going into the burn barrel, but gave back the poems. Then she left the room and never mentioned it again. Oh, but not before reminding me that 'exquisite' is spelled with an 'e' at the beginning *and* the end."

I laughed again. That sounded so much like Mrs. Swenson.

"I always did like your mom."

"She liked you, too, said you were one of the best students she ever had. As long as you're going to be in town for a while, why don't you drop by the house and see her? In fact, why don't you come for Thanksgiving?"

"Oh, I couldn't impose," I said, lifting my hand.

"You wouldn't be imposing. Mom always cooks enough for an army. And think of it this way—you'd be doing my dad a favor, saving him from one more round of dried-out turkey sandwiches. You've got to spend the holiday somewhere, don't you?" He cranked the steering wheel to the right, heading south on Bayshore. "What do you usually do for Thanksgiving?"

"Last year I ate a turkey wrap, sweet potato fries, and a Diet Coke in my hotel room while reading polling data and watching a rerun of *Dance Moms*."

"Gee. Sounds like fun," Peter said flatly.

"You're sweet to invite me, but I can't. Barney always had Thanksgiving with Alice, and this will be the first year . . ."

I let the rest of the sentence fade away and looked out the window, remembering that after Thanksgiving came Christmas, the holiday that

I'd always spent in sun-kissed Orlando, or Miami, or Charleston, or Bermuda, accompanied by my work and my sister.

This year I'd spend the twenty-fifth of December in frigid, frozen Nilson's Bay, with only Cousin Barney for company. The first year alone.

"So bring him along," Peter said simply. "My folks would love to have him too. Mom loves a full table. Seriously."

We turned into the parking lot of the church. Peter pulled up next to my car and set the parking brake.

"I don't know. I should really talk to Barney first."

"Fair enough."

We got out of the truck. I reached for my suitcase, but Peter beat me to it.

"I got it," he said, pulling it out of the truck bed and carrying it to my car.

"Thanks for the ride," I said.

I meant it too. It was nice of him to make sure I got home safely and then come to collect me the next day. I was sure he had better things to do.

"No problem," he said. "And, Luce, that stuff you told me last night? What happens in The Library stays in The Library. So don't worry about it, okay?"

"Thanks."

He bobbed his head, just once, and started to walk away from me.

"Peter!"

He spun around, looking startled.

"Yeah?"

"I . . . I just. Never mind," I said, realizing how panicked I had sounded. I waved my hand and let out a nervous laugh. "It's stupid."

"No. What is it?" Peter took a step toward me.

"I'm going to be here until New Year's. Seven weeks."

Still frowning, he nodded. "Uh-huh. So?"

"So . . ." I spread out my hands. "What am I supposed to *do* while I'm here?"

Peter took another step toward me, looking bemused, and kissed me on the forehead.

"Live," he said with a grin. "Just live."

❧ Chapter 16 ❧

Lakeview Trail, the aptly named road leading to a cluster of homes on the shores of Lake Michigan, about a mile and a half north of downtown Nilson's Bay, hadn't changed a bit. It was still narrow, unpaved, and studded with deep potholes that rendered the fifteen-mile-per-hour speed limit sign unnecessary.

The houses on Lakeview Trail had been summer

cottages back in the twenties and thirties. They were small and rustic and sat on tiny lots. The original buyers were working-class folk who couldn't afford more and were satisfied with simple accommodations in glorious surroundings.

The only reason our cottage sat on such a large plot of prime land, jutting out from the shore with an unparalleled view, was because my family, some of the earliest inhabitants of Nilson's Bay, had once owned more than fifty acres on the lakeshore. At some point, they realized they could make more money by selling the land than cultivating it, and so they did, one parcel at a time, as financial necessity required, until there were only two acres—the best two acres—left.

That was the land on which my ancestors had built their cottage. It had been passed down through the generations, eventually to my mother, then my sister, and now, assuming I could stick out the ridiculous required residency, to me.

By the time Alice and I were born, the neighborhood was settled. People were always upgrading, of course, adding a carport, a deck, vinyl siding, extra insulation, or improved plumbing, whatever was required to turn summer cottages into year-round residences; about half of the houses were now occupied full-time. But that was as far as it went. People fixed up what they had or bought, but nobody built new.

Until now.

It wasn't yet common—far from virulent—and perhaps only one plot in ten had succumbed, but here and there among the little cottages, I could see brand-new homes built on land laid bare when the old houses had been razed and the ground scraped clean, until no trace or memory of the former dwelling remained. These new homes were far from rustic. They were expansive. And expensive.

They gobbled up every available inch of ground, creating maximum square footage for their owners, people who lived here four or six or eight weeks a year but who had decided they couldn't do so without replicating their luxurious urban lifestyle amid this cluster of cabins on a remote piece of land in rural Wisconsin. The houses they built on those teeny cottage-sized lots had double garages and double entry doors, paved drive-ways and palladium windows. One had a wrought-iron gate across the driveway with an electronic keypad to keep away intruders.

"What intruders?" I said aloud as I drove past. "What are they so afraid of?"

It was crazy. And depressing.

I rounded the curve and took a left into the driveway, pulling up behind a blue 2001 Subaru, Alice's car, which had once been Dad's car. I twisted the key to turn off the ignition and sat there looking at the blue bumper, the not-too-clean rear window with a pink stuffed teddy bear suction-cupped on the inside.

It was strange to see it sitting there in the carport, right where Alice had left it, strange to think that both of its former owners were gone. I sat there for a while trying to get my head around it, but finally got out of the car and circled around the house to take a look at the lake, walking across the long expanse of lawn to stand at the water's edge, the spot where, if you keep your face fixed forward, you don't see a single object made by man and can imagine yourself in splendid isolation, the first human to draw breath here. Or perhaps the last.

It was breathtaking, especially on such a crisply cold but bright and sunny day in an autumn that was lingering long. Every breath of wind raised sparkling ripples on the endless blue-gray surface of the water and rattled the leaves of the trees, releasing showers of still brilliant yellow, gold, orange, and red foliage that floated to the ground like little flags of welcome.

I had always loved this view. Even as a little girl, running along on this same stretch of grass, playing tag or hide-and-seek or capture the flag, I would sometimes stop in my tracks, chest heaving for breath, just to look at the water, to watch the gulls soaring and calling overhead or the sun dipping toward the horizon. As a child, I hadn't yet heard the phrase "million-dollar view" and didn't understand that not everyone was lucky enough to have this kind of natural beauty right outside the door. And even this morning, when Peter had informed me that the lowball sales price of these two isolated acres would top four hundred thousand, I balked at such a figure.

But now, standing at the water's edge and gazing out on that truly magnificent vista, I understood completely.

I could have stood there for an hour staring at the lake, but it was chilly and I didn't have a proper coat, so after a few minutes I went back to the car, got my suitcase out of the trunk, and unlocked the cottage door.

I felt so odd, taking that first step through the door, like an intruder. The house was so incredibly quiet and still. It had never been like that when I was growing up.

When I'd come through that door as a girl, the first assault upon my ears was the barking of several dogs. We never had fewer than three in residence. Dad was a vet and tended to get on with animals better than with people. The next layers of the Toomey noise collage might include a roaring vacuum cleaner, feet walking on the poorly insulated floors of the upstairs bedrooms, a toilet flushing or a running shower in the bathroom, also upstairs, a banging of screen doors as kids and dogs ran in and out of the house, or Alice practicing an etude on our upright piano. There was always noise, always somebody around, always the sense of the house being too small and too crowded. But now . . . .

I stood in the foyer—really just a four-foot square of beige linoleum, a place for people to take off their snow boots or wipe their feet before walking onto the beige carpeting—and breathed in that strangely familiar aroma.

The house smelled like pine and vanilla and wool and mothballs and cooked meat and twenty other things I couldn't pinpoint but knew so well. It was the scent I'd never thought of as a scent because, growing up, it was all just air to me, the thing I inhaled and exhaled every day of my life. I had to go away and come back to recognize it as something unique to our house, but there it was. And all these years later, it still hung in the air unaltered, the smell of us.

I left my suitcase and briefcase on the floor, slipped off my shoes, the way Mom had taught me to, and walked across the carpeting and into the kitchen.

It was perfectly tidy, not a dish in the sink or a crumb on the countertop. Aside from the door shelves of condiments and such, the refrigerator was empty and perfectly clean. The floor was clean, too, and the dishwasher empty. A fresh kitchen towel hung over the handle of the oven door. I wondered if someone had come in to clean. Barney had said that one of the neighbors was taking care of the cats. Maybe whoever had done that had also taken it upon themselves to tidy the house as well.

The piano stood against the dining room wall opposite the china cabinet, where it always had. I found middle C and played a scale, pressing firmly against the ivory keys to bring forth the sound. It was tinny and a little out of tune. Maybe that was because of the humidity and being so close to the lake. Or maybe it just wasn't a very good piano.

When I was little, the house had been full of voices: my mother talking on the phone, planning the next neighborhood party or parish fund-raiser, Dad telling a patient how to get a Labrador to swallow a pill, Alice and me arguing over possession of the remote, yelling for Mom to referee, my parents' voices, sharp and shrill, overlapping in argument.

Back then, I used to play my music as loud as I could so I couldn't hear them fight. Now I'd have given anything to hear their voices, even raised in anger, anything to banish the silence. Had Alice wished the same thing? How had she endured the silence all these years? No wonder she kept trying so hard to get me to come home.

I circled back through the kitchen to the living room, past the stairway and hallway, and into the family room, looking at the pictures on the walls, the arrangements of objects on shelves, observing them from a distance the way you look at displays in a museum of history, artifacts that raised as many questions as they answered and had but little to do with me—except for the book, the papers and pencils. These were the only things in the house that hadn't been tidied up.

They sat on a little table in the family room next to a chintz-covered lounge chair, angled toward the window, facing the black walnut tree we used to climb when we were little.

The book, *The Encyclopedia of Animals*, was open, facedown, to an entry on meerkats. She'd been drawing meerkats, not copying the photographs but sketching them in completely different postures and groupings. The drawing pencils, in black, gray, tan, and brown, lay scattered haphazardly on the half-finished drawing, and a cream-colored afghan, another of my mother's creations, lay in a careless heap on the floor right next to the chair. It was as if Alice had only just gotten up to answer the phone, or the door, or run outside to get the mail and might return any minute.

I heard footsteps on the porch. My heart jumped and I spun around, startled. I heard children's voices, little-girl voices, high and shrill, and the sound of the doorbell. When I opened the door I saw two gray plastic boxes sitting on the porch and two little girls running away across the yard.

One was about eight, wearing jeans and a

Packers sweatshirt two sizes too big. The other was four or five, wearing a red sweater, pink tutu over black spandex shorts, and bright pink rain boots.

I called out to the girls and the older one turned around.

"Mom told us to bring back the cats!" she shouted while jogging backward. "She said to feed Freckles separately because she's too fat and will eat all of Dave's food if you let her."

"Thanks!" I shouted. "What's your name?"

"Ophelia!" she cried and then turned and ran off, adding to the distance between herself and the younger girl, who was running as fast as her stubby, rainboot-clad legs could carry her, the pink tutu bouncing with every step.

I called out again, asking their mother's name, but Ophelia disappeared through a little patch of pines, leaving behind the younger one.

"Felia!" the baby whined when her sister sprinted away. "That's not fair! Wait for me!"

Another person might have thought it was sweet and perhaps even smiled as they watched the ballerina in gum boots flounce off in pursuit of her older sister. But the sight of that little one chasing along behind the sister who so easily outpaced her made my throat feel suddenly tight.

There's no point in thinking about things you can't change, and so I don't. I try not to. But as I stood on the porch of our old family home and watched that little girl lumber off through the trees, crying for her sister to wait, the memories crowded too close.

My rain boots had been pink too. I, too, had been the second sister, forever falling behind, running the unwinnable race.

❧ Chapter 17 ❧

Alice was the smart sister. Unless you'd met her before the accident, you wouldn't know that, but it's true.

Alice had twenty-four IQ points on me. The reason I know that is because my father told me. The first time he said it, I didn't know what IQ meant, but I understood his tone.

I was a disappointment to my dad. One of many.

Raised on a not very prosperous farm north of Sacramento, Dad decided early on that education would be his ticket out of the hard, boring life in the country. But college and vet school tuition left him deeply in debt, and so when he graduated from the UC Davis School of Veterinary Medicine, he didn't have money to start or buy into a practice in the city. That was the first disappoint-ment.

He was offered only two jobs, one in Kansas

and the other in Wisconsin. Dr. Sutton, a sixty-three-year-old vet from Door County who was getting too old for the long hours and physicality of a large animal practice focused mostly on dairy cattle, promised to let Dad have the practice when he retired. Dad took the job, figuring that ownership of a lucrative practice would make up for having to live in the country and work with cows. Except it didn't work out that way.

By the time Dad took over the practice, farmers in the county were beginning to sell off their dairy herds. They couldn't compete with the big corporate operations. Before long, Dad's practice was struggling. He couldn't afford to expand the family cottage that my grandparents had deeded to them when Mom married Dad, or to buy a new car, or to go on vacation. He opened a small animal clinic, but it never brought in much. People preferred to drive their animals to the clinic down in Sturgeon Bay rather than go to my dad.

The truth is, people in the county never took to him. They felt that he thought he was better than them, and they were right about that. He was one of those people who deal with their insecurity by acting superior and end up coming off like egotistical jerks. It didn't help that he was married to my mother, a nice woman from a nice family who had lived on the peninsula for decades, but didn't treat her very well.

Nilson's Bay is the kind of place where you can dial a wrong number and end up having a twenty-minute conversation with whoever answers. Everybody knows everything about everybody, the good and the bad.

When it came to my father, it seemed like the bad always outweighed the good—partly because he could rarely see the good.

He was disappointed with his practice, prospects, and income, disappointed with his life and his wife, with a little house in a little town, with his failure to obtain all that he felt was due him. When my mother told him that she was expecting again and that the new baby would be born just seventeen months after their first child, whose arrival had further stretched their already tight finances, he was more than disappointed; he was resentful. His resentment toward my mother manifested itself in frequent arguments and constant criticism. He criticized me, too, but more often than not, he simply ignored me. In some ways, I think that was worse.

My mother tried to make excuses to explain away my father's indifference. But the older I got, the more hollow those explanations sounded. Though she'd originally converted to Catholicism just so she could marry my father, Mom was zealous in her faith and wouldn't consider divorce. As the years went by, she immersed herself more and more deeply in the life and work of the church, organizing events and fund-raisers, chairing the annual Bishop's Appeal, teaching catechism, and eventually becoming a lay minister. I don't doubt that her faith was a solace, but I'm also sure she was happy for any opportunity to get away from my father. Seeing her tireless efforts on behalf of the parish and undoubtedly knowing how difficult her marriage was, people often said my mother was a saint. She was a good person, and I know her faith was absolutely real and sincere, but . . . a saint?

I've sometimes wondered if, at some level, my mother didn't enjoy the sympathy that came her way. There's a fine line between religious devotion and martyrdom, and by the time I entered high school, I think Mom was starting to edge in that direction. After the accident, of course, the journey was complete. She became a martyr to her works of faith, to the brain-injured daughter whose spark of promise was forever doused, and to the misery of her marriage.

I've always wondered why Dad didn't seek a divorce. Though he was born and raised Catholic, he rarely attended mass. Every year my mother would write a check to the Bishop's Appeal and every year they would have a big argument about it. So it wasn't religious zeal that kept my father in the marriage. I think it was because he didn't want to risk losing Alice. She was the only thing in life that didn't disappoint him.

Alice was smart, like Dad. She had his scientific mind and shared his interest in animals. She was a good athlete, too, and fearless. She loved to skate and swim. She could ride any horse, no matter how wild, and climb any tree, no matter how high. Really, Alice could do almost anything she set her mind to. Before the accident, she was a straight-A student who planned to follow in her father's foot-steps and become a vet, as well as a better-than-average pianist and a talented artist.

Like I said, there was nothing Alice couldn't do. Including charm my dad. Let me tell you, *that* took some doing. I tried and failed for sixteen years. The only times my father seemed to notice me was when he was pointing out how far short of the mark I fell in comparison to my sister.

He was just a very critical, bitter, and deeply unhappy man. With time and distance—as well as a year of professional counseling—I can now look back logically and see that my father's dislike of me stemmed more from his personality flaws than from mine. But it wasn't as easy when I was five, ten, fifteen years old.

During those months of counseling, my therapist refused to believe me when I said I didn't resent my sister, but I truly didn't. Of course we had arguments—all siblings do—and I can't say I was never jealous of Alice, but I didn't resent her. Alice was good to me. She helped me with my homework and stuck up for me if Dad got too abusive. One time, when he said something demeaning to me when my friend Denise had come to spend the night, Alice refused to speak to him for two days. He was nicer to me after that, for a while.

And then, of course, Alice saved my life.

I was ten years old when it happened; Alice was nearly twelve. It was a Saturday in mid-March. Mom was at some meeting at church and Dad was out on a call. Alice and I decided to go ice-skating. It was a little late in the season, but still cold, and the ice on the north end of the pond was still plenty thick. We weren't being stupid or careless; we knew enough to check for things like that. Any kid raised on the peninsula would. But we didn't count on me losing control while I was attempting a spin, falling and sliding toward the south end of the pond, where the ice was thinner even though the water was deeper, and falling through.

I don't remember a lot about it, except that the water was so cold that it was actually painful. All that comes back in the dream. I can actually feel that cold piercing through me like thousands of needles, but I didn't start having that dream until a year or so after Mom and Dad died.

Alice risked her own life saving mine. She lay belly down on the ice, reached down into the hole, grabbed me by the hair, and pulled me out. It was incredibly brave of her, but also incredibly foolish; we both could have been killed. She should have run for help instead of trying to save me alone.

That's what Dad said later. It was the only time I ever heard him yell at Alice. She wasn't fazed a bit, though. She just looked at him and said that if she'd gone to get help, it would have been too late, which was probably true. I wouldn't have survived long at those temperatures, and the nearest house was a half mile down the road.

"I couldn't let her drown," Alice said simply. "She's my sister."

So how could I resent Alice? If not for her, I probably wouldn't be here.

News of how eleven-year-old Alice Toomey risked her own life to rescue her little sister spread quickly through Nilson's Bay and beyond. Somebody took it upon himself to call the papers, and soon reporters from as far away as Green Bay showed up on our doorstep wanting to interview my sister and take her picture.

Sometimes they wanted to talk to me, too, but quickly lost interest in a little girl who refused to smile into the camera and supplied one-word answers to their list of tediously similar questions. . . .

How did you feel when you fell through the ice?

Scared.

How do you feel now?

Fine.

Are you grateful to be alive? Do you think your sister is a hero? Do you want to be like her when you grow up?

Yes. Yes. Yes.

I was surprised that media people weren't more creative. They all asked the same obvious and meaningless queries, questions they already knew the answers to. I've been interviewed dozens of time since then, and my opinion of the media hasn't changed much. Maybe I expect too much. Few people are brave enough to pose a question unless they are fairly certain of and comfortable with the answer. I guess that's just human nature, isn't it?

Alice was more cooperative than I was, submitting to having her picture taken over and over, and more forthcoming in her responses, giving illuminating answers that were neither too long nor too short, coming off as precocious and heroic but humble. Eleven years old and she'd already mastered the art of the thirty-second sound bite. It was impressive.

On the fourth day the stream of reporters became a trickle, and on the sixth it stopped entirely. The news cycle turned and our lives went back to normal.

But people in Nilson's Bay have longer memories than the media. For months and even years afterward, they would talk about how Alice saved me, and though everyone already knew all about it, they'd ask my father, my mother, or Alice to tell the story, or they'd repeat it to themselves or one another if none of the principals was available.

If I was in earshot, they'd ask me the same questions that those reporters had asked. . . . *Were you scared? Are you grateful? Is your sister a hero? Do you want to be like her?*

Raised to be respectful of my elders, I said yes to everything, never pointing out that their questions were silly and that my answers should have been obvious.

Of course I was scared.

Of course I was grateful.

Of course I thought my sister was a hero. Everyone did.

Of course I wanted to be just like her.

I'd never wanted anything else.

A mournful yowl from one of the gray plastic cat carriers snapped me back to the present. I got down on my haunches and peered through the metal grating in front of the cages.

The carrier on the left held a sleek black cat with green eyes, skinny and skittish, who shrank back toward the rear wall of the carrier when I stuck a finger through the grating, trying to touch his fur. The one on the right contained a huge blue-eyed calico with brown, gray, and cinnamon fur and a white chest and nose, at least twice the size of the black cat.

I stuck my finger through the grate. "Let me guess. You must be Freckles," I said. "The food thief. Am I right?"

The cat stared at me for a moment, then yawned and turned her head away.

I carried both crates inside before I unlatched the doors. When I did, Dave, the little black cat, shot out of the crate and hid under the sofa. Freckles squeezed her bulk through the cage door, sauntered into the kitchen, sat down in front of the cupboard to the left of the sink, and started to yowl. Not surprisingly, when I opened the cupboard I discovered a bag of cat kibble and half a case of canned cat food.

Freckles began wolfing down a can of chicken liver and rice the moment I placed the bowl on the floor. I called and called and even meowed for Dave to come eat, but got no response, so I fixed up a smaller dish with kibble and wet food mixed together and set it on the floor, just at the edge of the sofa, before carrying my suitcase upstairs.

There were three bedrooms upstairs. The largest, facing the front of the house, had belonged to my parents. You'd have thought that the master bedroom would be on the side with the better view, but my father hadn't liked being woken by the morning sun reflecting on the lake.

The other two bedrooms, one on each side of the hall bath, had belonged to Alice and me. Alice's room was just the same, but mine had been turned into a sewing room.

So that left me with the choice of sleeping in Alice's bed or in my parents'—which seemed like no choice at all. Then I remembered the hide-a-bed in the living room sofa. My mother had nicknamed it the Iron Maiden and said it discouraged guests from overstaying their welcome. Not a very comfortable option, but it would have to do for now.

I left the suitcase in the hall and went back downstairs. Freckles was hunched down like a plump mushroom next to the sofa, scarfing down the food I'd left for Dave. I clapped my hands and hissed. Freckles looked up and then ran around me and up the stairs. Considering her weight, her speed was impressive.

I got down on my hands and knees and tried to coax Dave out of his hiding place, but he wouldn't move. All I could see was glittering eyes. I carried the empty food dish into the kitchen and rinsed it out.

And, after that . . . I sat down on a dining room chair and stared for close to an hour at the big round thermostat that sits outside the window. I didn't know what to do with myself.

"Just living" comes harder to some people than to others.

❦ Chapter 18 ❦

The next day, I called Jenna. She sounded harried.

The winning team had gone into full, victorious transition mode, and word had quickly gotten around the office that Ryland had tapped her to help manage the process. Every campaign donor, staffer, and intern within a five-hundred-mile radius was stopping by to congratulate her—and drop off a résumé.

The fourth time we were interrupted by someone who popped in unannounced and just wanted "thirty seconds" of her time, I told her to lock the door and turn off her office lights until we were able to finish our conversation.

"Maybe they'll think you've gone to lunch."

Jenna groaned. "I can't get anything done! I bought a door sign that says, 'Don't Even Think About Knocking: History Being Made.' Didn't help."

"Funny, but too subtle," I said. "Get a Doberman, one with really big teeth. Let's wrap this up before somebody else comes barging in. Now, before you forward any of those résumés for the slots in the DOJ, be sure to—"

"Run them by Joe Feeney," she said. "I know. You told me that twice already."

"I did? With all the interruptions, it's hard to keep track."

"How are you doing?" Jenna asked. "You sound tired."

"I didn't sleep at all last night." I yawned. "There's this metal bar in the sofa and no matter how you lay, it hits you right in the back. And then, just to make things extra fun, Alice's cat, the big one, jumped on me and started yowling at about two-thirty in the morning. Wouldn't leave me alone until I got up and fed her. The jerk."

Just then, as if she'd heard me, Freckles sauntered from the kitchen into the dining room and started to rub against my legs.

Jenna clucked her tongue. "You slept on the couch? What's wrong with the bedroom?"

I picked up my coffee mug and slurped my tea. Hopefully, the two bags of that nasty, perfume-tasting Earl Grey, which were all I was able to unearth in the kitchen, would deliver close to the same amount of caffeine as one cup of real coffee. Pathetic. How could Alice not have coffee? Or any cereal that didn't contain flaxseeds and raisins? The second I could summon up enough energy to get dressed, I was going to the grocery store for supplies.

"Nothing's wrong with the bedrooms," I said. "But I just don't . . . I don't know. I felt funny about sleeping in Alice's bed."

"Well, you can't sleep on the sofa bed for the

next seven weeks. Maybe if you change the sheets, get some new blankets, or move the bed to another part of the room it'll feel more like your own."

"Maybe. Listen," I said, changing the subject, "I know you're leaving for DC on Wednesday, but I need you to do me a favor before you go, kind of a big one."

"Okay," Jenna said.

She sounded hesitant, and I didn't blame her. She had so much on her plate, and, technically, she didn't really work for me anymore, but I just had to have someone go over to my apartment to open the door for the movers and hang around while they packed up my stuff and put it in storage. I'd tried to think of other people I could ask, but couldn't think of anybody who owed me that many favors—except Jenna. I'd hired her for her very first grown-up job, and now, not quite three years later, she was on her way to Washington. Plus, when I followed her to the capital in a few weeks, she'd undoubtedly be working for me again. As her benefactor and future boss, I was allowed to impose.

I explained what I needed, and she said, "So all I have to do is sit there while they pack? That's not so bad. I'll take my computer. Bet I'll get more done at your apartment than I would— No! Out!"

I jerked the phone away from my ear. Jenna's

sudden shout startled me so that it was an involuntary reaction. When I got back on I heard a *thunk,* as if she'd dropped the phone on her desk, and then her voice, still agitated but farther away. After a moment, she was back.

"Sorry. I had to yell at Graham Needham—"

"The weaselly press intern? The one who wears bow ties?"

"That's him. I told him three times that he has to put in his application and go through the process like everyone else, but he won't give up. He barged in without knocking. Brought me an azalea plant."

"Uh-huh. Because nothing says 'I'm the guy for the job' like a potted plant. You know," I said, glaring down at Freckles, who was still rubbing against my legs, feigning affection when all she really wanted was to be fed—again, "I was feeling bad about missing all the fun, but I'm starting to think there are worse things than being banished to the wilds of Wisconsin."

"There are," Jenna agreed. "Listen, I've got to go. When will your movers arrive?"

"Eight o'clock tomorrow. Should be done by lunchtime. There isn't that much stuff. And could you do me another favor? I wasn't planning on staying more than a few days, so I only brought a couple of outfits—"

"Two navy blue suits and a pair of khakis?"

"Something like that," I said. "I'm going to

172

need some warmer things—sweaters, jeans, jackets—just casual stuff, and some gloves and boots. Could you pull some stuff out of my drawers and send it up here?"

"Sure."

"Oh, and one more thing. . . . There's two cases of Samoas in the utility closet. Could you send one of them?"

"You want me to mail you a *case* of Girl Scout cookies?"

"Humor me, okay? Samoas are my comfort food. I need all the comfort I can get right now. Have you talked to the president-elect today?"

"Just for a second this morning. He added a name to the list of associate DOJ candidates. Why do you ask?"

"No reason," I said, taking a quick slurp of tea and pushing Freckles away with my foot. The cat took the hint and slunk off, giving me a spiteful glare. I glared back, unfazed. If Her Plumpness wanted another meal, she could go catch a mouse.

"Just wondering if he needs anything. The computer connection is fine here; I could work remotely with no problem."

"Lucy," she said in a tone that hovered somewhere between motherly and patronizing and was starting to irritate me, "it's not like everybody has suddenly forgotten about you—you're supposed to be resting."

173

"Yeah, well. Resting turns out not to be my strong suit. I'm better at doing."

"So do something. Go for a walk. Or shopping. Get a hobby."

"A hobby?"

"Don't make it sound like a dirty word. People can have lives outside of work, you know. I took up knitting last year. It's a great stress reliever. Plus I got all those cute scarves."

I remembered Jenna's scarves. She must have had twenty of them, all exactly the same except for the yarn. I'd have sooner poked a knitting needle in my eye than used one to make the same scarf two dozen times.

"I don't think I'm the knitting type. But it probably would be a good idea to get out of the house. Come to think of it," I said, "hold off on sending the clothes. I spotted a consignment shop in town. I think I'll go see what they've got."

"You still want the cookies?"

"Oh, yes. As quickly as possible. Express mail, dog sled, helicopter—whatever it takes. I'm in withdrawal."

"Drop them out the back of Air Force One?"

"Is that an option?"

Jenna laughed. "As long as you don't mind being the subject of a congressional investigation."

"So maybe just call FedEx instead."

"I'm on it, boss."

❧ Chapter 19 ❧

As I poured more hot water for another disgusting cup of Earl Grey, the first having failed to give quite the caffeine jolt I'd been hoping for, the phone rang—the house phone, not the cell phone.

Jenna was the only one who had that number, so when I answered I said, "Hey, can you send both cases of cookies? I really think I'm going to need them."

"Excuse me?"

The deep male voice on the other end of the line definitely did not belong to Jenna.

"Oh. Sorry! I thought you were someone else. Someone from my office. I was . . ." I stopped myself, realizing I didn't need to explain myself to a stranger.

"You know what? Let's just start over. Hello, this is Lucy Toomey."

"Lucy, this is Ed Glazier. I'm a builder, the owner of Peninsula Property Professionals. We've built three homes in your neighborhood in the last five years."

As he described the houses he'd built, I could picture them in my mind. None of them was anything I would have wanted, just too big for my taste and too . . . well, just *too*. Too much. But they'd been built with somewhat more taste and sensitivity for the surroundings than most of the surrounding McMansions. Glazier favored a sort of pseudo–prairie style with big, chunky pillars on the porches and leaded glass in the windows. His work was a nod to Frank Lloyd Wright that, if not completely convincing, made more sense in Wisconsin than the pseudo-Tuscan and over-wrought Greek Revival styles of some of the neighboring properties. And Mr. Glazier's houses actually left room for grass and some of the larger trees.

"I was talking to a Realtor friend of mine," Mr. Glazier continued. "He told me you might be considering selling your place. If that's true, then I'd sure like to discuss that with you."

"I'm not sure there's anything to discuss yet, Mr. Glazier—"

"Ed," he said warmly. "Call me Ed."

"Okay, Ed. But you're a little premature. I don't actually own the place yet."

Pausing now and again to take sips of my tea, I explained the unusual nature of Alice's will to Ed Glazier. I felt sure that the complexities of the situation would cool his enthusiasm, but I was wrong.

"I'm willing to wait. A piece of property like this, with that kind of lakefront view and that kind of size, doesn't come along very often. Even if you were ready to sell today, we wouldn't be able to start work until the spring."

"Right. And I won't be in a position to sell until at least . . ."

I paused, mentally calculating how long it would take me to make up the remaining weeks of residency Alice's will required, glancing at a wall calendar to estimate how many weekends I could slip away from Washington without jeopardizing my work, definitely not more than once a month.

"I can't see me getting possession of the deed until at least the end of April, possibly even as late as July."

"Well," he said, "April would be better than July, but, like I said, I'm willing to wait. I've had my eye on that land for a long time."

"Okay, then," I said, feeling kind of odd talking about selling our cottage to a total stranger, but also knowing that was what it would come down to in the end anyway. "So why don't we talk again in the spring. Say, March? I won't be around by then, but you can call my cell."

"Lucy, I don't mean to push you, but I'd really prefer to start the ball rolling now so I can start making plans over the winter and be ready to break ground in the spring. We've got a short building season here. I can't afford to waste a day of it."

"I appreciate that, Ed, but as I said, I really

can't make any agreements or sign any contracts until—"

"No, no," he assured me. "I'm not asking you to put your name to anything right now. I'd just like to present you my offer, see what you think, and come to an agreement. Kind of a verbal handshake. Lucy, I'm prepared to offer you five hundred and fifty thousand dollars for your property."

"*Five*-fifty?" I asked, certain I couldn't have heard him properly.

"Yes, five-fifty. That's more than it would appraise for, but I'm willing to pay that because it is such a unique piece of ground. Also," he said, and I could hear the smile in his voice, "because I'd like to come to an agreement with you now and keep it off the market and out of the hands of my competitors."

"You think there might be somebody else willing to pay more?"

"It's possible," he said plainly. "But I'll tell you something I know for sure. No other developer around here can offer you that kind of price *and* pay cash."

"Cash? You're just going to write me a check for five hundred and fifty thousand dollars?"

"Yes. You'll get paid the entire amount upon closing and won't have to pay a Realtor fee."

I took a sip of tea and gave myself a moment to think. In my experience, if something appears too good to be true, that usually means it is.

"Lucy," he said in response to my silence, "I'm not making you this offer just because I'm a nice guy. I'm doing it because I know I can make a profit on it. But I want you to know that I take a lot of pride in doing quality work and building beautiful homes that fit well within their surroundings. This land has been in your family for generations. There's bound to be an emotional attachment involved. You're going to want to pass this property on to someone who will see that it's developed with integrity, sensitivity, and a respect for your family history. I'm the man who can do that."

While Ed talked, I brought my hand up to my mouth and bit off an uneven piece of fingernail that was bothering me.

He was saying all the right things, bringing up the issues and emotions I hadn't even had time to process or put a name to yet. His assessment of my feelings and concerns was spot on. I was going to have to sell. Heck, I *wanted* to sell, but it was all happening so quickly. Still, I of all people could appreciate the need to get out in front of your competition and grab an early lead.

"Would you be building one house?" I asked. "Or two?"

"I'm honestly not sure yet," he said. "It would depend on what my architect comes up with, but my guess is that we'd put more than one

179

residence on the property. We'd have to in order to make a good return. But there's so much land there, Lucy. Plenty of room to build multiple dwellings without overcrowding the lot."

I thought about this for a minute. I wasn't too excited about the idea of knocking down the cottage to replace it with two big houses. But that was preferable to one ridiculously large mansion that would dwarf the rest of the houses in the neighborhood, wasn't it?

"Mr. Glazier . . . Ed, your offer is tempting. I can't pretend it's not. I'm about to move to Washington, DC."

"Yes, heard about that," he said. "Pretty exciting. I voted for Ryland. I'm expecting big things from him."

"You won't be disappointed," I said. "But back to the house. Having a half million dollars in my pocket would make moving to Washington a whole lot easier, but I'm just feeling a little overwhelmed. I can't quite come to terms with the idea of the house I grew up in just . . . . disappearing."

There was silence on the other end of the line. It lasted so long that for a moment I thought we'd lost the connection, but then Ed spoke and I realized he'd just been mulling over what I'd said.

"Lucy," he said slowly, "if I could develop the property without tearing down your house, would you be willing to sell?"

I took in a sharp, surprised breath, almost gasping. "Could you do that?"

"Yes," he said, his voice becoming lower and slower as he talked through the issues. "It'd complicate things, though. We'd have to do some major remodeling, probably knock down most of the interior walls. Maybe incorporate it into a larger structure. But . . . yes. I think it can be done while leaving all or most of the exterior walls intact. I've got a really creative young architect on my team. If anybody can do it, then Jocelyn can.

"Heck," he said, suddenly sounding more certain and robust, "I'll just tell her that is one of the conditions of the project; the cottage *has* to stay. End of story. So what do you say? Do we have a deal?"

I hesitated, but not for long. What more could I have asked for?

"Yes," I said. "We do. But I still can't put anything in writing, you know. Not until the cottage actually belongs to me."

"I understand," he said. "There's no paperwork yet. We'll have to get some lawyers involved when the time comes, but until then, the two of us know we have a deal. A verbal handshake, just like I said. Sound fair?"

"Absolutely," I said, smiling as I poured the last of my terrible tea down the drain and tossed the soggy tea bags into the trash. "More than fair."

❧ Chapter 20 ❧

Though it would be months until I had the money in hand, I was feeling pretty flush after my conversation with Ed Glazier. On the drive into town, I decided that I could definitely afford to splurge a bit.

Of course, there are limits to just how crazy a person can go in a consignment shop—that's kind of the whole point of buying secondhand—but if I saw something unexpectedly gorgeous, I'd get it. No hesitation, no second-guessing myself.

Second Act Consignments was small, but every inch of the shop was packed with tables and shelves and racks of clothing. There weren't any customers aside from myself. The ginger-haired girl standing behind the counter was so intent on talking to a lanky, long-haired boy wearing a wrinkled blue-and-green flannel shirt with a rip in the elbow that she didn't say hello or even look up when I came through the door.

I went to the nearest rack and started digging. The clothes didn't seem to be classified according to any discernible system—I found an almost new pair of size-six boot-cut corduroys hanging next to a size-fourteen prom dress with a bunch of the rhinestones missing. A size six might be wishful thinking on my part, but I draped the cords over my arm anyway and continued the search, unable to keep from noticing that the conversation between the teenage clerk and her Romeo was getting increasingly intense.

When I crossed the room to get to yet another table piled with haphazardly folded clothing, I heard a snippet of the conversation, which was really more of a monologue, since he seemed to be the one doing most of the talking. He said something about it being "time to make up your mind" and asking, "Who are you going to believe?" though the way he said it made it sound more like a demand than a question.

I didn't like the manipulative way that he was talking to her, but it really wasn't any of my business, so I kept shopping.

Before long I'd collected an armload of stuff I thought might work for me. Some of it was pretty cute. The pale blue, cable-knit cashmere sweater and the fawn-colored tweed jacket with suede patches on the elbows probably would have been way out of my budget if I'd been buying new, and they were both in perfect condition. My guess was they'd come from the walk-in closet of some-body who'd built one of those lakeside mini-mansions and was trying to make room for still more expensive things she wouldn't wear that often. Kind of a waste for them, but good luck for me—assuming they fit. I needed to try them on.

The boy was still there, standing behind the girl with his arms draped over her shoulders. I cleared my throat loudly, trying to get their attention. It didn't have any effect on the boy, but the girl was more responsive. She pushed his arms away like she was shrugging off a too-heavy shawl and hissed, "Stop it! I'm working. You're not even supposed to be here," then looked up at me, her cheeks a little pink.

I felt like it was a good sign that she at least had the sense to be embarrassed, because, *yes,* she was working, at least theoretically, and, *no,* he shouldn't have been there. I asked if they had a fitting room.

"Kind of," she said and pointed to her left.

I looked over my shoulder and saw a green curtain hanging across the far corner, hidden behind a clothes rack. I struggled to roll the rack out of the way. It wasn't easy with my arms full.

Behind me I heard another whispered conversation, more of an argument, and mostly unintelligible. But when I accidentally dropped some of the clothing I was carrying while pushing aside the heavy rack, the girl said, "Go away! I'm working!"

The boy snarled and stomped out of the shop. A moment later, the girl was by my side, crouched down next to me on the floor, helping to pick up the things I'd dropped.

"Sorry," she said without looking at me,

184

swishing her hand back and forth across the corduroys to erase a streak of dust they'd picked up from the floor.

"Don't worry about it. It's not your fault I'm a klutz," I said, pretending that both of us didn't know that she was apologizing for her behavior, not my clumsiness. Why make her feel worse than she already did?

She rolled the rack against the wall. I stepped into the corner and drew the green curtain closed and started trying things on. A couple of minutes later, I looked down and saw a pair of feet clad in black ballet flats.

"How's it going?" she asked.

"The black jeans were too big, but that's actually good news. Maybe I'm losing weight. The cords are good, though."

I slipped a soft gray sweater over my head and pulled back the curtain.

"What do you think?"

She looked me up and down.

"Nice! Those pants are a perfect fit. And that sweater looks really good on you. We've got a pink scarf with some little gray and black flowers that would go great with that. I'll try to find it for you. Oh, and did you see this?" she asked and held up a gorgeous black suede jacket with silver belt loops and subtle silver top stitching on the collar, cuffs, and pockets. "Just came in yesterday."

"Wow. That is beautiful." I reached out to touch the collar. It was wonderfully soft and supple. "How much is it?"

She made a sort of a wincing face, as if she was almost afraid to tell me.

"One hundred and twenty," she said apologetically. "But I think you'd look amazing in it."

She held out the jacket so I could slip my arms into the sleeves. I turned left and right, looking at my reflection.

One hundred and twenty dollars in a consignment shop in rural Wisconsin is serious money. But if I'd been buying new, it would have cost three or four times that much. And, after all, I had promised myself that if I saw something gorgeous, I'd get it. That black leather jacket definitely fit the description.

"I'll take it," I said, slipping out of the jacket and stepping back into the dressing corner. "Can you hang on to it while I finish trying on the rest of this?"

"Sure," she said with a smile. "I'll have it up at the counter for you."

Three hundred and twelve dollars later, I walked out of the shop with a brand-new wardrobe of old clothes, perfect for an extended sojourn in Wisconsin—casual, comfortable, and warm. And, if you didn't count the two pairs of jeans, there wasn't an inch of navy blue in the bunch. Joe would have been so pleased.

186

•••

Save-A-Bunch, the only grocery store in Nilson's Bay, isn't exactly a Whole Foods.

It was on the smallish side to begin with, and 80 percent of what square footage they did have was devoted to the sale of canned or frozen food. There was a small deli counter where you could get cold cuts and cheese sliced to order, but no specialty cheese section or olive bar. The meat counter had only a tiny selection of seafood, all of it previously frozen, which was odd considering how much fresh fish we had access to this close to Lake Michigan. The produce section was small, too, carrying only iceberg and romaine lettuce. The only available fruits were apples, oranges, bananas, four sad-looking melons, and six avocados, all as hard as rocks.

I wheeled my cart around the perimeter of the store three times, trying to figure out what I should buy. In the end, I settled on salad in a bag, pre-peeled baby carrots, potatoes, oranges, bread, canned soup and chili, frozen pizza, a pre-cooked rotisserie chicken, coffee, milk, cat litter, pretzels, and two boxes of Cap'n Crunch—regular and the kind with Crunch Berries.

I finished filling my cart and wheeled it to the front of the store. There were two checkout lines, but only one clerk. Rinda Charles was manning the register. My face broke into a smile when I saw her.

"Hi! I'm Lucy, Alice's sister. I'm so glad I ran into—"

"Got a rewards card?"

"Umm . . . no. I don't really live here now. Listen, I'm really glad that I—"

"Coupons?"

"Excuse me?"

"Do. You. Have. Any. Coupons." She uttered each word distinctly and a little louder than was necessary, as if I might be hard of hearing.

"No coupons."

With an expression as flat as her voice, Rinda started punching numbers into the register. Apparently, the store didn't have a computerized checkout system. Rinda had to key in the price of each separate item. It was clear that she'd memorized most of them, which was pretty impressive, but still inefficient. This was going to take a while.

"I'm Lucy Toomey, Alice's sister."

"I *know* who you are," she said, stabbing her forefinger against the register keys like she wanted to teach them a lesson. "I was *at* the funeral."

"Right. Of course."

This wasn't going very well. But Rinda was one of Alice's best friends and people respond differently to grief, so I decided to overlook her snippy tone.

"I saw you and your friends at the funeral and

really wanted to talk to you. But by the time I was able to get to that side of the room, you'd already gone."

Rinda went right on with what she was doing without giving any indication that she'd heard me. She weighed my oranges and keyed in the price before she shoved them across the counter into the bagging area and rang up the total.

"Eighty-one dollars and twenty-six cents."

I flipped open the flap on my wallet and pulled out a credit card.

"We don't take American Express," she said.

I flipped to another section of my wallet and reached for a pen.

"*Or* out-of-state checks."

I rolled my eyes. "Seriously? Come on. You know who I am."

"Uh-huh. Alice's sister. So you say. Since I've never seen you around here before now, I guess I'll just have to take your word on that. But even if you think you're all that just because you got yourself interviewed by some blowhard on television, and even if you do spend your life playing politics and figuring out ways to waste the taxpayers' hard-earned money instead of getting a real job, if you don't live in Nilson's Bay, we won't take your check. Store policy."

She pressed her lips together, crossed her arms, and stared as I took all the cash from my wallet and counted it out, giving me a little harrumph as

I asked her to take back one box of cereal and one of the frozen pizzas.

When she finished and announced the new, reduced total, I handed her the money and said, "Rinda. I'm starting to get the feeling that you don't like me."

She stabbed a button to open the cash drawer. "Thank heaven you're smarter than you look."

She handed me back my change with a triumphant little smile. I smiled back. I've always respected people who let you know exactly where they stand and what they think. It's so much easier to handle somebody who despises you outright than someone who pretends to be polite.

I dumped the change into the bottom of my purse. Rinda had given me back three dollars in quarters, even though there were plenty of bills in the register.

"Rinda, let me ask you something; does your dislike of me stem from the fact that I didn't come see my sister as often as you thought I should? Or because I work in politics?"

"Both," she answered. "But if you stuck around long enough for me to get to know you better, I'm sure I'd be able to find plenty of other reasons not to like you."

"Well, you might just have the chance," I said with my sweetest smile, enjoying the look of confusion on Rinda's face.

Really, if she thought I was going to burst into

tears over a few insults, she needed to think again. After thirteen years in the political arena, not only am I immune to the stings of verbal sparring, I actually enjoy them.

"I'm staying in Nilson's Bay until the end of December. Maybe even longer," I informed her, adding the last part just for the pleasure of seeing the distress in her eyes deepen. "So I'm sure we'll be seeing lots of each other."

"Not if I can help it," she said, giving another harrumph.

I began loading the filled grocery sacks back into my cart since it didn't look like Rinda was planning to do it for me.

"Since there's only one grocery store in town and I eat on a pretty regular basis, I don't see how you'll be able to avoid it," I said as I hefted the fourteen-pound box of cat litter onto the top rack of the grocery cart. "But you'll get used to me. I grow on people."

"I bet you do. Like fungus on a rotten log."

I laughed and prepared to push off, but not before remembering what I had wanted to say to her in the first place.

"Rinda, listen. I just want to thank you for making that quilt. It really was beautiful."

Her jaw twitched and tightened, as if she was swallowing hard. For a moment, I thought I saw a tear come into her eye, but she turned her back to me so quickly that I couldn't be sure.

She slammed the cash drawer closed.

"We didn't make it for *you*."

"I know," I said and started pushing my cart away from the counter. "But I thank you anyway."

And I meant it too.

The way that people had responded to them at the funeral told me that Rinda and her friends had been there for Alice when I couldn't be. People around town saw them as sisters of the heart, almost a single unit, the FOA. You never saw one without the others, they said. But what did they think of me? Her actual sister?

My guess was that Rinda's words summed up what a lot of people thought but were too polite to come right out and say.

Alice's sister? So you say. Since we never see you around here, we'll just have to take your word on that.

It was raining. I ran from the store to the car, the shopping cart clattering as I pushed it ahead of me, trying to jump across puddles and dodge the raindrops.

As I loaded the bags into the trunk, sniffling, my cheeks getting wet with a mixture of cold and hot drops, it occurred to me that I wasn't nearly as immune to the sting of a perfectly placed barb as I used to be.

❧ Chapter 21 ❧

In the following days, it felt like my life had abruptly shifted into low gear. The minutes, hours, and days plodded by without distraction or diversion. There was nothing to do but get through them as best I could.

I spent a lot of time thinking about Alice, of course. And my parents too. I spent one whole afternoon sitting in the middle of the living room floor, surrounded by family photo albums. Some of the pictures made me smile. Some made me angry. Some made me cry. Not just because they were gone and I alone am left, but there was some of that. And regrets. Plenty of those. Especially when I found Alice's sketchbooks and started looking through them.

There were the pictures of animals in them, of course, drawn in colored pencils. But there were also a number of landscapes that I recognized as scenes around northern Door County—Kangaroo Lake, the Cana Island lighthouse, the docks in Bailey's Harbor, the sod rooftop of Al Johnson's restaurant with its population of grass-munching goats, a particular rock formation and cluster of trees on the lakeshore near the north end of our property, the steps outside the library.

Most of the scenes were just that—drawings of scenery, executed in charcoal—but quite a few of them included people; really just one person, a girl.

At certain angles, especially from the side, the girl in the drawings actually looked a little like me. But not quite. Her eyes were wider set and her nose was definitely shorter than mine. She had a full lower lip, and in the sketches that showed her smiling, two perfect dimples indented her apple-round cheeks.

Another thing that struck me as odd was that even though the age of the girl in those drawings varied widely—in one she was barely more than a baby, pushing up from the ground with her bottom in the air, as though preparing to take some unsteady steps after a tumble; in another she was teetering on the edge of puberty, a slim shadow on her T-shirt indicating the swelling of barely there breasts; in another drawing she was a teenager, looking straight ahead, as if posing for the picture, with a challenging expression that, if you looked a little closer, didn't quite cover the uncertainty in her eyes—it was definitely the same person in each picture.

Who could it be? Until I found the sketchbook, I'd never known that Alice had any interest in drawing anything besides animals. And the intimacy of the drawings, the way Alice captured not just the physical presence but the emotional complexity of the girl, made me feel like this was someone she not only knew well, but cared about. This girl was important to Alice.

I looked through all the pages of the sketchbook, front and back, to see if she'd written any notes that might give a clue about the girl's identity, but didn't find anything. I wasn't really surprised.

After the accident, writing was difficult for Alice. Even on birthday and Christmas cards, she seldom wrote anything more than her signature, which was as painful and cramped looking as her drawings were lucid and free—just another of the many incongruities that a temporary lack of oxygen had inflicted on my sister's brain.

I searched through the papers on her desk, hoping to come up with a letter to or from the girl, a note, a photograph—but, once again, I came up empty-handed. The only way I could find out who that girl was would have been to ask Alice, but that door was closed forever.

As one day melted into another I became more conscious of what forever meant, of all the explanations and conversations that could have passed between us if I'd just listened a little harder, read between the lines, asked more questions. Now I was left with nothing but questions. And time. I was finding it hard to fill. Overnight I'd gone from never enough hours in the day to far too many.

I spent a lot of time checking my phone for

texts or e-mails, wishing that there would be some kind of transition emergency and that somebody, anybody, would call upon my services to deal with it. I called Jenna and Joe a couple of times, just to check in with the real world, but they were both distracted and busy, so I didn't talk for long. I know how irritating it is when some civilian calls wanting to chat when you're trying to work. Joe didn't try coaxing me to take a job with his firm again. He knew I'd be going back to work for Ryland the second I could escape Wisconsin. We both knew that. Why talk about it?

I thought about Peter a couple of times, too, wondering if he would call to follow up about Thanksgiving. But he didn't, and I soon dismissed his invitation as one of those things people say but don't really mean, the way old acquaintances meet on the street sometimes and hug and coo and promise to "do lunch" but never actually do, just trying to be nice. Or look nice. I understood. Happens all the time. I've done it myself, more than once.

It didn't matter. Barney and I would be all right on our own. I'd roast a chicken, make a salad, mash some sweet potatoes, and buy a pie from the bakery. After dinner I'd build a fire in the fireplace and we'd watch football and play Yahtzee. It'd be fine with just the two of us, cozy. And very quiet.

Aside from calling people who didn't have time

to talk and thinking about people who might have called but didn't, I also spent a good chunk of time trying to coax Dave to come out from under the sofa and eat. I was really starting to get worried about that cat.

On Wednesday, I spent one full hour on my stomach, peering under the little fabric flap on the sofa at two neon green eyes, trying to reason with him. When that didn't work, I opened a can of tuna. He did eat a little, but only when he thought I wasn't looking. When he saw me watching him, he zipped back into his couch cave. Still, it was progress. I was pretty sure that he wasn't sick, just sad, lonely, and confused. Well, that made two of us.

Other highlights of the week included a visit to the library to check out a "definitive" biography of Eleanor Roosevelt that I'd always promised myself I'd find time to read someday and several bracing walks along the lakeshore. The book was a disappointment, too big and too dry, but the walks were nice.

Though many of the trees were already bare, the colors of the remaining leaves were so vivid. I'd almost forgotten how beautiful fall was on the peninsula, when the clean and crisp November air made everything look somehow more vibrant, and how bright the sun shone on your face even as your exhaled breath froze into a frosty vapor.

But those bright autumn days wouldn't be

around for long. Soon the trees would be gray skeletons and it would be too cold for long walks. An icy crust was already beginning to form along the edges of the shoreline. Before long the sparkling waters of the bay would be filled with ice, not so much that it would freeze completely, but enough that ice breakers would be required so that fishing boats could get in and out of port over the winter. And when the snow came—and, really, it was surprising that it hadn't arrived already—the whole world would be soft, muffled, and still, wrapped in a cocoon of white until spring.

When I was little, I couldn't wait for that first snowfall, but not now. Snow, I was sure, would only make me feel more isolated, though it was hard to imagine feeling more cut off than I already did.

I kept telling myself that it was only for a few weeks and then I'd be able to pick up my life right where I'd left off, except with a half million dollars in my pocket, but it was hard to make myself believe it. I can't explain why, but I felt like my world had undergone a permanent shift. It would have helped if Tom had called, even once, to ask for my help or opinion.

It was silly to think that he should. The man was about to become the leader of the free world; he had a few things on his mind. And it wasn't like we'd been talking frequently before the election anyway. But the way he'd spoken to me on the morning of the funeral had made me think that was about to change. He wanted me to work for him, obviously, but I'd allowed myself to believe that he *needed* me. Of course, that was exactly what he wanted me to think. He could be very convincing when he put his mind to it. No one knew that better than me.

Why not? He is a politician. Convincing people, finding consensus, and winning the argument is his job. That's leadership. It was one of the qualities I'd first recognized and admired in him. But it didn't feel quite so admirable when it was turned on me. Sometimes it felt a lot like manipulation.

But that was only in my weaker moments. The problem was that, as the week wore on, my weaker moments occurred more frequently and lasted longer. Some of that, I realized, was pure fatigue.

My sister-imposed exile should have been a perfect chance to replenish my overdrawn sleep account, but it was impossible to get much rest on that sofa bed when I was spending the whole night rolling around, trying to find a halfway-comfortable position. Desperate for even one decent night's sleep, I tried putting the mattress on the floor, but it was so thin and the floor was so cold that I barely slept at all.

After that, I decided to finally bite the bullet and move into Alice's room. Jenna's suggestion to move the furniture, change the bedding, and make the space my own made sense. But two steps through the bedroom door, I stopped. Rearranging the furniture wasn't going to make this room mine. It would always be Alice's room. I could never banish my sister from this space, and I didn't want to.

But maybe we could share.

I opened my suitcase on the bed and carried my clothes into the closet, moving Alice's things aside to make space for mine. Then I did the same with the dresser, packing Alice's underwear, pajamas, tops, and pants tightly into the big bottom drawer, leaving the two smaller ones on top for my use. At some point, I supposed I should donate Alice's clothes to charity, but not yet.

While clearing out a drawer in the nightstand, I found one of Alice's unfinished quilting projects, a table runner with blue and green tulips. She'd been quilting it by hand. I remembered the other thing that Jenna had said, about how hobbies could relieve stress. As long as I was stuck here, maybe I should give quilting a try. It would keep me busy and it might be nice to make a quilt for my new place in DC.

I knew there was no point in trying to finish what Alice had started. I'd never be able to match those tiny little stitches that outlined each flower and seam. But maybe I could try something simpler.

I carried the unfinished runner down the hall to my childhood bedroom, now Alice's sewing room, and opened the big white armoire where she kept her quilting supplies. There was so much fabric inside, yard upon yard of it. What had she ever planned to do with all of it? But there were some really pretty greens. Maybe I would use some of those. Alice wouldn't mind. If anything, I suspect she'd have liked the idea.

The sewing machine stood in a maple cabinet in the corner, an old Singer that had once belonged to Mom. I didn't remember her ever using it. But I did recall Alice telling me a long time ago, maybe a couple of years after she dropped out of college, about taking it to Mr. Bjork, who fixed vacuum cleaners, lawn mowers, and snow blowers to augment his social security. He'd tuned up the old machine and, according to Alice, it worked fine after that. I didn't know how to use the machine or the strange collection of rulers and tools that I found stowed on shelves of the closet, but I could learn. That is, if I could find some kind of instruction books to tell me what to do. Surely Alice had some hidden away somewhere.

I moved things around in the closet, looking at the backs of shelves with no luck. A couple of promising-looking cardboard boxes only yielded more material, most of it pretty hideous—that must have been where she stored the ugly fabric.

Continuing the search, I lifted up a big piece of spattered canvas that looked like it had been used as a paint cloth and found the trunk.

Actually, it was a hope chest, not a trunk. It dated from the 1930s and had belonged to my great-grandmother, a chest of yellowish wood—some kind of pine, I remember Mom telling me—and lined with cedar to keep away moths that might eat into the bed and kitchen linens that young girls sewed or embroidered and stowed away until their weddings back in the day, back when the possibility of marriage to a good man usually marked the summit of female ambition. Seems kind of ridiculous now, but as a family heirloom it was sweet.

I liked to think about my great-grandma at the age of ten, or twelve, or sweet sixteen, diligently stitching linens that would be used for years to come, then folding them carefully and laying them in the chest as a down payment on the life she hoped to have and the family that, at that time, existed only in her mind.

I knelt down on the floor, fumbled with the latch, and lifted the lid.

The chest was filled with quilts, two big stacks of them, made with vivid fabrics of scarlet, amethyst, indigo, aubergine, and dozens of other hues. The colors were bright and fresh. The white or ivory backgrounds were crisp and unblemished. When I ran my hand across the patchwork star of red and blue, the fabrics felt perfectly smooth, but a little stiff, the way new clothes feel before the first washing.

These clearly weren't antiques. Alice must have made these quilts. As many as there were, she must have spent years accumulating them. Yet they looked and felt brand-new, as if they'd been folded up and hidden away the moment she'd completed them, carefully kept for the day when they might finally be needed, just the way our great-grandmother had stored her precious creations away when she was younger, protecting them safely in this very chest until the hoped-for husband should finally appear.

I pulled out the red and blue star quilt, unfolded it to see a border of stacked blue triangles, looked at the center section again, and realized that there was a secondary pattern of stars within the stars, subtle but distinct, that drew my eye and invited me to examine it still more carefully and search for other patterns that might emerge. It really was a beautiful quilt.

What was it doing here, hidden away in Great-Grandma's hope chest? What had Alice been hoping for when she made it?

I started taking out the other quilts and unfolding them one at a time. They were all so different in style, in pattern, in color scheme, and in size—some were small enough to fit in a baby's crib, others large enough to cover a queen-sized bed. As I looked more carefully at the complexity of the patchwork and the quality of the stitching, I could see how Alice's skills had increased with each new creation. But from the simplest to the most detailed, every quilt was stitched with skill and artistry, revealing yet another layer to the contradictions of my sister, whose handwriting was illegible, but whose drawings were exquisite, who couldn't balance a checkbook, but could perform complex functions of geometry while making a quilt, who talked so often and so long, but said so very little that I could relate to. The sister I had known for a lifetime. And not at all.

What could have inspired Alice to make all these beautiful quilts and then shut them up in a trunk? They deserved to be used and appreciated.

I decided to take one of the lap-sized quilts, made from rows and rows of brown and orange rectangles in graduating sizes stitched around center squares of red, downstairs to lay over the back of the sofa. It would be nice to sit under while watching TV at night. And I chose a larger quilt, the blue and red star design, to put on the bed in Alice's room . . . our room.

I began carrying the remaining quilts back to the hope chest, but as I passed the window something caught my eye, a flicker of movement. I hugged the quilts to my chest and ducked my head as I approached the low, gabled window and peered into the yard, which, despite all my raking, was carpeted with newly fallen leaves. At first, all I saw was the grass, the leaves, the bright blue sky, and the silver-gray waters of the lake glinting platinum in the sunlight. But then, where the yard gave way to the water, I saw something moving again and realized that someone was sitting in the old wooden glider, the once white-painted wood now exposed and faded to gray, staring out at the lake and rocking back and forth with slow, small movements.

The long hair and slim frame belonged to a woman, or perhaps a young girl, but I couldn't tell who it was or why she was sitting in our glider, looking at our view. Not that I was bothered by her presence, but it seemed unusual that someone would choose to sit in someone else's yard when everybody else's property looked out on a similar scene.

After a moment, she stopped rocking and tossed her head, sweeping her hair over her shoulder, turning just slightly to the right. It was a quick movement, but gave me a chance to see her face and realize that she was the same girl I'd seen in the consignment shop, the girl with the clingy boyfriend. She must live nearby. But why was she sitting in our yard?

Though I glimpsed her face for only a moment, she seemed sad to me. I thought about going outside to ask if she was all right. About then she jumped to her feet and ran off through the trees, making the glider swing vacantly for a long time after she was gone.

I went back to work and placed the first stack of quilts back into the chest before folding up the others. I grasped one of the larger quilts, with a pattern of rustic pine-tree blocks on an ivory background, and shook it out flat so it would fold more evenly. As I did, I noticed something was written on the back left corner of the quilt.

I flipped back the corner and took a closer look. The writing was small, black, and wobbly and definitely belonged to Alice. It said, "To Maeve" and the year, 2011. Nothing more.

Pushing the pine-tree quilt aside, I took hold of one of the smallest quilts, with bright, cheerful blocks in hourglass shapes on a background of white with hot-pink polka dots, and checked the back.

"To Maeve." This time the year was 2001.

I examined the back of every quilt, even those I'd already folded and put away in the hope chest. Every single one of them, eighteen in all, was labeled "To Maeve"; the words were all written in that same cramped hand, painstakingly penned by my sister, exactly the same except for the year. The years were all different, never two in the same year, from 1999 until 2016.

To Maeve.

In my entire life, I'd never known anyone by that name. But Alice had.

Alice had known her well enough to make eighteen beautiful quilts that she had never been willing, or ready, or able to give to her . . . Maeve.

❧ Chapter 22 ❧

When I went downtown later that afternoon, I ran into Peter Swenson. He smiled when he saw me lugging *The Definitive Biography of Eleanor Roosevelt.*

"Was it any good?" he asked doubtfully.

I nodded. Of course it was good. Six people with advanced degrees had given cover quotes testifying to this. The fact that I found it unreadable wasn't worth mentioning.

Peter fell into step next to me, shortening his long stride to match mine.

"Hey, I'm glad I ran into you. I was in Milwaukee all week on a case, but I was going to call to firm up the Thanksgiving plans. You're coming, right? Mom's planning to serve dinner at three, but she said to tell you and Barney to come at noon so you can watch the game. Fair warning—take it easy on Mom's cheese spread and pigs in a blanket. She always puts out way too many snacks and then gets all miffed if people don't take second helpings at dinner. If you've got some pants that are a little too big in the waist, wear 'em. Otherwise, you could end up in some serious pain by the time she brings out the pies. Pecan, pumpkin, and apple. If you don't try some of each she'll be devastated."

I smiled. All the talk of Mrs. Swenson over-feeding him aside, his eyes sparkled with an almost boyish enthusiasm, and it was really pretty cute. I'd always pegged the Swensons as being that kind of family, very close, with specific traditions, rituals, and recipes for different holidays. It must have been nice to grow up surrounded by that kind of stability.

"Peter, you're very nice, but your family really doesn't want Barney and me horning in on your holiday."

"Are you kidding? They're thrilled. Mom's so excited that she's talking about re-carpeting the dining room in honor of the occasion. Uncle Hugh can't wait to talk to you. Or at least chew you out a little. He voted for the other guy. Seriously, Lucy. You're kind of a big deal around here."

"Stop it."

"You are!" he protested. "Nobody from Nilson's Bay has ever been interviewed on CNN. And you're going to work in the White House. Every-body in town is talking about it."

I stopped at the bottom of the stone stairs in front of the library and turned toward him. "How do they know that? What have you been saying to people?"

Peter stopped, too, frowning at me as if he didn't understand the question.

"Nothing. You worked for the campaign. Everybody assumes you'll work for the administration as well. Of course they're talking about it. You know how people are in Nilson's Bay, Lucy. Everybody talks about everybody."

I took my eyes from Peter's, looked over his shoulder and across the street. Two old men in feed caps stood talking to each other. A mother with a set jaw was dragging her screaming toddler out of the drugstore and toward her car. One of the old men looked in my direction and then said something to his buddy, who turned his head to stare.

"Yeah, I remember," I mumbled. "That's part of why I left."

Peter's lips went flat. "So people don't gossip in DC?"

There was no need to respond. We both knew the answer. But the gossip was different in Washington. It wasn't about me.

"Don't be so sensitive. They're talking about you because they're proud of you. You're an inspiration. In fact," he said, sounding a little sheepish, "Mom's going to ask if you'd be willing to speak to the kids at the high school."

"What?" My head snapped toward Peter. "No!

209

I'm not a good public speaker. I work *behind* the scenes. That CNN interview? I almost passed out after it was over. I am not speaking to a bunch of high school kids, Peter. No way."

"You don't have to," he assured me. "But Mom's going to ask you about it, so I thought I'd better warn you."

I rolled my eyes. "Oh, great."

"But you're coming for Thanksgiving, aren't you? C'mon, Lucy. You have to. Mom is counting on you." He paused for a moment, and then, in a softer voice, he said, "So am I."

I looked at him and laughed.

"Oh, man. You really know how to lay it on thick, don't you? Does that really work?"

"Sometimes," he said. "Especially if I add the puppy dog eyes." He pulled a pathetic-looking face. "But . . . uh, no. Not really. Could explain why I'm thirty-six and still single."

"That might have something to do with it."

I glanced over Peter's shoulder again. The old guys were still staring. I considered sticking my tongue out at them, but decided to give them something worth talking about instead.

I pushed up on my tiptoes and gave Peter a kiss on the cheek—a kiss, not a peck, leaving my lips pressed against his skin for just a nanosecond longer than propriety and friendship dictated. I looked back toward the old guys and arched my eyebrows into a "How'dja like that?" expression.

They ducked their heads with embarrassment and quickly turned away.

Pleased with myself, I returned my attention to Peter. "Thanksgiving with the Swensons sounds terrific. What can I bring?"

The boyish sparkle came back into Peter's eyes.

"Not a thing," he said. "Just show up."

As I came through the library door, a woman with three slightly scruffy, jabbering little girls in tow pushed past me.

I recognized Daphne Olsen from the funeral. I thought about saying hello, but then, recalling my unpleasant encounter with Rinda, I decided against it. She didn't look like she was in the mood to talk anyway. The little girls bickered and whined and tugged at her jacket, demanding a ruling on whose turn it was to ride shotgun. Daphne, who was digging into her purse in search of cigarettes and a lighter, cuffed them away with her free hand like a mother bear batting away a bunch of unruly cubs and wearily uttered a series of benign threats.

Hardly anybody I know smokes anymore, especially if they have little kids. But on the other hand, if I had three yappy little girls dogging my every step, I might feel the need for a jolt of nicotine too.

I went inside, my footsteps echoing across the

small stretch of marble that led from the lobby to the checkout desk, and plunked down *The Definitive Biography*. A big white cat with patches of black sauntered out from behind the desk, rubbed up against my ankles for a moment, then jumped up onto the counter and started sniffing at the spine of the volume as if it were a fish that might have gone deliciously bad. I scratched him on the head.

"You must be Mr. Carnegie. You're awfully friendly," I said. "Why don't you come over to the cottage and give Dave some lessons?"

Mrs. Lieshout, who had been alerted to my presence by the ponderous thump of *The Definitive Biography*, approached the counter.

"How did you like it?" she asked brightly.

"I couldn't get through it," I admitted. "I kept dozing off."

Mrs. Lieshout leaned toward me. "So did I," she whispered, then opened the book cover and swept a scanning wand across a bar code inside the book.

"We've got another biography of Mrs. Roosevelt, you know. It's not as detailed as this one, but is far more readable. Would you like to check it out?"

"Not today. I was wondering if you had any books about quilting."

"What kind? Quilting history? Quilting as art? Quilting novels? Quilting instruction?"

"Instruction," I said, before adding, "They have novels about quilting?"

"Oh, yes. Very popular with our patrons, even the ones who don't sew."

She picked up the unreadable book, lifting with both hands, and dumped it into a wheeled bin with other books waiting to be re-shelved.

"Are you thinking of following in Alice's footsteps? She was a very talented quilter. Did you know she made a quilt for my granddaughter, Ashley, when she was born?" I shook my head. "So sweet of her," Mrs. Lieshout said and blinked a few times.

"I don't know if I'll be any good at it," I said quickly, moving the conversation into a less emotional direction. If Mrs. Lieshout started crying here in the middle of the library, I probably would too.

"But I've got some time on my hands, so it's worth a try. I've got everything I need as far as fabric and tools, but I couldn't find any books of patterns or instructions, and I looked everywhere. I thought maybe Alice got her instruction books here."

"No," Mrs. Lieshout said. "Alice mostly checked out movies, music, and books with animal photographs. She wasn't much of a reader. As far as I know, she didn't use any patterns for her quilts, or instructions. I think it was almost instinctual to her, the same way her drawing was.

You know how much value I place on education, but I do think that some people possess a kind of wisdom that can't be found between the covers of a book. Alice was one of them."

A minute before, I had been the one focused on trying to keep Mrs. Lieshout's emotions in check, but the tables had turned. Her eyes were dry and her tone almost philosophical, but my eyes were full and my throat so tight that I knew I was only inches away from launching into the full-blown ugly cry.

Mrs. Lieshout whipped two tissues out of a pink plastic dispenser standing next to the stapler and handed them to me. Then, without missing a beat, she scooped Mr. Carnegie up off the desk and carried him next to her chest like an infant waiting to be burped.

"Craft instruction books are all on the second floor," she said briskly. "If I'm not mistaken, quilting arts should be found in section 746.46. Follow me."

I did as I was told and trailed up the stairs after her, dabbing at my eyes with the tissues. Mr. Carnegie, his front paws resting daintily on her right shoulder like two white kid gloves, stared at me and flicked his tail.

❧ Chapter 23 ❧

There's a phrase somewhere in the Bible about shaking the dust off your feet when leaving a town that has made you unwelcome or unhappy. I'm not religious enough to be able to explain the original purpose of that act, but in my mind, it means you leave that place behind and never think of it or its inhabitants again.

When I left Nilson's Bay, just one day after my high school graduation, that was my intention. I wanted to shake the Door County dust from my feet and never think of or return to this place again. But now I'm back and I'm not sure I want to forget anymore. The longer I am here, the more I feel like I have to make sense of it, to see if Alice and Barney were right when they said I was remembering wrong.

Maybe that's why, as I was driving home from the library, I suddenly took a hard right onto a road that leads to Kangaroo Lake, where the accident happened.

Mentally, those two words are always capitalized for me, as if they are the title to a book: The Accident.

Well, maybe not a book. Maybe a chapter

heading, or the second act in a three-act play, the scene that separates the beginning of the story from the end, the pivot point that changes every-thing. That's what the accident was, the thing that changed everything.

When my sister's unresponsive body was pulled from the water on that hot day in August of 1996 and laid on the ground while a man performed CPR for what seemed like hours until she finally, finally, finally coughed up a lungful of lake water and began to breathe, everybody, including the doctors at the hospital, said it was a miracle that she'd survived.

I suppose that was true. But in some sense, Alice didn't survive the accident. Yes, she could breathe and talk and care for animals and draw beautiful pictures, but she wasn't the same person after that. Neither was I.

It was a Saturday in late August and time for the end-of-summer picnic for the high school kids. The Tielens family had nine kids in the school system, and so the picnic was always held at their house on Kangaroo Lake. Jeremy Tielens, seventh in the line of nine, was a year ahead of me in school.

The yearly gathering was something we all looked forward to. Even though Door County is surrounded by water on three sides, the waters of Lake Michigan are generally too cold for swim-ming even in summer, so getting an invitation to go swimming in one of the warm, private inland lakes was a treat, but swimming wasn't the only thing we were excited about.

For Door County kids, summer vacation was something of a misnomer. Most people who live on the peninsula full-time are self-employed. Summer, with its good weather and accompanying onslaught of tourists, was the time when they made most of their money for the year, and so it was all hands on deck.

Some kids worked on the family farms—planting or herding or weeding or picking or packing—and the children of entrepreneurs helped out at the family business. For example, Denise's parents owned a motel in Jacksonport, so she spent her summer cleaning rooms. Alice worked at the animal hospital, cleaning cages and assisting Dad in the clinic. He never asked me to help at the hospital, said I made the animals nervous, so I worked at Al Johnson's restaurant, serving and clearing thousands of plates of Swedish pancakes and meatballs for tourists.

After such a long and labor-intensive summer, we were almost looking forward to going back to school and to seeing one another at the Tielens' picnic. It gave us a chance to renew old friendships, catch up on the news, and, like the normal, healthy, hormone-driven adolescents that we were, show off for members of the opposite sex.

The girls always put a lot of thought into what

they should wear to the annual picnic. I'm less sure about the boys. No matter the occasion, they always showed up in the same jeans, T-shirts, and ball caps, but that didn't matter. From eighth grade on, I'd noticed that the summer months wrought an astounding transformation on the male members of our class.

They'd show up at the August picnic looking taller, tanner, and more muscular, mature, and desirable than they had when we parted ways in May. It really was kind of miraculous. I suppose the same thing must have been happening to the girls, but I didn't take much notice. Maybe the other girls got better looking over the summer months, but I was sure it wasn't happening to me, not at all.

I was small for my age, slow to develop, wore glasses, and had a bad overbite that required me to wear braces from the sixth grade on. The other day, I found some of my old school pictures while going through a box of photo albums. Sure enough, I looked just as geeky as I'd always felt.

But that summer, my sixteenth, it was finally my turn for transformation. My braces came off in June, and my long-awaited bust arrived not long after. In mid-August, I took a good chunk of the money I'd earned busing dirty pancake and meatball plates and bought a pair of contact lenses and a swimsuit just like one I'd seen on a *Sports Illustrated* model: bright yellow bikini bottom, belted and with a gold-tone buckle, and a matching bandeau top with another buckle in the middle that gathered the fabric and made the bust look bigger.

The contacts were one thing, but when my mother found out how much that swimsuit cost, she was furious.

"Ninety-five dollars! For *that!* Did they charge by the inch? If you think that I'm going to let you go down to the lake and parade around in that skimpy little . . ."

You get the idea. It's the same fight mothers and their teenage daughters have been having since the beginning of time. In the end, she did let me wear it. Well . . . it wasn't so much that she *let* me as that she hurried off to work at the church rummage sale and couldn't stop me.

It was an incredibly hot and humid day. When we arrived, Mr. Tielens was firing up the grill so he could cook some brats, and Mrs. Tielens was handing out glasses of lemonade. The girls squealed and hugged when they saw one another and the boys gave each other high fives and playful elbows in the ribs. Somebody brought a boom box—remember, it was the nineties—and started playing Green Day.

Carrying red Solo cups full of lemonade, we headed down to the lake to lay our towels out on the grass. Alice and her group, all rising seniors, set up camp next to a small cluster of birches. I headed in the opposite direction, far from them and closer to the water, to sit with Denise. I stretched out on the towel and, noticing Peter standing nearby with Clint and a couple of other guys, started applying sunscreen to my legs, belly, and breasts, taking my time and keeping my eyes down, pretending not to notice that he was watching me.

After a couple of minutes, the guys stripped off their shirts and jumped into the water. We girls sat on our towels to talk, tan, and steal glances at the half-dressed boys who were swimming and horsing around. Peter came swimming over toward our group with that cocky grin of his, then swept his whole arm across the surface of the lake, splashing water on me and my friends. I screamed, pretended to be mad, and jumped up from my towel and into the water. A five-minute water fight ensued.

Of course my feigned anger turned quickly to laughter. I was thrilled that Peter was paying attention to me. He grabbed one of my arms and I squealed and tried to wriggle away, but my heart rate about doubled. However, when he came up from behind, looped his arms around my waist, and lifted me halfway out of the water, saying he was going to get even by dunking me under, I screamed for real. A little splashing was one thing, but I'd spent an hour and a half doing my hair that morning.

Realizing my alarm was genuine, Peter put me down and let me go. Then Clint called and Peter swam over to see what he wanted, so I got out of the water and went back to sit on my towel.

Denise was grinning when I sat down. "Oh, geez! Oh, geez!" she hissed in a delighted stage whisper. "He picked you up and practically held you over his head like you didn't weigh anything!"

"Oh, stop it. He only lifted me halfway out of the water."

"He couldn't keep his hands off you, Lucy! He likes you! He really does!"

I stretched out full length on my towel.

"No, he doesn't," I said with a smile.

"Yes, he *does*," she insisted. "I took a look at the front of his swimsuit when he jumped out of the water, and his . . ."

"Denise!" I cringed and slapped her shoulder. "Quit it! That is so gross!"

Denise rolled her eyes, a smug smile on her face. "Oh, please. Spoken like a virgin. But I bet you won't be one for long, lucky duck. He is *so* cute."

Denise sighed and I closed my eyes, enjoying the sun on my wet skin and the sensation of having someone, at last, feel jealous of me.

"You know," she said, "if you play your cards right, you might even get it over with today. There's a bunch of trees and bushes over there on

221

the far side of the cove. After lunch, you could ask Peter if he wants to go on a walk. I'd cover for you."

"Eeww," I said again, opening my eyes.

"What?" Denise blinked, looking genuinely confused by my revulsion. "I think doing it outside would be romantic. Way better than in the backseat of Buddy's car; that's for sure." Denise rolled onto her left hip so she could see me better. "We went to the drive-in last weekend and it was so cramped and hot. The upholstery kept sticking to me."

I made a face. "Oh, ick! Denise!"

She shrugged. "You've got to do it somewhere."

"Well, *I'm* not doing it in the back of a car! Ever. And I'm not asking Peter to go for a walk and then trying to jump him. That's so forward."

"Forward?" Denise rolled her eyes again. "Geez, you sound like my mother. Yesterday, just because I phoned Clint to ask if he was coming to the picnic, she called me a chaser."

She was my friend so I didn't say anything, but Denise *was* a chaser. Just a few months older than me and she'd already slept with three guys. Her current boyfriend, Buddy, was a college kid who'd come up for the summer to wait tables at the White Gull Inn. Now that summer was coming to a close, she was obviously on the hunt for a replacement.

Denise sat up on her towel and tossed her head so her hair flipped over her shoulder. Clint noticed her, smiled a little. Denise smiled back and wiggled her fingers in a little wave. Clint elbowed Peter, who looked toward us and grinned that cocky, self-satisfied grin of his.

I turned my head away, lay back down on my towel, and closed my eyes again.

"The boy who wants me is going to be the one to do the chasing, not the other way around. Even if I have to wait."

"With an attitude like that," Denise said, "you could end up waiting a loooong time. Like until college. Or even till you're married! Like my folks did. By then you'll be too old to enjoy it."

Mr. Tielens called us for lunch when the brats were ready. It was so oppressively hot when we finished eating that even the girls abandoned their towels and got into the water. Somebody had the idea to organize some races. That's when it happened.

Alice was racing from the Tielens' dock, on the east side of the lake, to the west side. I don't know exactly what happened. Maybe it was too soon after she ate and she got a cramp? They say that's just an old wives' tale, but I can't think why else it would have happened; Alice was always such a strong swimmer. All I know is that she was there and then she wasn't. That's how it seemed.

223

But I didn't actually see it happen. I was on the other side of the lake.

I heard a commotion, looked up, and saw a crowd of kids standing on the shore, yelling and pointing to a spot far from the shore. Alice wasn't among them.

By the time I realized that, five of the older boys, including Peter, were swimming to the middle of the lake as fast as they could. Mr. Tielens was pulling a canoe off the grass and into the water. He climbed in and started paddling after the boys and yelled at his wife to dial 911.

Mrs. Tielens ran into the house and I dove into the water, swimming faster than I'd ever swum before, but the boys got there first. They flipped their bodies forward and kicked their feet up behind them like a school of playful porpoises, disappearing beneath the water for as long as their breath held out, then resurfacing to take another huge breath before diving down again.

As soon as I reached them I started diving, too, keeping my eyes open wide in the murky water, searching for my sister, the sensation of panic growing exponentially with each passing second. I went under two, three, four times, searching desperately and finding nothing. I broke through the surface again and heard more screaming from the shore, but this time it was different. There was a note of exultation in the cries of the girls on the shoreline.

Treading water and gasping for breath, I looked to my left and saw nothing, then paddled in a half circle to my right. Peter and Jeremy Tielens were swimming in tandem, each with one arm hooked under one of Alice's arms as they dragged her on her back toward the canoe. When they were close enough, Mr. Tielens grabbed Alice by the arm and pulled her lifeless, unresponsive body aboard. The hopeful cries from the shore became weaker and more tentative, then faded into silence.

I don't remember the swim back to shore, only that I was exhausted when I arrived. Someone, Mrs. Tielens, I think, wrapped a towel around my shoulders. I stood with the others circled around my sister, her skin slightly blue against the red spandex of her one-piece suit, and watched silently as Mr. Tielens performed CPR. I think I prayed, but I'm not sure now.

Mr. Tielens worked on her so long that the circle of onlookers began to diminish, as some of the girls gave up hope and drifted away, weeping.

At about the same time I heard the distant whine of sirens, Alice's inert body suddenly convulsed. Mr. Tielens shouted to his sons, Jeremy and Michael, who helped him turn Alice onto her side. Her body jerked again and she coughed, spewing out a murky mixture of lake water and phlegm. Alice's eyes were still closed, but she began to breathe on her own, her skin turning from blue to pink, like a chameleon adjusting to a new environment.

That was when I started to cry, to sob. She was going to be all right. The relief that washed over me was so overpowering that for a moment, I thought I might faint.

She wasn't all right. But we didn't know that for a couple of weeks.

The neurologist sat us down in the conference room in the hospital to explain the extent of the damage to Alice's brain and that we shouldn't expect her recovery to go much further.

"We can continue with rehabilitation therapies, but at this point," he said, "what you see is pretty much what you've got."

It wasn't a good meeting. Mom started to sob and Dad let completely loose on the doctor, who stayed surprisingly calm in the face of my father's attack. I guess he'd seen that kind of thing before.

After he left, Dad spun around and fixed me with eyes of ice. "Where were you, Lucy? Can you explain that to me? When your sister was drowning, where *were* you?"

It was the longest single utterance my father would make to me for the rest of his life.

But as it turned out, the neurologist's predictions were too dire. Alice's condition *did* improve.

Within a few months she was able to walk, but with a slight shuffle, able to speak and read and write, but laboriously, and to draw with surprising skill that only increased as the months passed. In fact, with the exception of her handwriting, all Alice's small motor skills remained intact and even improved with time. The collection of quilts she eventually left behind testifies to that.

It was really kind of miraculous; even the doctors admitted as much. My mother attributed Alice's remarkable improvement to the hours she'd spent in prayer, petitioning God and St. Agnes for healing. My father said that was a load of bull and pointed instead to the many hours he devoted to helping Alice with her physical and occupational therapy and to the fact that, unlike the doctors, he refused to give up on her or accept anything less than a complete recovery.

At some level, I suspect they were both right. Without their intervention and their ceaseless and utter devotion, Alice wouldn't have come back as far as she did; I have no doubts about that. For the first time since I could remember, they were on the same page. I'm not saying that Alice's accident suddenly united them in love; it didn't. But it certainly united them in purpose. They had only one concern and focus, and that was Alice's recovery.

I don't blame them for that—if I were a parent in that situation, I'd do the same thing. Alice needed them, but I could make my own way. I'd been doing it for years.

If I'm honest with myself, the thing that truly drove me to shake the Door County dust from my feet wasn't my parents' emotional abandonment of me. It was the things people around town said to me in the aftermath of the accident.

It was kind of like what had happened after Alice rescued me. No matter where I was or what I was doing, they'd ask me the same questions about how Alice's recovery was going, how my folks were holding up, how miraculous it was that she'd survived, and, of course, that unspoken question that they asked only with their eyes. . . .

Where were you?

As I stood at the water's edge and the biting wind of a fast-moving storm turned the skies to gray, I could see it all: the Tielens' house on the far side of the lake, the slate-gray boards of their neighbor's dock on the opposite shore, maybe a hundred feet from the place I now stood, and the spot in between, where my sister had almost drowned, the patch of brown earth where she had lain unconscious and blue before taking her first breath as a different being. I could see it all, every inch of it, and I knew exactly where I'd been on that day. What I can't explain is why, not even to myself.

And when I finally got back into the car, my fingers numb with cold even though I was wearing gloves, and drove back home, arriving just after dark, I understood that this dust I can never shake off, the day I can't change or atone for, the question will follow me wherever I go.

❧ Chapter 24 ❧

Mrs. Lieshout had suggested that I consider taking a quilting class or at least connecting with some of the local quilters, but I decided to tackle it on my own.

Lacking the IQ points Alice had—or had before the accident—I always had to work harder. There was no other option, and in time, I came to enjoy leaning in and figuring out how to do difficult things on my own. In time, *that* became my instinct, outworking everybody else to make up for my deficits. That's not all bad. At this point in my life, I feel confident I can understand and master anything printed between the covers of a book. Absolutely anything.

I didn't sleep very well after my visit to the library. The dream was back, but when I woke up the next day I decided it was time to quit brooding and get busy. As soon as I finished my breakfast, I grabbed a cup of coffee and went up to the sewing room and read both *Quilts for Beginners* and *The Novice Quilter's Handbook* from cover to cover twice, with a pad of paper nearby so I could jot down notes to myself.

After a while, Freckles came padding into the room, jumped onto the window seat, and curled up to watch me. Soon Dave showed up as well, standing at the threshold of the room to see what was going on. I was so happy to see him out from under the sofa at last, but resisted the urge to pet him, afraid that I might scare him off. After a few minutes, he joined Freckles on the window seat and started to purr.

Smiling at this small victory, I sat down at the Singer with the manual I'd finally located by lifting up the seat of the sewing stool and familiarized myself with the basic operation of the machine. Winding the bobbin was tougher than it looked. I was able to make it work on the second try, but not before untangling and unwinding about five miles of blue thread. Dave seemed fascinated with the thread, so I took the blue snarl and set it on the edge of the window seat. He batted it around while I threaded the machine and inserted the bobbin into the case according to the instructions.

Everything seemed fine, but when I tried sewing two scraps together, I ended up with a whole line of loose, messy loops of thread. Frustrated but determined, I completely unthreaded and rethreaded the machine. Four times. After the fifth attempt, my test stitches were perfectly straight and evenly spaced. I had no idea why, but decided not to question it.

The idea of tackling a big quilt was intimidating, so I flipped through the projects in the handbook and picked out a baby quilt made from four-patch checkerboard blocks alternated with big squares that looked cute and fairly simple. The fun part was picking out fabrics. I needed only three, but it took me close to an hour to settle on the right three—one with big, mostly green polka dots and just a touch of turquoise and a calmer turquoise floral that went perfectly with the polka dots. Those were for the checkerboard blocks. The big squares would be a simple white on white with a kind of starburst pattern.

Finally satisfied with my fabric choices, I got out Alice's green cutting mat, a rotary cutter—it looked like it was meant to slice pizzas—and a long, clear, plastic ruler.

The instructions said to lay the fabric on the mat, place the ruler on the edge of the fabric and measure in two and a half inches, use the rotary cutter to cut a long strip of fabric, then cut the strip into two-and-a-half-inch squares. It seemed simple enough.

But the thing about rotary cutters, I would soon learn, is that they are sharp. Really, really sharp. When you're using one, you should be very careful to keep your fingers, especially your thumb, planted securely on the ruler, well out of the way of the blade.

Unfortunately, I wasn't careful.

The blade sliced into the fleshy part of my hand, right below the thumb joint and across the top of my index finger too. I screamed and both cats bolted from the room in a panic. Freckles got tangled in my feet and almost tripped me. My hand hurt so bad that I thought I might pass out from the pain. There was blood everywhere—I mean *everywhere.* I couldn't see how deep the cut was, but I knew I needed stitches. The doctors' offices were closed by then, so I'd have to go to the hospital in Sturgeon Bay.

I grabbed the white starburst fabric and wrapped it around my hand to keep blood from dripping onto the carpet and hurried downstairs. Dave, his eyes wide with fright, was standing at the bottom of the staircase, but ran back under the sofa when he saw me coming. I went into the kitchen to get my purse and car keys, but quickly realized there was no way I could drive myself to the hospital. The wound was painful and bloody, but not life threatening, so I didn't want to call 911. I decided to see if one of the neighbors would be willing to drive me.

There were no signs of life at the three houses closest to me, but a white Subaru with a rusted fender was parked in front of the fourth house and the porch light was on.

The little girl who opened the door was my pint-sized neighbor with the pink boots. She looked at my face and then at my hand and started to scream at the top of her lungs. I didn't blame her. By that time the blood had soaked all the way through the white fabric, so I must have looked pretty gruesome, especially to the eyes of a five-year-old. A moment later, her older sister, Ophelia, the one who had sprinted past her just to prove she could, ran in to see what the commotion was about, and she started screaming too.

Maybe I should have just called for the ambulance.

A third girl, who had reddish hair, freckles, and a scowl on her face, appeared from a hallway, shushing the other two and pushing past them. Seeing me, her eyes went round and her face went white. For a second, I thought she might scream too.

Instead she opened her mouth and yelled, "Mom!" When no answer came she yelled again and louder, *"Mom!"*

An irritated adolescent voice from the back of the house yelled back. "She's having happy hour with the girls!"

"Go get her! Now!"

"You go get her! I'm trying to make dinner!"

"Juliet! Really! Go get Mom!"

"Viola, I *told* you, I'm busy! What's going on out there?"

The girl from the consignment shop, the same girl I'd seen sitting on our glider and staring out at the water, walked into the room, wiping her hands on a frayed kitchen towel.

"Ophelia! Portia! Will you two shut up and . . ." As soon as she saw me, Juliet dropped the towel. The two little girls ran to her and grabbed her around the waist.

"Excuse me," I said. "I'm really sorry to bother you, but I had . . ."

She ran out of the room before I could finish. The little ones ran after her, and one of them, the youngest, I think, started shrieking again. A door slammed and the cries of the little girl faded into the distance. The red-haired sister, Viola, stayed where she was and stared at me with a kind of horrified fascination.

After a moment she said, "I think Juliet went to find my mom. Do you want to come inside?"

I shook my head. "Probably not a good idea. I might drip blood on the carpet."

"Oh. Right." Another stretch of silent fascination and then a frown. "How did you do it?"

"Sewing."

Her eyes went wide again. "Does it hurt?"

"A lot."

The screen door slammed again. A confused,

234

panicked gaggle of girl voices with one lower, calmer, gravelly, grown-up voice, like the pulse of a patient bassoon in an orchestra of piccolos, came from the back of the house.

"All right, all right. Calm down. If she was able to walk over here on her own steam, it can't be *that* bad."

The girls, youngest to eldest, came through the door with their mother, Daphne Olsen, right behind. This was *her* house? These were *her* children?

I hadn't known that, but looking more carefully at the two littlest girls, Ophelia and Portia, I realized they were two of the three chattering children who had been with Daphne at the library the day before. Maybe the third girl was a friend of the other two? I'd been so distracted by pain and blood when I got to the door that I hadn't put two and two together.

Daphne seemed not the least bit surprised to see me standing on her doorstep. She walked up to me and, without asking permission, lifted up my hand and carefully pulled back the blood-soaked folds of fabric to examine the wound. She sucked a little air between her teeth as she saw the depth of the cut.

"Boy, you really did a number on yourself, didn't you?"

Before I could answer, she turned to her daughters and started issuing orders.

"Ophelia, run and get my car keys. Viola, go into the bathroom and bring a big, clean towel to wrap this in. Portia, quit crying. Juliet, give the kids their dinner and make them help clean up after. I'll call you from the hospital."

✇ Chapter 25 ✇

Thirteen stitches later, I was more or less as good as new—or at least on the road to that. Using my hand was a challenge for a while. Even by Thanksgiving I was still having enough trouble that Barney ended up cutting my turkey for me, which was a little embarrassing, but it was still a fun evening.

Once the turkey was reduced to a bony carcass and about the time it started to get dark, Peter's uncle Hugh slapped his hands against his thighs, looked at his wife, Eileen, and said, "Well, Mother, I guess we'd better be heading home."

Barney decided he should do the same.

"I've got to get up at four-thirty, but I'll tell you what, Ellen—that meal was worth staying up past my bedtime for. Best turkey I ever had in my life. And that apple pie? Better than my mother used to make. Of course, if Mom were still with us, I'd have to deny that," he said with a wink.

"Oh, I can't take too much credit," Mrs.

Swenson said. "You know where I got the apples to make that pie filling, don't you, Barney? From your farm."

Barney beamed. "Did you, now?" He put on his coat, ready to follow Hugh and Eileen out the door. I started to get up from my chair, but Karin, Peter's sister, grabbed my arm and pulled me back down.

"Don't go yet, Lucy! You can't!"

Karin had graduated four years after Peter and me, but she was already married. She and her husband, Jeff, lived in Appleton and had two adorable children, Kylie and Harry, ages three and one. The babies had been as good as gold during dinner, but were now asleep in their grandparents' spare room. Karin sat next to me during dinner. I remembered her as being terribly shy when we were growing up, but clearly she'd gotten over it.

In the moments when Mrs. Swenson wasn't plying me with more food and when Uncle Hugh wasn't quizzing me on my opinions on everything from the flat tax to congressional term limits, Karin regaled me with stories of the trouble she and Peter had gotten into when they were kids, including one about how, when Peter was nine and she was five, they'd decided to go downtown for some ice cream—in their dad's car.

With Peter taking the wheel and Karin on the floor pressing the pedals according to his instructions, they'd come within six blocks of the ice cream parlor before taking out a tree and a fence. Mr. Swenson had made Peter reimburse him for the three hundred and fifty dollars he'd paid to repair the damage.

"How long did it take you to pay Dad back?" Karin asked, smiling sweetly at her big brother.

Mr. Swenson, who had eyebrows as big and bristly as two gray scrub brushes, looked up from his plate. "I think he still owes twenty-nine dollars and forty-six cents. When are you planning on paying me back, son?"

"The second I win a big case, Dad," Peter said as he speared another piece of turkey from the platter and put it on his plate. "The very same day."

"So I shouldn't put down a deposit on that big diesel RV I've had my eye on just yet?" Mr. Swenson asked, lifting his eyebrows.

"I wouldn't."

They were a funny family, but affectionate toward one another and kind to me. Even though Uncle Hugh could get a little heated once he got rolling on politics, the arguments never became personal or crossed the line of civility. I kind of enjoyed sparring with Hugh. He had definite reasons for thinking the way he did, most of which I disagreed with 100 percent, but there was a clear logic behind his thought processes. I appreciated that, especially after being out of the political fray for so long.

In the middle of a heated debate about the Middle East that could easily have gotten out of hand, I grinned and said, "You know something, Hugh? I was worried that two months in Nilson's Bay might dull the edge on my partisan wrangling skills, but you're helping me stay in top form!"

Hugh threw back his head and laughed. Then we had more pie.

It was a much better Thanksgiving than I'd ever had growing up—that was certain. Most of our family holidays had ended in door slamming, shouting, or both. It was also better than all those Thanksgivings I'd spent eating at buffets in hotels or turkey sandwiches at my desk. Barney seemed to enjoy himself as well, and I was glad. I'd been worried that he might be feeling a little emotional in the face of this first holiday without Alice, but he seemed all right.

There was one moment when he looked across the table at me while Karin was in the middle of telling another story, his lined face very still and serious, but not sad, when I absolutely knew he was thinking what I was thinking: how much Alice would have loved this and what a shame it was that we'd never been able to share a Thanksgiving like this, all three of us.

Alice had been right. Nilson's Bay wasn't all bad. There were a lot of different ways to look at this town, all of them filtered through individual experience.

When I grew up, I couldn't wait to get away from Nilson's Bay. When Alice grew up, she couldn't bear to leave. After Peter finished law school, he couldn't wait to come back.

If I'd lived this kind of life, maybe I'd have felt the same way. If I'd had this kind of family, maybe my memories would be better.

Barney left, carrying foil-wrapped packages of leftovers. I said I should get my coat, but Karin was insistent.

"But you can't go! It's way too early. Mom and I need you to be on our team for Scrabble. We always play after Thanksgiving dinner; men versus women. Since I married Jeff, the guys have an unfair advantage. Two against three just isn't fair."

"You play Scrabble? I love Scrabble!"

"Hang on a minute," Peter said to his sister. "Talk about your unfair advantage. . . . This week I saw Lucy walking into the library returning a book the size of an encyclopedia. She's probably got a vocabulary that's just as big. I vote we flip coins to choose teams this year."

He dug into his pocket for a quarter. "If it comes up heads, Lucy's on my team. And if it comes up tails, I'm on Lucy's team."

"Uh-uh," Karin said. "Lucy's on our team this year. And you, big brother, are goin' down."

Mrs. Swenson, who continued to teach civics

and all four levels of history at the high school, asked about the book I'd returned to the library. When I told her the title of *The Definitive Biography*, she made a face.

"I just couldn't get through that thing. I'd read three pages and fall asleep."

"Me too."

"What? Wait a minute . . ." Peter said, his voice an accusation. "I asked you about it and you said it was good."

"And it is," I said. "People say it is. Reviewers and everything. But that doesn't mean I read it."

Peter narrowed his eyes. "Oh, you're sneaky. Now I really *do* want you on my team."

I laughed. "It's late. I really should be going."

"Why?" Karin asked. "It's a holiday. You don't have to get up early tomorrow, do you?"

"Well . . . no," I said, thinking how strange it was that, for the first time in years, this was entirely true. I didn't have to go anywhere or do anything the next day. I was on vacation.

"Karin's right," Mrs. Swenson said, "we really could use another woman on our team. Stay. You can have another piece of pie. You didn't try the pecan yet."

"Oh, I couldn't possibly," I protested, then turned to look at Peter. "Could I?"

The Swensons, like so many people on the peninsula, were of Scandinavian descent. They played their own version of the traditional board game; Swedish Scrabble, they called it.

All the words played had to be English, no exceptions, but when it came to spelling, there was a lot of leeway. As long as the letters you put down were more or less correct phonetically, you could spell the word pretty much any way you wanted. If anyone protested, you simply said, "Oh, but that's the Swedish spelling."

Most of the time, after some minutes of argument and rebuttal, the word was then allowed. Apparently, this rule had come about because Mr. Swenson's grandfather, Alrik, had been a first-generation Swedish immigrant who loved board games, but never completely mastered the idiosyncrasies of English spelling and grammar.

It was certainly one of the more interesting games of Scrabble I ever played. Definitely the most hilarious. In the end the women won, but only by six points. The men vowed revenge, and everybody said that, no matter what, I had to come back next Thanksgiving for a rematch. I said I'd seriously consider it. I meant it too.

After helping to put the game away, I said I really did need to get going. Mr. Swenson was starting to yawn.

Peter went to the closet to locate my coat and Mrs. Swenson scooted out to the kitchen to get the packet of leftovers she'd already made up for me. Karin gave me a big hug, and though I put out my hand to shake hands with Jeff and Mr. Swenson, they hugged me too.

Mrs. Swenson returned with the leftovers, asking if I was sure I didn't want to take one more piece of pie and saying that she hoped I'd come over again before I left for Washington. I promised I would.

Peter helped me on with my coat. "I'm just going to walk Lucy out to her car," he said.

"You don't have to do that. I'll be fine."

"Oh, let him, honey. It's so dark outside and you can't be too careful these days." She opened the door.

"Thanks so much for having me, Mrs. Swenson."

"You know, you're old enough to call me Ellen now."

"I know, but I can't. No matter how old I get, you're always going to be my teacher. My favorite teacher, by the way, so it's really a sign of respect."

"All right, I'll take it as that." She gave me one more hug and I hugged her back.

I started down the steps. Peter offered his arm to make sure I didn't trip in the darkness and I took it. When I got to the bottom step I heard the door open again and Mrs. Swenson's voice calling my name.

"Lucy, I almost forgot to ask you . . . while you're in town, would you consider coming to speak to my civics class? I'm sure the kids would be so interested in hearing about your experiences with the campaign."

I glanced at Peter. He pulled an apologetic face. "Of course," I said, smiling up at her. "I'd love to."

So many of the Swensons' neighbors had been hosting Thanksgiving celebrations that I'd had to park three blocks away. Now the street was deserted and still, illuminated only by the porch lights from a few houses whose inhabitants were still awake. The air had gone from chilly to so frigid that it stung my cheeks. I shoved my hands into my coat pockets, wishing I'd thought to bring gloves.

"Sorry about Mom's ambush," Peter said as we walked to my car.

"You warned me ahead of time, so it wasn't really an ambush. Besides, I kind of owe her. She was the one who got me interested in government in the first place. If you think about it, talking to her students is kind of a way of paying that debt. Or maybe paying it forward. Either way."

"You think there might be a young Lucy Toomey sitting in the front row of my mother's American government class?"

"Oh, I hope not. For everyone's sake. One Lucy Toomey is quite enough to unleash on this poor, unsuspecting world."

Peter looked at me, his forehead creased into a frown. "You're just kidding, right?"

"Of course I am. That was just banter."

"Was it? Because I can't always tell with you."

"Professional hazard," I said lightly. "That's what happens when you spend your life working in a profession where the objective is to utter a lot of words without saying very much."

"I see."

"Hey, Peter. Do you know of anybody in Nilson's Bay named Maeve?"

"Maeve? No."

"Did Alice ever mention anyone by that name?"

He narrowed his eyes and tilted his head slightly to the side, as if trying to recall such an incident.

"Can't say that she did," he said after a moment. "Why do you ask?"

"No real reason. It's just that I found these quilts. . . . Never mind." I shrugged. "I was just wondering."

We arrived at the car.

"Thanks," I said. "I'd have been fine on my own, but it was nice of you to walk me. Very gentlemanly."

"Well, like Mom says, you can't be too careful these days. The mean streets of Nilson's Bay and all that."

"Right. I read the police blotter in the paper this week; two incidences of theft! Somebody stole two bags of concrete from the back of a pickup truck and somebody else nabbed the garden gnomes from Mr. Teesdale's front lawn. It was a regular crime spree."

"I was over at the courthouse yesterday. Turns out the concrete just fell out of the back of the truck. *But,*" he said with a pointed arc to his brows, "the garden gnome caper remains unsolved."

"Good thing you're here to protect me."

I laughed and clicked the key fob. The car beeped twice and the headlights flashed as the doors unlocked.

"Hey, Lucy," Peter said. "I was wondering— how's your hand? Can you get it wet?"

"Well . . . no," I said and gave him a bemused smile. "Not for another week or so. Why do you ask?"

"I was wondering if you'd want to come ice fishing with me. If you catch something, your hands can end up getting a little wet. But another week should work out fine. We won't haul the ice shanty out for a few days. The ice isn't quite thick enough yet."

"Ice fishing?" I asked skeptically.

"Have you ever been?"

I shook my head and turned to face him, leaning against the front fender of the car.

"It's fun. And not nearly as primitive as it sounds. We've got a heater and chairs, even a TV.

246

But I never watch it. It's a good place to be quiet. Or to talk. What with the whole family being around, you and I didn't get to do much talking tonight. So anyway . . ." he said, giving his nose a quick pull. The gesture made me smile because I'd noticed his dad doing the exact same thing.

"I just thought you might like going out there. If you're not too busy."

"Busy doing what?" I laughed. "I'm unemployed, remember? I sit home all day eating cookies and being ignored by cats."

"You're on vacation," he corrected. "But that doesn't necessarily mean you're not busy. I thought you might be occupied making quilts or meeting friends."

I pulled my left hand from my pocket and held it sideways so he could see the line of jagged black stitches. "After this, I'm pretty sure that was my first and last attempt at quilt making. As far as friends—what friends do I have in Nilson's Bay anymore? I mean, aside from you?"

"Well, you finally got to meet Daphne. Since she lives in the neighborhood and everything, I figured—"

"You figured we'd become best buddies? Start a sewing bee? Not likely. I showed up on her doorstep after almost slicing off my own thumb and she drove me to the hospital. It was nice of her—I'm not saying it wasn't—but she almost had to, didn't she? I mean, what self-respecting

Midwesterner is going to let a neighbor bleed to death on her front porch? Neighborliness is built into our DNA, like the urge to eat cheese curds and root for the Packers. It's instinct.

"And aside from our mutual connection to Alice, I doubt we have much in common. Even if we did," I reasoned, "I think she's already got plenty of friends. Rinda and Celia, but I think she has friends in the neighborhood too. When I was standing on her porch, the oldest daughter . . ."

I paused for a moment, trying to recall the girl's name, annoyed that I couldn't.

"Juliet?"

"That's right! Juliet! And the other girls are Viola, Ophelia, and Portia. That's so weird. Who names their kids after Shakespearean heroines? I mean, who in Nilson's Bay?" I shrugged off my own question. "Anyway, I'm sure Daphne already has plenty of friends, because when I was standing on the porch, dripping blood, Juliet said her mother was at happy hour with the girls, so, yeah. Even if I wasn't leaving town in a few weeks, I'm sure Daphne isn't taking applications for new friends."

Peter had been standing with his arms crossed over his chest while I talked, waiting for me to take a breath. When I did, he uncrossed them and said, "Lucy, that thing you said before about working in a profession where the objective is to

248

utter a lot of words without saying very much?"

"Uh-huh."

"It's probably good that you're taking a vacation."

"Ha-ha," I said, batting playfully at his shoulder and then shifting forward so I was standing, ready to get into the car.

"So," he said, "since you have no job, no hobbies, no life, and no friends—I take it that means you're available to come ice fishing with me sometime?"

I thought about it for a second.

"Sure, why not? Could be fun."

"Good. I've got to go to Madison for a couple days next week, but I'll call you as soon as we haul the shanty onto the lake."

"Sounds good," I said. "Thanks for inviting me. And thanks for inviting me to Thanksgiving too. I had a really good time." I smiled and stuck out my hand.

"What?" he said and spread out his hands. "No hug? Everybody in the family got a good-bye hug from you, even cranky Uncle Hugh."

I rolled my eyes and took a step forward, into his open arms. He squeezed me and I squeezed him back, laying my head against his chest for a moment before looking up.

"That's better," he said. Then, without warning, he kissed me.

Not a kiss on the cheek, the way I had kissed

him in front of the library, but a proper, full-on, lip-to-lip kiss that lasted . . . well, I'm not sure how long. But it was a good while, several seconds at least. Though it seemed longer and yet much too brief.

When he finally loosened his hold on me, I took a step away from him.

"I don't think you should do that."

He tipped his head to one side, frowning. "Why not?"

Because I liked it, that was why. I liked it a lot.

When a person spends thirteen years working pretty much without a break, too busy to rest much or think much, too busy to eat or sleep or even breathe much—at least that's the way it felt sometimes—self-reflection is a luxury you can't afford. And if you're that kind of person, the so, so, so busy kind, chances are you don't *want* the luxury of self-reflection. Chances are you're avoiding it.

But with all this time on my hands and not enough activity with which to fill it, I couldn't avoid it—self-reflection, I mean. And one of the things I'd been reflecting on, one among the many, was the conversation I'd had with Joe just before the election, when he offered me a job over breakfast.

Joe had pointed out my ongoing pattern of getting involved with unavailable men, men whom I had little in common with aside from some connection to the political profession, who either traveled as much as I did or lived in some far-distant state, men I didn't have to see very often or risk getting attached to. Joe's theory was that I picked these men, the unavailable kind, on purpose, which was ridiculous.

But I could see how people might *think* that I had feelings for Tom. They might look at my devotion to getting him elected and mistake it for personal devotion, or even love. And okay, it might be true that I got myself involved in relationships that were doomed to fail because, subconsciously, I didn't want anyone to compete with my mission to help get Tom elected, but that was all over now. In less than two months' time, Tom Ryland would be sworn in as president. Mission complete.

Of course, I'd still work for him and work hard; I didn't know another way. But I wouldn't work quite *as* hard for him as I had in the past. He didn't require that level of devotion from me anymore. The time had finally come for me to have a life of my own: a house, furniture, pictures on the walls. And friends. Maybe even a cat—they were starting to grow on me. And a man, someone who cared about me most. Someone whom *I* cared about most.

And who knew, maybe even a family? There was still time. I wouldn't be forty for another four years, and I knew of plenty of women who didn't have their first baby until after that. And, I had to admit, seeing Jeff playing peekaboo with Harry across the table, how Kylie had fallen asleep on Karin's lap, that halo of blond curls resting on her mother's shoulder, had tugged at my heart. They were such beautiful kids; Harry's eyes were as blue and bright as could be, and Kylie's mouth was so perfect and pink, like a little rosebud, and seeing the two of them dressed in those jammies with the feet, yawning and waving as they were carried off to bed in their daddy's arms . . . well, it almost brought tears to my eyes. Wouldn't it be fabulous to have a family like that? Two adorable kids? A husband who is crazy about you? Someone to share your life with?

If there was one thing that these days of stillness and solitude had taught me, it was that I didn't want to spend my life alone. But that didn't mean I was willing to settle for just anybody. I'd been alive long enough to see the consequences that could result when a woman whose biological clock had started to strike twelve married in haste. I wouldn't make that mistake. From here on out, any man I dated would have to meet some very specific criteria.

That was why I'd called Terry Boyle and broken up with him last week. He didn't care about me most, and if I'd had any doubts about that, they were shattered by the way that Terry received the news—dispassionately, as if it didn't much matter one way or the other to him.

I don't know why I was surprised. That was the way he approached just about everything, including sex: with a definite lack of passion. Still, it would have been nice if he'd displayed a little distress, a *hint*. At least for form's sake.

Instead, he said, "Well, okay, Luce. I understand. Listen, I've got a conference call in a few minutes, but give me a call when you get to DC, okay? We'll do lunch."

Well, good riddance. The next guy I let myself get involved with would be the polar opposite of Terry Boyle. He would be kind, strong, smart, funny, loving, passionate, and, most important, available. He wouldn't live more than ten miles from me, twenty at the most, because the thought of being farther from me than that would be agony, for both of us.

That would be part of the passion. It would be a thing we shared for life and for each other. I wouldn't settle for less. Not anymore. That was another thing that Alice's death had taught me, that life is short and time is too precious to waste or to spend going through the motions.

And if I couldn't have the real thing with someone who was genuinely available, then I'd just as soon abstain, thank you very much.

And since Washington is a thousand miles from Wisconsin, I couldn't let myself get attached to

Peter Swenson. I wouldn't. No matter how much I liked how he kissed. And I did like it. Too much. Much too much.

But I couldn't tell him that.

I took another step back and opened the door of my car.

"I've been sniffling all week," I said. "I think I'm coming down with something. I'd hate for you to catch it."

❦ Chapter 26 ❦

Growing up in Nilson's Bay, I spent more than one Halloween trick-or-treating in snow boots and with a parka over my costume, so I knew how fortunate we were that the weather had continued to be cold but bright and sunny so late in November. But it wouldn't last. The forecast was calling for storms early in the week.

I spent the Saturday after Thanksgiving raking up the last few leaves so they wouldn't rot underneath the snow and burn the lawn come spring, bleeding the outdoor faucets and wrapping them in old towels and plastic bags to make sure the pipes didn't freeze, locating the shovels and ice scrapers, and making sure that the snowblower had plenty of oil and gas and that I still remembered how to start it. Once that was done, I drove to town for rock salt from the hardware store, groceries from the market, and movies from Redbox.

I came home feeling pleased that I was ready to handle the winter's icy blast and even a little excited about the prospect of snow. I decided to take a nice long walk along the lakeshore. It might be my last chance to do so for some time, maybe even forever, since I'd be selling the cottage in the spring.

The trees were completely bare by now, stark and skeletal, but still beautiful, like pen-and-ink drawings superimposed upon a canvas of bright blue. I was wearing a sweater under my coat, gloves on my hands, and a thick pair of wool-blend socks inside my boots, so even though the temperature was hovering just above twenty degrees, I was perfectly warm.

After cutting through the neighbors' backyards, I reached the edge of the forest and the start of a trail that led to the far side of the bay. The trail, a deer path that had become more established when people started using it, wasn't maintained by anyone, so I sometimes had to climb over rocks or fallen tree limbs to follow it, but that was part of the attraction for me; it was a great workout.

I walked for about two miles to a big fallen tree that hung out over the edge of the water. I climbed out onto the trunk to catch my breath and enjoy the view for a few minutes before turning around and retracing my route through the woods and then the yards that backed up to the shore. I was so entranced by the sight of the sun beginning to sink toward the water that I didn't notice Daphne Olsen sitting outside in a lawn chair until I heard her calling out to me.

"How's the hand?" she asked, blowing out a column of cigarette smoke and gesturing with the wineglass she held.

"Better," I said. "The stitches come out soon."

"Good! So you'll be able to start quilting again."

"Oh, I'm pretty sure that little escapade marked my first and last attempt at quilting. Thanks again for driving me to the hospital."

She dismissed my gratitude with a wave of her cigarette before putting it to her lips and taking another deep drag, making the tip glow orange. I walked across the grass toward her, trying not to look too surprised as I got closer and saw a half dozen chickens with rust-colored feathers milling about at her feet, pecking at something on the grass and also occasionally dipping their beaks into a wide-mouthed wineglass that was filled with golden-colored liquid that looked exactly like the liquid in Daphne's glass.

"Is that . . . ?"

Daphne nodded and blew out another breath of smoke.

"Cherry Riesling," she confirmed and then looked down at the birds. "I get it from the winery

256

in Fish Creek. Pairs well with macaroni and cheese. They've got a lingonberry wine, too, but that's got a little too much bite for me. We like our wine a little on the sweet side. Don't we, girls?"

She put her cigarette between her lips, took a couple of potato chips from a little bowl she was holding on her lap, then crushed them between her fingers and tossed them on the grass, creating a flurry of flapping and excited clucking.

"You give your chickens wine? And potato chips?"

"Uh-huh. Every day after work I come out here with my chair, my chips, and my wine and have happy hour with the girls. At least when the weather is decent," she said. "This'll probably be our last happy hour until spring."

I watched, fascinated, as the biggest hen pushed one of the smaller ones away from the glass and dipped her beak several times in succession.

"Can that be good for them?"

"Well," Daphne said, taking a quick puff of her cigarette, "I've lost plenty of chickens to foxes, but not a one to booze. So far. But Matilda here might prove to be the exception."

She nudged the fat hen away from the glass with her foot. "Get away from there, Tilda. You big hog. Give somebody else a chance, why don'tcha?"

The hen clucked softly and waddled unsteadily away in search of more potato chip crumbs.

Daphne tilted her head far to one side, squinting through the sunlight to see me.

"The way I look at it, the girls work hard and so do I. We all deserve our little pleasures, don't we? If that means we end up shaving a little time off the clock, then so be it." She inhaled deep and long, then tilted her head back and blew smoke slowly, almost delicately, through the curve of her lower lip. "We all end up under the dirt eventually. Or in the pot. Any way you look at it, every goose gets cooked in the end."

"You work at the . . ." I paused, almost but not quite able to recall what she'd told me during my pain-pill-fogged attempt at small talk on the drive home from the hospital.

"The minimart out on the highway," she said. "But that's just during the cold weather. In the summer, I'm a flagger for a road crew. Miserable work, but the pay is good."

"That's right," I said, wincing with self-annoyance. "You told me before. I should have remembered."

She shrugged and dropped her cigarette butt onto the grass before grinding it out with her shoe. "You were kind of out of it during the drive home."

"Those pills they gave me were way too strong."

"Speaking of medication," she said, lifting her glass, "would you like a drink? There's half a bottle left in the kitchen."

I hate Riesling. Of course, I'd never tried the cherry variety, but I was pretty sure I'd hate that even more.

"Oh, thanks. But I'm sure you've got better things to do than sit here with me."

"Not for a while. Juliet makes dinner on Saturdays when I work—always the same thing, macaroni and cheese with hot dogs—but it's great not to have to cook after I've been on my feet ringing up blue raspberry slushies and lottery tickets all day. Really," she said, nodding toward a nearby stump, "pull up a chair and stay a while. It'd be nice to have an adult conversation before I have to go inside and referee my kids."

She sighed. "Lucy, you are looking at the Midwestern distributor of female children. And every single one of them is going through a stage. That's the polite word for it—a stage. I could come up with a few more choice expressions, but I don't know you well enough for that yet. Are you *sure* you don't want a drink?"

I shook my head, but sat down on the stump. Daphne took a sip from her glass and then, seeing that Matilda was about to belly up to the bar again, reached down and poured the contents of the other glass out onto the ground.

"*You* have had enough," she scolded. "You big lush."

The bird turned her head to the side, glaring at Daphne with one beady eye, and then tottered off.

"So I was wondering about your girls," I said. "I mean your daughters, not your chickens. Very unusual names. Are you a big Shakespeare fan?"

"I am! In high school the teacher made us read *Julius Caesar* and *Romeo and Juliet*. Except for the sex and the murder, everybody hated them. But not me. I just loved every word, even the ones I didn't understand."

Eyes gleaming, she stared out at the horizon and recited, "'My only love sprung from my only hate! Too early seen unknown, and known too late!'"

She sighed and closed her eyes, as if savoring the lingering taste of poetry on her tongue.

"I couldn't get enough," she said. "I went to the library and checked out every Shakespeare play I could find, the tragedies, the comedies, and the histories. The sonnets, too, every single one of them."

"Does your . . ." I was about to say "husband," but then I remembered that, during the drive, Daphne had told me she wasn't married. Never had been. "Does the girls' father like Shakespeare as much as you?"

Daphne lit up a new cigarette and took a long drag, as if she needed to think awhile before deciding what or how much she could share with me.

"Juliet's father was a lance corporal in the Marines. I met him at a dance and lived with him for two weeks before he shipped out. The only thing I ever saw him read was *Mad* magazine. I met Viola's father at a biker bar. I'm not sure he knew how to read."

She gave me a wry smile and tapped her finger against the top of the cigarette, even though there wasn't enough ash to flick away yet.

"Ophelia's father worked on the construction crew with me, came up from Arizona for the season to run the paver. He read the *Weekly Standard*. At the end of the season, he went back to Arizona. Turned out he had a wife he kind of forgot to mention. Two-timing jerk. I'd never have given him the time of day if I'd known about that.

"Now, Portia's father was different," she said and took another quick drag before going on. "Very smart guy. He ran the Tilt-A-Whirl ride at a carnival. I met him at an Oktoberfest. You remember how those rides look? All painted red with kind of a half dome over the top, so you can't really see inside? Well, he rigged up some kind of remote control device so he could start or stop the ride without having to actually be at the controls. That way, if it was after hours and nobody was around, he could just hop into one of the cars, bring along a friend, and ride as long as he wanted."

She put her smoke between her lips, moving her head slowly from side to side, and inhaled. "Let me tell you, that man could go a *long* time. It was impressive."

"Wait a minute." I laughed. "Are you saying that Portia . . ."

Daphne nodded. ". . . was conceived on a Tilt-A-Whirl. Uh-huh."

My jaw went slack. I was sure she was kidding. I waited for her to wink or laugh, but she just kept on talking as if her admission were nothing out of the ordinary.

"Tony read books, real books. Hemingway." Her lips flattened into a line. "Well, that tells you all you need to know, doesn't it? Biggest misogynist in literature. One of them." She shook her head. "Anyway, Tony left with the carnival. I'd always known he would."

"But if you knew he was going to leave . . ." I paused, frowning, still not quite sure if I really understood or believed what I was hearing.

"Why did I let myself get mixed up with him in the first place? Because I don't really care for men," she said simply.

"Oh, sure, listening to me talk, knowing that I have four daughters by four different fathers, you probably think I'm a great big slut. But those four men were the only men I've ever been with and the sum total of my encounters with them can be counted on both hands and two toes. And half of those were with the Marine. Either I cared more about him than the others or I got more self-control as I got older."

I leaned forward, resting my elbow on my knee

262

and propping my chin in my hand as I sorted out the math in my head.

If Daphne had had only four lovers in sixteen years, then our love lives were on a pretty even pace. I'd actually had one more boyfriend than she had. And even with the challenges of time and distance that marked nearly all my relationships, my physical encounters with my boyfriends had been significantly more numerous than Daphne's.

But hers sounded a lot more interesting.

A Marine. A biker. A burly construction worker with big biceps and a tight T-shirt. A hard hat. A tan.

Okay, maybe the philandering construction guy hadn't had a tan. Or big biceps. Daphne hadn't actually described what the man who had fathered Ophelia looked like, but I was pretty sure that he and all the rest of them were a lot more masculine, capable, and passionate than Terry Boyle or any of the slick suits I'd dated in the last sixteen years.

I couldn't picture Terry or any of my old boyfriends spending their time and energy figuring out how to jury-rig a remote control in hopes of luring a woman onto a carnival ride for lascivious purposes.

It must be kind of exciting to be lured. I'd never been lured. Not once.

In the usual and entirely predictable course of my love life, when I went to bed with a man the first time, I knew in advance it was going to happen. So did he. We'd been through the obligatory three dates, assessed each other's strengths and weaknesses, and, on occasion, run a background check, and decided to move ahead with the relationship.

Though we never actually discussed it beforehand, we both knew that the fourth date would end at his place or mine—carpets vacuumed and sheets changed for the occasion—and that we would go to bed, right on schedule and according to plan. There was no mystery to it, no surprise, no pursuit, no passion—simply the conclusion of a transaction whose outcome had never been in question.

Even when I was sixteen years old and decided to rid myself of my virginity, tired of being among the ignorant and uninitiated, anxious to be an adult and stupidly believing that this would speed the transition, I had looked over the available candidates and decided that Peter Swenson was the most likely and potentially most responsive, weighing my options, confident in the successful outcome of my mission. And who knows? If I'd picked any other day but *that* day, the day of the picnic and the accident, it might have happened just exactly the way I'd planned it.

Now I was glad it hadn't. It would have made things awkward between Peter and me. And wouldn't it have been sad if that time, with Peter, whom I liked a lot, would have been just like the other times—something happened because I had determined in advance that it would?

No passion. No pursuit. No heat.

I looked at Daphne.

You did it in a Tilt-A-Whirl? Damn, girl!

I smiled. "I don't think you sound like a big slut."

"Good," she said, crushing out the second cigarette. "Because I'm not. The way I see it, I'm a giant panda."

"Excuse me?"

"A giant panda," she repeated, and then, seeing that I wasn't following her, she continued. "Not an *actual* giant panda. It's a simile. I'm *like* a giant panda. I read in a book that giant pandas only ovulate and mate for two or three days once a year. So I'm like that, see? Except with me, it's every four years."

She started counting off on her fingers. "I was eighteen when I had Juliet. Four years after that, I had Viola. Four years after Viola, I had Ophelia. And four years after *that,* I had Portia."

"So Portia is four now?"

"Uh-huh," Daphne said in an ominous tone. "Which means I'm due. That's why, when I moved to Nilson's Bay after she was born, I made a conscious effort to seek out the company of women. I met Alice, and then, through Alice, I met Rinda and Celia. I figured they'd reel me in if I started to veer off course. Two years ago, just to hedge my bets, I decided to start having happy hour with the girls instead of going to The Library."

"The library? But I just saw you there last week."

Daphne lowered her chin and raised her brows, giving me a "think about it" sort of look.

"Oh, wait. You mean the bar, not the building."

"Right. In addition to the four-year time frame, the common component in the conception of all my darling daughters was a lethal combination of alcohol and men. I don't consider giving up men that much of a hardship, but I'll be danged if I'm giving up Riesling. Or potato chips."

She held out the bowl and I took a few.

"It's going pretty well so far, but I won't feel safe until Portia turns five in May. Of course, technically, if I were to get pregnant tomorrow, then the baby wouldn't be born until after Portia's birthday, but still. I'm just not going to feel like I'm out of the woods until Portia blows out all five candles on her cake."

She put a chip in her mouth and chewed it thoughtfully. "There's this guy who comes into the minimart to buy beef jerky and M&M's who looks just like Ryan Reynolds. He's a long-haul trucker, so I don't see too much of him, but when I do . . ."

Moving her head slowly from side to side, she pulled another cigarette halfway out of the pack and then slid it back, apparently thinking better of it.

"If he starts coming more often, I might have to quit my job. At least until May. The man makes me nervous."

"I can see why," I said.

Matilda, who had eaten all of the available potato chips, waddled over and stared me down with her beady black eyes. More from fear than from benevolence, I crumbled a chip and tossed it on the ground.

"I'm nervous about Juliet and that boyfriend of hers too," Daphne said.

"The skinny guy with the long hair? I saw him at the consignment shop."

"That's him. The one who hangs on to her like a three-toed sloth." She growled and took a small sip from her glass.

"Juliet is so smart," she said, frustration creeping into her voice. "She could be anything she wants to be! But this boy is putting pressure on her to stay here after graduation, and if she does . . . Listen, I don't regret moving here one bit. If Juliet wants to come back to Nilson's Bay after college, I'd have no problem with that. But first I'd like her to finish her education and experience life a little. 'Ignorance is the curse of God. Knowledge the wing wherewith we fly to heaven.' *Henry the Sixth, Part Two*," she informed me.

"With all my love of Shakespeare, do you

know that I've never actually seen one of his plays performed on a real stage? I want better for Juliet."

"Can't you just tell her to stop seeing him?"

"Tried that. Didn't work." She picked up three chips and ate them, one after another.

"Sometimes I almost wish I *did* have a man in my life. Maybe a father would be able keep her in line. But who knows? My father didn't have much success with me. He knocked me around plenty, but it didn't keep me away from the Marine. If anything, it drove me to him."

She sighed heavily and then shrugged. "But enough about me. How are *you* doing? I mean since Alice is gone? I wanted to talk to you at the reception after the funeral. . . ."

"I thought you were avoiding me."

Daphne tilted her head to one side and frowned. "Why would you think that? I just had my hands full was all. Celia was such a wreck that I didn't feel like I could leave her."

"She seemed pretty torn up."

"We all were. But Celia is so tenderhearted, and that day of all days, Pat decided to pick a fight and threaten to leave. That's her boyfriend. He knows *exactly* how to push Celia's buttons."

Daphne's eyes grew dark. She took a big swig from her glass.

"Come to think of it," she said with disgust, "I take back what I said before about wishing I had a man around. Men are so manipulative! And Celia has a gift for terrible relationships, poor thing. Before Pat it was a guy named Don, worked in a dry cleaners in Sturgeon Bay and ended up taking *her* to the cleaners. I didn't really think anybody could treat her worse than Don, but I was wrong. Pat is always picking at her, starting fights or flipping out because some other guy looked at her sideways, and threatening to leave. It's a complete control thing, but Celia just doesn't get it. She's so young and so sweet, and she just wants to be loved. It's always the sweet ones who get their hearts broken, isn't it? Probably explains why mine is still intact, being made of stone and all." She winked.

"Yeah. Not buying it," I said with a smile. "I suspect you're a lot softer than you like to let on. Can I just say something? I know it sounds stupid, but I'm so relieved to know that you weren't avoiding me during the reception. I was sure you all hated me."

"Don't be silly," Daphne scoffed. "I don't hate you. And Celia doesn't hate anybody; it's just not in her." She picked up her glass. "Of course, Rinda is a different can of worms. She *definitely* hates you. . . ."

Daphne tipped up her glass, leaving me hanging while I waited for her to swallow the last drops of wine.

"That's kind of the way she is. Rinda loves

fiercely and hates the same way. But I wouldn't let it bother you. In a lot of ways, she's even more sensitive than Celia. But she'll warm up to you once she gets to know you. You'll see."

"Oh, I doubt that," I said, recalling the way Rinda had glared at me in the grocery store. "And even if that were true, I won't be here long enough for her to get to know me. I'm off to Washington right after Christmas."

"That's right," Daphne said with a frown. "I forgot about that."

Evening twilight was quickly giving way to darkness. I heard the high, nails-on-chalkboard squeak of a screen door opening, followed by the soprano piping of little Portia's voice, calling from the doorway.

"Mommy! Juliet says to tell you that it's time for dinner!"

"Be right there, honey!" Daphne got up from her chair and looked at me. "Care to join us?"

"I've got to get home and feed the cats."

She folded up her lawn chair. I got up from the stump and started walking across the grass toward the cottage, smiling when I saw Daphne *chook-chooking* to the hens, using the lawn chair to herd them toward a coop that stood closer to the house.

After she opened the door to the coop and the first of the chickens went inside, Daphne looked up and called out to me. "You doing anything after dinner? I've still got that half bottle of Riesling. I could bring it over to your place."

"I'm really more of a scotch drinker, but come on over," I called back. "About seven?"

"You sure? I don't want to bother you."

"You won't be," I said. "It'd be nice to have some company."

❦ Chapter 27 ❦

A few minutes after seven, just as I was throwing half of a pretty awful frozen pizza into the trash can, the doorbell rang.

Daphne Olsen was standing on the porch with a nervous smile on her face, holding a half-empty bottle of Riesling and a plate covered with aluminum foil.

Celia Brevard and Rinda Charles were with her.

"Surprise! Celia and Rinda were already coming over for a little girls' night gathering and I didn't think you'd mind if I brought them along. The more the merrier, right?"

I stood there, temporarily frozen to immobility by the enmity of Rinda's cobra-like stare.

Daphne cleared her throat. "Can we come in?"

Her voice jolted me back to sensibility. "Oh, yes! Sure. Come right in."

I opened the door wider to let them pass.

Daphne headed immediately for the kitchen, making little kiss noises at Dave, who had come out from under the sofa as soon as he heard her voice, following right behind her, meowing plaintively.

In contrast to the bright, almost whimsical wardrobe she'd worn to the funeral, Celia was now dressed in a black zip-front dress with a bustier-like bodice attached to a short, ruffled skirt and black lace-up booties. However, I noticed she had added a streak of bright blue to her blond hair since I'd last seen her.

She politely introduced herself, but her eyes were shiny and her chin quivered as she attempted a smile. For a moment, I was afraid she might burst into tears, but Daphne, who was now holding Dave in her arms, poked her head out of the kitchen and said, "Celia, run in here and help me, will you? I can't remember where Alice kept the paper napkins."

I knew exactly where she kept them: to the right of the refrigerator, third drawer down. My guess was that Daphne knew that, too, but she was assigning Celia a task as a distraction from the wave of grief that accompanied her first entry into the cottage since Alice's death.

"Excuse me," Celia murmured and scurried off toward the kitchen, leaving me alone with Rinda.

"Nice to see you again," I said.

"Oh, I am *sure* that's not true."

She stepped through the doorway and set her purse down on a nearby table.

"Let's clear some things up right now. I am here for three reasons and three reasons only. The first is Alice. Daphne told us that you were trying to teach yourself how to quilt, and as near as I can tell, that is the only time you've done anything that Alice wished." She stuck out her index finger and pointed it right at my nose. "The *only* time! So I feel duty bound to help make that wish come true.

"The second reason is Alice again. Not you— Alice. No matter how I feel about you, she would not have wanted to see her little sister's hand hacked off like a piece of meat." She shook her head and scowled even more deeply. "What kind of fool doesn't move her fingers out of the way when she's cutting fabric? Are all the overpaid, do-nothing bureaucrats in Washington as brilliant as you?"

She raised the remaining four fingers on her hand, holding it flat in front of my face. "Never mind," she said. "I already *know* the answer.

"The third reason I am here is because of Jesus," she declared, lowering her hand and lifting her chin. "My Jesus said we must offer forgiveness if we hope to receive it. So I offer you mine. For the terrible way you treated my sweet Alice, never *once* coming home to see her even though she begged you to year after year, for your selfishness, and even for your participation in an election that is going to lead this country further down the path to perdition, I forgive you. But only because Jesus says I have to."

She scowled and pointed her finger at me again. "And just because I forgive you doesn't mean that I like you. So don't go thinking that it does."

"Fair enough," I said. "Because I don't think I like you either."

There was a little spark of something in her eye, a glint that could have been shock or respect or some combination of the two.

"All right, then. Now we understand each other."

"We do."

"Good."

I closed the front door. Celia, who was smiling for real now, came running out of the kitchen, holding a plate in her hand.

"You've got to try one of these bars. They're the best!"

Rinda picked one up and nibbled at the corner.

"Good," she said, sounding a little surprised. She took another bigger bite and raised both eyebrows. "Daphne made these?"

"Uh-uh," Celia said. "Daphne brought cheese and crackers, remember? We found these in the kitchen."

"I made them," I said. "It's an old family recipe: You Like-A Me Bars. I don't know if they go with cherry Riesling or not, but I guess we can find out." I took the plate from Celia's outstretched hands and marched off toward the kitchen. Celia trailed behind. Upon reaching the doorway, I looked over my shoulder at Rinda.

"Well? Are you coming?"

It was awkward for the first few minutes. Even the administration of refreshments didn't quite help the ladies loosen up. And why would it? In spite of our mutual connection to Alice, we were complete strangers.

Once everyone had a bar and a beverage in hand, Riesling for Daphne, Celia, and me—it actually wasn't too bad with the cookies—and a cup of tea for Rinda—maybe that was why Alice had that box of Earl Grey—we went up to the sewing room. Celia started to sniffle as we climbed the stairs, and the others were quiet too. Upon entering the room they just stood there, looking around the room. It was almost exactly as Alice had left it.

"It still smells like her," Celia said softly.

"It does," I agreed. "I keep waiting for her to walk through the door. Hey, I'm glad you're here. I wanted to ask you something. Who is Maeve?"

"Maeve?" Daphne frowned and looked at Rinda, who shrugged. "No idea."

I opened the trunk and showed them the pile of quilts, flipping over the corners so they could see the labels on the back. None of them had ever seen the quilts before or heard Alice mention anyone named Maeve.

"That's so weird," Celia said. "I thought Alice showed us all of her quilts. I've never even seen most of these fabrics before."

"Maybe she made them before we met her?" Daphne offered.

Rinda frowned and pointed to one of the quilt labels. "No. Look at the date on this one—2014. I moved here in 2010 and started sewing with Alice the same year. You moved to Nilson's Bay and joined us a couple of years later, and Celia came in the fall of 2013. For some reason, she must have decided to keep these a secret from us."

Rinda leaned closer, squinting as she studied the stitches on the quilt, an eight-pointed star design made with a range of pale-blue and sage-green floral fabrics with touches of metallic gold on the leaves, set on a cream-colored background.

"Beautiful work," she said quietly. "Alice was really something. Sweetest woman on the face of the good Lord's earth and just about the best quilter I ever met. And yet," she went on, flipping the quilt back so she could look at the label that, once again, had words written in Alice's laborious script, "even writing her own name was so difficult for her."

"So you never heard her mention anyone by the name of Maeve? Not even in passing?" All three of the women shook their heads. "I don't get it. Why would she make all these quilts for someone and then not only not give them to that person, but also not even show them to her three closest quilting buddies? It doesn't make sense."

They all agreed, but as Daphne pointed out, a lot of things about Alice didn't make sense.

"On the one hand, Alice said whatever came into her head without filtering a word of it." Daphne chuckled to herself. "That made for a few uncomfortable moments around town, but nobody could be mad at Alice for long. She wasn't ever mean, just one hundred percent honest and completely open. But then, every once in a while, sometimes right in the middle of one of her monologues, those real long ones—"

"Oh, Lord, but Alice could talk," Rinda interrupted. "She could just go on and on when she took a mind to. I met her in the quilt shop over near Fish Creek about a week after we moved here. I was buying fabric for a new project and Alice just came over and started talking my ear off, asking what I was planning to make and where I lived and the names of my children and if I had any pets and I don't know what all. At first I just thought she might be the local crazy lady. Then I saw that the clerks in the shop really liked her and talked to her kindly and just a little slowly, like you might speak to a child, so I realized she must have some kind of disability, you know. I thought she must be slow, but then she pulled out this quilt she was working on, this very complicated appliqué block with a basket of flowers, and I didn't know what to think. Anyway, Alice just kept following me around the shop, talking a blue streak while I shopped."

Rinda paused for a moment and smiled, wide and bright and real, the first time I'd seen her smile like that. "We'd just moved to town and I didn't have a job yet, so I was trying to be careful about money. I went over to check out the sale rack and I pulled this yellowy-green bolt off the shelf that I thought might be okay for a backing. So Alice sees this stuff and says, 'That's the ugliest fabric I ever saw in my life. Why would you buy that?' I told her it might be ugly, but it was only two dollars a yard."

Rinda's eyes crinkled at the corners. "And then Alice puts her hand on my arm and looks at me all serious and says, 'Rinda, it is possible to pay too *little* for fabric.'"

Rinda started to laugh and the others laughed with her. So did I. That was Alice, we all agreed. Honest to a fault, completely open with her thoughts and feelings.

"Except when she wasn't," Daphne said, picking up her comments where she'd left them before Rinda's interruption. "Every now and then, she'd suddenly get very quiet. Right in the middle of a sentence, she'd just clam up and stare off into space. I'd ask her if something was bothering her, but she always said no. You know what people in town call the three of us, don't you?"

I nodded. "The FOA—Friends of Alice. Because you never saw one without the other three."

"That's kind of an exaggeration," Daphne said. "I mean, we weren't together all the time. We all had lives to lead, but we were pretty close to her."

Celia tipped her head to one side, as if some new thought had just occurred to her. "Which is kind of strange when you think about it. I mean, Alice lived here her whole life, knew everybody in town from the time she was a little girl, but the three people she picked as friends were three people who had just moved here."

"That was just Alice's way," Rinda said. "She never could resist a stray. I think that's how she saw us, as three strays who needed rescuing."

"And yet," Daphne said, "for all that we knew Alice as well as anybody in town did, there were times when I felt like I didn't know her at all."

I knew exactly what she meant.

After I folded the quilts and put them back into the trunk, Daphne insisted that I show them the quilt I'd been planning to make when I sliced up my hand. I pulled out the bag where I'd stowed the fabric and pattern book upon my return from the ER and laid everything out on the table.

I could tell they weren't as excited about my

choices as I'd been, and I had to admit, after looking through all of Alice's pretty, vibrant quilts, it did seem a little on the dull side.

After a moment, Celia, who was always very encouraging—I guess you have to be if you're going to teach art to middle schoolers—said, "Well . . . it's definitely a good pattern for a beginner. And that's a nice blue."

"It's a boring pattern," Rinda countered. "And a namby-pamby blue."

Boring? Namby-pamby? And she was the one who'd been telling stories about how overly frank Alice could be? But . . . it was hard to argue with her observations.

"I was worried about making something too busy or complicated, you know? The first time out, I figured I wanted to play it safe."

"Yeah, well. You succeeded," Rinda said. "That quilt is safe as a bowl of oatmeal and just as bland. Or it will be, when you finish it. Except I don't think you will ever finish it. You'll get sick of it halfway through, put it aside, and then never quilt again because you'll have convinced yourself that quilting is boring."

She gave me a look of disdain. "Just because you're making a beginner's quilt doesn't mean you have to play it safe. Look at Alice's quilts; even her early work—not a dull one in the bunch. Alice was willing to take chances. A quilt is only as boring as the person—"

"I think what Rinda means to say," Daphne said, jumping in and shooting her friend a "Be nice!" look, "is that you might want to think about spicing this up a little. There's nothing wrong with the fabrics you picked; I just think you might want to add a few more to the mix."

"And maybe find a pattern that's a little more exciting," Celia added. "The basic idea here isn't bad, but let's maybe just use this as a jumping-off place. Where did Alice keep her graph paper and drawing pencils?"

"Ummm . . ." I turned in a circle, trying to remember where I might have seen drawing supplies.

"Here they are," Daphne said, bending down and opening the bottom drawer of the painted white dresser that stood on the far wall. She handed a pad of paper and box of pencils to Celia.

"Thanks!" she said, and set to work.

While Celia scribbled away, Daphne gave me a lesson on how to cut blocks using a rotary cutter and ruler *without* drawing blood and Rinda sat down at my sewing machine, trying to figure out why it was skipping stitches.

"Here's the problem!" she said triumphantly, holding something that looked like a big dust bunny between her fingers. "You could knit a sweater with the amount of lint in that bobbin case. Your tension was off too. Were you messing with those knobs?" she asked and then answered her own question. I guess the guilty look on my face must have given me away.

"Well, don't! Not for any reason! I've got them all set perfect now, you hear?"

"Yes, ma'am!" I said, snapping my fingers to my forehead in mock salute. Daphne guffawed, nearly swallowing the piece of nicotine gum she'd been chewing. Rinda didn't so much as crack a smile.

A few minutes later, Celia finished sketching out a new, much more interesting design for my quilt project and held it up so we could all see.

"Don't worry," she said when she saw the look of concern on my face, "it's really not that much harder than the pattern you picked before."

She'd kept the blank blocks as they were in the original, saying this would give me a good place to do some quilting or even some free-motion embroidery.

"Daphne can help you with that part," she assured me. "She's got a real feel for free-form quilting and embellishing."

I nodded, but honestly, I had no idea what she was talking about.

The rest of it made more sense to me. Celia had traded out those big, boring four-patch blocks with smaller nine-patch checkerboard blocks, each six inches across. Using her pencils, she had colored in some of the little squares within the blocks and left others blank, creating a secondary crisscross pattern that would stretch from one corner of the quilt to the other.

"See?" she said, looking up at me, her eyes bright. "Doesn't that look more interesting?"

It did. Even I could see that.

"You know," she said slowly, tapping her pencil thoughtfully against her lips and holding her sketch at arm's length, "maybe we shouldn't leave those crisscross blocks white. I feel like I've seen that so many times. You can use any color you want as long as it's consistent through the pattern. Why not try something a little more daring? Is there a color you really like and think you look good in but are afraid might be too wild to wear to the office?"

I didn't have the heart to tell her that my entire work wardrobe consisted of navy blue suits and sensible shoes.

"Orange?" I said uncertainly, because it was the first thing that came to mind.

"Perfect!" Celia exclaimed. She grabbed a pencil from the box and started filling the previously blank squares in the blocks with bright orange. "See what it does to those blues? Not namby-pamby now!"

She was right about that. My dull, safe quilt design was coming alive! I couldn't wait to start sewing, but first I needed to find more and better—more exciting—fabrics to make it with.

Everybody helped. For close to an hour, we sat

cross-legged on the floor of the sewing room "auditioning" combinations of fabrics, surrounded by piles and piles of blue and orange yardage pulled from Alice's stash.

"Stash," I was informed, is the name quilters use to refer to their fabric collection. Apparently, the bigger the better. I was starting to see why. I bet we had to consider fifty or sixty blues before finding just the right fabric to use in my quilt.

"I've been quilting since I was a little girl," Rinda said, "and I'm still trying to build up my stash. Won't be satisfied until I have achieved SABLE. I think I'm just about there."

"SABLE?" I asked.

"Stash Accumulated Beyond Life Expectancy," Rinda said with a grin.

Celia looked around at the piles of blue, orange, and white fabric heaped on the floor and her smile faded. "I guess Alice achieved SABLE," she said softly, and her eyes began to well.

Rinda put an arm around Celia's shoulders. "Yes, she did, sweetheart. I know you miss her. We all do. But isn't it wonderful that Alice's stash is getting a new life?"

Celia blinked a few times and tried to smile through her tears. "It is," she said. "I'm glad Lucy's here."

Rinda squeezed Celia's shoulder and then looked up at me.

"So am I," she said.

❧ Chapter 28 ❧

When the phone rang a week later, I thought it might be Daphne answering the message I'd left asking what kind of batting I should buy for my quilt. But it was Joe Feeney, calling from Washington. When I told him why I didn't have much time to talk, he started to laugh.

"High school kids? You're giving a speech to a bunch of high school kids?"

"It's not exactly a speech," I said, shifting the phone from one hand to the other and reaching out to pet Dave, who jumped onto the sofa and started head-butting me. Now that he'd gotten used to me, he was getting to be an attention hog.

"It's more of a question-and-answer session about the American political landscape. Why are you laughing?" I asked, grinning. "I've been grilled by the hard-boiled members of the national press corps. You don't think I'm up to the task of taking questions from a bunch of teenagers?"

"It's just hard to picture you talking to a bunch of kids. I never thought you liked them."

"What do you mean? Of course I like kids. And anyway, I'm doing it as a favor for my old high school civics teacher."

"Well, that's commendable," he said. "Molding

the minds of the next generation and all; I've met some of them and they could use some molding. It's a nice thing. Very patriotic. I'm impressed."

"Yeah, I can tell," I said, scratching Dave under the chin, then reaching over and doing the same for Freckles, who had hopped up onto the sofa to make sure Dave wasn't getting all the attention.

"But you're feeling more settled in now, right? You sound a lot better."

"I am. But it's still hard to make myself believe that Alice is gone forever, especially being here. Sometimes," I said, almost to myself, "it feels like she's still here, standing in a corner or watching me through a window."

"She's haunting you? That must be unsettling."

"No," I said, annoyed because of the skepticism I heard in his tone, but more annoyed with myself for being unable to explain what I meant. "It's not like that. It's more like she left some of herself behind in the walls and the floors and the books, like there's something she wants to tell me."

"And she left behind clues?"

"Kind of," I said. "Not exactly."

"Huh," he said. "Did you ever find out who she made all those quilts for?"

I shook my head. "No. I asked her friends, but they'd never heard her mention anyone named Maeve. They'd never seen the quilts before either, which is really strange because Alice always showed them her projects. I asked a few people around town, too, and even did an online search and spent a day combing through records at the library. Came up empty-handed. There isn't anyone with a first name of Maeve in the whole county."

After studying both the quilts and the multi-aged sketches of the anonymous girl, I'd decided that Maeve must have been a sort of imaginary friend for Alice. But I didn't say anything about that to Joe. I felt guilty enough, thinking my sister had needed to invent a friend to fill the void left by our parents' deaths and my absence. I didn't want Joe turning it into some kind of joke. I don't mind him teasing me, but I didn't want him teasing me about Alice.

"Gosh, Nancy Drew! Sounds like you've got a mystery to solve! Good thing. You must be bored out of your mind up there. You need a project."

"Actually, I'm pretty busy. Not crazy busy, just busy enough. Which is good. Speaking of busy," I said, looking up at the kitchen wall clock, "I'm supposed to be at the high school by eleven and I haven't shoveled the driveway yet."

"It snowed again?"

"Uh-huh. Another five inches last night."

Joe made a groaning noise. "How can you stand it? I hate snow. Every inch adds a half an hour to my commute."

"But there's no traffic here," I explained. "And people know how to drive in snow without crashing into each other. It's actually kind of exciting when a big storm comes through. The wind howls and blows so hard that the windows rattle and the chimney whistles, but the whole world has been transformed. Everything is perfectly quiet, still, and wrapped in white."

"Very poetic, I'm sure."

"It is." I laughed. "Stop being so cynical. I've even been thinking about getting some snowshoes."

"Snowshoes? What are you, an Eskimo?"

"I like getting out into nature."

"Since when?"

"Joe," I said flatly, "can I help you with something? Or did you just call to make fun of me?"

"As it turns out, I do need your help," he said. "Making fun of you is just an added bonus. Would you be interested in taking on a short-term consulting project while you're up there? We just took on a new client, a developer out in California who's putting in two big new sub-divisions out in Orange County; fifty-five and up communities. It's not the kind of project we usually handle, but this guy has deep pockets and wants to hire the best.

"There are some issues with land use and water rights ordinances," he continued. "Our West Coast office is handling the lobbying effort with local officials and the state legislature. We're going to need a marketing campaign to sell the citizens on the idea. Or at least keep them from fighting it. It

has to look like a movement that sprung from within the community; you know what I mean. Very grassroots. We'll need a name that people won't associate with the developer or his money, call it the Committee for Affordable Senior Housing. Something like that."

"Joe, I can't go to California right now. I've got to rack up as much residency time here as I can before I leave for DC, remember?"

"I don't need you to actually implement the campaign. Just craft the concept and message, work out the timelines, budgets, lists of key contacts and target audience, draft some language for editorials and letter-writing campaigns, that kind of thing. I just need a blueprint that my people can work from, Lucy. It's right up your alley and it'll give you something to do during your exile in the wilderness. And it pays ten thousand dollars," he said. "No need to thank me. Think of it as my Christmas present to you."

Ten thousand dollars? Lobbying definitely paid better than government work. But there was a reason for that. People who can afford to hire big lobbying firms have the money to buy the access and influence to change the rules and stack the deck. I didn't like the sound of what Joe was describing, a dummy committee and a high-dollar campaign that looked like a grassroots community movement but was really just a cleverly disguised marketing campaign, designed to help one very

wealthy individual mold public opinion and reshape the law so he could become still wealthier.

Still, I thought as I pushed Freckles off my lap and carried my empty coffee cup into the kitchen, whether I helped out with this effort or not, the campaign would undoubtedly go forward and the subdivisions would be built. And the money would sure come in handy. My paychecks had stopped when the campaign ended. It would be nice not to keep dipping into my savings, not to mention earning some extra cash to buy furniture for a new place in DC.

I wanted a condo or town house that was no more than five metro stops from the White House and that also had outdoor space—real outdoor space, not one of those sad little balconies that make you feel like you're about to fall off the edge of the building as soon as you step out onto them. Getting what I wanted was going to take every dime of what Mr. Glazier was willing to pay me, plus a good bit more. Real estate in DC was incredibly expensive. I'd spent a lot of time on sites that sold patio furniture and had my eye on a kind of outdoor living room suite with a sofa, two side chairs, a coffee table, and blue-striped, all-weather cushions and a matching umbrella. It cost forty-six hundred dollars, but came with a lifetime warranty.

Joe could make fun if he wanted, but the last four weeks had taught me that I really was an

outdoor person, that access to nature was central to my happiness. I wouldn't have an incredible lake view or a big yard with hundred-year-old trees when I moved to Washington, but with an extra ten grand in my pocket, I could create a beautiful outdoor oasis or pocket garden.

I turned on the faucet and rinsed out my cup.

"What kind of a time frame are we looking at?" I asked.

He sucked in a breath and let it out slowly. "Yeah. That's the tricky part. I need it by December twenty-second. My client is leaving for a three-month world cruise on the twenty-fourth and wants to see everything beforehand. A package with research materials, proposed schematics for the subdivisions, and background information on the company is already on the way to you, rush delivery. Should arrive by three o'clock today, assuming the sled dogs don't get lost."

"You expect me to start today? Joe . . ." I protested, but he didn't pay any attention.

"I'm flying to LA for the presentation on the nineteenth," he said. "Thought I'd stay on and spend Christmas in Malibu. If you weren't busy serving your sentence in the Frozen North, I'd ask you to join me."

"Joe, are you kidding? A full-scale campaign, something that's ready to present to a client, will take at least eighty hours!"

"Ummm . . . I'm thinking more like a hundred.

Look," he said, his tone turning from jovial to apologetic, "I know it's a lot to ask in a short time, but you're the absolutely best person for the job. Nobody on my staff has your instincts on this kind of thing—that's why I wanted you to come work for me. You understand how to organize people, how to cast a vision, and then get everyday Joes and Janes working together to make it happen."

"Yeah, but you're not asking me to cast a vision for the common good. You're asking me to make people *think* they're supporting the common good when what they're really supporting is something that is only good for Mr. Deep Pockets Cruise Around the World Real Estate Developer."

"Lucy," he said, drawing out my name, his voice low and placating, "what's so terrible about creating housing options for senior citizens?"

"Tell me something: What's the price of the lowest-priced unit in this development?"

Joe was quiet for a moment. "Six hundred and twenty-two thousand dollars."

"I'm hanging up now."

"Wait! Don't!"

I didn't say anything, but I didn't hang up either. We've been friends a long time, so I at least owed him the courtesy of listening to him.

"Lucy, I could really use your help. We're swamped and half my staff is leaving on vacation in the next ten days."

"But I'm *already* on vacation. Remember?"

"I know. But this isn't a real vacation, is it? I mean, it's not like you're lying on a beach in Hawaii. You called me yourself, whining that you were lonely and bored."

"Okay, first off, I never whine. Second, that was three weeks ago. Now I'm enjoying the time off. Do you know how long it's been since I've had the time to even take a deep breath?"

"Couldn't you breathe deeply while you work? If you move your desk to the window you can stare out at the tundra and watch the reindeer herds running by."

"Very cute. This may not be a beachside paradise, but there *are* things to do here and I'm busy doing them. Alice's friends helped me start making a quilt with her old fabric. Do you know something?" I said, hearing the surprise in my own voice as I asked and answered my own question. "I like them. Daphne is a high school dropout who quotes Shakespeare and has happy hour with chickens. Celia is a twenty-five-year-old middle school art teacher and is working on an installation for walls of the town hall featuring old dial-up telephones she's decorated with paint and beads and feathers and any other weird thing she can find. Rinda is a black, evangelical, recovering alcoholic who moved here from Chicago."

I laughed. "I've got to tell you, Joe, these aren't the kind of people I thought I'd find in Nilson's Bay! But then again, I didn't expect to find myself here, ever again. That's why I like them, because we're all a little bit . . . off. We get together to sew twice a week. If I don't finish this quilt before I start my new job, I probably never will. And I *want* to finish it, as sort of a testament to Alice. This way, even after I sell the cottage, I'll have a piece of her. It will be kind of like we made it together."

Dave rolled onto his back and stretched his front paws up over his head, signaling that he wanted his tummy rubbed. I squatted down and obliged him, smiling as he closed his eyes and started to purr.

"For the first time in years, I'm going to have a real Christmas," I said. "With a tree, decorations, and everything. I'm even thinking of hosting a little party. The Swensons had me over for Thanksgiving. It would be nice to reciprocate."

"The Swensons," Joe said. "They're the ones with the son, right? Your boyfriend from high school? So you're going out with him now?"

"Peter wasn't my high school boyfriend," I said, "and we are not going out. He's a nice guy with a nice family who was also Alice's lawyer. He was just elected to the town council."

"Oh, no. So he's a politico?" A grumbling groan came through the line. "I know you dumped Terry Boyle, but I figured you'd take a little time before finding a replacement. Especially after all those very sage insights I made regarding your unfortunate relationship patterns. Luce, if you have to revert so rapidly to type, couldn't you pick a boyfriend who has at least some chance of making the cut long term? Somebody with at least a little ambition, who doesn't live on the dark side of the moon? Sure, I *guess* you could have chosen an even lower-level public servant from an even more remote region, but it's hard to imagine who—an assistant sheriff from the wilds of Wyoming? A dog catcher from Ketchikan?"

"Quit being such a snob! There's nothing wrong with serving on the town council. Considering how thankless and miserable those jobs are, it's amazing anybody is willing to serve in local government—especially anybody as smart as Peter. But thank heaven they do, because somebody has to.

"And I told you, Peter is not my boyfriend. Don't you ever listen? He's just an old friend who has been kind enough to help me out after Alice's death and to keep me from getting bored while I'm stuck here. Did I tell you that he coaches hockey for five-year-olds? They're adorable. I went to watch one of the games last weekend. They looked like a squad of drunken bumble-bees, buzzing around the ice and bumping into each other, falling down and then getting back up. Peter is incredibly patient with them. This weekend, he's taking me ice fishing."

"Ice fishing," Joe deadpanned. "As in standing

around a hole in subfreezing temperatures waiting for fish to bite?"

"It's not quite that primitive. There is some kind of a shelter to keep you out of the weather. But yes," I said, frowning a little as I realized what kind of picture I was painting, "that's more or less the idea."

"Uh-huh. And you find that more appealing than staying in your nice warm house and working on an interesting project that will net you a few thousand dollars?"

"It isn't an interesting project, Joe. It's a scheme to help one rich man get richer by skirting a whole bunch of very good laws. And even if it weren't, I've made up my mind to spend my time here doing things that I enjoy with people I enjoy."

"Like your friend Peter. Well," he sighed, "at least we know he really *is* your friend and not your boyfriend. Can't see him trying to make a big move on you while ice fishing." He let out a short laugh.

"But really, Lucy, are you sure that you couldn't spare just a *few* days to knock out this campaign? If you pulled a few marathon days back to back, I bet you'd have it done in a week. I know how you can produce once you get into the zone, Lucy. You're a machine."

"Yeah, and when I get to Washington I'm going to have to be a machine again for the next four years. Maybe eight. Which is why I'm going to relax and enjoy myself while I can. Life is short."

"All right, all right. I won't beg. I know your implacable voice when I hear it." He groaned. "I hope you enjoy your Christmas season. Mine has just gotten a lot more complicated."

"I'm sorry," I said, and meant it.

"At least *one* of us will have happy holidays," he said.

"Hey! Did I tell you? The library is sponsoring a snow sculpture contest! Doesn't that sound like fun?"

"Snow sculptures? Ice fishing? Quilts?" Joe made a *tsking* sound with his tongue. "Who are you and what have you done with my friend Lucy? Don't tell me you've gone off and decided to be happy. What a waste of a promising career."

"Ha-ha. It's a break, Joe, not a lifestyle transformation. And I intend to enjoy it while it lasts. In another month, I'll be back to work and back to my cranky, overwrought, overworked self. Promise."

"Well, that's a relief. All that homespun happy talk was starting to make my teeth hurt. Just too sweet." He laughed. "Well, I'd better let you go. Have a nice Christmas, kiddo. See you in DC. Oh, wait! Speaking of DC, have you talked to Ryland lately?"

"No, not since the funeral. But I didn't expect

to. He's got a few things on his plate, you know. Why do you ask?"

"No reason," Joe said quickly. "I was just wondering if he's been calling to check in. He's always depended on your advice."

"He has armies of people to advise him. More now than ever."

"Bet their advice isn't as good as yours. You've always known how to handle him."

"I never handled Tom Ryland. I may have nudged him now and again, but I didn't handle him. He didn't need it. He's a pro."

"Yeah. I'm sure you're right. Well, I'd better let you go. See you in a few weeks. And, hey! Next time you talk to the office, put in a good word for me, will you? I want good seats at the inauguration."

I smiled. "I'll see what I can do."

❧ Chapter 29 ❧

Shoveling the driveway took a little longer than I'd thought it would, and so I didn't get to the school until about ten minutes after eleven. Mrs. Swenson, bundled up in a coat, scarf, and snow boots, was standing in front of the entrance, pacing.

"So sorry I'm late!" I called as I jogged up the

sidewalk to the door. "You didn't have to come out to meet me. It's been a while, but I still remember the way to your classroom."

I laughed and gave her a hug. She gave me a quick hug in return and off we went, walking quickly past the principal's office and the trophy case. I would have liked to have slowed down and have seen if they still had the plaque that listed Alice as captain of the 1995 girls' track team, but Mrs. Swenson was holding on to my arm, propelling me down echoing, empty corridors that smelled like floor wax, cafeteria taco meat, and disinfectant. Every high school I've ever been in smells just the same. It's weird.

"Lucy," Mrs. Swenson said as we rushed down the hallway, "I probably should have asked if it was all right beforehand, but . . . I told one of the other teachers that you were coming. I just couldn't help myself. I'm so thrilled that you're here! Anyway, she asked if she could bring her students too. I didn't think you'd mind."

"Oh, that's all right," I said. "A few more won't make any difference."

It was a small school so the news that one more class would be joining us wasn't a big concern.

"How many is she bringing? Ten? Fifteen?"

"Well, that's just it. I told that one other teacher, but she told a couple more, and then somebody went and called the superintendent, and next thing I knew . . ."

I stopped in the middle of the hallway. I wasn't moving one more inch without better information.

"Mrs. Swenson? How many kids are we talking?"

She turned around to face me, took in a breath, her lips pressed tight together, and then blew it out. "All of them. Every student from ninth grade on up. From both schools."

"*Both* schools? What are you talking about?"

Mrs. Swenson spread out her hands helplessly. "The superintendent decided we should include the students from Sturgeon Bay too. She thought it wouldn't be fair for them to miss out. Oh, Lucy! Don't look at me like that. You can't blame her for being excited. To think that you grew up right here in Nilson's Bay, went to our schools, sat in *my* classroom! And now you're going to work at the White House! You can't blame us for being proud.

"The buses from Sturgeon Bay arrived about twenty minutes ago. We moved everything to the auditorium. Wait till you see! There's not an empty seat in the house!"

I felt beads of sweat popping out on my forehead. "The auditorium?" I asked weakly. "How many does it hold?"

"Three hundred and twenty-five, but we've got a few more than that. Some of the teachers had to stand in the back with the reporters."

"You invited the media?"

"I didn't invite them. They just showed up. Not too many, maybe six or seven. But," she said in a voice that was meant to be reassuring and then grabbed my arm again and started pulling me along, "I told them that you're *only* taking questions from the students. They can listen and take pictures, but that's all!"

"Mrs. Swenson, you really should have told me about this before."

"I know, I know. But I honestly didn't realize things had gotten so out of hand until yesterday, when the superintendent called. At that point, I thought telling you ahead of time might make you nervous. Also," she said, a slightly sheepish expression on her face, "I was worried that you might cancel."

She knew me too well.

Taking questions from a handful of teenagers was one thing, but speaking to an audience that numbered in the hundreds and doing so in front of a gaggle of reporters was a whole different ball of wax! I've never enjoyed public speaking. I can do it if I have to, but I don't love it, not like Tom. He always found it energizing, but I'm always drained after giving an interview or a speech, even to a small group. That's why he's the president-elect and I'm happy to stand in the background. Far, far in the background.

We reached the double doors of the auditorium.

I could hear the rumbling murmur of voices and shuffling of feet coming from inside.

Three hundred and twenty-five people! Wasn't there some way to get out of this? But after taking another look at Mrs. Swenson's face, I knew there wasn't. She really *was* excited, and proud that I'd been one of her students.

Let's hope that she felt the same way an hour from now.

"Ready, dear?"

"Oh, I doubt it."

"Lucy," she said, in a tone that was half-scolding and half-mothering, "remember when you took my debate class? You always got so nervous, but you never lost a debate. Not one. This is even easier than that. Everyone in there is on your side, excited to hear what you've got to say. Trust me. You're going to be fine."

"If you say so."

Figuring there might be a photographer in there, I brushed my hand quickly across my jacket to make sure there weren't any unsightly flakes on my shoulders, and ran my tongue over my teeth to feel if there might be anything stuck there. Then I took a big breath. I could do this.

"Okay. Ready."

Mrs. Swenson reached for the door handle. "Oh, Lucy. One more thing. Right before your talk? They're going to give you a key to the city."

My eyes went wide. This was really too much!

But before I could protest or change my mind about changing my mind, the doors swung open and I was greeted by the sound of three hundred clapping, stomping adolescents, who, I was sure, were way more excited about missing their third-period class than they were about listening to some old broad gab about government. Though cell phone coverage is lousy in Nilson's Bay, it seemed like every kid in the room had one and was using it to snap pictures of my entrance.

When my eyesight recovered from temporary flashbulb blindness, I walked toward the stage at the front of the room. And who was waiting there to greet me? Peter Swenson.

He had a big silver key in his hands and a big smirk on his face. He knew that I was hating this, and yet there he stood, enjoying my misery.

If there hadn't been so many witnesses, I'd have walked right up there and kicked him in the shins, maybe even higher. But there *were* a lot of witnesses, so instead I walked up the stairs, shook his hand, accepted the key, and posed for pictures.

It honestly wasn't as bad as I had anticipated—or would have anticipated, had I known about it in advance. Maybe it was a good thing that Mrs. Swenson hadn't told me about it until the last minute. Still, even though things turned out for the best, she should have told me ahead of time.

So should Peter; it was his fault that I'd gotten into that mess in the first place. At least . . . I thought it was. Okay, maybe not his fault exactly, but Mrs. Swenson was his mother and so, somehow or other, that meant he was responsible.

Anyway, it went off pretty well. My throat felt really dry at first, so I took a big drink of water from the bottle on the podium, choked, and started coughing, but after that, I was okay. The kids asked good questions—really intelligent questions about the nature of partisanship, the two-party system, the influence of money on government, and how we can get people from all points on the political spectrum to work with common purpose instead of spending all their time wrangling and harassing one another. I don't know that I had any deep insights or real solutions, but, as I told the kids, the fact that they're concerned about this even at their young ages was a really good sign because change is created by the people who care enough to ask questions and show up.

Juliet was sitting in the fourth row and gave me a shy little wave when I stepped up to the podium. I winked so she'd know I'd seen her. She didn't raise her hand during the presentation, but afterward she came up to talk to me. I had the feeling she wanted to ask me something, but her boyfriend —I think his name is Josh, but Daphne just calls him The Sloth—came up and stood next to her, sighing and shuffling his feet, and generally making his boredom clear. After a minute she looked at him and then at me and asked if it would be all right if she came over to the cottage sometime. I said yes. Daphne's right. She's a bright kid. She could do anything she wants with her life, as long as she manages to untangle herself from The Sloth.

A lot of other people wanted to talk to me, too, mostly students and teachers, but a few people from the community as well. Mrs. Lieshout was there and stopped to give me a hug. "We're all just so proud of you, Lucy Toomey!"

Once the crowd thinned out, the reporters asked me to pose for a few more pictures. Like they hadn't had time to get what they wanted during the forty-five minutes when I was speaking? Who were they trying to fool? I'm not stupid; I knew they were just using this as an excuse to get closer and ask me questions, in spite of Mrs. Swenson's ban on it. But trying to make nice with the media is a sort of default mode for me, and they were just local people trying to make a living reporting local news, so I said yes.

The questions were all softballs, stuff about how it felt to be back in Wisconsin, and if the school had changed much since I'd graduated, and who my favorite teacher was back in the day, etcetera. You know, human interest stuff. After a while, somebody asked if we could get a few more shots of me receiving the key to Nilson's Bay and so they found Peter and had him stand next to me and smile as we shook hands and held the key. Yeah, I know. Really an original shot, right? But, like I said, they were just local reporters.

Or so I thought.

After a couple of minutes, one of the reporters, a skinny guy with glasses and greasy hair, held a tiny recorder out to me and yelled out, "Lucy, are you looking forward to working at the White House?"

"Well, it's a little premature to discuss that. The president-elect hasn't even been sworn in yet, but certainly I'd be thrilled to serve if given the opportunity."

"Is there any reason to think you won't get that opportunity? After all, Tom Ryland likes having a cadre of young female staffers working for him, doesn't he?"

"What?"

The question took me by surprise; it wasn't the kind of thing a local reporter working on a puff piece about a hometown girl who made good would ask. Unless this wasn't a local reporter.

I dropped my smile and Peter's hand. "Excuse me, who are you and who do you work for?"

"Brandon Kimble. I'm with JaybirdNews.com," he said and started lobbing questions faster than I could answer or even take them in.

"Lucy, how many women does Tom Ryland have on staff? When you were on Ryland's staff, you traveled with him extensively, didn't you? Stayed in the same hotels? Why did you suddenly stop traveling with Ryland? Why did you step down as campaign manager?"

"I stepped down as manager because I'd never run a national campaign. At that point, we needed someone with more experience, and so I stepped aside and handed the reins to Miles Slade. Which, seeing as Candidate Ryland is now President-elect Ryland, seems like it was a pretty good decision."

I grinned, trying to make light of the question. The other reporters, who had stopped taking pictures by now and were just standing around listening to Brandon Kimble batter me with questions, chuckled at my answer. Brandon just kept at it.

"But why did you stop traveling with Ryland?"

"Because I was working on other projects at that point."

"Isn't it true that Ryland likes to travel with young, pretty women?"

This was not going in a good direction. If Tom had been standing there, enduring a barrage of questions by some reporter who was clearly on a fishing expedition for something salacious, I'd have pulled him out of there but quick, making some excuse about being late for a meeting or something. That's what staff does. But I didn't have a staff. Walking off in a huff, which was what I felt like doing, would only fan the flames of prurient interests, so I'd have to figure out a way to get myself out of this.

"Well, I don't think of myself as all that young anymore, but I'm glad you think I'm pretty. And no, I'm not going to give you my phone number."

That got a big laugh. For a moment I thought I was out of the woods, but Kimble just wouldn't give up. He shouted to make himself heard above the laughter.

"So is that why Ryland stopped having you travel with him? Because he preferred the company of younger female staffers?"

"What!"

My jaw dropped to my chest. The first rule when dealing with nosy reporters is to never let them see you sweat or take you by surprise. I blew it on both counts. But, in my defense, I hadn't planned on fielding questions that day. I wasn't prepared, especially not for a question that was so blatantly, over-the-top sleazy and rude!

"Lucy, your former assistant, Jenna Waters, who is only twenty-four, is working on the Ryland transition team. Whose idea was it to promote her so quickly? Yours or President-elect Ryland's?"

I started to stutter, literally stutter. My mind was whirring, but I couldn't formulate a coherent sentence. Suddenly, I felt a hand on my arm. Peter gently pulled me one step backward.

He took one step forward, said, "Hey, guys, this has been fun, but Lucy's old teachers have planned a private little celebration for her. She's got to go before the ice cream melts," and then placed his arm near my back without actually touching me, escorting me out of the room, like a faithful sheepdog putting himself between the lamb and the wolf pack. It was the same move I'd performed when Tom got himself in too deep with the press.

"So this is what it feels like to have a staff," I whispered as Peter and I, both smiling and looking straight ahead, walked briskly to the door.

"What?"

"Nothing," I said out of the side of my mouth. "Thanks for rescuing me."

Peter shifted his gaze sideways so he could see me. I did the same and saw that he was smiling that same cocky, self-satisfied little smile. It wasn't as broad as before, but it was there.

"Anytime," he said.

Peter wasn't kidding about having ice cream and cake with the teachers. He led me to the principal's office, making a joke about it having not changed a bit since he was last there, and showed me the wooden chair outside Mr. Derby's door with the initials "P.S." carved into the right arm.

"I spent a lot of time in that chair," he said.

"I can tell. Nice job on the carving. I love how you turned the periods into little flowers. Very creative."

Peter grinned. "Woodshop was the only class I ever got an A in."

Mr. Derby didn't mention Peter's early career as a low-level delinquent when he saw us. In fact, he shook Peter's hand, gave me a big bear hug, and introduced us both to the superintendent, saying he'd always known that the two of us would go far.

"Some students just have that spark, know what I mean?"

It was a nice little party, short but nice. Mrs. Swenson brought a homemade yellow sheet cake with chocolate frosting, and Mr. Crenshaw, who was still teaching algebra, brought a tub of vanilla ice cream. We sat around on plastic chairs, balancing our plates on our knees and visiting until the bell rang to signal the end of the lunch period, when the teachers had to get to their classes.

After we said good-bye to Mr. Derby and left the office, I thanked Peter again for saving me from the clutches of that reporter.

"But," I said, lifting an eyebrow at him as we wended our way through the corridor, dodging kids who were scurrying to get to class before the second bell, "that doesn't mean I'm going to forgive you for that crazy business with the key. Why didn't you tell me about it? Or about the fact that my quiet little Q and A to a handful of your mom's students had turned into a media event?"

"Don't blame me!" Peter exclaimed, lifting his hands to protest his innocence. "I didn't know a thing about it until I showed up today."

I shot him a look. "I see. So instead of going to your office and practicing law today, you just woke up and said to yourself, 'I think I'll drive over to the school and say hello to my mother.' And when you arrived, somebody just handed you a giant key and told you to stand at the front of the auditorium and present it to me."

"Pretty much," he said. "Except for the part where I was talking to myself. My trial ended a day earlier than I thought it would, so I decided to take the day off to come watch your talk and then take you ice fishing. We hauled the shanty out onto the ice just yesterday. When I showed up, everybody was all in a panic because you were late and the mayor was sick with stomach flu. Mom asked me to step in for him and so I did."

I gave him a hard stare. "Well. You still should have told me. Or somebody should have."

"You can take it up with Mom; I am totally innocent here. So what do you say? Want to go ice fishing?"

"I'm not really dressed for it," I said, looking down at my outfit. Even though it was snowing, I figured this was a somewhat formal occasion and I'd dug a pair of khakis and my blue blazer out of the closet and put on a pair of brown loafers with a little bit of a heel.

"No worries. I figured you'd be dressed up, so I brought a bunch of Karin's old stuff in the truck."

"You did?" I smiled as we walked through the front door and into the freezing air. "Well, aren't you the well-prepared little Scout?"

"I try."

"I don't know. I was planning to work on my quilt this afternoon."

"It's not going anywhere, is it? And anyway," he said, jerking his chin in the direction of my car, which was parked on the far side of the lot, "it might be a good idea to go hide out somewhere for a couple of hours."

I turned to follow his gaze and saw that reporter, Kimble, standing next to my car with his back turned toward us, smoking a cigarette and waiting for me.

"Man. He doesn't give up, does he?" I shook my head and looked at Peter. "You're right. An afternoon of ice fishing suddenly seems like a very good idea."

❧ Chapter 30 ❧

I changed into a pair of boots before getting out of the truck, but I really wasn't dressed for the weather. By the time we got inside the ice shanty, I was shivering.

Peter tossed me a bag filled with clothes. "You can change in the bathroom."

"There's a bathroom?"

I went through the door Peter pointed to and sure enough found a tiny bathroom with a chemical toilet and even a little sink. I took off my khakis, jacket, and blouse and then pulled on a pair of jeans and a blue-and-white Nordic sweater.

Peter was kneeling down next to a dormitory-sized refrigerator when I came out of the bathroom. "Warmer now?"

I nodded. Peter held a beer out to me and I gave him a look.

"We're not working today," he said. "C'mon. It's part of the experience."

While Peter turned on the heater and prepared our fishing gear, I sipped my beer and took a little tour of the ice shanty. It wasn't large, maybe ten by ten feet and entirely paneled with knotty pine, but it was a lot cuter and more comfortable than I'd imagined.

Besides the bathroom, there was a kitchenette with a two-burner stove, the refrigerator, and a small countertop. A Formica-topped kitchen table with chrome trim and two chrome chairs with white trim and padded seats upholstered in red vinyl, like something you'd see in a 1950s diner, stood next to that. There were red-and-white gingham curtains hanging at the two tiny windows and red-and-white quilts with matching pillow shams on a set of bunk beds tucked in the corner. The red theme was even carried over to the two benches, upholstered in vinyl to match the kitchen chairs, that sat on either side of the ice holes.

"You got yourself quite the fancy clubhouse here," I said. "I was picturing something a little more man cave than *Better Homes and Gardens*."

"Oh, yeah . . . well. Mom got to it a couple of years ago. Decided she'd fix the place up as an anniversary present for Dad. It was pretty rugged before that."

I walked over to the propane-powered space heater and turned around so I could talk to Peter while warming my backside.

"And from the way you're saying it, should I assume that he might have preferred if she'd just left well enough alone?"

Peter flipped open the lid of a black plastic box loaded with fishing lures and started attaching them to our lines.

"Let's just say it was a good thing I was able to talk her out of tearing out the paneling and putting up wallpaper."

"Well, I think it's nice." My behind was getting too hot, so after a minute I walked across the room to the bed. "So do you actually sleep out here?"

"Not very often," Peter said, keeping his head bent low as he worked. "It's more for naps. Ice

314

fishing isn't just about the fish, you know. Some-times it's about just getting away by yourself for a while."

"So it really is your little clubhouse," I said and opened the door on the cabinet on the wall. "Oh, my gosh! You've got a TV in there! And a DVD player!"

"Dad was going to hook up a satellite dish, too, so he wouldn't miss the games when he brought his buddies out to fish. But he doesn't bring the guys out here much now."

"Why not? I think it's darling." I took a bigger swig from the bottle in my hand and sat down on the bench next to Peter.

"Yeah. So does Mom. But when a guy describes his ice shanty to another guy, 'darling' is not one of the preferred adjectives. All set," Peter said, putting the poles aside. "Now we just need some bait."

He reached into the tackle box, pulled out a jar, and unscrewed the lid.

"Eeeww!" I cried when he stuck his fingers inside the jar and pulled out four fat, squashy, disgusting, white creatures. "Are those maggots?"

"They're waxies—the larvae of white caterpillar moths. Whitefish love 'em." He opened his palm and showed them to me. "Here. Put two on the hook."

I cringed and drew back. "I am *not* touching those things!"

Peter rolled his eyes. "Fine. I'll do it."

After the poles were baited, he opened two covers in the floor of the shanty. Looking down, I could see several inches of white ice and then the clear, cold water. Peter showed me how to drop the line and told me how much to let out.

"Now what?" I asked when he handed me the pole.

"Now we wait."

"For how long?"

"As long as it takes," he said. "Ice fishing is all about patience."

"Sounds very Zen. You know that I tried yoga once and was asked to leave in the middle of the class, right?"

Peter smiled. "How about if I turn on some music and get you another beer? You hungry? I brought cheese curds and a bag of Chex mix."

In spite of Peter's unfortunate love of seventies rock, the music helped me relax. So did the beer. The cheese curds were yummy, too, and the way they squeaked when I bit them made me smile. Alice and I had loved that when we were kids.

After a little bit, I started to understand what men see in ice fishing. There's something peaceful about removing yourself from the distractions of life, having nothing more pressing to do than hold on to one end of a stick while talking with an old friend.

I'd seen Peter a few times since my return, but there'd always been other people around and whenever I asked him questions he tended to dodge them and start asking his own, bringing the conversation back around to me. But the quiet atmosphere of the ice shanty helped loosen his tongue.

"So," I said, "you didn't start practicing law until you were thirty-two. Did you take a break between college and law school?"

"More like a break between college and college. I dropped out in my freshman year."

"I didn't know that. Why?"

"Well," he said, looking up at me and pausing for a moment, as if trying to decide how much to say, "the official line is that I decided that I wanted to give professional hockey a try before it was too late, and I did play on a minor league team for two seasons. But hockey was kind of an excuse. The real reason I dropped out is that I couldn't handle the work, but if I said that to my mom, she'd have shown up at my dorm with a list of tutors, some kind of new calendar system to get me organized, then given me a lecture about buckling down and trying harder."

I frowned and took another tiny sip of my beer—two was my limit and I wanted to make it last. It was strange to hear Peter talk about his mom like that. I'd always thought of her as the perfect mother and the Swensons as the perfect family. When I was in Mrs. Swenson's class, sometimes I'd have a guilty fantasy that my real parents had been killed or kidnapped—that version was slightly less guilt inducing—and that the Swensons would adopt me and Alice and I'd live happily ever after with this very nice, very normal, regular family with parents who never spoke a harsh word to me or each other and never made me feel like a disappointment.

I'd always thought he was the one kid in our school who'd had it together and was comfortable in his own skin, content with his life. I guess it just goes to show you that no family is perfect and that everybody, no matter how happy they appear to be, has their own secret regrets, disappointments, and doubts.

"I'm sure she just felt like . . . I mean, if your mom is a teacher . . ."

"Mom was trying to help," he said, lifting his hand to stay my sympathy. "I always knew that. It had to be frustrating for her, spending her life helping other people's kids succeed academically and not being able to do the same for her own. She was always so sure that if I just tried a little harder . . . You know what my reputation was in school: a cheerful, charming, but slightly arrogant jock who wasn't all that bright and didn't care. I did care. And I did try, way harder than my folks or anyone else realized. It didn't make any difference. So after a while, I fell back on what I *was* good at, sports.

"The only reason I got into college in the first place was because I held the county record for stolen bases. But the baseball coach was kind of a jerk, believed in the 'break 'em down to build 'em up' school of coaching. That didn't work with me. I didn't need to feel any worse about myself than I already did, you know? One day, in the middle of practice, I walked off the field, packed my stuff, and left. I blamed it on the coach, but, truth was, I just couldn't handle the pressure."

"Kind of like what happened to Alice," I said. "After the accident, we knew she'd never be a vet, but my parents kept pushing her. And that wasn't all bad. If not for them, she'd probably never have been able to live independently or have a normal life. But there were limits to what she could do. Dad just couldn't accept that.

"When I left for school, Alice did too. She enrolled in a two-year veterinary technician program in Madison. She was great with animals, got a B in her husbandry class, but flunked all her science classes. I think it must have hit her hard. She remembered what she'd been like before. Up until then, I don't think she'd gotten any grade lower than an A-minus. Anyway, she dropped out. She was so down that my parents sent her off to live with Dad's sister, Peggy, in California for a few months. That was the beginning of the depression. Sometimes it got so bad that she ended up in the hospital."

"I know," he said. "Alice and I spent a lot of time together when I wrote her will. She was my first client; paid me one hundred dollars and a goldfish."

I chuckled. "Sounds like Alice. But tell me the rest of your story," I said. "How did you go from college dropout to lawyer?"

Peter took a quick swig from the bottle that was sitting next to him on the bench before going on. "Well, after two seasons and two concussions, I figured out that playing pond hockey with your buddies is different than playing on a real team with guys who've been training their whole lives. I didn't want to come home twice a failure, so I moved to Milwaukee, got a job in a sporting goods store, an apartment with two other guys who were just as lost as me, smoked a lot of weed, and drifted.

"A year after that, Dan, a retired special education teacher looking to earn a little extra cash, started working at the store. One day he took me out for a beer and asked what I was doing with my life, said I was too smart to be spending it selling hockey sticks and jock straps. So I told him the whole story. The condensed version—a lot quicker than I'm telling you," he said, with an embarrassed little smile.

"Keep going," I urged him, sensing the approach of a happy ending. "Please. What did he say?"

"He told me he thought I might have a learning disability and gave me the number of a doctor friend of his. I took the number, but didn't call the guy. But Dan kept after me."

"And?"

"And Dan was right. I have ADHD and some issues with speed of information processing. It was a relief to hear that there was a name for what was wrong with me, but a part of me wasn't convinced. I spent so many years thinking of myself as a thickheaded jock that it was hard to put that aside. Anyway, the doc prescribed some medication and I enrolled in one class at the community college. The doc helped me get extra time on my exams and Dan tutored me, helped me work on my reading comprehension and organizational strategies. Sure enough, I earned a B in Introduction to the Novel. I worked incredibly hard and it paid off. Not just in terms of the grade. That one class taught me that I wasn't dumb.

"It took me six years to finish my bachelor's because I was working part-time. I took out loans for law school. Since I was already twenty-six when I started, I decided I better bite the bullet and get it over with. And I did."

"Do you still take medication?"

"No," he said. "I was able to focus better as I got older. I've read some studies about that. A lot of people with ADHD have trouble with executive functioning when they're young, but the brain eventually catches up. That's what happened to me. I wasn't dumb; I just needed time and some extra help."

"I never thought you were dumb," I said. "I just thought you didn't care about school."

"Yeah. That's what everybody thought. But . . . hang on." He sat up very straight, took the fishing line between his fingers, and gave a tug. "Never mind," he said after a moment. "Thought I might have had a bite. They're sure slow today."

"Did your mom feel bad that she wasn't able to figure out what your learning issues were?"

"Terrible. I think she apologized to me about fifty times for that. But it wasn't her fault. She wasn't trained in special education, and even if she had been, I did a good job of covering up. A lot of kids with learning problems withdraw or act out or become depressed, but because I was good at sports, I had something to kind of hang my hat on. I might not have made honor roll, but man . . ." He grinned and checked his line again. "When I'd slide into third and the hometown crowd went crazy, I felt pretty darned good about myself."

"Yeah," I said, smiling and taking the last cheese curd from the bowl, "I'd kind of noticed that about you."

"Hey, you can't blame me. There's not one teenage boy in fifty who wouldn't rather score the winning run in the hometown tournament than get an A on his history exam. Everybody knows that jocks get all the cute girls," he said, and then paused for a moment. "Well, almost all the cute girls. Now and then one gets away. Well, really just one. The best one."

I blushed. Actually blushed! I couldn't help it. Not only that, but his words and the way he said them, not with his usual cocky grin, but with a simple, almost nostalgic kind of smile, his tone just a tiny bit wistful, made my breath catch in my throat—and a cheese curd along with it.

No kidding, I started to choke. And it wasn't a momentary blockage, easily cleared with a polite cough or two. No, no, no. This was a full-on, hacking, face-reddening, "does anybody here know the Heimlich maneuver?" choking. It was so bad that Peter dropped his fishing pole, came over to my side of the room, and started pounding on my back.

"You okay?" he asked when I finally stopped hacking and started breathing again, his expression worried.

My eyes were tearing and my throat was still tight, but I bobbed my head and lifted my hand to wave off his concern. "Fine," I rasped after a minute. "Cheese curd. Went down the wrong pipe. But I'm—"

I didn't get a chance to finish my sentence.

Before I knew what was happening or could fully catch my breath, Peter locked me in his arms and kissed me, just like he had on Thanksgiving. It was a really, really good kiss. Even better than the first.

Of course, it is possible that, having not been kissed like that in so very long, which is to say passionately, the pleasure of that kiss had been heightened by extended privation, the way a piece of rich, delicious dark chocolate tastes even richer and more delicious after you've been dieting. But I don't think so.

All I know for sure is that I was grateful to be sitting down, because if I'd been standing, my knees would probably have buckled under me. Seriously. I've read a number of novels in which the hero's kiss leaves the heroine feeling faint and always thought it was silly, completely unrealistic. But at that moment, I suddenly understood what swooning meant.

Maybe that was why, even though a part of my brain knew that this was a bad, bad idea, I kissed him back, because I felt faint, or was suffering from acute kiss deprivation, or because it didn't seem quite real. Whatever the reason, I lifted my arms around his shoulders, let my lips fall slightly apart, and kissed him. It just felt so incredibly good. I didn't want him to stop.

And then, in case I hadn't been thrown off balance enough, he made another surprise move, the kind of thing I was *certain* never happened except in books, movies, or the late-night fantasies of kiss-deprived women; he picked me up! No kidding! Without ever taking his lips from mine, he kind of scooted off the bench, scooped his arm under my legs, and starting carrying me across the room toward the bed.

It was, without question, the single sexiest thing I have ever experienced in my life. He lifted me up like I was nothing! And as he did, a thought popped into my head: *He planned this all along. . . .*

Peter had come out here the day before, filled the fridge with snacks and beer, set the radio to what he thought was a romantic station (though he sadly misjudged that part), invited me out here, and wore down my defenses by plying me with liquor and opening up to me and becoming irresistibly vulnerable, all in anticipation of the moment when he would kiss me like I'd never been kissed in my life, and carry me to the bed, and . . .

He'd lured me! He had lured me to his ice shanty the way that the carnival guy had lured Daphne onto the Tilt-A-Whirl, both among the least likely possible spots for an assignation, knowing that we wouldn't be expecting it! Hoping to catch us off guard and in a moment of weakness! Joe Feeney was right—I'd never have imagined Peter trying to make a move on me while we were ice fishing. If I had, I never would have agreed to come along. I thought we'd go to some tin shack and sit huddled around a hole in the ice wearing parkas and mittens and shivering. I had no idea there'd be music and conversation and beer and a *bed*.

Peter knew that I wasn't expecting this. And that was why, after I'd rebuffed his earlier advance, he had brought me here. No, *lured* me here!

This revelation was so surprising, comical, and—I'll admit it—oddly flattering that it actually made me feel a little giddy. If Peter's lips hadn't still been pressed to mine, I might have started laughing. But when he actually set me down on the bed, pulled away, and made a move to pull his sweater over his head, I came to my senses—quickly.

"Oh, Peter." I clutched at his wrist. "I can't. This is a bad idea."

"Yes, you can," he said. He loosened my hand from his wrist. "And it's an incredibly good idea. One I've been working on since we were both sixteen years old. Let me show you."

He turned my wrist upward, uncurled my clenched fingers, one at a time, then pressed his lips to my palm. Where had he learned that? How did he know that the feeling of his lips, so soft and sure and slow, would make my heart pound like a conga line and fill me with the urge to throw him down onto the bed?

I pulled my hand away and held it tight against my chest. "No, Peter. I can't. Really. I can't afford to let myself get mixed up in a relationship with anybody right now, especially someone who lives thousands of miles from DC. If I let myself get caught up with you, it'd be for all the wrong reasons."

"So you're saying you'd just be using me for sex?" He pressed his lips together and furrowed his brow as if considering the implications of my statement. "I can live with that," he said, and reached for me again.

I scooted to the far end of the bed, dodging his grasp. "No! Peter, I mean it! This is a really bad idea! I'm going back to DC in just a few weeks and you . . . Ack!"

A sudden clatter of plastic against wood as my fishing pole was jerked from the holder made me yelp with surprise. The pole started skittering across the floor toward the open hole in the ice.

"Grab it!" Peter yelled.

I lunged for the pole, but he got there first, snatching the handle only a moment before it disappeared into the water. Kneeling on the floor, he tried to reel in the line as quickly as he could. The fight and weight of the fish made the pole bend so far that I thought it might snap in two.

"Whoa! This is a huge mutha!" Peter exclaimed, his eyes bright with excitement. "Luce! Help me out here! Grab the line and pull him in!"

Though flustered and a little unsure about exactly what I was supposed to do, I followed his instructions, clutching at the fishing line and pulling it in, hand over hand, drawing the enormous whitefish toward the opening in the ice. The water was clear blue. When I looked down, I could see the fish, twisting and fighting to get away, silver scales glinting like star points in the water.

"Oh, it's beautiful!"

"Sure is!" Peter cried, moving closer and bending down to get a better look. "Man! Look at that bad boy! He's gonna be too big for the frying pan!"

"Frying pan?" My eyes went wide as I realized what he was saying. "Peter, we're not going to *eat* this fish!"

"Of course we are," he said, looking as if he thought I'd lost my mind. "What else should we do? Adopt him? Hang on!"

The silver leviathan wasn't giving up easily. It twisted its body from side to side, banging into the bottom of the ice, as if it had an understanding of its own size in relationship to the opening and knew that it would never fit through unless it was in a perfect, nose up–tail down position. Peter cursed and pulled up the sleeve of his sweater and plunged his arm into the frigid water.

Moving quickly, I untangled myself from the loops of fishing line, grabbed the tackle box, and scrabbled frantically through the various compartments, searching. I found the wire cutters just as Peter sat back on his haunches, grinning from ear to ear as the silvery head of the enormous white-fish emerged from the hole.

"Look at that! What a beauty! He's got to be eleven or twelve—"

In one quick and unexpected movement—if not for the element of surprise I'd never have managed it—I shoved Peter aside as hard as I could, sending him sprawling, then snipped the line and pulled the hook from the fish's mouth.

"Lucy!" He rocked forward and made a grab at the line, but he was too late; I released the fish into the water. He peered into the hole with his mouth ajar as the silver streak made its escape and disappeared into the depths.

He sat back on his haunches again, staring at me with a mixture of anger and confusion. "Are you insane? That was our dinner!"

I got up from the floor, wiped my wet, freezing hands on my pants, and sat down on the bench across from him.

"I'm not hungry."

❧ Chapter 31 ❧

Actually, I was hungry. So was Peter. Cheese curds and a few handfuls of Chex Mix don't quite constitute a well-balanced meal. And so, after we got back into the truck, I suggested we go to the fish boil at the White Gull Inn. It was kind of a peace offering. After all, not only had I rebuffed the man's sexual advances, I'd released his dinner into the wild. I couldn't blame him for being mad.

"I'm sorry," I said. "But I just couldn't bear the idea of eating such a beautiful, wild creature."

He turned the ignition switch, revving the engine a couple of times to warm it up after sitting so long in the cold. "The whitefish we'll eat at the boil were beautiful, wild creatures too."

"I know. But I wasn't the one responsible for killing them."

"What difference does that make?"

I clicked my seat belt together. "I don't know, but it does. Anyway, do you want to go or not?"

"Okay," he said, his expression softening as he shifted the truck into gear.

"Just one thing. I'm buying." He started to protest, but I cut him off. "No! I want to pay this time. I owe you a fish. And, Peter . . . after

330

this? If we go anywhere or do anything together, we split the bill. I meant what I said in there. I'm not getting myself tangled up in another dead-end, long-distance relationship. I'm done with all that. My next relationship is going to be with some-one who is *the* one. Or at least has the potential to be the one. And if I never meet that guy, then so be it. I'm not settling for anything less than the real deal. But," I said, looking to my left so I could see his face, "I am still taking applications for friends. So if that sounds good to you . . ."

Peter shifted his eyes from the road to my face. "Not as good as letting you use me for sex, but since that doesn't seem to be an option . . ."

"It isn't," I said. "I mean that."

"Okay," he said with a shrug, conceding more quickly and easily than I'd supposed he would. "Friends."

"Good," I said and fixed my eyes on the road. "Friends."

During the summer, the White Gull Inn in Fish Creek is *the* place to go for tourists and vacationers wanting to take part in a traditional Door County fish boil. From May through October, the White Gull hosts three boils a night, four nights a week. During the winter, they have only one boil a week, on Friday night. Since only the hard-core populace of the peninsula is crazy enough to think that standing around a giant cauldron of potatoes and fish bubbling over a big open fire in twenty-degree weather is fun, most of the wintertime guests are locals.

There were about fifty people in the crowd, and we knew quite a few of them. It was almost like going to a neighborhood party. Father Damon was there with his brother, Bill, who had driven up from Eau Claire for the weekend, and Mrs. Lieshout was there, too, with her husband, Lars, and her in-laws. We saw Mr. and Mrs. DeVine too. They told me they came to the boil almost every Friday night. "Only during the winter, though," Mrs. DeVine said. "Too many people in summer, but when the snow comes, I'm looking for any excuse to get out of the house."

"And away from the kids," Mr. DeVine added, smiling as he put an arm around his wife's waist.

I spotted Celia standing off to one side with a burly, almost hulking man who was holding a tumbler of brown liquor. I figured he must be her boyfriend, Pat. I considered going over to say hello, but they seemed to be in the middle of an intense, somewhat unpleasant conversation. Celia looked up with shiny, tear-filled eyes and warned me off, so I decided to stay put.

The rest of us stood around the fire pit, bundled up in sweaters, boots, and hats, holding steaming cups of hot cider or something stronger in our gloved hands as we chatted with our neighbors and watched the white-haired boil master stand crackling cedar logs vertically against the sides of the cylindrical pot so the boil would stay strong even after he added pounds and pounds of red potatoes and fish, and at least a couple of quarts of salt to the water.

The heat of the fire was intense, the yellow-gold glow of the flames piercing the darkness and casting dancing shadows across the faces of the people and the silhouetted circle of surrounding trees. The million stars in the sharp cold of the winter sky sparkled brilliant and bright, like scattered diamonds on an infinite field of black velvet. It was beautiful and sort of mystical, possibly even a little bit pagan, like a solstice celebration in the palace of some ancient Viking king.

"Admit it," I said to Peter when he returned from the bar with two more cups of hot cider, "this is way better than a fish fry in your dad's shanty."

"Maybe. But only because I'm here with you, old pal. Old buddy. Old BFF." He shot me a bad-boy grin over the rim of his mug and took a sip.

"Don't be a jerk," I said and elbowed him in the ribs. He elbowed me back and I smiled, happy that we'd moved past the awkward part.

When the boil master announced that the fish was just about ready, everybody gathered closer to see the highlight of the evening: the boil over. I noticed that Celia wasn't in the crowd. I looked over my shoulder, wondering where she could be, just in time to see Pat slam his empty highball glass down on a table and storm off, with Celia following close behind, apparently trying to placate him.

Poor Celia. Daphne told me that Pat was really a nasty piece of work, very controlling, but Celia couldn't seem to see it. Should I go after her? Tell her to come back to the fire and just ignore him, that by chasing after him, she was only getting sucked into his manipulation? Should I? I didn't know her all that well yet. Maybe she wouldn't appreciate me butting in.

I felt a hand on my arm and turned around. "Watch!" Peter said. "He's just about to throw on the kerosene!"

Sure enough, a moment later the boil master tossed a tin can full of kerosene onto the fire. There was an enormous *whoosh!* The flames shot up five or six feet, like something out of a disaster movie, and even though this was the moment we'd all been waiting for, the crowd drew back and gasped, then laughed, then repeated the entire sequence when the boil master threw a second can of kerosene onto the flames to make sure that every last bit of the oils and impurities that the salt had drawn from the fish and to the surface boiled over the top and onto the flames, leaving nothing but perfectly seasoned potatoes and clean, firm, fresh-tasting whitefish.

When the flames died down, the boil master yelled, "Dinner is ready, folks!" and everybody clapped.

Two men in white kitchen aprons slid a long wooden pole through the metal handle of the boiling basket that held the fish and potatoes, lifted it from the cauldron, and carried it into the dining room, where it would be seasoned with lots and lots of butter before it was put onto the buffet table to be served with lemon slices, coleslaw, fresh-baked bread, and cherry pie for dessert. It wasn't fancy or complicated or nouveau, but it was delicious and the people had been coming to the White Gull in droves to enjoy the exact same menu since 1961.

Peter and I got in line behind Father Damon and his brother. We chatted a little bit while waiting our turn. Father Damon laughed when I told him that the FOA was helping me make a quilt.

"I know, right? I'm the least crafty person on the face of the earth."

"That's not why I'm laughing," he said. "I'm laughing because, somehow, that's exactly what I thought would happen. Alice told me that she wanted you to come home, see her quilts, meet her friends, and maybe even take up quilting yourself. She said it would do you good. And look! It's happened just like that. One way or another, Alice always did manage to get her way."

"You're right about that," I said.

Funny thing, just a couple of weeks ago that observation might have made me tear up, but now it made me smile. I was glad I could remember the good things about Alice and glad that other people remembered them too. And I was glad that, however belatedly, Alice had gotten her wish, glad for both of us.

For a minute, I thought that Father Damon might invite Peter and me to join him and Bill at their table, but he didn't and I was relieved. Not that I wouldn't have enjoyed their company, but I'd been thinking about some questions I wanted to discuss with Peter privately. Maybe Father Damon felt the same way.

Once we sat down and got organized, buttered the bread and removed the bones from the fish, I cut right to the chase.

"You know, I was reading an online transcript of the last meeting of the village council . . ."

Peter's fork froze midway to his mouth. He stared at me as if I'd suddenly grown a second head. "You did? Why? Who *does* that?"

"People do," I said defensively, feeling the color rising in my cheeks. "I do. Why wouldn't I? And I think it's a good idea to post them on the town Web site. Wasn't that why you did it? Because you want people to be well-informed?"

"I guess," Peter said. "Honestly, I think we just started doing that because it made it easier to comply with some open meeting regulations, and to make sure we weren't misquoted by reporters or irate citizens. I didn't think anybody would actually read it. At least, not normal people." Peter put a forkful of fish into his mouth and chewed. "Boy, you really are bored, aren't you?"

"Anyway," I said, ignoring his question, "I read the transcript. You're really good. No, I mean it!" I protested in response to the skeptical expression that came to his face. "You were obviously well prepared and asked really good questions about the upcoming spring street repairs. And you were right about not going with the cheapest bid; the materials used by the company that turned in the next-lowest bid are much better quality. It's going to save the town thousands in the long run. And I thought it was great that you were able to get the council to go along with you and trim some other items from the budget so the library can stay open longer on Saturdays. That'll be a big help for students and working people."

"It wasn't a big deal," Peter said with a shrug. "Just common sense."

"It was leadership," I countered. "And it's not something that everybody has. Neither is common sense, especially in the field of politics, but that's another subject. My point is, you're really good at this and you seem like you like it.

Have you ever thought of taking it further?" He reached for another piece of bread and started spreading it with butter. "Peter?"

He put down the butter knife. "Further how?"

"Politically. I mean, there's nothing wrong with serving on the village council, but have you considered aiming higher? Maybe running for state senator? And if that works out, who knows?" I said, using my fork to carefully lift a lattice of bones from another piece of whitefish. "You might even be able to run for Congress."

"Why in the world would I want to do that?"

Now it was my turn to look at him as if he were the one who'd grown two heads.

"What do you mean, why would you want to? Because it's . . ." I put down my fork and cast my eyes up at the ceiling, searching for an explanation.

"Because that's supposed to be the next thing?" Peter offered. "The natural progression for anybody with any ambition? Because I'd have more power and influence in Madison or in Washington than I'd have in Nilson's Bay?"

"No," I said, trying and failing to keep my tone from becoming resentful. But, really! He sounded so smug. "Although you would. And anyway, what's wrong with having a little more power and influence? In the hands of the right person, somebody honest and decent, with a good heart and good leadership, power and influence can be used to help people! That kind of attitude is just . . . You know what, never mind. I'm sorry I mentioned it."

I dropped my fork and knife onto the plate. I wasn't hungry anymore.

"I'm sorry," Peter said, spreading his hands in a conciliatory gesture. "I didn't mean to offend you or to imply anything negative about your work. It's important to get good people elected to office at all levels, and you—"

"It certainly is! And the reason we don't have more good people willing to run for office is because of critical, judgmental, thoughtless people who constantly make critical, thoughtless comments about any elected official who casts a vote that is even slightly counter to their personal beliefs, accusing them of being in it for power, or influence, or to boost their own egos! In that kind of environment, what sane, decent person would want to get into public service?" I grabbed the lip of the table with both hands and leaned so close we were practically nose to nose. "And when good people *won't* run for office, do you know who is left to do it?"

"Egomaniacs who are in it for power and influence?"

"That's right!" I exclaimed, throwing up my hands in frustration.

Peter took one of my hands and pulled it back down to the table. "Okay, Luce. Let's just take a deep breath and calm down, okay? People are staring."

I shifted my eyes from right to left. He was right. People were staring, but when they saw that I saw them, their eyes darted away.

"Sorry," I mumbled.

"It's fine. You don't need to apologize for being passionate. And I agree with everything you said."

"Then why won't you consider running for higher office?" I said, leaning closer, but keeping my voice low. "Peter, you're a natural leader. Think of all the people you could help! If you're worried about raising money for a race, I know a lot of people who could help. Seriously, all I'd have to do is call some people in the party and—"

He laughed and held up his hands. "Whoa! Let's just slow down for a second. I already *do* help people. I'm convinced that I have a bigger impact here locally than I ever would at the statewide level. Do you know why? Because you don't need to ascribe to any particular ideology to figure out how to fill potholes or keep the library open. Right now, it's very clear where my loyalties should lie—with the people of this town, those who voted for me as well as those who didn't. But when you start taking money from a party or from big donors, it's natural that they are going to expect you, if not precisely to vote how they want you to, then at least to champion their ideology. I don't want any part of that, Lucy."

"Look," I said, "I agree with you. The whole system of parties and money in politics is really messed up. But it's the only system we've got, and until it changes—"

"Until it changes," Peter said, taking a last bite of coleslaw, "I'm going to keep serving at the local level, where I know I can get more done in one year than I could in a decade of partisan bickering in Madison. The other thing I'm going to do," he said, putting his fork down on his plate, "is see about getting us some dessert." He looked up, craning his neck as he searched for our waitress. "Do you want your pie plain or à la mode?"

After a little bit of wrangling, Peter finally did let me pay the check—our dinners, delicious and served in a beautiful atmosphere, ran only about twenty dollars each. A similar meal in DC would have cost twice as much. More things to appreciate about life in a small town, I thought as we headed out to the truck. I was starting to wonder if I shouldn't take a little bit of the money from the sale of the cottage and buy a condo here in Door County. Nothing big or elaborate, just a place that I could rent out now and use as a second home someday, when Ryland was out of office and my life was less complicated. Something to think about.

The sun sets early in winter, and once we left the relatively populated domain of Fish Creek and headed east across one of the county roads toward Bailey's Harbor, the drive home was pitch-black and a little bit spooky. Peter was quiet, focused on driving, and I said nothing to distract him. At this time of year, on a dark and potentially treacherous road that could be hiding black ice around every curve, you're suddenly very respectful of the awesome power and danger of nature.

We drove that way, which is to say in silence, for some time. But when we rounded a curve I spotted a quick glint of something unidentifiable in the headlights and shouted, "Look out! On the right!" and instinctively braced my arms against the dashboard.

Peter shot a quick glance in my direction, then took a tighter grip on the wheel and steered the truck deliberately to the left without swerving while pressing his foot on the brake pedal firmly enough to bring the truck to a stop, but not so hard that he risked going into a skid.

We came to a stop in the middle of the deserted road. "What was it?" Peter asked.

"I'm not sure. I couldn't see anything but a flash in the headlights. Maybe the eyes of a deer?"

At that moment, I was startled by another flash, a glimpse of something moving in the darkness. I gasped and clapped my hand instinctively against my chest, and then slumped with relief when the something stepped out of the shadows and into the bright beam of the headlights.

I opened the door and jumped from the cab of the truck. Peter grabbed the emergency blanket he kept under the seat and followed right behind me.

"Celia!" I cried. "We almost hit you! What in the world are you doing out here in the freezing cold?"

"Sorry," she said, hanging her head as Peter wrapped the blanket around her shoulders. "Pat kicked me out of the car." She sniffled. "And the house."

❧ Chapter 32 ❧

It was too late to do anything about Celia's predicament that night, so I made her a sandwich and a cup of hot tea and put her to bed in my parents' old room. In the morning, I phoned Daphne and Rinda and scheduled an eleven o'clock strategy meeting in my living room.

Celia had been living with Pat since the previous May. She paid him eight hundred dollars a month in rent, but Pat owned the house, so even though it was lousy of him to throw her out with no notice and in the middle of winter, he was within his legal rights to do so.

Rinda clucked her tongue at Celia, who was

sitting in the corner of the couch, in something close to the fetal position, looking small and miserable.

"Didn't I tell you that this would happen?" Rinda asked as she paced from one end of the living room to the other, never taking her eyes off Celia. "Didn't I warn you about him? And didn't I tell you that living in sin with a no-good, worthless man—and, honey, *any* man that asks you to live in sin is worthless—would lead to nothing but heartache and shame? Didn't I?"

Celia nodded and Rinda resumed her harangue.

"A man who loves you, truly loves you, will offer you a ring and a *home*. 'And the two shall become one,' " Rinda said, lifting her chin high and pointing an index finger at Celia.

"That's what the Word says, and that is what is *right!* But you wouldn't listen to me, would you? No, ma'am. You had to do it your way, just ignoring God's good word and my good advice. And now look at you! Tossed out on your behind in the middle of winter. Hmph." Rinda crossed her arms over her chest and took a deep breath.

Daphne, taking advantage of the momentary silence, looked at Celia and sighed. "Poor thing. Don't be so hard on her, Rinda. 'Love looks not with the eyes, but with the mind. And therefore is winged Cupid painted blind.' *A Midsummer Night's Dream*, act one, scene one."

Rinda put a hand on her hip. " 'Let marriage be

held in honor among *all*,' " she countered, " 'and let the marriage bed be undefiled; for God will judge the immoral and adulterous.' Hebrews, chapter thirteen, verse four."

"I know," Celia said in a piteous voice, looking from Daphne to Rinda and back again. "I'm sorry. I'm an idiot."

Rinda's expression softened.

"Oh, honey. Aren't we all? Idiots and sinners and hopeless romantics—wishing for something better. Well . . ." She sighed. "What's done is done. Learn from it, but don't dwell on it. We've got other problems to deal with now, like finding you a place to rent."

Celia shrank even farther into the corner of the couch and looked at me, her eyes begging me to intervene.

"Yeah," I said slowly. "That could be a problem. Celia doesn't have money for a rental deposit. Seems she loaned Pat twenty-three hundred dollars last month, everything she had in her bank account, and he hasn't paid it back."

"What!" Daphne exclaimed. "Celia, are you crazy? 'Neither a borrower nor a lender be'! Why would you lend money to a man who hasn't worked steady in three years?"

"He told me that if he got his car fixed he'd *get* a job," Celia said. "He said they were hiring at the winery."

"And you gave him every dime you had so he

could get a job selling liquor," Rinda said sarcastically. "Makes perfect sense. Because people who own a winery are going to be anxious to hire the town drunk. And *did* he get his car fixed?"

"Well . . . he told me that he bought a new set of plugs and belts and was going to put them in himself, but . . ."

Celia moved her head slowly from side to side and sniffled.

"Wait a second," I said. "Pat's car isn't working? Whose car was he driving last night?"

"Mine."

"So . . . he kicked you out of your *own* car and then drove off and left you by the side of the road in the dark and freezing cold?"

Celia nodded.

Rinda stopped her pacing and stood right in front of Celia. Now she had a hand on each hip.

"Didn't I warn you? Didn't I tell you that you can't trust an alcoholic? That he will break your heart and drink it dry? Didn't I tell you how I nearly bankrupted my family and destroyed my marriage before I finally put down the bottle? 'Wine is a mocker, strong drink is raging: and whosoever is deceived thereby is not wise.' Proverbs, chapter twenty, verse one."

Daphne, who had been nodding in agreement as Rinda spoke, added her two cents. " 'O thou invisible spirit of wine, if thou hast no name to be known by, let us call thee devil.' *Othello*, act two, scene three."

"Amen!" exclaimed Rinda.

"I just thought it would be different this time," Celia whimpered. "I really thought he was trying to get his act together. I just wanted to help him."

Tears formed in Celia's eyes and her shoulders wilted, making her look even more pitiful.

"Oh, I know you did," Rinda replied more gently. "You meant well. But, honey, believe me when I tell you that Pat has got to help himself. He's got to *want* to change. Nobody can do it for him. Not even you."

"You're right," Celia conceded. "I just . . . never mind. You're right. If I didn't know that before, I do now."

Daphne sat down on the couch and put her arm around Celia.

"Lord, what fools these mortals be," she sighed. "You deserve better, sweetie. You deserve someone who will love you and cherish you and treat you like a queen."

Celia laid her head on Daphne's shoulder.

"Right now I'd just settle for getting my car back and getting my stuff out of his house. I don't even care about my clothes so much. I can get new ones, I guess. But I want my paintings and quilts and photo albums. Pat texted me in the middle of the night. He said he changed the locks on all the doors."

"Celia," I said, "when you loaned him the money, I don't suppose you made him sign anything saying how and when he'd pay you back, did you?"

She shook her head. I'd expected as much. Celia was far too innocent and trusting; she really believed that Pat would use the money to fix his car and then pay her back when he had a job.

"Well," I said, "unless Pat suddenly grows a conscience . . ."

"Hmph!" barked Rinda, making clear her opinion on the chances of that happening.

". . . I doubt you'll ever see that money again. He'll probably claim you gave it to him as a gift. But he can't keep your car and he can't prevent you from getting your stuff."

I picked my cell up off the coffee table. "Let me call Peter. I'm sure he'll know what kind of paperwork we'll need to fill out to get a judge to force Pat to give back Celia's car and let her collect her possessions."

"Paperwork? A judge?" Rinda shook her head in disgust. "Isn't it just like you to go running off in search of a lawyer and begging the government for help instead of taking matters into your own hands? I say we just drive over there, bang on the door, and tell Pat he'd better open up."

"And if he won't?" I asked.

Rinda sniffed and scowled, considering the question. "Then we'll just cross that bridge when we come to it. Maybe he'll let us in and maybe he won't. But if he does, it'll be a lot cheaper and faster than dragging Pat into court. Anyway, we don't lose anything by trying."

"Rinda's right," Daphne said, " 'The fault is not in our stars but in ourselves.' "

Rinda put a hand on her hip. "Now, isn't that what I just said?"

Daphne patted Celia on the arm and then stood up. "C'mon, girls. Let's drive over there and try to reason with him."

"And if that doesn't work," Rinda said brightly, as if the idea had just come to her, "we can try snipping the electrical connection to the house so it'll get so cold and dark that he *has* to come out and talk to us." She slipped her arms into her coat. "I've got a pair of wire cutters in the glove box."

Rinda marched out the front door with Celia in tow. Daphne and I brought up the rear.

I whispered to Daphne out of the side of my mouth, "She's just kidding, right? About the wire cutters?"

Daphne shrugged. "Could be. With Rinda, you never can tell. 'And though she be but little, she is fierce.' "

Thankfully, we didn't have to resort to Rinda's wire cutters.

When we knocked on the door, Pat peeked out through the curtains, but wouldn't open the door.

Fortunately, I'd been quietly texting Peter during the drive to Pat's house, telling him what was going on, and he arrived on the scene about the time Rinda was rifling through her glove box.

He knocked on the door but, like us, got no answer. Raising his voice loudly enough for Pat to hear, he told Pat that if he didn't open the door, give Celia her car keys, and let her collect her things, he was going to take Celia to the police station and help her press charges against him.

"For what?" Pat shouted back.

"Auto theft and attempted murder."

"Attempted murder! I never laid a hand on her!" His words were slurred, not a lot, but enough so I knew he'd been drinking.

"You shoved her out of her own car and left her by the side of the road, miles from the nearest house and inadequately dressed in subfreezing temperatures. If we hadn't come along when we did, she might have frozen to death," Peter said calmly. "In all fairness, I probably wouldn't be able to make an attempted murder charge stick, but I'm pretty sure we could get a conviction for attempted manslaughter. Either way, it's going to cause you a lot of problems and some time as a guest of the state."

"Are you crazy? We had a fight is all! It's not a crime to have a fight with your girlfriend. And I didn't shove her out of the car! She yelled at me to stop the car and then jumped out on her own! I told her to get back in, but she wouldn't listen."

"That's not what Celia says," Peter said, leaning casually against the door. "So I guess it'd be your word against hers, but, Pat? I gotta tell you, Celia is going to be a much more believable and sympathetic witness than you."

Pat started to curse a blue streak. When we heard a big *thwap* sound followed by more cursing, Celia shook her head and explained. "He punched the wall with his fist. He does that when he's mad."

After the cussing died down a little, Peter said, "But, you know, we really don't have to go through any of that. If you'll just open the door and let Celia get her car keys and anything else that belongs to her, everybody can go on with their day and leave the police out of it. Whaddaya say, chief?"

For about a minute, nothing happened. We just stood there and waited, our breathing creating clouds of vapor in the air. But then we heard the sound of a key being turned in a lock and Pat opened the door. There was black stubble on his face and he was wearing the same clothes he'd worn the night previous, but he didn't seem quite as burly or as menacing as before. His eyes were red—not bloodshot, but red on the rims, as if he'd been crying.

Without looking her in the eye, Pat put a set of car keys in Celia's hand and stood aside so we could file past. I could smell liquor on his breath.

In the end, what might have been a potentially dangerous drama was played out in relative calm. Pat sat at the kitchen table with his head in his hands, not saying anything to anybody, while the rest of us, with Peter standing guard, helped Celia pack her things and carry them to the cars.

It was too much for one vehicle, so we loaded the clothes, books, cosmetics, and whatnot into Celia's trunk and the art supplies and paintings into Rinda's van. After a quick discussion in the driveway, it was decided that Celia would move in with me for a while.

"Are you sure?" she asked when I made the offer. "I mean, you don't really know me that well."

"You were one of my sister's best friends," I said. "What else do I need to know? Alice was an excellent judge of character."

"I'd love to have you stay with us," Daphne said, "but with me and the girls . . . we just don't have any extra beds."

Rinda didn't say anything, neither offering to let Celia stay with her nor giving an explanation as to why she couldn't. That surprised me a little. I know that Rinda loves Celia like another daughter. So does Daphne. They're both very protective of her, which is good. Celia is a doll, but a little naïve; she could use a little protecting.

"I really don't mind," I said. "In fact, I'll be

happy for the company. And it would be a help to have somebody stay in the house and take care of the cats after I go back to Washington."

"I can pay you," Celia said stoutly. "Eight hundred a month, just like I did Pat."

I waved off her proposal. "No. You can help with the groceries, but that's it. You need to save up money for a rental deposit. You're welcome to stay for a few months, but you'll need to find a new place after I sell to Mr. Glazier."

"It's so sad to think of you leaving and selling Alice's cottage," Celia said.

"I know. But it just doesn't make any sense for me to hold on to it anymore. And like I told you before, the cottage will still be there. Mr. Glazier promised that he'll leave the exterior walls of the cottage intact. It's pretty amazing that he was willing to agree to that."

Celia bobbed her head, conceding my point. "But it won't be the same."

"Nothing ever is," Daphne said. "You can't help things changing."

"I know," Celia said with a pout. "Doesn't that suck?"

We finished just in time for Peter to get to the ice rink. His tiny players had a game that afternoon.

"Want to come along?" he asked, rolling down the window of the truck so we could talk. "We're playing a team from Sturgeon Bay. I hear they've got a six-year-old on the squad who's nearly four feet tall. Should be quite a battle."

I whistled low, mirroring his tongue-in-cheek tone. "Wow. Hate to miss that. But I should really go back to the house and help Celia settle in. You understand."

"Sure, sure," Peter said. His grin disappeared so quickly that I had the feeling he also understood what I wasn't saying, at least some of it.

I'd texted him only because I was worried about what might happen. If Rinda broke out her wire cutters, somehow, I knew Peter would come up with a way to defuse a potentially explosive situation. It was kind of an emergency. But I needed to keep a little distance between me and him. His clipped tone of voice told me that he understood that. But what he didn't get was that I wasn't withdrawing because I wasn't attracted to him; quite the opposite. I'd lain awake half the night thinking about him. And that kiss.

For a couple of days, at least until the memory of that spectacular, passionate, brain-numbing kiss and the feeling of giddy surrender that flooded my body when he'd picked me up in his arms faded a little, I needed to stay away from Peter Swenson. But as I looked into his gorgeous, soulful brown eyes, I realized that a couple of days might not be enough.

Peter turned the key in the ignition and the truck came to life.

"Thanks so much," I said. "This could have gotten ugly if you hadn't been here."

"No problem," he said, refusing to meet my gaze. He rolled up the window, shifted into gear, and drove off.

"See you later!" I called, lifting my arm high.

I'm pretty sure he heard me, but he didn't wave back.

❧ Chapter 33 ❧

With all the cargo, there was space for only two passengers in each vehicle, so Daphne drove back to the cottage with Celia and I got into Rinda's van. Celia drove right off, but as we were starting to back out of the driveway, Rinda hit the brake and then put the van into park.

"Hang on a minute," she said, switching off the ignition and opening the door. "There's something I need to say to Pat."

My pulse started to race. Heaven only knew what Rinda might say to Pat. Or how he might react.

"Are you sure that's a good idea?"

She didn't answer, just grabbed her purse off the floorboard and hopped out.

"I won't be long," she said.

I watched her stride up to the door like a woman on a mission; the square set of her shoulders and every step she took spoke of determination. I shouldn't have let Peter leave until the rest of us did. He'd have known what to say or do to ward off a confrontation between Rinda and Pat. But I knew she wouldn't listen to me.

I sat in the passenger seat, watching anxiously as Rinda hammered on the door, hoping that Pat would refuse to open it. But he did open it and Rinda went inside. The door closed and I sat there, waiting.

Fifteen minutes later, about the time I was thinking I should knock on the door myself to make sure that everything was all right, Rinda came outside. She climbed in the van, backed out of the driveway, and headed down Birch Street without saying a word.

The suspense was killing me.

"Well? What took you so long? What were you doing in there?"

"Talking to Pat," Rinda said calmly, her eyes glued to the road. "And giving him tracts."

"Tracts?"

"Uh-huh. One from my church and the other from Alcoholics Anonymous. They meet in my church every Monday and Thursday."

She started humming a little tune as she drove, a snippet of some hymn, as if she had suddenly gotten into a very good mood.

I sat there for a moment, trying to make sense of it. Only a couple of hours before, Rinda had been masterminding a plan to lay siege to Pat's house and, on the drive over, had voiced a few other creative ideas on how her wire cutters might be used to inflict a few further lessons on that "no-good, worthless fornicator." And now she wanted to invite him to church? I didn't get it.

"So . . . did he read them?"

"No. Mostly he sat there feeling sorry for himself and blubbering about Celia. He's not ready to read them yet. But someday he might be. He said I could leave them on the table and that's a start. And he let me give him my phone number too."

My eyes went wide. "You gave him your phone number? Why?"

"Because someday he *is* going to be ready. And when that day comes, I told him I'd be his AA sponsor."

Rinda went back to humming and driving and I just sat there for a second, trying to digest this information and to make sense of the walking bundle of contradictions that was Rinda Charles, ultimately deciding that it couldn't be done and I'd just have to accept her as she was.

"That was really nice of you," I said, but Rinda shrugged off the compliment.

"No. I'm just doing unto others what some-body else already did for me. That's all. But you know what is nice?" She turned her head so she could see my face. "You watching out for our Celia. Taking her into your home."

Now it was my turn to wave off words of praise. "Oh, that's not anything. I don't mind. I like Celia."

Rinda turned her gaze forward again. "So do I. I would have asked her to come live with Lloyd and me, but . . ." She sighed.

"What is it?" She dismissed my question with a wave of her hand. "Come on. I can tell that something is bothering you."

"Nothing. It just wouldn't be a good time to have somebody move in with us. I'm going to have to put our house up for sale."

Since the night when Daphne showed up at my door with the remainder of the FOA in tow, we'd gathered together a few more times for "quilt-ins," as Rinda termed them. In that time I'd learned a lot about quilting and even more about my fellow quilters. Quilting, I'd noticed, loosened tongues even faster than liquor did. However, conversation among quilters tends to be a lot less rambling and make a lot more sense than conversations among your average group of barflies.

It won't leave you with dry mouth or a headache the next morning either. But that's another issue.

The point is, though our time together was short, I'd already learned a lot about the FOA. I knew all about Celia's unhappy childhood that kept her looking for love in all the wrong places. I learned more about Daphne's history and her struggles trying to raise four girls on her own. I'd learned about Rinda too.

I knew that Lloyd, her husband of thirty-one years, had been in the Marines when they met and that Rinda had started drinking during his long and lonely deployments. Eventually, Lloyd gave her an ultimatum and Rinda started going to AA. Lloyd retired from the military and they decided to move to Door County because they thought life in the country would offer fewer temptations and a lower cost of living. They'd invested their life savings so Lloyd could open his own HVAC business and worked hard to finally purchase their own home, a three-bedroom, two-bath bungalow with a garage and a peekaboo view of the bay. Rinda loved that house and often pointed to it as evidence that if people would just work a little harder and solve their own problems, they could "pull themselves up by their bootstraps."

And now she was going to sell? Something must be really wrong.

"Lloyd hasn't been feeling very good," she admitted. "We went to the doctor and it turns out that his kidneys are failing. Eventually, he's going to have to have a kidney replacement, assuming we can find a compatible donor. Everything is all right for the moment; the doctor said that he can go at least a year and maybe a few before he'll need a replacement, but he just can't keep working like he has been. It's such physical work and he gets tired so easily. Looks like he's going to have to retire early, sell the business.

"At first, I wasn't too worried, at least not about that part. With what he can get for the business, plus his military pension and my job, I figured we'd be able to get by. But I just found out that someone is buying the Save-A-Bunch. The new owners are going to put in a lot of those automated checkout counters. They won't need so many cashiers. Since I was the last one hired . . . ."

"You'll be the first one fired. Oh, Rinda. I'm so sorry."

"Me too. We'll make it somehow or other," she said, her brave-sounding words a sharp contrast to the worried expression on her face.

"But you know how it is around here. Most of the retail work is seasonal, and that's all I know how to do. I'll find another job in the spring. But in the meantime, we've got to tighten our belts. The house is our biggest expense. We just can't afford to keep it."

I told her again how sorry I was. What else was there to say?

"You know something else that really gets to me?" she asked, and then answered her own question. "The people buying the market aren't even from here. It's some investment group out of

California. And yet, they're just going to waltz into town, tear down the old store, and build a new one. I love the old building. It's been Nilson's Bay's only grocery store since 1922. It has history! And character! But this thing they want to build . . ." Rinda shook her head and curled her lip.

"It's like something you'd see in a strip mall in Mendocino—because it is. It looks exactly like all the other stores in that chain. Fake adobe on the exterior. Adobe! In Wisconsin!"

"That's crazy," I said. "That won't fit in with the rest of downtown. And you're sure they're going to tear the old store down completely?"

"Oh, not just the store—the old Herzog building, too, so they can expand the footprint of the market and add more parking. I saw the plans. They're going to put in one of those ready-to-go meal counters, an imported cheese section, an olive bar, a café with an espresso maker—stuff they can charge higher prices for—and then decrease the amount of shelf space for basic groceries, like baking supplies and canned goods. But they're going to raise the prices for that too. I know that the tourists like all that fancy, prepared stuff, but what are the people who live here year-round supposed to eat? I can't afford the time or gas to drive all the way to Sturgeon Bay just so I can buy a can of corn or a bag of flour!"

"No, and you shouldn't have to. That's terrible."

As Rinda turned the van onto Lakeview Trail, she pressed her lips together, exposing a web of worry lines around her mouth. "I don't know how we're supposed to pay more for groceries when I'm about to lose my job, but I guess we'll just have to figure it out. What else can I do? You can't fight city hall."

I turned in my seat and stared at Rinda with a mixture of confusion and amusement. Didn't she realize who was riding in her car?

"Don't be silly!" I exclaimed. "*Of course* you can!"

🍃 Chapter 34 🍃

Our quilt-ins are kind of a movable feast; everyone takes turns hosting. We were supposed to meet at Rinda's house that evening, but since we were already at the cottage after having gotten Celia moved in, we just decided to stay put and sew at my house.

It was kind of an exciting night for me because my quilt top was nearly complete. The only thing I had left to do was sew the batting to the front of the quilt and then hand-stitch it to the back. Rinda had promised to help and teach me how to miter the corners so they'd look tidy and sharp. I'd wanted to use the easier "self-binding" method, where you just cut the backing wider and then fold it, iron it to the front, and stitch it down, but Rinda made a face and then suggested I "jazz it up" by adding prairie points to the binding, a row of colorful triangles to add dimension.

"Don't be such a chicken! You can do it. I'll show you."

She'd said the same thing about having me do the quilting myself on my good old Singer instead of sending it out to a professional.

"I don't hold with that. All these people who piece their tops but hire somebody else to do the finishing . . . Hmph. They're not quilters. They're toppers!" she declared, curling her lip in a way that made it sound almost like a dirty word.

Frankly, I'd been pretty darned impressed with myself just for finishing the top, and it would have bothered me not one whit to be called a topper—until Rinda started giving me a hard time about it. But the idea of quilting the top was far more intimidating than piecing it. Ripping out a seam in a piece of patchwork isn't so bad, but removing stitches quilted through two layers of fabric plus a center batting is complicated. I was terrified that after so many hours of hard work, I'd end up ruining the quilt. But in the end I caved in to peer pressure and did it myself.

And, believe me, even just doing basic stitch-in-the-ditch quilting, sewing into the seam lines so my mistakes would be less noticeable, wasn't as easy as Rinda had made it sound, but, I had to admit, I felt a certain pride in knowing I'd done the whole thing myself and could legitimately claim the title "quilter" as my own. And, considering it was my first quilt, it really had turned out pretty well.

I'd worked hard on it, but I knew that the real reason I was sitting in the sewing room with an almost completed quilt top on my lap that night was because of the FOA. Daphne, Rinda, and Celia had made it their mission to ensure that I finished my project before the end of my final sojourn in Nilson's Bay, knowing that once I returned to DC and plunged back into the swift current of politics, I wouldn't have time to quilt, not for years. Or perhaps ever.

I knew I would miss those quiet hours at the sewing machine, the way my worries would recede and my imagination would drift when I submerged myself into the steady *thunkedy-thunkedy-thunkedy* of the needle moving over and through the fabric, the sense of satisfaction I felt when I lifted the presser foot, snipped off the thread, opened the patch or block or row to the right side of the fabric, and saw what a pretty combination the colors made and how neatly the seams met.

I would also miss these evenings with the FOA, the pride I felt when showing them what I'd been able to accomplish since the last time I'd seen them, the excitement of seeing what they were working on, too, and the connections we created as we worked together to correct a mistake or tackle a problem. And it was amazing how much pleasure I got from something so simple, or the sense of accomplishment I derived from something as basic as joining one square of fabric to another, but my vacation was fast coming to a close, the days flying far more quickly than I could ever have imagined.

Soon I would pack my bags and leave this house I had grown up in and this town that held so many memories, good and bad, but more good than I had been willing to acknowledge until recently. Yes, I would return to Nilson's Bay, but only briefly, to finish the last of my Alice-mandated residency and sign over the deed to a home that represented a huge part of who I was and what had made me this way. It would all belong to someone else then.

I hadn't wanted to come home for a day, let alone two months, but now that my time here was coming to a close, I felt a little sad.

But still, I had this quilt, and I was grateful for that.

Whenever I saw it or touched it, I would remember this room, the hours I had spent here, and the supposedly simpleminded sister who had a wisdom I could never hope to match, whose legacy brought me home.

And, of course, I would remember Rinda and Daphne and Celia. They were without question three of the oddest women I'd ever met—especially when encountered as a set. But, eccentricities aside, they were as good a trio of women as you could hope to meet. The fact that, out of all the available candidates, Alice had picked these three to be her best friends was more evidence of my sister's inexplicable wisdom. I really was going to miss them.

After I left we might exchange Christmas cards, or maybe, if they ever came to DC, I'd take them to lunch and arrange a private tour of the White House. Aside from that, it was doubtful our paths would cross again. But I would miss them. I knew they'd only helped me out of a desire to honor Alice's memory, but had I been able to stay, I think they might have become my friends too.

All day, ever since that uncharacteristic moment of vulnerability in the van when Rinda had confessed her problems to me, I'd been thinking about ways to stop the demolition of the market and, in turn, save Rinda's job. I'd trotted out a couple of different possibilities to Rinda during the remainder of the drive, but she'd told me, in pretty clear language, to butt out of her business.

But I couldn't. The whole time Rinda was helping me sew those prairie points, I was thinking about how I could help her. Alice wasn't the only doggedly determined Toomey sister. And I just couldn't sit there and do nothing, not when I knew in my heart that there was a possibility of helping!

So after my beautiful blue, white, and orange quilt was finished and we were sitting in a circle, each holding one edge of the quilt and hand-stitching the binding, I spilled the beans and told Daphne and Celia about Rinda's predicament.

She was not pleased.

"Who said you could—!" she sputtered. "Didn't I tell you to keep that to yourself?"

"No," I said. "And even if you had, I'd have ignored you. Why shouldn't they know?"

"Because there's no point in getting people upset about things that can't be helped. Now look what you've done. Celia! Stop crying! Everything is going to be fine."

"But what about Lloyd?" Celia said, fighting to keep her lip from quivering. "And your house!"

"The doctors say that Lloyd will be fine for now, but he needs to take better care of himself. They're putting him on the list for a new kidney and, God willing, one will be available by the time he needs it. Lloyd and I are leaving this in God's loving hands. And as far as the house . . ." Rinda said stoutly, "it's just a house. It's not like we'll be homeless."

"But you love that house," Daphne said.

"No," Rinda corrected. "I *like* my house, but I

love my husband. Lloyd's health is all that matters." Daphne gave her a doubtful look and started to say something, but Rinda cut her off. "Now, don't you start in too. It's just a house. The Lord giveth and the Lord taketh away, blessed be his name."

"Listen to me," I said sharply. "This *can* be helped. We need to take this up with the village council, and—"

"Pfft," Rinda puffed, and then rolled her eyes. "As if anybody ever got anywhere by relying on the government to solve their problems."

"Rinda! Will you just shut up and listen for a minute!" I shouted, loudly enough to make Rinda jump in her chair and shock Celia from her tears. Daphne just grinned as if she were enjoying the show.

"Don't you get it?" I stabbed my needle into the batting, let the quilt drop into my lap, and clapped one hand onto my chest. "We *are* the people! The government exists and functions of, for, and by us!"

Rinda scowled at me, but she didn't argue. I stayed quiet, knowing that she was at least thinking about what I'd said.

"Maybe," she said, "but I think it's too late for that. The plans are all finished. I just don't see how—"

"But I *do*," I said urgently. "This kind of thing— grassroots, hands-on political campaigning—is my job. And, not to brag, but I'm really good at it! Just the other day, a man called me up and offered me ten thousand dollars to sketch out a plan to help his client drum up community support that would help him win government approval to create a new housing development. I said I wouldn't do it because the project was sketchy, definitely not in the best interests of the community. But this! Preserving a historically important building? Staying true to our traditions and the unique, rural character of life on the peninsula? Saving jobs? That's the kind of project I'm more than ready to support. And if we can get the word out, I know there are plenty of other people who will feel the same."

As I talked, Rinda's hostile scowl softened into a frown of concentration. When I finished, she pressed her lips tightly together and blew out a heavy breath through her nose.

"I don't know. Seems like a long shot. And ten thousand dollars? Where would we get—"

"Rinda!" I shouted again and threw up my hands. I couldn't help myself. "I am not going to charge you a ten-thousand-dollar consulting fee! I'm not going to charge you anything. I'm doing this because it's the right thing to do!

"Look, I know that you and I could not be on more opposite sides of the fence when it comes to a whole range of issues and attitudes, but as different as we are in ideology and methodology,

I have come to see that your heart is absolutely in the right place, and that you are a caring and compassionate"—I smiled—"if somewhat intolerant woman."

Rinda's scowl returned, but I paid no attention and kept talking.

"Now, if I can ascribe good intentions to you, why can't you do the same for me? Because really? It's starting to hurt my feelings."

I blinked a few times and pretended to sniffle. Rinda's brow went smooth and her lips flattened into a line as she fought, and nearly succeeded, to keep herself from smiling.

"Hmph. You politicians. Always ready to make a speech, aren't you?"

"I'm not a politician; I just work for them. And in this instance, I think you'd really call me more of an activist."

"Just as bad," she grumbled. "Worse!"

She hesitated and I could see in her eyes what was holding her back, the fear of hoping for something she wanted so badly, of trying and failing and then having to resign herself all over again.

"You think there's really a chance?"

"I do," I said. "There's no guarantee, but it's definitely worth a try."

"It would be such a load off Lloyd's mind if we could keep the house," she mused. "He's been so upset, feeling like he's let me down . . . foolish old man . . . he's never let me down a day in my life."

During this entire exchange, Celia and Daphne had been sitting by silently, Celia's eyes darting from Rinda's side of the quilt to mine and back again, Daphne keeping her head down, continuing to stitch, neither of them missing a word.

Now Daphne looked up. "You know what King Lear said—nothing will come of nothing." Celia bobbed her head in agreement. Rinda still had doubts.

"And you really think that the council will listen to us?"

"If by us, you mean you, me, Daphne, and Celia—the answer is no. We're going to need more people. A lot more people. And a plan."

I picked up my needle again, pinching it between my thumb and forefinger, and started stitching again.

"Daphne, when is Winter Fest?"

"On Saturday."

"Okay, so we've got to hurry. Here's what we're going to do . . ." I said, and smiled wide because, not to brag, but I *am* good at this.

Really good.

❧ Chapter 35 ☙

"Mrs. Lieshout!"

I stood next to an archway of ice, artfully carved with a design of white-blue roses and vines, like a summertime arbor that had been magically frozen in full bloom, and waved my arm over my head to get the librarian's attention. She turned around, eyes searching the crowd to see who had called her name, her face lighting up when she saw it was me.

"Lucy!" She walked toward me quickly, weaving through the clusters of people on the sidewalk and a clump of giggling preteen girls as she passed the elegant, life-sized sculpture of St. Lucia, the Swedish saint whose name day coincides with the start of the holiday season, complete with a crown of boughs and lit candles, and another, more abstract sculpture, an enormous six-foot-high pyramid composed of hundreds of perfectly formed snowballs.

"Isn't this fun? Only the third year of the festival and look at this crowd!"

She opened her arms as if to give me a hug, but then, remembering the big paper cup full of hot chocolate she was carrying in her hand, laughed and pulled back.

"Oops! I'd better be careful or I'll end up spilling cocoa all over that pretty white sweater. Where did you get it?"

Anxious as I was to steer Mrs. Lieshout to my desired topic of conversation, I knew it would be best to bide my time and make a little small talk. Nobody likes being pushed. And anyway, I was kind of pleased with my bargain.

"The consignment shop. Fourteen dollars. Cashmere."

"Fourteen dollars!" Mrs. Lieshout's eyes went wide. "Oh, I have been shopping at the wrong stores!"

"I've got an in. Juliet keeps an eye out for things she knows I might like and then calls me." I laughed. "I think I've bought more clothes in the last month than I did in the last five years. I'm hoping Santa brings me some bigger suitcases for Christmas."

The light of Mrs. Lieshout's smile dimmed a little. "That's right. You'll be leaving soon, won't you? Say, how is your quilting coming along? I forgot to ask when I saw you at the fish boil. And how is Peter?"

She craned her neck, as though expecting him to pop out from behind the nearest bush, as though wherever Lucy Toomey went, Peter Swenson was sure to follow.

"I guess he's fine. I haven't heard anything to the contrary," I said, moving past the question, ignoring the little flash of speculation I saw in Mrs. Lieshout's eyes. "And my quilt is all finished. I've even started another! It's red and white. I was inspired by some of the pictures in that book you suggested I check out. I don't think I'll be able to finish it before I go, but the FOA kind of gave me a nudge. The theory is that if I finish the top while I'm here, I can quilt it after I get to DC. We'll see."

"Sounds like a good idea, a nice way to relax at the end of a long day. I know it's selfish of me because you're going to be doing such important work, but I do hate to see you leave Nilson's Bay." She sighed and then swallowed hard. For a moment, I thought she might actually tear up.

"Oh," she said, waving her hand and forcing a smile, "I'm getting sentimental in my old age. Or maybe stuck in my ways. I just hate to see things change."

There it was—my opening. I nodded understandingly.

"I know what you mean. Did you hear about the Save-A-Bunch?"

"What about it?"

"An investment company from out of state is buying it and planning to tear it down—the Herzog building, too—to make room for a bigger store, a supermarket. Of course, that store will have all kinds of amenities that we don't have now. Take-out meals, an espresso bar. That sort of thing." I gave a disinterested shrug. "I guess some people might like that, the tourists and such, but—"

"An espresso bar? What do we need that for? People have been getting their coffee at Dinah's for years and nobody has complained yet. What will happen to her business if she has to start competing with the market?"

"Nothing good is my guess. I'm concerned that this expansion could hurt several of our small businesses and cost people their jobs. I heard they're going to let go of at least half the clerks and replace them with those computerized checkout counters."

"No," said Mrs. Lieshout, her voice low and her tone scandalized. "That's terrible. Have you ever used one of those things? They're so confusing! If you want to buy produce or anything without a bar code, then you have to look up the codes yourself. It takes forever! And then that irritating computer voice keeps barking orders at you. 'Remove items from the belt! The bagging area is full! Enter your rewards card! Take your change!' " She shuddered.

"So dehumanizing. No conversation. No 'How are you today, Mrs. Lieshout?' Or 'How are things down at the library?' No civility. No pleasant exchanges about the weather or suggestions for how to cook that pork roast you just bought on special."

"You're right," I said in a commiserating tone. "They have them in all the big cities now. Makes me feel like a cog in a wheel instead of a valued customer. The companies that put those machines in always say that they're faster and more convenient for customers, but everybody knows it's about eliminating jobs and adding to profits. I heard that the new company plans to get rid of all the box boys."

"So you'll have to bag your own groceries? And carry them out to the car?"

I nodded and Mrs. Lieshout clucked her tongue.

"What are the older people in town supposed to do, the ones who have a hard time walking, let alone lifting heavy bags? And what about the young people who've always saved for college by bagging groceries? And Mr. Lindstrom? He's been working as a box boy ever since he retired. He counts on that extra money to supplement his social security. Surely they won't eliminate his job?"

"From what I heard, all the box boy jobs will disappear."

"Well, that is just awful."

"And, of course, on top of all that, there's the issue of the demolition. Knocking down those buildings will change the entire landscape downtown."

Mrs. Lieshout's expression went from concerned to alarmed.

"Think of the precedent that would set! It's bad enough that so many of the old cottages have been bulldozed to make way for those McMonstrosities. If they can knock down the market and Herzog building, then what's next? The church? The town hall? Even the library?"

There it was. The connection I'd been waiting for her to make.

The thing that Joe Feeney and his deep-pocket developer didn't understand is that a truly effective grassroots campaign isn't a commodity you can buy. You can nurture and nudge it into being, but, as the name implies, a real grassroots movement grows organically, as a response to a genuine need within or threat to the community. And, as I had explained to Rinda, Daphne, and Celia that night at our quilt-in, the person or persons who head it up have to be insiders, energetic leaders whose lifetime of service to and residency in the community command respect, with a purity of purpose that made them above reproach.

Mrs. Lieshout fit the bill perfectly. She was one of the most energetic and well-respected women in Nilson's Bay and also, once she was truly motivated, one of the most pushy. And, for Mrs. Lieshout, no motivation could be stronger or more urgent than thwarting a perceived threat to the beloved, historic library to which she had devoted her life.

"Well, we simply cannot stand for this!" she declared, her eyes glittering with determination, her chin jutting like a knife point. "This is not only a threat to the livelihood of many of our citizens, but to our entire way of life. We've got to let people know about this. We've got to organize and agitate and stop this cancer before it spreads!"

"I couldn't agree more," I said and reached into my pocket to pull out one of the flyers that Celia and I had designed and printed out earlier in the day. "A few of us have already started working on it."

I handed her the flyer and she perused it quickly, nodding as she skimmed the bullet points outlining the negative effects that the proposed new market could have on the economy and character of the town.

"This is good," she mused as she read. "Though I do see that you've used 'devastate' twice in the same document. You might consider another, more descriptive word . . . perhaps 'decimate'?"

"Good suggestion."

"Oh, and Lucy . . . you really must be a little more judicious in your use of exclamation points—only one per sentence. Give people a little credit for common sense. Just lay out the facts rationally. You don't need to resort to ebullience or overdramatics."

"You're right," I agreed. "We'll change that for the next printing, once I finish handing these out."

"The sooner the better! Here," she said, and took half the stack of flyers, "let me help you. You couldn't pick a better time or place than here at Winter Fest—half the town is here!"

"I've already got people handing out flyers at all the entrances."

"You do?"

She looked at me curiously and I grinned. Knowing that the hook was now planted firmly in her mouth, I could reveal my hand.

"Uh-huh. And if you'll turn over the flyer, you'll see that we've already scheduled an organizational meeting next week." I grinned. "We're holding it at the library. And you're facilitating the discussion."

Mrs. Lieshout flipped over the paper and started to read. And then to frown.

"Seven o'clock on Monday? In the Lundstrom Room? You shouldn't have done that, Lucy. Not without consulting me first."

She looked up at me with a serious expression. I felt my heart sink. Apparently that hook wasn't planted quite as firmly as I'd thought.

"I'm sorry, Mrs. Lieshout. I just thought that—"

"You *can't* have a meeting in the Lundstrom Room. The Mystery Mavens book group has it that night. And, anyway, Lundstrom can only hold twenty people." She thought for a moment. "Let's use the Carnegie Room instead."

"Okay, sure. Good idea."

"Right. Well, I'd better get going. My hot chocolate is getting cold. Oh, Lucy, can you drop some more flyers off at the library? I want to post some on the bulletin boards. See you Monday?"

"Yes, ma'am. Absolutely."

Since Mrs. Lieshout had taken half of them off my hands, it didn't take long to chat people up and distribute the rest of my flyers, which meant that I had time to walk around and check out the ice sculptures before meeting up with the FOA for the tree lighting in front of town hall.

Winter Fest, with its accompanying ice sculpture contest and tree lighting, was the brainchild of some of the local merchants who were looking for a way to lure tourists up to the peninsula for just one more weekend before winter set in. It was a good idea.

I'd stopped by The Library earlier that day—the bar, not the building—to eat a basket of wings and ask Clint if I could put our flyers up on the stalls in his bathroom. He told me they were booked solid for dinner that night.

"Couldn't fit one more person in here unless we greased 'em up wid Crisco," he said, the gap in his front teeth showing when he grinned. "But Roberta had a good idea. We're gonna grill a buncha brats, put 'em on sticks, and sell 'em from a stand on da sidewalk," he told me.

He'd also surprised me by asking if Peter would be joining me for lunch. When I said no, why would he, he'd frowned and looked flustered.

"Oh, nothin' . . . I just thought that you and Peter . . . Well, you know. You'd been coming in together pretty regular for a while, and I just thought . . . Never mind," he said, and started vigorously scrubbing the already clean table with a rag. "Sometimes people just decide to take a break. None of my business."

"We're not taking a break," I said. Clint flashed a smile and I jumped in to clarify my statement. "You can't take a break unless you've got something to take a break *from*. Peter and I aren't a couple. Never were."

"Okay. Sure." Clint looked down and started wiping the table again. "Like I said. None of my business."

People gossip like crazy in Nilson's Bay. I guess it's the same in most little towns. Especially in winter—what else is there to do? But the fact of gossip being a common occurrence doesn't make it less annoying. Though I felt guilty every time I saw Peter's number on my phone and ignored it—three times during the last week— keeping my distance was the smart thing to do. In the end, it would be easier on both of us.

I walked past The Library and, sure enough, the two little Spaids, Kayla and Ricky, were standing behind a card table, wearing white aprons over their jackets, selling bratwurst on sticks. Their parents were inside tending to the sit-down diners, but the kids seemed to be handling everything well, even though the line to purchase their wares was ten people deep. It was the same story outside of Dinah's Pie Shop, where Dinah was selling hot, individual apple or cherry pies with the crust folded to make them easy to carry, as well as coffee, hot chocolate, and hot cider. Dinah saw me walking by and raised her arm over her head.

"Lucy! I saw Daphne Olsen a little while ago. She brought me one of those flyers. You can sure count on me being there for the meeting! I'll bring a couple of pies for the refreshment table." She paused to take fifteen dollars from a man wearing a down jacket and one of those knitted jester hats with bells on the tassels and hand him five pies in exchange. "If I haven't sold them all!" She laughed.

I waved and walked on.

It was nice to see so many free-spending travelers thronging the freshly shoveled sidewalks, but it was even nicer to see so many familiar faces, people who had known me and whom I had known from childhood. In the eighteen years since I had left this town behind, hoping never to return, I had traveled to every major metropolitan area in America and had met with some of the most influential leaders in the country, and during my fifteen minutes of fame after the Iowa caucuses, my face appeared on millions of television sets all over the country. But in spite of all that, there was no one city, town, or hamlet in the country, except this one, where scores of people recognized me, called me by name, and looked happy to see me.

It was a good feeling. But also a lonely one.

Everyone walking down the street, stopping to buy bratwurst, or to get their picture taken with a live reindeer brought in for the occasion and decked out in a red halter and jingle bells, or to *ooh* and *aah* over the prizewinning, incredibly lifelike ice sculpture of a mother polar bear with twin cubs gamboling at her feet, was walking with someone else, traveling in herds: families with little children or elderly parents, groups of friends, couples holding hands. It seemed like I was the last lone person on the face of the earth, the only person alive who was not connected to some other person by birth, or love, or both. I was an orphan.

It was a strange thing, and terrible to admit, but after my parents died I didn't miss them that much. I know how awful that makes me sound, but . . . I'd been away from home for so long, almost never seeing them or talking to them— even when I did call, my father refused to speak to me—and I was so busy living my life, trying to latch on to that brass ring that would fill the constant void and somehow redeem me, that weeks could pass without my ever thinking about them.

And then they died.

I came home for a few days, did my duty, attended the funeral, comforted Alice and helped her get organized, arranged for part of my paycheck to be direct deposited into her account every two weeks, signed the necessary papers, and left. The whole thing had taken less than a week. And then everything went on like it always had. I didn't miss hearing from them because I'd never heard from them much to begin with. Before long, the weeks that passed without a thought of them stretched to months and then to never. Almost never.

With Alice, of course, it was different. I talked to her almost every day, but I wasn't . . . engaged. Not really. She would talk and I would listen, sort of. More often than not I was either half-asleep or working on the computer during our conversations, giving her what attention I felt was owed, paying her bills, doing my duty. Because I knew I owed her that. Because I felt like . . .

It didn't matter. Nothing I knew, or felt, or feel could change what had been. I'd spent twenty years trying to accept that truth, or at least not dwell on it.

Now there was no one whom I belonged to and no one who belonged to me. Not even here, in the only place on the face of the earth where people recognize my face and know me by name.

I missed Alice. Really missed her. And not just the old Alice, the Alice golden child who I chased across lawns and through woods in a pair of too-big pink rubber boots, the sister I could never catch up to. I also missed the Alice I left behind, who woke me in the night and droned on and on about things and people and places I had worked so hard to separate myself from. I missed the slow and steady, pedantic and plodding sister who never gave up and who summoned home her selfish second sister in the only way left to her, issuing the invitation I could not refuse and did not deserve. I missed the Alice who disappeared under the water on a hot day in August and emerged more mortal, more simple and simulta-neously more complex, wiped free of memory and malice, the one who couldn't understand why I wanted to forget, who could not grasp that there are moments and acts that completely sever the life that was from the life that is, moments beyond redemption, and homes you can never return to.

I missed Alice. I missed everyone.

❦ Chapter 36 ❦

It was only four o'clock, but the light was already fading from the sky.

In another hour it would be dark, and when the assembled onlookers finished singing "O Tannenbaum," mumbling through the verses, but jumping in and singing lustily along with the chorus, and the mayor pushed the button to illuminate the thirty-foot-tall Christmas tree, making the five score strings of lights glow white-gold in the darkness, everyone would gasp and then applaud, as though they'd never seen an electric lightbulb before.

But you can't really blame them. On a cold December night when the setting of the sun causes the temperature to drop twenty degrees in as many minutes and turns your fingers into ice pops even through your gloves, there really is something miraculous, and hugely comforting, about the existence of electricity.

The police had closed five blocks along Bayshore to traffic the night before, giving the ice sculptors a spot to work on their creations through the night and leaving plenty of room for pedestrians to admire the completed sculptures the next day. The sidewalk concession booths had been set up by local merchants.

Before making my way to the tree lighting, I bought a snow cone from Heller's Ice Cream Haven, not because I really wanted one, but because I felt a little sorry for Mr. Heller. Though he'd tried to get into the spirit of the occasion, putting out a chalkboard sandwich board that said "Embrace the Cold!" on one side and "Snow Cones! The Original Ice Sculpture!" on the other, and offered holiday-inspired flavors like Pink Peppermint and Spicy Cinnamon, his was the only food booth without a line.

"Thanks," he said as I handed him a five-dollar bill, his voice a little despondent. "I tried to think up something different, but in this kind of weather people want something hot. Maybe next year I'll give hot fudge sundaes a try."

"How about hot cocoa floats? Take the big foam cups you use for milk shakes, then fill them with hot chocolate and put in a scoop of vanilla ice cream."

"And maybe a candy cane stir stick?" His face lit up. "That's a great idea. Thanks, Lucy."

I took my three dollars change and my snow cone and walked down the street toward town hall. The cinnamon snow cone was better than I'd thought it would be, but Mr. Heller was right. In this kind of weather, I would have preferred something warm. When I was out of sight of the ice cream shop, I dropped the cone into a nearby trash can.

Looking up, I saw the top of Peter's head sticking up above the crowd on the opposite side of the street and called out to him. He turned at the sound of my voice and I started walking toward him. There was no hint of a smile on his lips, no cocky, teasing grin in response to my greeting. His expression was totally neutral. I lowered my arm to my side, feeling suddenly foolish, the way you feel when you start yoo-hooing to a long-lost friend at a crowded party who ultimately turns out to be a stranger.

We met in the middle of the street, in a some-what less crowded spot between two ice sculptures where somebody had decided to park three snowblowers.

"Hi."

"Hi."

I smiled and waited for him to smile back, but he just stood there, hands in his pockets, being Switzerland.

Finally, I asked, "Did you see the polar bears?"

"Yeah. Really something."

I nodded. "Hey," I said. "I'm sorry I haven't returned your calls. It's just been a really busy week. I've been working to organize support to help stop the sale and demolition of the Save-A-Bunch."

"I know," he said. "About fifteen people have

stopped me to talk about it since I got here."

"Yeah? That's great!" I couldn't keep myself from smiling. Already the word was spreading.

"Listen, we're having a meeting on Monday at the library. It'd be really great if you could stop by and say—"

He shook me off before I could even finish my sentence. "Can't."

"Oh. Have you got another out-of-town trial?"

"No. Just can't make it."

"You can't? On a Monday? Why not? I know how you feel about these kinds of issues and about preserving the places and traditions that make Nilson's Bay unique. Not to mention supporting small business. I mean, we've talked—"

"Lucy." He held up one hand. "Stop right there."

His expression went from neutral to stern. I did stop, but more because I was surprised by his response than because he told me to. He paused, frowned, shoved his hands deeper in his pockets, and then, after leaving me hanging for a good five seconds, looked up.

"Mrs. Lieshout tracked me down a few minutes ago. She wanted to give me her opinion about the market, which was fine. When she was done, she made a point of telling me that you were handing out flyers over by the ice-carved archway. I guess she figured I'd be looking for you. And a few minutes before that, when I was standing in line to buy my brat, Clint came out of the restaurant to resupply his kids, then came over to pat me on the shoulder and give me his sympathy, said that he'd heard you and I were taking a break."

I felt my jaw clench. Clint! Hadn't I *told* him?

"And just before you waved to me, Mr. Coates flagged me down to ask about the town getting a dog park. But not before asking how we were and if you were still planning to move to Washington."

"I know," I said. "I've been dealing with the same kind of thing. But you know how things are around here. People see a single man and a single woman going to dinner or having a conversation on the street and they immediately assume that—"

"Exactly. They immediately assume that there's some kind of romantic involvement going on. Even," he said, his gaze becoming suddenly steely and his language lawyerly, "after it has been made eminently clear that there is absolutely no possibility of such a thing occurring."

My jaw dropped. "What? So you're not willing to get behind the effort to save the market just because I don't want to go out with you? You can't be serious," I said, shaking my head with a mixture of disbelief and disappointment. If that's how he felt, then Peter was not the guy I thought he was.

"First you lure me out to your ice shanty and try to jump me. *Then* you hold the market demolition over my head because I won't play ball." I let out an incredulous gasp. "And people say *Washington* is the hotbed of dirty politics!"

"Hang on!" Peter barked, loudly enough so a small knot of passersby, fortunately no one I recognized, turned to look. I shot Peter a look and he lowered his voice.

"Just hang on right there, Lucy. That is *not* what I said!"

I leaned closer, furious, practically hissing at him, "You implied—"

"I implied nothing! And if for once in your life you'd shut up and quit assuming that you know everything about everybody, even what they're thinking, then I might have a chance to explain myself."

He glared at me, daring me to interrupt or argue and thereby prove his point. I wouldn't give him the satisfaction. I clamped my lips together and crossed my arms over my chest.

"This has nothing to do with you and me. Nothing. The reason I can't attend the meeting on Monday, or any future meetings, is because I don't think it would be right for me to take a position, or even appear to take a position, on this issue before it comes up for a decision before the council."

"Are you done?" He nodded. "I see. So because you're afraid that people will think you're being influenced by your . . ." I was about to name a part of his anatomy but, angry as I was, decided to take the high road. ". . . girlfriend, you've decided not to support a grassroots effort to save a business that is key to maintaining the character and economic viability of this town."

"No," he said, in a maddeningly calm tone. "What I said is it doesn't make things any easier if people were to assume that my feelings toward you might be influencing my vote. But even if that weren't the case, I can't take a position, one way or the other. Not right now."

"Why not? That's crazy! Peter, I *know* whose side you're on here. Why not show your hand?"

"No!" he said. And then he growled. He actually growled! And pointed his finger at me. "This is what I'm talking about! The way you assume things, the way you constantly jump to con-clusions. You do *not* know what I think about this issue or any other. Hell, Lucy! Half the time, you don't even know what you think, let alone me!"

"What's that supposed to mean?"

He lifted both his hands and looked away. "You know what . . . never mind. Forget I said that. It doesn't matter."

He hesitated for just a moment and scratched his forehead, the way he does when he's thinking. I again asked him to explain that last statement, but he cut me off.

"Lucy. Listen to me. This is not about you or

me or the two of us together or not together. I'm just trying to do the right thing here."

"By *not* taking a position on important issues?"

I shook my head and dropped my arms to my sides. He was new at this. Maybe he didn't understand the rules of the game.

"Peter, it is perfectly legal for you to adopt and express a position on a given issue ahead of an actual vote."

"Gee, Luce. Thanks for clearing that up for me. Because, seeing as I went to law school and all, I wasn't quite sure."

"Hey! No need to get snarky! I'm trying to help."

"Well, don't! I don't need that kind of help, okay? Lucy, I'm not talking about what is legal. I'm talking about what is *right*. I'm getting all kinds of opinions from people on both sides of this, which is great. That's how democracy works. But until this thing comes up for a vote, I intend not only to appear neutral and open-minded; I intend to *be* neutral and open-minded. So please don't stand there and try to lobby me, okay? I'm getting enough of that as it is."

"Lobby you?" He nodded and I rolled my eyes. "Oh, give me a break. So you're above politics? Is that it?"

"Politics is your line of work, Lucy. You're good at it and I respect that. But I'm not a politician. I'm a public servant. I'm not perfect by a long shot. Nobody knows that better than you do, and I apologize for"—he pulled his hands out of his pockets, rubbed his neck, and then put them back in—"being so . . . aggressive in my attentions. But I happen to find you attractive and I can't apologize for that. Not any more than I'm going to apologize for trying to do the right thing as best I know how."

So he was a noble public servant while I was just a lowly, scheming politico?

It was not the first time I'd heard that line, generally from the kind of grandstanding politicians who put the "crave" in "craven." Sometimes from members of the general public, people who immediately suspect the worst of anybody who gets involved in politics. I was used to that kind of accusation and I'd learned not to let it bother me.

But this was different. This was coming from Peter, who knew me better than that. Or so I'd thought. I guess I'd been wrong.

I'd never felt so discounted—or so judged—in all my life.

"Well, if that's how you feel . . . I guess it's a good thing that I *didn't* return your phone calls. You know, I was just walking down the street a few minutes ago, looking at all the couples and the families. And I was just feeling so . . ."

Suddenly, inexplicably, my throat got tight and I felt tears form in my eyes. I looked away, over my right shoulder, and blinked a couple of times, embarrassed in case he should see me crying and think it was over him.

"So what?" he said, and took a step toward me, his voice suddenly softer. "What were you feeling?"

"Doesn't matter," I said, blinking quickly. "I get it now. I have to go. I'm supposed to meet some people at the tree lighting. See you around, Peter."

I turned away and started walking, then jogging down the street, pushing my way through the throng. Behind me, I could hear Peter's voice calling my name, but I kept my head down and my feet moving until the sound started to fade away and I didn't have to hear, or to think, about him anymore.

Just keep walking, I said to myself. *You know how to do this. You've done it before.*

❧ Chapter 37 ❧

By the day of the meeting, I was fine. I was over it.

The holidays are always a terrible time for single people—all that emphasis on family, kiddies dancing joyfully around the tree while Mama and Papa sneak a kiss under the mistletoe, all those sappy, sentimental movies on television, the equally sappy and sentimental carols crooned from every spot on the radio dial and every loudspeaker in every retail establishment—no wonder I'd been feeling emotional.

In previous years, I'd been working so hard that I'd been able to ignore most of the holiday hoopla until I'd hop on a plane to meet Alice at some nice, warm spot for a Christmas that had little to do with family dinners and nativity scenes and everything to do with lying poolside and working on my tan while simultaneously catching up on my e-mail. If not for Alice's insistence on our presence at midnight mass in whatever church was nearest to our hotel on Christmas Eve and the next-morning ritual of stockings and gift giving, I might not even have known it was Christmas. That would have been fine with me. Christmas is an insidious, emotionally manipulative holiday. What with Alice's death coinciding with the holidays, and the snow, and being back home for the first time in years, it was easy to see how I'd allowed myself to get sucked into it.

But now I was over that. Well and truly over it. I'm not saying that I suddenly turned into some unfeeling, insensitive pillar of salt. Nor was I doing a turnabout on my feelings about Nilson's Bay; on the contrary, I recognized that my coming home was a good thing, that it had helped me find a certain amount of peace regarding Alice's death, and even though I still hadn't unraveled the mystery of Maeve and probably never would, I had gotten some insight into my sister's life.

It was just that after a bit of reflection, I recognized the source of my melancholy and the season that had primed me to become emotionally vulnerable to Peter and his unkind and unfair commentary. Having recognized the problem, I was able to explain it rationally and prescribe myself an antidote, the medicine that never failed me: work.

And not just any work, though I did make some calls to the office in DC to see how things were coming along with the transition and I did check in with Jenna, but meaningful work that would help Rinda and others keep their jobs, would preserve an important though unrecognized historic building, and would protect the town from the economic and cultural ravages of a bunch of greedy people who didn't care a rat's rear end about Nilson's Bay and the people who live here.

Peter's sensibilities might be too delicate to fully engage on behalf of his constituents, but mine weren't. I've never backed away from a fight. And this wasn't just me fighting for the sake of it. Winning this fight would actually help my fellow man. If you can think of a better way to celebrate Christmas, the birth of the one who instructed us to love our neighbors as ourselves, then I'd like to know about it.

Our first big organizational meeting was set to take place that night. With the help and input of Mrs. Lieshout and the FOA—particularly Celia, since school had let out for the holiday and she had plenty of time, not to mention proximity since she was living with me—we had rewritten and reprinted the flyer, posted copies on every bulletin board in Nilson's Bay and the surrounding towns, crafted a press release and sent it to various news outlets in the county, and made phone calls inviting people to the meeting. We were ready. If everyone who said they were coming actually showed up, we'd have upward of forty attending, a pretty impressive showing in a town this size.

I'd also spent a lot of time doing research on the investment company that was buying the store—they were hugely profitable—and what had happened to the small businesses in other localities after the company had opened similar stores. A lot of them hadn't survived. I was boiling down that information and putting it into bullet points that could be handed to attendees and members of the press.

Though we didn't yet officially exist as a group, it was decided that Mrs. Lieshout would facilitate the meeting. I was sure that by the end of the night, she would be elected as chair of the Nilson's Bay Heritage Protection Committee and that the name, though still unofficial, would also be voted upon and adopted.

We'd done an amazing amount of work in a short time. Now we were just handling the final details of logistics and refreshments. Dinah had confirmed that she would bring three dozen of her fold-over fruit pies, Rinda was mixing and bringing a big batch of punch, and, with Daphne's help, I would bake a few batches of You Like-A Me Bars. We decided to do the baking at her house. Celia was out running a few last-minute errands, but would join us at the library that evening.

"Welcome to the asylum!" Daphne said when she opened the door. "Can I take your coat?"

It was an appropriate greeting.

The television was blaring, even though no one was watching it. The whine of a blow-dryer and the wince-inducing squeal of badly played violin music came from the general direction of the bedrooms. Ophelia and Portia, with beach towels trailing from their shoulders like capes, were running through the living room, shouting and leaping and whacking each other with long cardboard tubes that had once held wrapping paper.

" 'I have no words!' " Ophelia cried. " 'My voice is in my sword!' "

She leapt onto a chintz ottoman and thrust the long cardboard cylinder at her sister's shoulder. Portia then jumped onto the sofa, nearly knocking over a table lamp.

"'Yield thee, coward!'" Portia shouted and started thwacking her sister repeatedly over the head, her expression full of murderous glee that quickly turned to frustration.

"Mom!" she whined as Daphne hung up my jacket. "Ophelia won't yield!"

"I don't have to!" Ophelia countered. "Malcolm dies offstage!"

"But he still dies! Mom!"

Daphne hung my jacket up and slammed the closet door. "Girls! That's enough! Go outside and play. Why are you so obsessed with *Macbeth* anyway, you little barbarians?"

"It's got the best fight scenes," Portia said, hopping down from the couch.

"It's too violent," Daphne said. "If you *have* to play *Macbeth*, then why not be the Weird Sisters instead? Suits you better."

"But it's just me and Portia," Ophelia reasoned. "We'd need a third witch."

"Well, it's not like we're lacking in that department," Daphne said in a half mumble. "Viola! Come out here and play with your sisters. They need another witch!"

The scraping of the violin ceased, mercifully. Viola came into the room with her instrument at her side and a scowl on her face.

"Mom! I'm too old to play *Macbeth*. And I've got to practice."

"And *I've* got to be able to hear myself think,"

Daphne said, clicking off the television set. "Seriously, Viola, take them outside to play for an hour or so. I'll pay you three dollars."

Viola's forehead creased as she considered the offer. "Four," she said after a moment. "And I get to do the 'fair is foul' speech."

"Five," Daphne countered. "And you've got to check on the chickens while you're out there."

"Deal," Viola said and turned to her siblings. "C'mon, weird sisters."

The girls bundled up and went outside. I followed Daphne into the kitchen and started unloading recipe ingredients from the grocery bags I'd brought. Daphne made coffee. A moment later, Juliet popped in, her hair sleek and shining, wearing a sweater and wool skirt with cute brown riding boots.

"Gotta run, but do I look okay?" she asked.

"Fantastic! Good luck!" Daphne made a kiss noise at her. Juliet grinned and disappeared.

"What was that about?"

"Juliet has an interview. She's applying for a summer internship at the state capitol this summer."

"Yeah? That's great!"

Daphne pressed the brew button on the coffee maker. "When The Sloth heard she might be going away, he got all pissed and gave her an ultimatum—him or Madison. She told him to have a nice summer."

Daphne threw up her hands.

"Hallelujah! Thought she'd never get rid of that loser!"

"Good for her! It's about time," I said.

"Sure is. And I've got you to thank for it. Your talk at the high school really inspired her."

Daphne opened the cupboard and pulled out two coffee mugs, humming to herself.

"You seem awfully happy today," I said as I started unwrapping the sixteen sticks of butter that would be required to make four pans of bars—no wonder they taste so good. "Is this just because of Juliet? Or is something else going on?"

Daphne's eyes danced. She pressed her lips together and blew up her cheeks like a squirrel hoarding nuts, as if she was bursting to share her news.

"So you remember the truck driver who kept stopping into the store to buy jerky and M&M'S?"

"Daphne, no! You made a deal with yourself, remember? No more giant panda! You can't afford to get pregnant now, and even if you could, where would you put another baby? You're out of bedrooms."

"No! It's not like that," Daphne said, grinning as she filled the coffee mugs and handed one to me.

"His name is Myron. He's from North Carolina, but spends most of his time on the road. Anyway, he came into the store last week and bought some jerky like he always does, and we chatted a little bit like we always do, and then he asked me if he could take me out for a cup of coffee after work, and I said okay."

Daphne pulled a chair out from the kitchen table and sat down. I left the butter to soften and went to join her, sipping coffee as she continued her story.

"So," she said in a hurried and breathless voice, leaning toward me, "we walked over to the doughnut place and got some coffee and talked, and then he asked me if I wanted to see his truck."

"Let me guess. His truck has a sleeper cab."

"It does," she confirmed. "But I climbed in anyway because he's really cute and nice and, by that time, I was feeling a little . . . well, you know."

"Not good," I said and blew on my coffee. Daphne went on with her story, ignoring my comment.

"So we get in the cab and he shows me the controls and how the radio and the refrigeration system works and then asks if I want to see the sleeper and I said okay—" I started to scold and she lifted her hand to stop me. "Hang on. Let me finish. Anyway, we climb in there. I just thought it would be a bed, but he customized it so there's cabinets and a kitchenette and a sofa and even a shelf for books! And what do I see on his shelf?" she asked, her eyes sparkling in anticipation of my answer.

"No," I said, *thunking* my coffee cup down on the kitchen table. "No way!"

Daphne bobbed her head excitedly. "Yes! Yes way! *The Complete Works of William Shakespeare!*"

"I can't believe it."

"It's true! He had the sonnets and everything! Well, the second I saw those books, I went into full-bore, hard-core panda mode. I grabbed him and kissed him like there was no tomorrow. And then do you know what happened?"

"Well, yeah," I said. "But I'd just as soon you didn't share the details."

She shook her head hard, like a dog just come in from the rain.

"Uh-uh! No! I kissed him and he kissed me back, but just for a second. Then he pulled back and said that he thinks I'm beautiful, but he doesn't believe in premarital sex. Myron is a Baptist!"

"He's a . . . and you didn't?" Daphne bobbed her head again. "Really? And you're happy about that?"

"I know it sounds crazy, but it makes me feel like he's interested in *me*." She pressed her palms urgently to her breast. "That he's interested in who I am, and what I like, and what I think—not in how quickly he can get me on my back. And do you want to hear something else? Something amazing?"

I nodded.

"He said he'd like to take me out to dinner the next time he comes through town. He said he'd like to take me out *every* time he's in town! And this summer, he wants to take me to the Shakespeare festival in Bailey's Harbor. And *then* he said he'd like to be my boyfriend. Can you believe that? He actually used the word—'boyfriend'!"

She laughed, looking younger and happier than I'd ever seen her look before.

"Well, for a minute I just thought he was crazy. But I figured I knew how to bring him back to earth quick, so I broke the news to him; told him I had four daughters. Do you know he didn't even blink an eye? He just said we'd have to get more tickets for the plays!"

"He did? Daphne, that's wonder—"

I wasn't able to finish; she talked right over me.

"Isn't it? We sat in there for the longest time, talking. He told me about growing up in North Carolina, getting baptized in the same river where he caught catfish when he was little, and how he got laid off from his job in an auto factory and decided to go into business for himself driving trucks. I told him all about my life, and the girls having four different dads, and just . . . just everything! And he just listened.

"And then! You won't believe this, Lucy. He sat there and read sonnets to me. Sonnets! He's got this deep voice; it's like thunder rolling in across the bay. You know, I always thought that English accents were sexy, but until you've had a man with a beard and a deep voice and a North Carolina drawl read Sonnet one-sixteen to you, you don't know what sexy is. Oh, Lucy! I am in love! For the first time in my life, really and truly!"

She clamped her hand to her heart, closed her eyes, and threw back her head, enraptured.

" 'This is the very ecstasy of love:/Whose violent property fordoes itself/And leads the will to desperate undertakings/As oft as any passion under heaven/That does afflict our natures. . . .' "

"*Romeo and Juliet*?"

"*Hamlet.*"

She popped her head up and opened her eyes and giggled.

"You think I've lost my mind, don't you?"

I did a little. But she was happy, so why say something to spoil it?

"Well," she went on, "maybe I have. But I never, ever thought I'd fall in love. Heck, I never even *wanted* to fall in love! At least, that's what I told myself."

Daphne's voice grew softer, as did the gleam in her eyes, softening but not dimming, the giddy girlishness of the moment before replaced by an expression that was reflective and mature but still slightly amazed.

"I didn't believe that there could be somebody

out there who was really right for me—a man who was handsome and kind and decent and real, and a good listener. A man who cares about the things I care about, shares my interests. A man who loves kids and Shakespeare. And me. I mean, what are the chances of finding a guy like that? A million to one, right?"

"Two million."

Daphne wrapped her hands around her coffee cup and nodded slowly, her gaze shifting to a distant spot somewhere past my shoulder.

"Two million," she mused. "Like winning the lottery without ever buying a ticket. What are the chances? I know this is crazy. I hardly know him, even though it feels like I've known him forever. Maybe he'll change his mind about me. Maybe I'll never even see him again. And if I do—if he does come back and he doesn't change his mind and this thing turns out to be the real thing—it would change my whole life. And his . . . It's crazy. A chance in a million. Two million! But when the chance comes along, and you find that somebody who fits you so fine, like a hand in a glove, you'd be crazy not to take it."

Her eyes shifted back to mine, as though she'd just remembered I was sitting there, and she grabbed my hand across the table. "Am I right?"

"You are," I said, unable to keep the rasp from my voice. I squeezed her hand. "Absolutely right."

• • •

After we finished the baking, made pizza for the kids, and cleaned up the kitchen, Daphne and I drove over to the library to get ready for the meeting. Rinda met us there, and Lloyd came along too. He started trying to help me set up the chairs, but Rinda put a stop to that.

"Lloyd, are you crazy!" she snapped. "Put that down and come help me with the food!"

He grinned, gave me a "What can I do?" look, and went to help his wife.

"Lucy," Rinda called to me over her shoulder, "where are the napkins?"

"Celia's supposed to bring some from the discount store. Guess she's running late."

Rinda grunted and went back to work, grumbling the whole time at poor Lloyd, who just smiled and kept putting cookies on platters.

"Can you believe he spent twenty years in the Marines?" Daphne whispered to me. I shook my head and we both laughed—quietly.

We planned to set up about forty folding chairs, but when Mrs. Lieshout came in, breathless and nervous and wheeling a podium, and said that they'd been getting calls about the meeting all day, we decided to set up fifteen more chairs, just in case. And sure enough, when seven o'clock rolled around, every one of those seats was occupied. We had to set up six more for latecomers.

Mrs. Lieshout ran the meeting well, kept things moving along in an orderly fashion, as I'd known she would. People posed intelligent questions, were highly motivated without being hysterical, and were eager to pitch in. After some discussion, they settled on a three-prong attack consisting of a petition drive with people volunteering to take shifts on the sidewalk near the market to collect signatures, a letter citing specific economic concerns to be drafted and signed by the local merchants and sent to the village council, and a phone tree to alert others to the issues and encourage them to show up when the question came before the council, sometime after the New Year.

Of course, I would be long gone by then, but that was all right. With Mrs. Lieshout firmly at the helm and with so many energetic volunteers at the ready, I was certain that the council would have to put a stop to the demolition and that Rinda would be able to keep her job and her house.

My work was done here.

❦ Chapter 38 ❦

The meeting adjourned around eight-forty and still Celia hadn't shown up. I tried texting and phoning, but got no answer.

"Could she have been in an accident?" I asked Daphne as we were refolding all those folding chairs.

Daphne shook her head. "No. We'd have heard something. You said she was going to get together with a friend?" I nodded. "Maybe they were having fun and she lost track of the time. Or maybe she forgot the meeting was tonight. You know how flaky Celia can be."

"Flaky, but not that flaky," I said. "We talked about it just this morning. She was going to post more flyers for me, buy the napkins, and bring them to the meeting. She's been such a help all week and she's really worried about what will happen to Rinda if she loses her job. She wouldn't have forgotten. I know she wouldn't. Seriously, what if something happened? What if she met up with Pat and decided to move back in with him?"

Daphne placed another chair in the rack and stopped to consider this. "No. She wouldn't do that," she said, but I could tell by the look on her face that she wasn't really sure about that.

In the end, there was nothing left to do but go home. We'd driven in Daphne's car, so she dropped me off. When we pulled into the driveway, the lights were on and Celia's car was parked near the garage.

"See?" Daphne said. "She probably dropped by the house after seeing her friend, got involved painting something or quilting something, and totally forgot about the meeting. She *is* that flaky!"

"Guess so," I said with a smile, and then got out of the car.

When I went inside, the living room, dining room, and kitchen lights were all on, but Celia was nowhere to be seen. I went from room to room, shutting off the unneeded lights and feeling a little annoyed. I was happy to have Celia stay with me and I didn't want any rent, but electricity is expensive and I didn't appreciate her wasting it. I'd have to talk to her about that later.

I heard the sound of footsteps overhead and went upstairs.

"Celia!" I called as I reached the top of the staircase and started walking down the hall to my parents' old room. "Are you all right? You missed the meeting. And you really should have been there. It was great. We had over sixty people! Mr. and Mrs. Binder are going to head up a petition drive and . . ."

I stopped in the doorway. An open suitcase, half filled with clothing, was lying on the bed. Celia stood in front of the chest of drawers with her back to me.

Oh, no. She *was* moving back in with Pat!

"Celia," I said and came into the room. "Celia, don't. You can't go back to Pat. He's got a serious problem, and if you go back to him, it'll just make it easier for him to avoid dealing with it. Remember what Rinda said? How it takes some time before . . ."

Celia turned around to face me. Her eyes were red from crying.

"I'm not moving back in with Pat," she said, her voice surprisingly strong in spite of her tears. "But I can't stay here anymore. Not now that I know what you're up to."

"What I'm up to? What are you talking about?"

"About that," she snapped and pointed to a photocopy of a drawing, a pen-and-ink architectural schematic.

"What is it?" I asked. Celia crossed her arms over her chest and glared at me. I picked up the sheet of paper and looked closer.

It was for some kind of town house development, eight total units contained in two buildings, three stories with garages on the bottom and patio decks on the upper floors. There were paths and a pool, and next to the pool, a clubhouse. The clubhouse windows were tall and wide with striped awnings and there was a porch with stocky stone columns, giving the building a sort of pseudo–Craftsman style, but the walls, the foot-print of the building, were familiar. I looked down at the lower left corner and saw the words "Lakeview Village" written in block letters.

"Where did you get this?"

"My friend Krista works for an architecture firm. Peninsula Property Professionals is one of their big clients." Celia raised one eyebrow in a sort of "gotcha" glance and then turned to the dresser and continued emptying it.

"Krista knew Alice, too, got a kitten from her a couple of years ago. And she knew that Alice was my friend. We met up for a drink and I was telling her all about how Pat threw me out, and how you guys helped me get my stuff, and that you were letting me live with you. And then she pulled *that* out of her purse."

Celia dumped an armload of clothes into the suitcase and shut the lid, pressing down hard so she could close the zipper, then set the suitcase on the floor.

"You said that the developer was going to leave Alice's cottage the way it was. How could you lie to us like that?"

"I . . . I didn't lie to you. I didn't know anything about this. Mr. Glazier said that he wouldn't tear down the cottage or change the exterior walls, and he said, with the lot being so large, he'd probably have to build more than one house, but he never . . ."

I spread out my hands helplessly. The drawing fell, fluttering to the floor like a desiccated autumn leaf. "Celia, I didn't know anything about this."

"Sure you didn't," she scoffed. She walked to the door, carrying her suitcase, and then turned to face me. "How could you not know? You're always so on top of everything, always so in control. There is no way this could have slipped past you.

"You're such a hypocrite!" she cried, her eyes swimming with tears. "All the baloney you fed us about wanting to guard the character of the town and the lifestyle of the peninsula being more important than money! And about how you hated to sell the cottage, but you just had to, because it was your duty to go to Washington and help the president fix the country and save the world and—"

"Celia, that's not fair! I never said anything like that!"

"Maybe not," she said petulantly, the tears spilling over and running down her cheeks, "but you made it sound like that. You said that even though you had to sell, you'd make sure that Alice's cottage, that her memory, would be protected. But you lied! Maybe the walls of the cottage will still be there, but it'll be crawling with cars and people and noise. They'll put in parking lots and take out the trees and block the

414

view. But you won't care because you'll have pocketed your money and skipped town!"

She sniffled and swiped her hand across her eyes. Her voice was angry.

"On that first night after you cut your hand, Daphne had to talk us into coming over here and helping you with your quilt. She said we should give you a break because you were lonely and sad, and that different people show their grief in different ways. But Rinda said it was all an act. She said that if you'd really cared about Alice, you'd have come to see her a long time ago and that you'd only shown up because you knew there'd be money in it for you. Rinda was right. You never cared about Alice! You don't care about anybody!"

"That is not true." I was trying to keep the edge from my voice, but it wasn't easy. Celia didn't know what she was talking about.

"I took care of Alice for *years* after our parents died. I took her on vacations and talked to her almost every single day. I made sure she was safe and that she had everything she needed. I deposited money into her account every month, even though it meant I couldn't afford to buy a home of my own. And even though it hurt when my parents left everything to Alice, the house and the car and absolutely everything, I didn't fight that. I could have, but I didn't."

"Why would you?" Celia spat. "Alice was the

one who was really hurt. She couldn't take care of herself all alone, but you could. You had everything you needed!"

"Not everything," I said. "I needed my parents' love. I never had that, but Alice did. She had all of it."

Celia made a face of disgust and swiped at her eyes with the back of her hand. "So you took that out on Alice? You never came to visit her because you were mad at your parents?"

"No! It had nothing to do with Alice! I never came back here because I *hated* this place! Alice said I was remembering wrong, but she was the one who didn't remember. The accident wiped everything clean for her. She couldn't remember, but I *could*. And I do! No matter how hard I try not to. I'll never be free of those memories!"

I swallowed hard and shook my head from side to side. "You don't know what you're talking about, Celia. They weren't your parents and you weren't there. I never took *anything* out on Alice, never. I've spent the last twenty years of my life trying to make it up to . . ."

I stopped in midsentence, screwed my eyes shut, and lifted my hand to Celia's face. It wasn't her business. She didn't know. She couldn't understand. And I didn't have to explain myself to her. I wouldn't.

"Believe me or don't believe me," I said evenly. "I don't care. But I'm telling you the truth.

416

When Mr. Glazier told me about his plans for developing the property, I had no idea this was what he had in mind."

"I don't believe you," Celia said. "Not anymore. Neither will anyone else."

She picked up her suitcase and walked down the hall and the stairs and out the door. I didn't try to stop her.

❧ Chapter 39 ❧

I went to bed feeling pretty rotten and, not surprisingly, woke up the same way. The house was so quiet without Celia. Amazing how quickly I'd gotten used to her presence.

Standing next to the coffee maker with Dave and Freckles winding around my legs, waiting for the pot to fill enough so I could sneak a cup, I decided that I wasn't going to give in to gloom. I would go about my day as if nothing had happened, do the things I'd planned to do, beginning with the Christmas tree.

Celia and I had bought a tree from the Kiwanis lot earlier in the week and had planned to decorate it and the rest of the house after the meeting at the library. I'd just go ahead and do it on my own. I thought about calling Barney and inviting him to come over for dinner, but then remembered he was at a fruit growers' conference. Well, maybe I'd work on my new quilt instead. Or rent a movie and make popcorn. Or try out my new snowshoes. A little exercise would do me good. One way or another, I was going to salvage the day.

After drinking my coffee and feeding the cats, I built a fire in the fireplace, found some Christmas music on the radio, and set to it. Getting the tree to stand up straight in the stand was a little tough to manage on my own—I really should have stuck with that five-foot tree instead of letting those guys from Kiwanis talk me into a seven-footer—but it all worked out.

I untangled the lights, wrapping them carefully and evenly on the branches so there were no bare spots, and then put on the ornaments, making sure that the fragile and expensive glass ones were placed near the top, out of paws' reach. The cats, Freckles in particular, were already showing a dangerous fascination with the decorations on the lower branches.

I had just put on the last ornament and plugged in the lights, and was standing back to admire the effect, when the doorbell rang. Peeking through the window, I saw Peter at the door. The sight of him standing there lifted my spirits a little. Maybe it wasn't too late to make things up between us.

I greeted him with a smile and invited him inside, asked if he had time for coffee. He accepted, but seemed nervous while I prepared a fresh pot, taking his hands in and out of his pockets and clearing his throat.

His discomfort was understandable. We hadn't parted on very good terms, but I was ready to overlook that. I'd been thinking about him an . . . well, I'd been thinking about a lot of things since I'd seen him at the festival. I figured that his sudden appearance meant he'd been doing the same thing.

There was so much I wanted to say to him, speeches I'd been mentally rehearsing for the last day or two, but he was the one who had taken the initiative, so I thought it would be better—and yes, less embarrassing for me—to let him speak first. Then, as soon as he broached the subject, I'd jump in and let him off the hook, and we could move on from there as if nothing had happened and make a fresh start. But he certainly was taking his time working up to it.

Waiting for the coffee to drip, we made small talk about the weather and how we couldn't believe that it was only a few days until Christmas. He was nice enough to ask how things had gone at the meeting and said he was happy it had gone well, which, in light of our last conversation, was big of him.

I filled two mugs with coffee and set them on the table along with a plate of leftover bars in case he was feeling hungry.

"So," I said with what I hoped was an encouraging smile, "is this just a social call? Or is there something you wanted to talk to me about?"

He took a big gulp of coffee, as if he were trying to fortify himself for what was to come next.

"Yes, there is. But first, I want you to know that I . . ."

He stopped for a second and looked up at the ceiling, clearly at a loss as to how to begin. It was really kind of sweet.

He cleared his throat and tried again. "Lucy, before I say what I've come to say, I want to tell you that I'm sorry."

I smiled. "You don't have to apologize. I think we both said some things we wish we hadn't, so let's just call it a wash and move forward. Okay? I'm pretty sure I already know what you're here to say anyway."

Peter tilted his head to the side, giving me a quizzical frown.

"No, I don't think you do." He took a breath. "What I wanted to say is that I'm sorry I couldn't be more forthright with you about this before, but, professionally, I really couldn't talk to you about it. But something has happened to change that."

"Professionally? So, this has something to do with Alice?"

"Yes." He took an even bigger gulp of coffee. "As you know, Alice hired me to create a will for her. But that wasn't the only thing she asked me to do for her. When she first came to see me, right after I moved home to Nilson's Bay and started my practice, it was because she wanted me to help her find someone."

He looked at me for a moment, as if hoping that I'd take it from there, but I honestly had no idea what he was talking about.

"She wanted me to find Maeve," he said.

It took a second for his meaning to fully sink in.

"But . . . but I asked you if she'd ever mentioned anyone named Maeve and you said she hadn't."

"No," Peter said, his eyes solemn and his voice even, "I said that I couldn't say that I had. And it was true; I couldn't. Alice told me about Maeve in confidence, as her attorney, and because of that—"

"You knew? And you didn't tell me? Not even when I came right out and asked?" Peter started to answer, but I didn't give him the chance. I wasn't in the mood to listen to any more lawyer-speak. "What right do you have to keep secrets about *my* sister?"

"Because they were Alice's secrets, not yours!"

His raised voice and the sudden flash of his eyes startled me into silence. He took a couple of breaths and went on, his voice low and deliberate.

"Even after her death, unless there was some

421

compelling reason to do otherwise, I had a duty to keep her confidence."

"And now there's a compelling reason?"

"Maeve is Alice's daughter."

My mouth dropped open. For a moment, I forgot to breathe.

"Her daughter? Is this some kind of joke? Alice was never pregnant. She never even had a boyfriend! Not after the accident."

"Yes, she did," he said. "Well, I assume there was a boyfriend. Honestly, it could have just been some guy who took advantage of her. Alice never wanted to talk about it. You know how she was."

I started to nod, but then realized that maybe I really didn't know how Alice was.

"She never shared more than the basic facts," Peter said. "All I know is that she got pregnant while she was away at school, working on her veterinary tech certification. Your parents convinced her that she couldn't keep it, that she wasn't capable of taking care of a baby, and made arrangements for her to go away to have the baby and then give it up for adoption. They told her that she could never tell anyone about it, not even you. They said if people knew it would make the family look bad and hurt your dad's practice."

I let out an incredulous huff. They didn't need Alice's help with that. Dad had been perfectly capable of hurting his practice all on his own.

"Alice was always sad about giving her baby

up for adoption," Peter continued. "She thought about her all the time. After a couple of years, she became so depressed that she tried to kill herself."

I'd always known about that part. Mom had found her lying on the floor, unconscious. She called me from the emergency room, completely hysterical. I told her everything was going to be okay, even though I didn't know if it was, but somebody had to calm her down. I packed a bag and went to the airport, but before I could board the plane, Mom called again and said that Alice was awake and would be all right, but they were transferring her to a psychiatric hospital and that she wouldn't be allowed visitors, so I shouldn't come after all. Alice was in the hospital for three weeks and I sent postcards almost every day, most with pictures of animals, but she never answered. After she was released, she didn't want to talk about it. Neither did my parents, even when I asked my mother directly.

"That was the first time she'd ever told anyone about the baby," Peter said, "during that time in the hospital. Alice said it made her feel better just to be able to talk to someone about it. The doctor said that even though Alice wasn't in contact with Maeve, she might want to make something for her—"

"The quilts," I whispered.

And the drawings too. Though she hadn't inscribed them, I knew without being told that the dozens upon dozens of drawings were of Alice's daughter, the way she had imagined her for all those years as a baby, a toddler, a girl, a teen, and the life they might have had together.

"So she made a quilt for every year of Maeve's life," I said, "hoping that someday she would find her and be able to give them to her in person."

"That's right," Peter said. "After I moved back to Nilson's Bay, she came to my office and asked if I could help her get in contact with Maeve. I tried," Peter said earnestly, "but it was a closed adoption, so I couldn't track her down. I did help Alice register with several reunion registries. It was a long shot, but I hoped that once Maeve turned eighteen, assuming she even knew she was adopted, she might go searching for her birth mother. Now she has. Maeve—her name is Jennifer now—called my office yesterday."

I started to cry. How could I not?

Everything about Alice's life and death, her unfulfilled promise and longing, and the secrets she'd felt she had to keep, even from me, was not as tragic as knowing that the child she had carried and borne but never known and, yet, who was never far from her heart, not even for a day, had finally come looking for her. But come too late.

I pressed my hand hard against my mouth, barricading the sobs that threatened to escape. My shoulders shuddered with silent convulsions as the tears trailed down my cheeks. Peter moved his chair back, as if he might come to comfort me, but I raised my arm to warn him away. I didn't want to be comforted. I didn't want him.

"Why?" I choked when I was finally able to speak. "Dear God, why now? Why let her die before she had a chance to meet her daughter? What was the point?"

When God shared no answer, I posed the question to Peter. He offered no explanation either, just sat there helplessly.

"I thought . . ." he said hesitantly, casting his eyes over his shoulder as if embarrassed by my tears, or perhaps by his inability to stop them. "I thought you'd want to meet her, to give her the quilts. She's coming up the day after tomorrow. I made a lunch reservation for you at the Harbor Fish Market in Bailey's Harbor. It's quiet there and I thought you'd prefer that to—"

"You should have told me about her before," I said, as the tears of my grief grew hotter and harder, turning to anger.

He turned his head toward me, his gaze steady and final. "I couldn't."

"You should have gotten Alice to tell me. If she'd just have told me, then—"

"I tried to, but she wouldn't . . ." He stopped himself. His lips became a line. "She wouldn't do it."

"You should have made her!"

His eyes flashed and he slammed his hands hard against the table, shoved his chair back, and sprang to his feet, his body unfolding sharp and fast like a jackknife ready to slice.

For a moment I thought he would shout back and I was glad. I wanted him to be as angry as I was, to feel what I was feeling, to know his own failure the way I knew mine. But he didn't shout. Instead his voice became low, hard, and cutting.

"I couldn't make Alice do, or feel, or see *anything*. Not any more than I can you. I don't know what more you expect of me, Lucy. I don't know what you want."

I shook my head, turned my face to the wall. When I turned back, he was gone.

❧ Chapter 40 ❧

It came back that night, the dream.

It had been at least three weeks since I'd walked across the white plain and the earth had opened up, swallowing me whole, plunging me into the icy, suffocating depths, but Celia's harangue summoned it back into being, in the extended version that came to me shortly before Alice's death, the dream where she saves me, but then, the tables turning, I am unable to save her. And this time, there was something more.

Unable to grab hold and haul Alice back to the surface, I put my head into the hole and then slipped through to follow her, my arms stretched out and pointed purposely toward the abyss. I couldn't see Alice, but I knew she was just ahead of me, somewhere, hidden in the black. I was frozen with cold and nearly out of air, and frightened, knowing that, in a moment, I wouldn't be able to stop myself from opening my mouth and trying to breathe, that I could not override eons of instinct, and that doing so would mark the end. And I was right.

With my lungs about to burst, my mouth opened in a desperate gasp. I was flooded by water and fear and relief. Terrible relief. And a single thought that shone quicksilver bright in my brain.

Just let it be over.

I woke with a start, the way I had on that night when Alice's final phone call splintered my dream, but this time there was no rude ringing phone and no patient and persistent sister, begging me to come home and remember rightly.

And still, it wasn't over. It never would be. Not unless I figured out a way to finish it.

❧ Chapter 41 ❧

Though I had never in my life needed wise counsel more than I did that day, there wasn't anyone to talk to. Celia and the rest of the FOA were obviously not speaking to me, and I wasn't speaking to Peter. Barney was away at his conference, and Joe Feeney was on a flight to Los Angeles, probably to meet with his deep-pocket developer client.

I even tried getting hold of Jenna, not that I thought she'd have much to offer or add, but I was desperate to talk to someone—anyone. My own thoughts and uncertainties were circling in a continuous loop, as pointless as a dog chasing its own tail.

Finally, I got into the car and started driving with no particular destination in mind, just wanting to get out of the house and outrun the tangle of emotions that clung to me like spider-webs. I drove out to the lighthouse, now closed for the winter, then turned around and drove back, went past the turn for the house and back through town, passing the town hall, the market, the bookshop, the library, and The Library. I nearly passed St. Agnes's too. But then, suddenly, without really knowing why, I took a sharp, hard right, turning so quickly that the rear tires fishtailed and almost hit the curb.

The big oak doors to the church were unlocked, but heavy. I had to pull with both hands to open them.

I went inside, hearing my footsteps echo against the stone floor, breathing in the church scent of my childhood, a perfume mixed from dust and candle wax and damp wool. The dim winter sun coming through the banks of stained glass windows bathed the walls and floors in dull red, gold, and blue. The doors swung closed behind me with a soft but solid *thump*. I walked up the center aisle and, four pews from the front, crossed myself and sat down on the right-hand side.

It was incredibly quiet and still. I had a sudden feeling of—I don't quite know how to describe it—of expectation, I guess. As though I'd been summoned for an audience with some ancient and august monarch.

I sat there, waiting for something to happen. Nothing did.

After a few minutes I glanced down to my right and saw a book lying on the pew next to me, a copy of Augustine's *Confessions*—a book my mother had pored over constantly. It was still there, sitting in the bookcase at the cottage. I'd never opened it, but now I did and began to read. . . .

For it is thou, O Lord, who judgest me. For although no man "knows the things of a man, save the spirit of the man which is in him," yet there is something of man which "the spirit of the man which is in him" does not know itself. But thou, O Lord, who madest him, knowest him completely. . . . Therefore, as long as I journey away from thee, I am more present with myself than with thee. . . . I would therefore confess what I know about myself; I will also confess what I do not know about myself. What I do know of myself, I know from thy enlightening of me; and what I do not know of myself, I will continue not to know until the time when my "darkness is as the noonday" in thy sight.

The things I knew about myself, the things I had journeyed so long and hard to escape, had pursued me just the same. The actions I'd refused to acknowledge and memories I'd tried to expunge are written with indelible ink. I could not erase them. God knows I tried.

God knows. So who am I running from?

The answer was suddenly clear. Only myself.

There was a *click-click-click* and the overhead lights illuminated in three groups—back, center, and front. Father Damon's voice echoed off the high ceiling and limestone walls.

"Lucy? Is that you?"

He walked up the aisle and I quickly swiped at my eyes with the back of my hand.

"I was just coming to hear confessions. I don't get many takers in winter; maybe it's too cold to sin," he said. "But just the same, I'm here every Wednesday from noon to one. Just in case someone needs me."

He stopped at the end of the pew and turned to face me.

"Is there something I can help you with, Lucy?"

I told him everything. Not just about Peter and Celia and Maeve, but everything, the things I had never told anyone. We didn't go into the confessional; it was too late to hide behind a screen. Instead, we sat turned toward each other in the pew, face-to-face, talking. Actually, I did most of the talking. Father Damon responded now and then or urged me to go on, but mostly he just listened. There was a lot to listen to.

On that day, the day of the picnic, I'd had this plan—this stupid, childish plan—to get Peter's attention. I took the tip money I'd made at the restaurant, everything I'd earned for a month, and bought a bikini from one of those expensive boutiques in Fish Creek where the tourists go. It cost me a fortune and it was tiny and my mother would have had a fit if she saw it. I knew that so I hid it in the bottom drawer of my dresser, underneath a bunch of winter sweaters, because I didn't think she'd go looking in there.

She didn't. But Alice did.

She was looking for a pair of pink shorts she thought I'd borrowed, found the bikini, and showed it to Mom. Mom was furious and she yelled at me. And Alice? Alice just stood there, right behind Mom's right shoulder where she knew I could see, smirking.

I was angry. I was so, *so* angry. Not so much because she'd ratted me out, but because she enjoyed doing it. And also because, after Mom went off to church and Alice and I drove to the Tielens' house for the picnic, she kept teasing me about it, needling me about trying to flaunt myself and saying that, just because I'd finally grown a pair, did I really think that the boys were going to take any notice of me? And that even if they did, it would only be because they'd be hoping to cop a feel and that I'd be making a fool of myself, parading around in that outfit.

I'm not sure I could have put it into words back then, but I think I'd been anticipating the picnic as the day of my transformation. Not just the day when I'd capture Peter's attention—though I wanted that, too—but the day when I would become someone . . . different. Someone that other people wouldn't be able to overlook anymore. But Alice spoiled it for me, made me doubt myself, made me afraid that everything she'd said was true. That's why I was so angry. At that moment, I honestly think I hated her.

Of course, it was silly to think that a new bathing suit was going to change the course of my life, but I was sixteen. At sixteen you still believe in transformation. And I wasn't really wrong. In a sense, that bikini did change my life. Alice's too.

I wish I'd never laid eyes on it.

I was starting to feel that way even before we arrived at the picnic, but it was too late by then. The bikini was the only thing I had on under my shorts and top, and it was so incredibly hot. I told Denise I wanted to sit down on the far side, away from the crowd, but mostly away from Alice and her friends, who were already sitting there like a flock of fat hens, looking at me and snickering in a way that would make it clear that I was the one they were laughing at.

All of a sudden I thought, *Screw them!* I whipped off my top, stood there with my hands on my hips, and just stared daggers at them. After a minute or so of that, they started looking away and then turned their backs, trying to pretend I didn't exist. I stood there for a while more, just to make them miserable. While I was doing that, of course, everybody got a good look at my new bikini and my new bod, especially the boys.

It wasn't like they suddenly started swarming; they were more subtle than that. But not a lot more. I could feel their eyes on me.

At first I felt embarrassed. But after a little while I realized that the boys, unlike Alice and her crowd, weren't laughing at me. If anything, they were drooling. I was enjoying their reaction, the sense of power it gave me. For a minute, it felt like my fantasy was coming true, that this really was the day of my transformation.

The fantasy didn't last long.

I stretched myself out on the towel, making it even easier for the boys, and Peter in particular, to get a good look. Denise was sitting next to me, jabbering away about boys and sex, the two topics that dominated about 80 percent of her conversations. She was going on again, like she always did, about how I was probably the last virgin in our grade.

In retrospect, I realize that wasn't true, but at the time I actually believed her. It made me feel backward, as though I were wearing a really ugly outfit that I needed to shed as quickly as possible. But at the same time, I really didn't want to go through with it. I wanted that first time to be special, and everything Denise was describing to me sounded like the exact opposite of that, just steamy and sticky and cheap.

Anyway, I was starting to rethink the whole idea.

I wanted the boys—well, one boy, Peter—to notice me, but I wanted him to notice *me*. Not just my boobs and my body. But when he jumped out of the water and I saw that he was . . . aroused, I started remembering all the things that Alice had said in the car on the way over and I felt embarrassed and even angrier than I had before.

It was so ridiculous—it was just sister stuff, an older sister putting the younger in her place, the way siblings have done since the beginning of time, but for me, right then, it was more than that. It felt like she'd ruined everything, not just the day, but the whole way I saw myself in it. And the way I saw other people too. I suddenly felt like I couldn't trust my feelings for anyone else, or their feelings for me, and that I never could again.

Later, right after lunch, I saw Alice talking to Peter, flirting with him. She was doing it just to get to me, and it did. I walked over and challenged her to race me to the dock at the far side of the lake.

I don't know why I thought that was the way to get back at her, but at the time, it seemed like it was. Of course, Alice took me up on it. She was a much better swimmer than I was. She was probably the best in the whole school, as she was the best at so many things. But I was determined to redeem the day she had ruined for me and, for once, to be better than my sister.

We got into the water up to our ankles and everybody gathered on the shore to watch. Peter wished me good luck, but I'm sure he didn't think I had a chance. Nobody did.

Somebody shouted, "Go!" We dove into the water, and sure enough, Alice shot past me. I think she was swimming as fast as she'd ever swum, but so was I. All that fury I was feeling coursed through my arms and legs, making them whir like well-oiled pistons. Nothing could stop me. I wasn't going to give up for anything!

I sensed that I was closing the gap, could feel the flutter of Alice's kicks troubling the water just ahead of me. That's when I started to hear it, the muffled sound of voices, of clapping and cheering, getting louder as I came closer and threatened to rob Alice's lead. The sound affected me like a syringe full of adrenaline, filled me with an energy and determination I'd never had before.

Though my arms were aching and my lungs felt ready to burst, I kept swimming, faster than ever. I could feel Alice next to me, could sense her presence and her desire to stay ahead. We battled side by side for a few seconds until, finally, I passed her.

And when I did, she suddenly just wasn't there anymore. I didn't know if I was getting faster or if she'd just given up, but it didn't matter. I kept going, buoyed by the euphoria of knowing I had bested my sister and the roar of the crowd thrumming in my ears, a roar that got louder and more frenetic with each passing moment.

I thought they were cheering for me. I truly did.

It wasn't until I reached the finish, grabbed the dock with both hands, and then leapt up and thrust my fist into the air in triumph that I understood that the frenzied shouting from the shore didn't signal excitement at my victory, but terror at my sister's disappearance.

The instant I knew what was happening, I joined in the search, but it took so long before she was found; she was under the water for so long. . . . I was too slow. Too late. Too busy beating her to even notice what had happened to her.

After they dragged Alice from the water and laid her on the shore, after she finally started breathing, the paramedics wouldn't let me ride with her. There wasn't room in the ambulance. Mr. Tielens drove me and followed right behind, those red lights flashing in my eyes like a strobe.

My parents arrived in separate cars, but at nearly the same moment. I'm not sure how long it was after I got there, but not a long time. I was still in my swimsuit, my hair dripping, my T-shirt sticking to me.

Mom started asking me questions, but I couldn't answer. I was crying too hard. The doctor came into the waiting room, told us that Alice was alive, but the prognosis wasn't good. He said there was always hope, but he didn't look like he believed it.

When the doctor left, Dad turned on me and started screaming, louder than he ever had screamed at me before, calling me all sorts of filthy names, pointing to my wet shirt, which was almost transparent over my breasts, screaming at me, "Where were you? Where were you? She saved you! You'd have frozen under the ice without Alice! Where *were* you?"

When she survived, everybody said it was a miracle. But in some sense, Alice—the Alice I knew—really did die that day. The Alice I knew was smart and quick and competitive, and, sometimes, a little bit cruel. Not often, but often enough. It wasn't a cruelty that was out of the ordinary for a teenage girl, an older sister trying to keep a younger sister in her place; even at the time I knew so, but that doesn't mean it didn't hurt.

Sometimes, when a person dies young, her survivors unconsciously revise her history, choosing to recall only what was good, the acts of kindness and inclinations to nobility, beatifying her memory until she becomes in death what she never was in life: a saint.

But that wasn't what happened to Alice, not exactly.

The Alice who disappeared beneath the waters that day was not a saint, but the Alice who awoke and inhabited my sister's body after the accident was, or something near to it.

She was slow and kind and endlessly patient. She struggled and stumbled and made everyone she ever met admire her and feel ashamed of their

438

own pettiness and dissatisfactions. Me most of all.

Alice's unfailingly sweet nature and endless patience, the fact that she never complained or cast a word of blame in my direction even though I know she understood what she was like before and how much the accident triggered by my actions had narrowed her boundaries, were an ongoing reproach to me.

Before she died, Alice accused me of remembering wrong. But the truth is, I didn't want to remember at all. Remembering only reminds me of all the ways I failed her.

I can never forgive myself.

Father Damon didn't say a word, not until I finished. Then he took my hand in his. "It's God's place to forgive, Lucy. It is yours to accept that forgiveness."

"I don't know if I can believe that, Father. It seems like an out, like I'd be letting myself off the hook. If there was just something I could do, some way to make up for—"

He sighed. "Lucy, what penance could anyone require of you that you haven't already laid upon yourself? Almighty God chooses to pardon you; what right have you to reject that pardon?"

He was quiet for a moment, waiting for me to respond, I suppose. When I didn't, he said, "Do you remember the story of the woman caught in adultery in the gospel of John?"

"Not really."

"The people of the town dragged her out with the intention of stoning her to death," he said. "This was the legal sentence imposed for that crime. But Jesus put a stop to it, saying that whichever of them was without sin should cast the first stone. One by one, knowing that this was a standard they couldn't meet, the crowd dispersed.

"When they were all gone, Jesus looked at the woman, wanting to know where her accusers had gone. 'Does no one condemn you?' he asked. When she answered no, he said, 'Neither do I condemn you. Go now, and sin no more.' "

He looked at me with an expression of such compassion that I had to swallow back tears again.

"If Alice didn't accuse you and God doesn't condemn you, why are you standing stubbornly in the same spot, year after year, waiting for your stoning?"

He got up and made the sign of the cross over me, raising his voice so that the sound of it reverberated to the rafters and fell upon me like a hard and cleansing rain.

"Lucy Toomey, go and sin no more! Be joyful! Be grateful! Forgive others as you have been forgiven! Everyone—Peter and Celia and Alice, and even your mother and father. Let the past be past and the dead rest in peace. Live a life that is worthy of this love so freely given," he commanded, then repeated the words of absolution.

"Amen," I whispered and wiped my eyes one last time. "Thank you, Father."

"Lucy? One more thing. Tonight before you go to bed, and every night hereafter, get down on your knees and pray, pour out your heart to God and let him pour out his heart upon you."

He smiled. "That's not a penance, my child. It's a gift."

✖ Chapter 42 ✖

Once again, I didn't sleep much, but not because I was plagued by guilt or sorrow or bad dreams.

After I returned home, I reheated some leftover lasagna and pulled a chair up close to the window so I could eat while looking out at the frozen lake, thinking how beautiful it was in winter, and how it would be even more beautiful with the coming of spring and summer and fall.

After I rinsed my dishes, I bundled back up, went out to the woodpile, and brought in as many logs as I could carry. I started a fire in the fireplace and sat cross-legged in front of it with a glass of wine and a pile of Alice's old sketch-books, turning the pages very slowly, taking my time, marveling at her talent, missing her terribly, knowing I always would, and thinking.

I closed the last sketchbook just as the last log

split in two and fell from the grate, releasing a burst of bright orange sparks that rose into the black recesses of the chimney like a swarm of midnight fireflies. I carried my wineglass back into the kitchen, turning out lights as I went, and rinsed the glass in the sink. The tail of the Felix the Cat wall clock swung from right to left in constant rhythm and the eyes followed along, wide and unblinking, as if it were just as shocked as I was to realize it was almost morning.

After getting into bed, I closed my eyes, ready for sleep, but then remembered what Father Damon had said and rose again to kneel by the bed, saying prayers, giving thanks, asking for pardon and protection and guidance, some kind of sign, that would bring resolution and clarity to the jumbled tug-of-war that was playing out in my mind.

That was all. I got back into bed and fell immediately asleep, waking only five hours later yet feeling refreshed.

When I pushed back the quilts and looked out the window, I saw that more snow had fallen while I slept, covering the muddy tracks in the driveway, leaving every surface clean, smooth, and glittering, as if the entire world were making a fresh start.

Lunch with Maeve—I mean Jennifer—was wonderful. And kind of miraculous.

I was anxious on the drive to the restaurant, so much so that I actually felt a little nauseous. There was so much that could go wrong here. It was bound to be an emotional meeting for her. Surely she had been disappointed, even grief stricken, to have discovered her birth mother's identity only to be told that Alice had died only weeks before. She might be teary. She might ask questions I wouldn't know how to answer. She might have been raised in an unhappy home, or spent her whole life feeling unloved, unworthy, abandoned —not every adoption story turns out happily, does it? She might feel angry, bitter, resentful. She might be looking to lash out at someone. I didn't mind that so much—I could take it—but I was so afraid I wouldn't know what to say, how to comfort her. After the confrontation with Celia and then with Peter, I just didn't think I could handle one more emotional scene. And it was obvious that I was no good at all in those kinds of situations.

Driving past the sign to Bailey's Harbor, it occurred to me that I should have brought someone with me. Maybe Father Damon? He'd been a priest for something like forty years; by this time he had to know what to say in every situation, no matter how emotional. For a moment, I thought about turning the car around, driving back to Nilson's Bay, and begging him to come with me, but that would take at least twenty-five minutes and I was already five minutes late. Damn. Why hadn't I thought of bringing the priest before?

I found a parking space down the block, turned the key off in the ignition, and sat there for a few seconds, breathing deeply, trying to calm the butterflies in my stomach. It didn't really help. I was so nervous that I almost got to the door of the restaurant before realizing I'd left the bag with Alice's sketchbooks and had to go all the way back to the car to get them. While I was there, I grabbed a stack of paper napkins I had stowed in the glove compartment, thinking that, if things did get emotional and Jennifer started to cry, I could at least hand her something to wipe her eyes.

Arriving at the door a second time, I felt another jolt of panic as I realized that I had no idea what Jennifer looked like. Judging from the number of cars parked on the street, the restaurant was crowded. How would I know her?

As it turned out, the restaurant was only moderately full, but the bar, which stands at the front of the old building, was doing a brisk business, hosting a company Christmas party. I walked past the big aquarium by the door, pushing my way through clusters of chattering coworkers enjoying holiday cheer and trays of appetizers, until I reached the reservation desk in the restaurant.

"Reservation for Toomey," I told the woman at

the desk. "Sorry, I'm a little late. Has my guest arrived?"

She ran her finger down a list of names and frowned. "Toomey?" I nodded in confirmation. "Oh, wait. Your guest arrived a few minutes ago, but she didn't want to sit down without you. She said she'd wait for you out front."

I looked back over my shoulder, scanning the crowded room, half of whom were youngish-looking women. "Any idea which one? We've never met before."

"Over there," the hostess said, pointing in the direction of the fish tank. "The girl in the denim jacket."

"Thanks."

I pushed my way back through the scrum of bodies, murmuring apologies, until I saw a woman with shoulder-length brown hair, wearing a jean jacket, standing with her back to me, bending down and staring at the fish. I must have walked right past her before. I took a deep breath and tapped her on the shoulder.

"Jennifer?"

She straightened up and turned around. Her eyes, bright blue, were set a little wider than mine, and her nose was just a little shorter.

"Lucy?"

When I nodded, her full lower lip bowed into a smile, revealing two dimples in her apple-round cheeks. I started to cry.

She was Maeve. She was Jennifer. She was the girl in the sketchbooks, Alice's little girl.

Though I hadn't been quite willing to admit it, a part of me had worried that I wouldn't like my niece. I mean, just because we shared some similar DNA didn't necessarily mean we would be in sympathy. She might have been sullen, or spoiled, or silly, or shallow, or just plain uninteresting. But I needn't have worried.

Jennifer was bright and lively and openhearted and looked miraculously, amazingly, exactly like the girl in Alice's drawings. Exactly.

And I don't mean that she just looked like that now, as a young woman of eighteen, no. Alice had captured her perfectly at every stage of her life. I knew because Jennifer had thought to bring along some scrapbooks of her own life, with pictures of her adoptive family, their tidy little home in a suburb of Minneapolis, their vacations to Florida and San Francisco and, yes, even to Door County, her graduation from nursery school, from kindergarten, from middle school, from high school, pictures with her friends, her little sister, her dog and cats, her classmates, her church camp counselors, swim coaches, and piano teachers, and pictures of birthday party after birthday party.

The locations and settings in Alice's sketches were different from those photographs, but in each year of life, Alice had captured her perfectly and imagined her happy. And she was.

"How did she do it?" Jennifer asked, her voice nearly breathless with wonder as she flipped slowly through page after page of Alice's sketches. "They look just like me! How did she know?"

I wiped my eyes with the last of the paper napkins I'd brought from the car before putting it in my pocket with its sodden companions.

"Because you were never far from her heart," I said, sniffling. "Come on out to my car. There's something else I want to give you."

Even though I was a complete wreck, going through a whole pile of paper napkins during lunch, Jennifer had done a pretty good job keeping a handle on her emotions. But when I opened the back of the car and started pulling out quilt after quilt, she lost it. So did I. Again. I should have brought more napkins.

"She made these for me? All of them?" Her disbelieving eyes swam with tears.

"One for every year of your life," I said. "Because there was never a year, or a time, not even for a moment, not even when she had to give you up, that she didn't love you."

We hugged and cried and hugged some more, but it was all right. We had good reason to cry, to shed happy tears and sad.

The time went too quickly. Jennifer had to

drive back to Minneapolis to help her mother with Christmas preparations, but we promised to keep in touch and see each other again soon. We got out our phones and took a series of "selfies" to mark the day; then I helped load the quilts into Jennifer's car.

"Alice would be so proud of you," I said as we hugged good-bye for the fifth time. "So proud. I'm proud of you too."

Jennifer tipped her head to one side, smiled and bit her lower lip simultaneously, just the way Alice used to when she felt embarrassed but also a little pleased.

Jennifer got into her car and I stepped up onto the curb to watch her drive away, but when she turned on the motor I remembered something.

"Hold on! Wait!" I cried, leaping forward and banging on the window, which Jennifer quickly rolled down. "You told me you've been accepted to Kenyon in the fall, but you didn't tell me what you're going to study."

"Environmental studies with a minor in biology. But what I'd really like to do is be a wildlife photographer. It just seems like the perfect combination of the things I love best: animals and art. I know it's a long shot," she said with a giggle. "There just aren't that many wildlife photographers out there, but the world needs at least a few, right? I can't see any reason why I shouldn't be one of them."

"Neither can I. Bye-bye, Jennifer."

"Bye, Lucy." She shifted the car into drive and started to press the button to roll up the automatic window, but stopped herself. "Hey, do you mind if I call you Aunt Lucy?"

"I'd like that," I said.

She grinned. "Okay! And, also . . . Aunt Lucy, I was wondering . . ."

She stopped and ducked her head, suddenly bashful.

"What?"

"Never mind," she said. "It was kind of a dumb idea."

"Go ahead," I urged. "I want to know."

She hesitated. "Well, I was wondering if—and it's totally okay if the answer is no," she assured me, her expression wide-eyed and earnest. "I mean, you barely know me and it's kind of an imposition, but . . . do you think that maybe, during summer vacation, I could come up and stay with you for a day or two? I'd just really like to see where you and my mother grew up."

I never saw that coming. For an instant, her question stopped me dead in my tracks, but only for an instant. Almost as soon as the words were out of her mouth, I knew what the answer was, for Jennifer and for me.

"Nothing could make me happier," I told her.

I was never more sincere.

I stood waving my arm high over my head until Jennifer's car turned the corner and disappeared. As soon as it did, I got into my car and pulled my phone from my purse. Now that I knew what I needed to do, I saw no point in putting it off, not any of it.

I took a deep, decisive breath, hit the correct listing on my screen, and asked the operator to put me through. It didn't take long.

"Lucy? I didn't expect to hear from you until after Christmas. Are you all right?"

"I am, Mr. President-elect. In fact, I'm better than I've been in a long, long time. But, sir? There is something I need to tell you."

⚜ Chapter 43 ⚜

"You did what? No way! You didn't. You're just messing with me, aren't you? Trying to get back at me," Peter said, looking up from the pile of papers that sat on his big oak desk.

I couldn't blame him for doubting my truthfulness. No one who really knew me would ever have believed I could turn down a job in the White House so that I could stay in Nilson's Bay, Wisconsin. Even me. But as soon as I finished the conversation with Tom, explaining my reasons

450

and—after a degree of argument and pleading that I couldn't help but find flattering—received my former boss's blessing and said good-bye, I knew I had made the right choice.

"It's not a joke," I said, keeping my face absolutely stern so he'd know I meant business. "I am not going back to Washington. I'm going to stay here."

"And do what?"

"No idea," I said, letting out a nervous little laugh. "But I think I should wait until the end of the year before making any decisions."

Peter's eyebrows lifted. "What? Lucy Toomey without a step-by-step strategic plan? Just flying by the seat of her pants? That's something I never thought I'd see."

"Me either. It's kind of scary," I said. "A bit exciting. But mostly scary. I haven't been without a job since I was fifteen years old."

"So you're serious? You're really going to live in Nilson's Bay full-time?" I nodded, and the skeptical expression on his face faded, but slowly, as if the meaning of my words was taking time to sink in. "Well, that's great. I'm glad."

"Are you?" I asked, unable to keep the hopeful edge from my voice. "Because I wouldn't blame you if you weren't. I was pretty awful when you came over to tell me about Jennifer. I'm really sorry. It was just such a shock and . . ."

Peter shook his head and raised his hand to stop

my words. "It's okay, Lucy. I understand. I'm just glad everything worked out so well with Jennifer. It sounds like you made a real connection with her. Besides, if we're going to apologize, I'm the one who should go first."

"You mean for not telling me about Jennifer before? You were just trying to do what you thought was right," I said. "Just like you were trying to do the right thing by not taking a position on the new market before you heard all sides of the argument. Don't apologize for having high ethical standards, Peter. I admire that about you. The world needs more people like you, especially in public office, and I was wrong to give you such a hard time. Sometimes, I just see what I think needs to be done and I just . . ." I shrugged and looked away, embarrassed as I remembered how harsh I'd been with him.

"I get so involved in what I'm doing that I can't see that there might be another side to the issue or a better approach. I just can't let go. I'm like . . ."

"A dog with a bone?" Peter grinned and I chuckled.

"Yeah. I guess it's one of those things that just comes with being a Toomey."

"That's all right," Peter said, getting up from his desk and walking to a filing cabinet on the other side of the room. "And as long as we're handing out compliments, your passion is one of the

452

things I admire about you. But I still owe you an apology."

He walked across the room and opened the drawer of the cabinet, standing with his back to me as he spoke, as if he couldn't quite bring himself to face me.

"Peter, you don't have to—"

"Just let me do this, okay? Last time I tried to apologize to you, it didn't work out very well, but I need to say this. I was really short with you that day at the festival, downright rude. And it didn't have a thing to do with my professional ethics. There was nothing high-minded or noble about it." He paused for a moment, riffling through the files until he found the one he wanted, then pulled it from the cabinet and turned toward me.

"Even though you told me that you were only interested in being friends, I didn't really believe you. I thought maybe you were being coy, or that you just needed time. I thought I could change your mind." He shrugged. "It was stupid. You told me exactly how you felt, but . . . when you started keeping your distance, I was hurt. And mad. And I wanted to make you feel as bad as I did. Like I said, stupid. Anyway . . . I'm sorry. I hope you'll forgive me."

"Only if you forgive me," I said. "I guess we've both had our moments."

Peter's expression softened. He walked around the front of his desk. "Then we'll call it even, eh?"

He stuck out his hand and I shook it, sealing the bargain. It was all very cordial and civilized, friendly, and yet the feeling of his skin against mine, the simple touch of his hand, felt like an electric current running from my palm to my arm and all through my body, and the feelings and thoughts I had for him at that moment went far beyond friendship. But, after the way I'd treated him . . .

"I'm glad you're staying, Lucy. I really am."

"Me too," I said, taking in a deep breath and then letting it out, forcing myself to let go of his hand. "But I'm not quite sure how this is all going to work out. I mean, the cottage is paid for and I've got a little in savings, but at some point, I'm going to have to get a real job. And I doubt there's a whole lot of call for retired political operatives here on the peninsula."

"No, but there's lots of other places that need them." He slid his hands into his pockets and shifted his weight back, leaning against the lip of his desk. "If Joe Feeney was willing to hire you for one consulting job, I bet he'd be willing to hire you for others. I'm sure other people would too. And I wouldn't completely dismiss the idea of finding work around here. You made kind of a splash spearheading the movement to halt the demolition of the Save-A-Bunch."

"That wasn't me. That was a community effort, grassroots stuff."

"Maybe. But you were the one who spread the seed and wielded the watering can, and everybody knows it. And I think you're about to become even more popular around here," he said, his eyes twinkling, "because I got a very interesting phone call this morning. Seems the attorneys for the company that purchased the Save-A-Bunch property have decided to retract their request for a building permit. They've decided that, instead of knocking down the building, they'd like to keep the existing structure but remodel it with input from the community. How do you like that?" he asked, grinning because he already knew the answer.

"Really? That's great! Will Rinda be able to keep her job?"

"Maybe," he said, "but I doubt it. They still need to make a profit, and putting in those computerized checkout lines will help them do that. But, hey, it's a start. At least they're willing to negotiate."

"Well, we'll just have to convince them to hold on to the existing staff," I said, lifting my hand to my mouth and biting the edge of my thumbnail, considering the various plans of attack. "Maybe if we started a letter-writing campaign . . ."

Peter laughed and pushed himself up off the desk. "There she is, the pushy, passionate Lucy I've come to know and love, the woman who really believes it's possible to change the world and just won't give up until she does. But I thought you weren't going to make any moves until after the first of the year."

He circled to the back of his desk, sat down, and started shuffling through a pile of papers.

"Okay, good point. I should probably hold off for a little bit. Nothing is going to happen before Christmas anyway. But," I said slowly, drawing out the word, "I did have one thought. And it involves you."

"Uh-huh. Well," he said, glancing up briefly and then going back to his paperwork, "if it involves trying to talk me into running for anything, the answer is no. I told you before, I'm happy right where I am."

"And I'm happy you're happy," I said, lifting my hands as a testament to the purity of my motives. "I wouldn't dream of trying to change that. What I had in mind is something that doesn't require quite as big a commitment, at least not to begin with."

He pushed aside the papers, giving me a curious little frown and his complete attention. "Such as?"

"Asking your mom if Cousin Barney and I can join your family for Christmas dinner?"

"That shouldn't be a problem. In fact, she already asked me to ask you."

"Okay, good. So that's all settled."

"All settled," he echoed, smiling again. "Anything else I can do for you?"

"Well, since you mention it, I was wondering if—assuming Christmas goes okay—you might want to spend New Year's Eve with me. And maybe Valentine's Day?"

A small smile spread across his lips. "Well, let me see . . ." He stroked his beard in pretended concentration. "Hmm. Yes. I think I can pencil you in."

"Good. And if that goes well, maybe St. Patrick's Day? And Easter? May Day? Memorial Day? The Fourth of July?"

He stopped, put down his pen, and looked at me for a long moment.

"Not a problem. Every major holiday, every minor one, and all the days in between; they're yours for the asking, Lucy."

I pressed my lips together, took a breath. "Well, then . . . I'm asking."

"Consider it done. Anything else?"

"One more thing," I said softly. "You remember how you kissed me that time?"

He got up from his desk and came toward me, his suddenly serious eyes fixed upon mine, making my heart pound.

"When? The time when I walked you out to your car? The time I lured you out to the ice shanty? The time I carried you in my arms?"

"Yes. That," I stammered. "All of it. Both. I mean . . ." Once again, I was reacquainted with the meaning of the word "swoon." I had to close

457

my eyes. When I opened them again, his arms were around me. "Just kiss me," I whispered. "Kiss me and don't stop unless I ask you to."

He lowered his lips to mine.

"I can do that."

❧ Chapter 44 ❧

Eventually, I did ask Peter to stop.

It wasn't easy, believe me, but there was one more thing I had yet to do. "Besides," I said, "I'd like to take our time and do this right."

"Oh, I intend to," Peter said, with that cocky, self-assured grin that reminded me of all the things I loved about him, and he reached for me again.

I laughed and slipped from his grasp, reluctantly.

"You know what I mean. I don't want to rush things. For once in my life, I want to be wooed, romanced. I want to cherish every moment with you."

"Lucy Toomey, it is my intention to woo you, romance you, and cherish you for the rest of my life. However, if we have to play by the rules in the meantime, so be it. But don't expect me to make it easy for you."

He reached for me again. This time I let myself be caught.

· · ·

The FOA was scheduled to quilt at Rinda's house that night. When I pulled up, I saw Celia's and Daphne's cars parked in Rinda's driveway just as I had expected.

What I didn't expect was that the front door would open even before I had a chance to ring the bell and that I would see Rinda, Daphne, and Celia standing on the other side of it, dressed in coats, hats, boots, and scarves.

"Oh," I said, feeling awkward. "I should have called first. I didn't realize you'd be going out."

"Since the person we were going out to see was you, it turns out you saved us the trip." Rinda looked me up and down and scowled. "I know that leather thing looks good on you, but don't you have a real coat? That thing isn't even lined, is it? Get in here before you catch your death of cold."

I came inside, but it felt a little awkward to be standing there in a circle in Rinda's foyer, all of us still wearing our coats. "Aren't you quilting tonight? Why were you coming to see me?"

"We were coming to apologize to you. I mean, *I* was," Celia said sheepishly, looking down at her feet and then up again, words of apology tumbling from her lips like water from a broken dam. "I was so awful to you! Not only that, I was one hundred percent wrong. I did a little more investigating and found out that what you said

459

was absolutely true—you didn't have any idea of what the developer was really planning for the property. You never signed off on any of it. I'm sorry, Lucy! I was so horrible to you—"

Celia started to blink her eyes, but I cut her off before she could work herself up to tears.

"It's okay. Mr. Glazier talked a good line, and, in all fairness, I think he really was trying to do the best he could to preserve the cottage and still turn a profit. And why shouldn't he? That's his business. He was totally up front about the need to put more than one home on the property in order to get back his investment. But it never crossed my mind that he was talking about more than two houses. So you're not the only one at fault here, Celia. I should have asked him for more specifics."

Celia shook her head vehemently. "Don't let me off the hook like that, Lucy. I owe you an apology. When you told me you didn't know what he was planning to do with the property, I should have believed you. Or at least given you the benefit of the doubt. Because that's what friends do for each other."

As Celia said the last, she glanced at Rinda and Daphne in turn, locking her eyes with them in a way that gave me to understand that she'd picked up this bit of wisdom from the two of them.

It made me smile to think of Daphne, and especially Rinda, who had taken her sweet time warming up to me, defending me on the basis of friendship. But there was no doubt in my mind now. We truly were friends.

What miracles these last six weeks had wrought.

I'd returned home steeped in grief, reluctant to stay. But if I was being honest with myself, reluctant doesn't begin to describe my feelings about the way that Alice had engineered my exile to Nilson's Bay. Adamant opposition came closer to my true response, and even that was a polite way of putting it. But now I realized that Alice had known exactly what she was doing. She'd brought me home, forced me to stay put, slow down, and confront my past. As well as my present.

It's not that I regretted the time I spent working for Tom Ryland. I still believed that the work we did together was important, and I knew that, as president, he was going to do good things for the country. I'd always be proud of that. But somewhere along the way, I'd forgotten the old adage that we should work to live, not live to work.

Alice helped me remember that. Once again, my sister saved my life, gave it back to me.

That's a debt I couldn't ever repay, but I knew Alice wasn't looking for that. She wanted me to live, just live, happily and with an open heart, to put aside the past and embrace the future. And that's what I'm going to do.

"Friends assume the best about each other,"

Celia said, looking me right in the eye. "And I didn't do that. Please forgive me."

"Forgiven and forgotten," I said, and then gave her a big hug. Looking over her shoulder, I could see Daphne smiling. Rinda gave me an approving nod.

"Well, I'm glad we got that cleared up," Rinda said.

"Thanks," Celia said when I let go of her. "I know it's just a house and that my memories of Alice will outlast it, but the thought of it being turned into a condo clubhouse and that you were okay with that . . . It was kind of like losing her all over again. And, in a way, it felt like I was losing you too. I completely overreacted. I'm sorry."

"Celia, you're forgiven. Really. You don't need to apologize again. And I've got good news—there will be no condos built on the property and the cottage will *not* be turned into a clubhouse. I called Mr. Glazier earlier today and told him that the deal is off. I'm not selling the cottage to him."

Celia looked at Daphne and Daphne looked at Rinda, who looked at me.

"Well, then . . . who are you going to sell it to?"

I grinned, anticipating their reactions when I shared my news. "Nobody. I'm keeping the cottage. I've decided to stay in Nilson's Bay permanently."

"What? You're kidding!"

"You mean you're not going to move to Washington?"

"That's great! When did all this happen?"

I laughed. Their response was just what I'd thought it would be—shock and disbelief followed by delight.

"Just today," I said. "Matter of fact, a *lot* has happened today. Actually, in the last couple of days. All of it good! I drove here because I couldn't wait to share the news. But," I said, looking from one smiling face to the next, "do you think I could possibly do that sitting down?"

Two minutes later, we were all seated in Rinda's living room. Rinda, who seemed a little embarrassed by her earlier lack of hospitality, was fussing and taking coats and making noises about bringing out food, but I told her to forget about that.

"Food can wait," I said. "I don't have a lot of time, and there's so much to tell you that I'm not even sure where to begin."

But begin I did, from the beginning.

I told them about Peter coming over to tell me about Maeve/Jennifer, and how Alice had made all those quilts and drawn all those pictures for the daughter she'd barely met and yet somehow knew completely. I told them about my fight with Peter, how angry I was, and my sleepless night, and my visit with Father Damon. When I got to that part, Rinda closed her eyes in rapture, clapped her hands to her breast, and murmured, "Thank you, sweet Jesus, for answered prayers!"

And I told them about meeting Jennifer.

When I showed off the pictures I'd snapped with my phone camera, they crowded around the screen to *ooh* and *aah* and coo as if I'd been showing them pictures of an adorable new baby. And in a way, I guess I was. She was Alice's baby and she was absolutely adorable.

"And smart and interesting and well-spoken and happy," I said. "She's just an all-around terrific kid! And she wants to come up again and spend some time at the cottage, maybe this summer. And when she's here, you'll all get to meet her."

"That would be fantastic!" Celia exclaimed, clapping her hands.

"Does she quilt?" Daphne asked.

"If she doesn't, then we'll teach her," Rinda said.

"Absolutely," I agreed. "You know, meeting Jennifer is what really helped me make up my mind about staying. I think maybe that's what I wanted all along."

Daphne raised her eyebrows at this and I revised my answer.

"Okay, maybe not all along." I laughed. "But for at least the last couple of weeks. But I just couldn't admit it. I mean, for so many years I've been feeling this lack, an empty spot in my life, a hunger for something more. I thought that reaching the top of my field would fill the void, that working in the White House would prove to the world that I was worth something, and that when I moved into that West Wing office, I'd finally be happy."

I let out a little huff, amazed that I could have been so dense.

"But as I was sitting there with Jennifer, I realized I already *was* happy. And satisfied. And when she asked if she could come up and see me again because she wanted to see where Alice had grown up, I knew I couldn't sell the cottage. I just . . ."

I had to stop a moment. I pressed my hand to my mouth, trying to keep my emotions under control. Daphne put her arm around me and gave me a squeeze.

"It's okay," I assured her when I was able to speak again. "I'm just so grateful. It's been an amazing day. Oh! And I almost forgot! I've got more good news!"

I told them what Peter had told me about the market being saved and, hopefully, Rinda's job as well.

"That part's not certain yet, but I think our chances are pretty good. The fact that they want input from the community is a really good sign. We've just got to help them find ways to make the investment worth it."

"Well, that is good news," Rinda said with a smile. "But, I'm not sure I'm going to need that job anymore." I gave her a curious look and she went on to explain.

"Lloyd and I've been talking things over the last few days. This news about his kidneys has kind of gotten our attention, helped us start thinking about what we want to do with what's left of our lives. I'll tell you one thing: I don't want to spend mine standing at a cash register, ringing up cans of beans. Lloyd just can't keep working the way he has been, and he's ready for a change too. He'd like to do something more creative. So would I. That's why we've made a decision." She paused, looking from one face to the next. "We're going to sell Lloyd's heating and air-conditioning business and the house, and—"

"The house!" Daphne cried.

"You can't!" Celia protested. "You love this house!"

Rinda crossed her arms over her chest and glared, waiting impatiently for them to finish.

"I told you before," she said, "I like my house. But I *love* my husband. And I want to spend more time with him. That's why we've decided to sell the house and the business and use the money to buy the Comstock building."

"The one where the antiques store used to be?" Daphne asked. "It's been empty for at least two years."

"Which is why we think we can get a good deal on it."

"Why would you want to?" Celia asked.

"Because." Rinda smiled. "I'm going to open a quilt shop. It's something I've had in the back of my mind for a long, long time. If I don't do it now, I never will." I frowned and started to raise some questions, but she cut me off. "I know it's risky. A couple of shops have opened and closed on the peninsula in the last few years, but I think we can make it. For one thing, I think we can rent out the upper floors as office space, so that will give us some extra income. I'm going to teach classes and hold some special workshops in the summer for projects that can be completely finished in just two or three days. I think that'll appeal to the tourists. Lloyd is going to help me out in the shop, at least as much as he can, but he's also going to start a side business, long-arming."

"Longarming?" I asked, my eyebrows arching. "You mean he's going to get one of those huge professional quilting machines and finish people's quilts for them? I thought you said that people who don't quilt their own quilts aren't real quilters, just toppers."

Rinda sniffed. "I know. But if there are people out there who want to be toppers instead of quilters, who am I to tell them they can't?"

"You didn't have any trouble telling me," I

mumbled, but Rinda kept right on talking as if she hadn't heard.

"And I think Lloyd would be good at it. He's always drawing and sketching. Do you see that?" she asked, pointing to the wall and a watercolor of the seascape with a lighthouse in the background. "He painted that himself. He's very artistic, and, of course, he'd be good at the technical side of it too. He's always been great with machinery. Anyway, if people insist on having somebody else finish their quilts for them, then why shouldn't Lloyd be the one to do it?"

"Makes sense to me," Celia said. "He can fulfill his creative side and he'd only have to take on as many customers as his health would allow."

"Right," Rinda said, taking a big breath, her face breaking into a smile again. "Anyway, we've been praying and talking it over for the last couple of days, and we feel like this is the right thing to do. We're meeting with the Realtor in the morning and putting an offer in on the building."

"Well, I think this calls for a celebration!" Daphne said.

"You're right!" Rinda slapped her hands against her thighs, stood up, and started issuing instructions. "Celia, baby, come on into the kitchen and help me slice that chocolate cake I made. There's a bottle of sparkling cider in the refrigerator too. I've been saving it for a special occasion. Daphne and Lucy, you two go set up the sewing machines. I know Lucy forgot to bring hers, but we can manage with three. I've got a binding I need to stitch."

Daphne touched four fingers to her forehead in a mock salute and said, "Aye-aye, Captain." Celia jumped to her feet and started to follow our hostess. I got up, too, and grabbed my leather jacket from where I'd left it on the back of the sofa.

"Listen, I hate to miss the party, but I can't stay. I promised Peter I'd meet him for dinner at The Library."

Rinda, who was already halfway to the kitchen, spun around to look at me. "You're having dinner with Peter? Why? Did you forget that it's quilt night?"

"Well, no . . . I mean, yes . . . It's just that . . ."

Rinda scowled and put a hand on her hip. "It's just that what? Spit it out!"

I opened my mouth to explain and, inexplicably, started to laugh. Hard. And for a long time. It was crazy! I couldn't stop myself. I tried, but I couldn't. I just stood there laughing, giggling like a thirteen-year-old girl and feeling twice as giddy.

Celia giggled, too, but nervously, as if she didn't quite know how to respond. Rinda just kept scowling at me, irritated and completely confused. Daphne's face lit up like a Christmas tree, and she ran over and threw her arms around me.

"No way! Really?" she cried.

Still giggling and now to the point of tears, I bobbed my head in mute confirmation.

"Oh, Lucy! That's fantastic!" she exclaimed and squeezed me even tighter.

Celia, who by this time had figured out what was going on, squealed and threw her arms around us both. "I'm so happy for you!"

"What?" Rinda barked and threw out her hands.

"Don't you get it?" Daphne said. "Lucy's in love!"

"I am," I said, suspending my laughter just long enough to confirm it.

Rinda rolled her eyes and groaned, "Oh, no. Not you too! It was bad enough when it was just Daphne. Now we have to put up with two grown women getting all giddy and going on and on about their—"

"Rinda," Celia said sweetly, "why don't you shut up and get that bottle of cider? I think it's time for a toast, don't you?"

Rinda narrowed her eyes, giving Celia a momentary glare. Then she smiled. "You're probably right," she said, and went off to the kitchen.

By the time she returned carrying a tray with four orange juice glasses and a bottle of chilled sparkling cider, explaining that they didn't have wine goblets, I had regained my composure. Celia took over from there, pouring the cider and passing out the glasses. When everyone had one, we got to our feet and stood in a circle.

"So does this mean I'm an official member of the FOA?" I asked.

"The Friends of Alice?" Rinda cocked her head and gave me a curious look. "Honey, you always were."

"And now you're our friend too," Celia said, her face beaming.

"I know. I'm glad," I said. "So who's making the toast? Daphne? Does Mr. Shakespeare have anything appropriate for the occasion?"

"Mr. Shakespeare has something appropriate for *every* occasion. Tonight it's from *Richard the Second*."

Daphne lifted her glass and the rest of us followed. " 'I count myself in nothing else so happy as in a soul remembering my good friends.' "

"Amen," Rinda said.

❧ Chapter 45 ❧

Three days until Christmas and I'd run out of wrapping paper. Again.

But my miscalculation was understandable. After all, I'd never had so many presents to wrap before. In years past, my gift list had been limited to Alice, Joe Feeney, Jenna, and Mr. and Mrs. Ryland. I'd always sent a present to Barney, too, but that I'd had shipped directly from the catalog company, a box of apples and cheese. To a guy who grew apples for a living. What had I been thinking?

The answer was: I wasn't. I'd seen Christmas as just another task to check off my to-do list.

This year it was different. I had a lot more people in my life than ever before, which meant I had a lot more gifts to buy for them. I wanted every single one of them to be special.

Peter helped me pick out presents for his dad, his sister, her husband, and their two kids, as well as Uncle Hugh and Aunt Eileen. But I'd picked out Mrs. Swenson's gift, a bottle of perfume, on my own. I got a set of studio-grade drawing pencils for Celia, a bust of Shakespeare for Daphne, beautiful soft knitted berets and matching gloves for her girls, in each of their favorite colors, and a new Bible with a pink leather cover for Rinda. Father Damon and Mrs. Lieshout would be getting gift certificates to Dinah's Pie Shop.

For Barney, I'd chosen a new barn coat and matching hat, both with sheepskin lining, to replace the old ones he'd just about worn threadbare. A little pricey, but I figured I ought to make it up to him after all those years of fruit boxes.

Peter would be getting a new ice-fishing rod and a pair of beautiful, hand-stitched, leather gloves, very soft and warm. They'd come in handy when we went to Washington for the inauguration.

That was my present from the president-elect. The tickets had just arrived in the mail, along with tickets to one of the balls. I wouldn't want to live there, but Washington was a nice place to visit, and that's what I intended to do: see every single monument and museum, just like the rest of the tourists, marveling at our history and taking pride in the miracle of our democracy, just like the rest of my countrymen. I couldn't wait.

But, before I got to do any of that, I had to buy some more paper and finish wrapping the rest of the gifts. And make a couple as well.

I was stitching up some catnip toys for Dave and Freckles. I thought about new cat beds, but realized they'd still insist on sleeping with me—and waking me up in the wee hours so I could feed them. Well, it was really just Freckles who did that. Dave sleeps right through the night. And right on my pillow.

I was making a little scrapbook with photos of Alice and the rest of the family for Jennifer. I wouldn't be able to finish it in time for Christmas, but I didn't think she'd mind.

I was making something else for her, too, another quilt. But that's for later, for her birthday, when she comes up to visit in July. She called me the day after she left and asked if that date would work. Of course I said yes.

And then, as soon as I hung up I went into the sewing room and started picking out fabrics for her quilt, purples and white, the school colors for Kenyon College. I picked out a pattern, too, called New Year's Star. It leaves a lot of white in the background that Celia says will be a good place to show off some fancier quilting and these skinny, V-block stars that remind me of exploding purple firecrackers.

I was worried that it would be too hard for me, but Rinda and Daphne have been helping talk me through it, and so far, so good. I think Jennifer will love it. It's turning out beautifully so far. Everything is.

Dear Reading Friend,

Early in our marriage, my husband and I were fortunate to spend a couple of years living in Wisconsin. In fact, our first son was born there and proudly roots for the Packers to this day. During those years, my family and I had many opportunities to make day and weekend trips to Door County, walking along the shore, picking apples, enjoying fish boils at the White Gull Inn, and taking pictures of the goats grazing on the roof of Al Johnson's restaurant.

When I was thinking about where I might want to set my novel about two sisters, one who can't wait to get away from home and one who can't bear to leave, the Door County peninsula came immediately to mind. Thirty years had passed since my last visit to "The Door," but when I returned there to spend a few days researching the area, I found it just as beautiful and enchanting as I did when I was a new bride and young mom. If you've ever been there, I'm sure you know just what I mean.

And if you've never been to Door County, do take the opportunity if it ever comes your way. You'll have a wonderful time. But until then, I hope you enjoyed taking this little armchair visit to one of the most delightful spots on earth, home to some of the kindest and warmest people you could ever hope to meet.

Though Door County is a real place, the town of Nilson's Bay is a product of my imagination, an amalgam of so many charming little towns on the peninsula, with a few flights of my own fancy thrown in, just because I could. One of my greatest pleasures in writing comes when I am creating a new little town, deciding how the streets are laid out, where people like to gather most, what the shops sell, what the residents are like, and, of course, what unique stories they have to tell. When I'm writing about a place like Nilson's Bay, I can see every street corner and building, hear the call of the gulls flying overhead and the waves lapping against the pier, breathe in the scent of butter and baking apples coming from Dinah's Pie Shop. I can see the characters walking down the sidewalks, hear their conversations as well as if we were dear friends, which, of course, we are.

I hope that you experience that same sensation when reading *The Second Sister*, that you feel like you know the characters as friends and, for a few hours at least, consider yourself a temporary resident of Nilson's Bay, and that, after the story ends, you find yourself wanting to return. If that's the case, drop me an e-mail or note on my Facebook page and let me know.

As I write this, I cannot honestly say if I'll write more books about Lucy, Rinda, Daphne, Celia, and the other residents of Nilson's Bay—there are just so many, many stories in my head, more than I could write in three lifetimes—but I do take reader response into account when choosing future projects, so do feel free to weigh in. I always love hearing from my readers.

You can write to me at . . .

Marie Bostwick
P.O. Box 488
Thomaston, CT 06787

Or "like" my Facebook fan page at www.facebook.com/mariebostwick. (And if you also check the "Get Notifications" item from the pulldown menu, you'll get all my posts. I'm there every day.)

And remember, if you register on www.mariebostwick.com, you'll not only be subscribed to my monthly newsletter (which has information on all my doings, as well as book recommendations, recipes, fun links, contests, and other tidbits I know you'll enjoy), you'll also be able to down-load free companion quilt patterns and recipes from many of my books, including The Second Sister.

Usually when I finish a new book, my dear friend Deb Tucker, creative kingpin of Studio 180 Design, and I collaborate to create a new free downloadable quilt pattern as a gift to my lovely readers. However, Deb is extraordinarily busy right now, working on a pattern book to be released in the spring of 2015 with some of her gorgeous Hunter's Star designs (can't wait to see it!). So that means that this time I'll be doing the design for the companion project on my own. I've decided to create a pattern for Lucy's first project —a jazzed-up nine-patch in blue, orange, and white. It's going to be a fun quilt to make, something even a beginner can handle, so be sure to register on my website so you can download it as well as the other free patterns that are available there.

Even though Deb isn't available to create a companion quilt with me for this book, you can find full-sized patterns for quilts from my past books available for purchase on her website. Be sure to check them out at www.studio180design .net. (And while you're at it, take a look at Deb's fabulous tools and rulers, too—they've made me a much better quilter!)

I hope you enjoyed reading *The Second Sister* as much as I enjoyed writing it. This is my eleventh full-length novel. Every time I think about that, I am amazed, grateful, and mindful that it would never, ever have happened without the loyalty and support of readers like you. Thank you so much.

Blessings,

Marie Bostwick

About the Author

Marie Bostwick was born and raised in the Northwest. In the three decades since her marriage, Marie and her family have moved frequently, living in eight different states at eighteen different addresses, three of them in Texas. These experiences have given Marie a unique perspective that enables her to write about people from all walks of life and corners of the country with insight and authenticity. Marie currently resides in Connecticut, where she enjoys writing, spending time with family, helping out at church, gardening, collecting fabric, and stitching quilts.

Please visit her on the Web at:

www.mariebostwick.com
on Twitter, at twitter.com/mariebostwick
and on Facebook,
at facebook.com/mariebostwick

Center Point Large Print
600 Brooks Road / PO Box 1
Thorndike, ME 04986-0001 USA

(207) 568-3717

US & Canada:
1 800 929-9108
www.centerpointlargeprint.com